'Holiday r
out,' she m

'That's what I've ...

'Keep reminding me that this is nothing more than a few weeks of fun, okay?'

Finn rubbed his jaw. He had to acknowledge that it would be easy to forget who they were and why they were here. They were on a fake honeymoon—emphasis on the *fake*—surrounded by romance and luxury, and they might easily get swept away and inadvertently slip on a pair of those rose-coloured glasses.

He—they—had to keep their eyes open, their heads in the game.

Callie turned her head and sent him a small, almost sad smile. 'We're on the same page?'

He rubbed his hand over his jaw before nodding briskly. 'Just to be clear—are you saying that you'll sleep with me?'

The tip of her tongue touched her top lip and he saw her skin flush with anticipated pleasure. Yeah, she would be his as much as he would be hers. Tonight.

Callie held his eyes as she sucked in her bottom lip. 'Well, sleeping isn't what we would be doing, exactly.'

Dear Reader

When I wrote THE LAST GUY SHE SHOULD CALL I got so many messages from readers asking for Callie's story. Something about the vivacious, independent, flirty character grabbed them, and—Callie being Callie—she hasn't stopped nagging me for her happily-ever-after since then!

When a condom falls from the pocket of a gorgeous blonde's jacket into his lap on a flight back from New York to Cape Town, travel writer Finn Banning knows that Callie Hollis is trouble with a capital T. She's bold and flirtatious, and somehow he finds himself in a discussion about his upcoming wedding and her feelings about love and marriage… She's cynical and sceptical and she doesn't buy into the concept of happy-ever-after. But Finn needs a wedding planner, and Callie gives him the name and number for her friend Rowan, who is doing just that.

Three months later the wedding is off and Finn finds himself all at sea. He's not particularly upset about losing his fiancée, but he is devastated at the loss of his dreams to have a family. He also has a huge problem in that he's been contracted to write a series of articles for an important publication on upmarket honeymoon destinations, to be researched while he's on his honeymoon, and he can't let them or the magazine down.

Nobody is more surprised than Callie when she finds herself agreeing to act as Finn's fake wife. But needs must: she needs to vacate Cape Town to avoid meeting up with her mother, who left her and her brother Seb when they were very young, so she jumps at the chance to spend three weeks with the über-delicious Finn Banning at various luxury honeymoon destinations in Southern Africa.

It's a perfect arrangement—she'll be his rebound girl and he'll be a fling, and in three weeks they'll wave each other goodbye. *Hmm…I don't think so!*

I hope you enjoy Callie's story as much as I loved writing it.

Happy reading!

Joss xxx

Come and say hi via Facebook: Joss Wood Author or Twitter: @josswoodbooks or visit www.josswoodbooks.com

THE HONEYMOON ARRANGEMENT

BY

JOSS WOOD

MILLS & BOON

Published in Great Britain 2015
by Mills & Boon, an imprint of Harlequin (UK) Limited,
Eton House, 18-24 Paradise Road, Richmond, Surrey, TW9 1SR

ISBN: 978-0-263-25394-8

Harlequin (UK) Limited's policy is to use papers that are natural, renewable and recyclable products and made from wood grown in sustainable forests. The logging and manufacturing processes conform to the legal environmental regulations of the country of origin.

Printed and bound in Spain
by CPI, Barcelona

Joss Wood wrote her first book at the age of eight and has never really stopped. Her passion for putting letters on a blank screen is matched only by her love of books and travelling—especially to the wild places of Southern Africa—and possibly by her hatred of ironing and making school lunches.

Fuelled by coffee, when she's not writing or being a hands-on mum, Joss, with her background in business and marketing, works for a non-profit organisation to promote the local economic development and collective business interests of the area where she resides. Happily and chaotically surrounded by books, family and friends, she lives in Kwa-Zulu Natal, South Africa, with her husband, children and their many pets.

Other Modern Tempted™ titles by Joss Wood:

YOUR BED OR MINE?
MORE THAN A FLING?
FLIRTING WITH THE FORBIDDEN
THE LAST GUY SHE SHOULD CALL
TOO MUCH OF A GOOD THING?
IF YOU CAN'T STAND THE HEAT…

This and other titles by Joss Wood are available in eBook format from www.millsandboon.co.uk

To Sandi, so far away but still so close to my heart.
Also for Sandi's Chris, who brings my little technie toys.
Thanks bunches!

PROLOGUE

'MINIMALISM, MODERNISM OR IMPRESSIONISM?'

Finn Banning looked up from his seat in business class into the lovely face of a navy-eyed blonde with her hand resting on the seat in front of him. A ten-second scan told him that her body was long, lean and leggy, her waist tiny, her bright blonde hair falling way past her shoulders. Another five seconds of looking into those impish flirty eyes told him that she was Trouble. With a capital T. God, he hoped she wasn't sitting next to him on this long-haul flight back to Cape Town from JFK.

Over the past two months his life had been turned upside down and inside out and he didn't want to make small talk with a stranger—even if she was supermodel-gorgeous.

But he couldn't help the corners of his mouth kicking up in response to the mischief in those amazing eyes.

'Graffiti,' he replied when she cocked an arrogant sculpted eyebrow.

Her mouth twitched in what he suspected was a smile waiting to bloom.

'Whisky or bourbon?'

'Beer.'

She tipped her head and tapped her foot, encased in what looked to be, under the hem of dark jeans, low-heeled black boots. 'Rugby or cricket?'

He'd never played either as he'd spent every spare moment he had at the dojo. 'I was on the UCT crochet team.'

Her mouth twitched again with amusement as the other eyebrow lifted. 'You went to the University of Cape Town? Me too! What year? Degree?'

'Journalism. Is there a point to these questions?'

'Sure. I'm trying to decide whether you're worth flirting with or whether I should ignore you for the rest of the flight.'

She flashed him a megawatt smile that had his groin twitching and his heartbeat jumping. An elegant hand gestured to the empty seat next to him.

'My seat.'

'Ah…' he replied. Of course it was.

Finn watched as she tossed that bright head of relaxed curls and pushed some of them out of her eyes. Reaching for the strap over her shoulder, she dropped her leather rucksack to her feet and shrugged out of her thigh-length brown leather coat to reveal a taut, tight white T-shirt that covered small and perky breasts. *Nice.*

She folded the coat and stood on her toes to push it into the bin above their heads and that white T-shirt rode up to reveal a tanned, taut stomach and a beaded ring piercing the skin above her belly button. He watched, bemused, as she picked up the leather rucksack, pulled her tablet and earphones from the bag and tossed them on the seat. Holding her rucksack in her hand, she pulled a shawl from it, and as the bag tipped a thin, familiar silver foil packet fell out of a side pocket and landed on his thigh.

Finn picked up the condom and held it between his thumb and forefinger, waiting for her to look at him. When she did, instead of giving the blush he'd expected, she just flashed him another lightning bolt smile and nipped the condom out of his grip.

'Whoops! Maybe I should introduce myself before I throw prophylactics in your direction. I'm Callie Hollis.'

'Finn Banning.'

She wasn't shocked that he wasn't shocked, Finn thought as she tucked the condom into the back pocket of her jeans. Then again, after eight years as an investigative journalist before switching over to travel journalism nothing much shocked him any more. He'd seen the worst of what human beings could do to one another and, since it wasn't the first time he'd had a condom tossed in his lap by a beautiful woman, it didn't even make a blip on his radar.

Callie brushed past his knees and dropped into the seat next to him, wiggling her butt into the soft cushions and letting out a breathy sigh. She was all legs and arms and he would bet his last dollar that she hated economy class as much as he did—at six-two, for him it was like trying to sit in a sardine can—and that she figured the ridiculous price for a business class ticket was worth every cent.

Callie dropped her head back against the seat and then rolled it in his direction. 'So...married or single?'

'Why does it matter?' he asked.

Callie grinned. 'Well, I do this flight every month or so, and it's been a *looooong* time since I've had someone sitting next to me who I'd want to flirt with—normally my travelling companions are old, dull or ugly. And besides, when the guy is as hot as you flirting is fun—and I'm really good at it.'

He had no problem believing that and told her so. 'It must be because you're so shy and timid,' he added, his tone super-dry.

Callie laughed—a deep, belly laugh that made his stomach clench and his groin jump. 'That's what my best friend Rowan says all the time. Anyway, we were talking about flirting... If you're single you get the full treatment. If you're married I behave like a normal person.'

'I'm in between. I'm engaged.'

'Pooh.' Callie pouted. 'Well, your loss—because I flirt really, *really* well.'

He absolutely believed that.

Callie wiggled in her chair again, and tucked her legs up and under her. 'So when are you getting married?' she asked, and he could see that she'd dialled back the charm.

'In three or so months' time.'

She fiddled with the clasp of her seat belt and looked at him, puzzled. 'I don't get the whole marriage thing. What's your reason?'

Finn stared past the lovely face to the darkness beyond her window, frowning when a quick, instinctive answer didn't fall from his lips. Shouldn't that be a minimum requirement when he was contemplating spending the rest of his life with someone?

Her question raised all the issues that he'd been struggling with lately. Were he and Liz doing the right thing by getting married just because Liz was five or so weeks pregnant? It was the twenty-first century—they didn't need to get married to keep living together, to raise a child together. Were they complicating an already complicated situation? It wasn't as if their relationship had been fantastic lately, and he was mature enough to know that a baby was hard work and might put more strain on the frayed rope that was keeping them together.

On the other hand, being parents might bring them closer…

God—a baby. He was still taking it in. He wanted to be an integral part of his child's life and he was excited about becoming a dad. Maybe the birth of his own child would fill the hole that had appeared in his life when James died three months ago. A birth for a death, it seemed…*right*.

Fitting. Fated.

Finn rubbed his jaw. He was approaching his mid-thirties

and he wanted to be a brilliant father to someone. James had been one to his stepbrothers, to him. He wanted to create a family of his own—something he'd only truly experienced when he was fourteen and he and his mum had joined the Baker gang—a single dad and his three sons. He wanted to be part of something bigger than himself and he and Liz had been good together once. Maybe they could be again. Actually, they didn't have an option. They *had* to make it good again.

'So, why are you getting married?' Callie asked again.

He frowned at her, warning her off the subject. 'None of your business.'

Callie's low chuckle floated over him. Warning ignored, then.

'Of course it's not, but I'm always fascinated as to why someone would be interested in tying themselves down for ever and ever and ever…'

'Love?'

'*Pffft.* That's just an easy excuse—a myth perpetuated by movies and books.'

'You don't believe in love?' Finn asked, intrigued despite himself. Because, deep in his soul, he wasn't sure if he believed in the fairytale version either.

To him, love was taking responsibility, showing caring, companionship and loyalty, and he firmly believed in those. Besides, Liz hadn't got pregnant by herself, and if he was part of the problem then he would be part of the solution.

Right now it seemed that marriage *was* the solution.

He saw something that he thought was sadness flicker in Callie's eyes.

'I believe the only pure love people have is for their children, and some people don't even have that. No, love is a generic term we use to feel safe. Or comfortable? Possibly co-dependent?' Callie suggested, twisting in her seat as the aircraft started to move down the runway.

'Is that what you see love and marriage as? Co-dependency?' He couldn't believe that he was having a conversation about his upcoming marriage with an absolute stranger. Reticence was his usual style, along with reserve and caginess. He *asked* the questions, dammit, he didn't answer them.

Callie shrugged. 'I think that a lot of people use love and marriage as an escape from whatever is dragging them down. Just like some people escape to drugs in order to feel happy, others escape to love.'

Whoa. He was occasionally cynical about love and relationships, but she made him look like an amateur. He was cautious, thoughtful and rational about the concept. He took his time to become fully invested in a relationship and he never made quick or rash decisions. Which was probably why he was feeling so out of sorts about getting married—he hadn't had nearly enough time to think the whole situation through, to process the changes.

And he was still dealing with the death of the only father he'd ever known. Finn pushed his fingers to his right eye to stop the burning. Would he ever get shot of this ache in his heart?

Callie placed the tips of her fingers, the nails shiny and edged in white, on the bare skin of his forearm. 'Sorry—I'm being an absolute downer. I'm just naturally sceptical about love, marriage and relationships. It's a crap shoot and I'm not much of a gambler.' Callie bit her bottom lip. 'I admit that I'm a little too outspoken and opinionated—'

He couldn't help his sarcasm. 'A *little*?'

'Okay, a lot—but I do wish you happiness and success.' She tucked her foot up and under her backside again, and sighed theatrically. 'Both my brother and father—neither of whom I thought would *ever* get hitched—are getting married within the next couple of months, so I'm going to have to learn to keep my cynical mouth shut.'

Despite having only known her for twenty minutes, Finn knew that was impossible.

'Thank goodness that Rowan—my best friend, who is about to marry my brother—is an event planner and she's organising both their weddings. I just have to show up and look pretty.'

Pretty? She could don a black rubbish bag and still look stunning, Finn thought. Those eyes, those cheekbones, that pink tongue peeking out from between those plump lips… He wondered what she would taste like, how those breasts would fit into his hands, about the baby softness on the inside of those slim thighs…

Whoah!

What the hell…? Rein it in, bud, before you humiliate yourself. You're engaged, remember? An almost father, an about-to-be husband.

Knowing that she'd said something of importance that he hadn't picked up because in his head he'd been tasting her skin, he mentally rewound. 'Wait…you say your best friend is a wedding planner?'

'Mmm. Actually, she does all sorts of events, but she's great at weddings.'

'My partner—fiancée—is going nuts. Apparently there isn't a wedding planner in the city who'll take on organising a wedding at the last moment.'

'When are you getting married…tomorrow?'

'As I said, we'd like to get it done in three months or so.'

Liz wanted the wedding done and dusted before she started to show as she wasn't comfortable displaying her baby bump to her conservative relatives.

'And finding a wedding planner is something I have to do in the next couple of days.'

'Why isn't the bride-to-be looking?' Callie asked. 'Shouldn't that be her thing?'

'Liz is in Nigeria for the next six weeks, so finding a wedding planner has become my job.'

'What's she doing in Nigeria?'

God—more questions. He didn't think he'd met anyone more inquisitive and so unreservedly blatant about it. *So, Sherlock, why haven't you shut her down yet?*

'Liz is a consulting engineer working on an oil rig.' He saw her open her mouth and held up a hand to stop the next barrage of questions. 'This friend of yours…the wedding planner? Is she any good?'

Callie nodded. 'She really is. She started off by doing kids' birthday parties and then she did a Moroccan-themed wedding which was amazing. In eighteen months she's done more than a few weddings.'

'Can I get her number?'

'Sure.' Callie nodded. 'If you allow me one last word on marriage.'

'Can I stop you?' Finn raised a dark eyebrow. 'And just *one* word? How amazing.'

Callie ignored his quiet sarcasm. 'It's not from me but from Nietzsche…'

Good looks and good brains too? Callie was quite a deep little package.

'Nietzsche, huh? Do enlighten me.'

'He said something about love being many brief follies and that marriage puts an end to said follies with a single long stupidity.'

Huh. Some German philosophers and some navy-eyed blondes were far too smart for their own good.

'I need a drink.'

Callie grinned. 'People frequently say that when they're around me.'

Finn didn't find that hard to believe. *At all.*

CHAPTER ONE

Three months later...

CALLIE, ABOUT TO pull the door open to their favourite watering hole, the Laughing Queen, frowned as Rowan held the door closed and stopped her from walking inside.

'What?'

Rowan narrowed her eyes at her. 'Can you try and remember that this is a *business* meeting? That my client and his fiancée have called their wedding off two weeks before they were supposed to say I do. Do *not* flirt with him!'

Callie, purely to wind Rowan up, flashed her naughtiest smile. 'Why not? Maybe me flirting with him will cheer him up.'

'Don't you dare! I swear, Cal, just behave—okay?'

'I always behave!' Callie protested. Okay, that wasn't true, so she quickly crossed her fingers behind her back. For most of her adult life, whenever she'd found herself back in Cape Town, she had normally ended up in this bar, getting up to some mischief or other. Jim and Ali, the owners, loved her because she always got the party started and they ended up selling much more liquor than normal.

'Just no dancing on the bar or impromptu line-dancing, okay? Or, if you have to, pretend that you don't know me.'

'Hey! I'm not so bad!'

Rowan was thinking of Callie's early twenties self, or

maybe her mid-twenties self…maybe her six-months-ago self. The truth was that it had been a while since she'd caused havoc in a pub. Or anywhere else.

Normally, whenever she was feeling low or lonely, needing to feel outside of herself, she headed for the nearest bar or club. It wasn't about the alcohol—she'd launched many a party and walked out at dawn stone-cold sober—it was the people and the vibe she fed off…the attention.

So why, after a decade, was she now boycotting that scene? Had she totally lost every connection to the wild child she had been? That funny, crazy, gap-toothed seven-year-old who'd loved everyone and everything. That awesome girl she'd been before everything had changed and her world had fallen apart.

Sadness made her throat constrict. She rather liked the fact that at one point in her life she'd been totally without fear. That was how she usually felt in the middle of a party she'd created: strong, in control, fearless.

Maybe she should just start a party tonight to remind herself that she could still have fun.

When she repeated the thought to Rowan, her mouth pursed in horror.

'You are hell on wheels,' Rowan grumbled, letting go of the door handle and gesturing her inside.

'And *you* were a lot more fun before you got engaged to my brother,' Callie complained, stepping into the restaurant. She waved at Jim, who was standing behind the long bar at the back of the large harbour-facing restaurant. 'What happened to my wild, backpacking, crazy BFF?'

'I'm *working*.' Rowan said through gritted teeth. 'This is my *business*.'

Seeing that Rowan looked as if she was about to start foaming at the mouth, Callie slung an arm around her shoulder. 'Okay…chill. I'll behave.' She couldn't resist another dig. 'Or at the very least I'll try.'

'I was nuts to bring you along tonight,' Rowan complained, leading them to an empty table in the corner and yanking out a chair.

Callie took the seat opposite her and flipped her hair over her shoulder. Seeing Rowan's irritated face, she realised that she might have gone a little too far, so she placed her hand on hers and squeezed. When Rowan's eyes met hers Callie met her dark eyes straight on. 'Relax—I'll behave, Ro.'

Rowan scrunched her face up and when she opened her eyes again let out a long sigh. 'Sorry. It's just that I feel for this guy. I mean, can you imagine calling it quits so close to the wedding?' Rowan picked up a silver knife from the table and clutched it in her hand. 'What could have gone so badly wrong so late in the day?'

Callie heard the unspoken question at the end of Rowan's sentence. *And what if it happens to us?*

'Easy, Ro. Seb adores you and nothing like that is going to happen.'

'Bet Finn didn't think that either,' Rowan muttered.

Finn? Callie stared at her. Finn Banning? The guy on that flight back from JFK? The one she'd never quite managed to forget? The one she'd recommended Rowan to as his wedding planner? Black hair cut short to keep curls under control, utterly mesmerising grape-green eyes and that wide-shouldered, long-legged, slim-hipped body. The man who had starred in quite a few of her night time fantasies lately.

'Finn? You've got to be sh—' Callie caught her swear-word just in time. With Rowan's help she was trying to clean up her potty mouth. And by 'Rowan's help' she meant that she had to pay Rowan ten bucks every time she swore. It was a very expensive exercise. 'You've got to be *kidding* me.'

Rowan placed their order for a bottle of white wine with

a waitress before answering her. 'Sadly not. Anyway, he's the strong, stoic, silent type—not the type of guy who you can commiserate with. So don't let on that you know.'

Of course she wouldn't. She was loud and frequently obnoxious, but she wasn't a complete moron.

She had a low-grade buzz in her womb at the thought of meeting Finn again—jilted or not. She still had a very clear picture of his super-fit body dressed in faded jeans, his muscles moving under a long-sleeved black T-shirt, sleeves pushed up to his elbows lounging in the seat next to her; his broad hand, veins raised, capable and strong, resting on his thigh. His quick smile, those wary, no-BS-tolerated eyes…

She had amused him, she remembered, and that was okay. He'd looked as if he needed to laugh more. And, more worryingly, those hours she'd spent with him were the last she'd spent in any concentrated, one-on-one time with a man.

Maybe she was losing her mojo.

'So, how long are you in the country for this time?'

Rowan changed the subject and Callie sighed with disappointment. She wanted to gossip a bit more about the luscious Finn.

As a fashion buyer for an upmarket chain of fashion stores Callie was rarely in the country, constantly ducking in and out of the fashion capitals of Europe and in New York and LA. Trips back home were rarely for more than a week or two—three if she was at the end of a three-month rotation. Wasn't she due for a three-week break soon? Hmm…she'd have to check.

'I'm flying out to Paris in a little while and will be away for a week.'

'Aren't you sick of it, Cal? The airports, the travelling, the craziness?' Rowan asked. 'I could never imagine going back to my old lifestyle, kicking it around the world.'

'But, honey, you stayed in grotty hostels and hotels. I travel the easy way—business class seats, expensive hotels, drivers, upmarket restaurants and clubs.'

Rowan had been a backpacker—a true traveller. Callie wasn't half as adventurous as her friend; unlike Rowan she'd never visited anywhere that wasn't strictly First World.

Upmarket First World. She was that type of girl.

Callie frowned. Rowan had a look in her eye that told her that she was about to say something she wouldn't like. She'd been on the receiving end of that dark-eyed look many times since her childhood and she leaned back in her chair, resigned. 'I know that look. What's wrong?'

Rowan pulled in a long breath. 'I don't know… I'm just concerned. Worried about you.'

Callie fought the urge to roll her eyes. 'Why?'

Rowan stared down at her hands. 'Because…um…'

'Jeez—just spit it out, Rowan,' Callie said, impatient.

Rowan's eyes flashed at her command. 'Well, okay, then. Seb and I are concerned because we think you might be becoming…what's the word?...brittle, maybe.'

What? 'Why?'

'You gobble up life, Cal, like nobody else. You love people and you talk to anyone. Within two seconds everyone adores you and wants to be your best friend. You are the only person I know who can walk into a party and within half an hour have everyone doing shots and then the conga. Men want you and girls want to *be* you.'

Well, that was an exaggeration—but it was nice that Rowan thought so. 'So where does the worry and the brittle part come into it?'

'Being bubbly and funny and outrageous has always been a part of you, but we sort of feel like you've been acting lately. It's almost as if you're trying a bit too hard…'

'I am not!'

Callie instantly denied the accusation. Except that Rowan's words stung hard enough for her to know it was the truth. And hadn't her recent actions shown her how hard she now had to work to dredge up the flirty, party-hearty girl when it had used to be constantly and consistently easy for her?

Maybe she was getting old. Or bored. Or maybe she just needed sex. Or all three.

Rowan traced the pattern of a bold flower on the tablecloth with her finger. 'I read an article the other day about people feeling out of sorts as they approach thirty,' Rowan explained. 'Maybe you're wondering if you're on the right path, whether your life makes sense.'

'Of course my life makes sense,' Callie retorted.

She earned spectacular money doing a job she could do with her eyes closed, she was constantly meeting new people, buzzing from cosmopolitan city to cosmopolitan city. Dinner in Paris…lunch in Rome. Looking at beautiful clothes and making the decisions on what to buy and for whom. She dated cosmopolitan, successful men.

She loved her job. She'd always loved her job. She *still* loved her job…okay, mostly loved her job. She'd been doing it for a long time—she was allowed to feel iffy about it occasionally.

Over the last six months the designers seemed to have become a lot more diva-ish, the cities a bit grimier, the hotel rooms even more soulless than normal. The men more man-scaped than she liked and a great deal more bland.

Maybe she needed a holiday. Or an affair…

'And how's your love-life, Cal? Who's the lucky guy of the moment?'

There Rowan went again—reading her mind. When you'd been friends with someone for more than a quarter of a century it happened. Often.

Callie sipped her wine before answering. 'I'm currently single...'

'You're *always* single,' Rowan corrected her.

'Okay, if you're going to be pedantic then I'll say that I'm currently not sleeping with anyone. Is that better?'

She dated lots of different men and slept with very few of them. Despite her party-girl, flirt-on-two-legs reputation she was very careful who she took into her bed. And she usually found out, during dinner or drinks, that they were married, bi, involved, arrogant or narcissistic. So she normally went to bed alone.

'Marginally. So why aren't you tearing up the sheets with some hunk?' Rowan asked.

Callie twisted her lips. 'Not sure, actually. Nobody has interested me for a while.'

Rowan shoved her tongue into her cheek. 'How long is a while? A week? A month?'

Callie looked at Rowan and tried to ignore the flash of hurt. She knew that Ro was teasing, but saying it like that made her sound like a slut—and she wasn't. She really wasn't. She didn't bed-hop or treat sex casually, but neither was she a nun.

'I haven't slept with anyone for about five, maybe six months,' she admitted quietly.

Rowan instantly looked apologetic. 'Sorry, honey, I didn't mean to sound judgemental. Teasing, maybe—judgy, no.' Rowan waited a beat before speaking again. 'Why not, Cal? You like men and men like you.'

Callie wished she could answer her but she couldn't—not really. Like her avoiding the party scene and her occasional dissatisfaction with her job there was no reason—nothing she could put her finger on. She just hadn't met anyone lately whom she wanted in her bed...in her body. Nobody she liked enough to make the effort.

She just couldn't put her finger on why, and she was

getting a bit tired of her self-imposed celibacy. She liked sex—she needed sex.

'I genuinely don't know, Ro. It just hasn't happened lately and I refuse to force it.' Callie shrugged before sitting up straight and putting a smile of her face. 'Anyway, it's not the end of the world. I'll find someone sooner or later who I'll want to tumble with. In the meantime I have a great, interesting life.'

Rowan bit her lip—a sure sign that she was about to say something that Callie might not like.

'Is it possible that your life is *too* great?'

'Huh? What?' Callie wrinkled her nose, puzzled.

'Your life is so busy, so crazy, and you are so virulently independent—do you have any room in it for a man? A lover? Someone who might be something more than a temporary arrangement? Can it be, darling Cal, that you're too self-sufficient and busy for your own good? Or is it a defence mechanism?'

Okay, had Rowan acquired a psychology degree along with her engagement ring? What was this all about?

'What is *wrong* with you? I came out for a drink—not to be analysed.'

Rowan pulled a face. 'We both had screwed-up childhoods, Cal. My parents and their inability to see me—your mum leaving when you were a little girl. Our push-the-envelope crazy antics got worse and worse the older we got and ended up with you writing off your car when you were eighteen. I landed in jail shortly afterwards.'

'Just for a weekend.'

'That was long enough. That was a hell of year, wasn't it?' Rowan shook her head at the memory.

It had been a hell of a year, indeed, Callie agreed silently.

'After both incidents we…settled down, I suppose.

We're so much better adults than we were kids,' Rowan continued.

'Speak for yourself,' Callie muttered. All she knew for sure was that she'd felt more alive when she was a kid and a wild teenager than she did now. Right now she just felt…*blah*. Not brittle—just *blah*. As if she was a cardboard cut-out of herself.

Rowan sent her a quick, worried look. 'While we're on the subject of your mother, I need to tell you that…'

They were on the subject of *her mother*? Since when? And, oh, hell *no*—they were not going to go there. Not tonight, not tomorrow, not ever. Her mother was long, long gone and not worth wasting time and energy discussing. They most certainly were not on this subject and would never be…

Good try, Ro.

Callie quickly shook her head. 'Don't.'

Rowan held her stare and Callie knew that she was debating whether to get pushy and pursue the topic. Luckily Rowan's mobile rang and she scooped it up off the table. Judging by the soft look on her face, she quickly deduced that it was her brother Seb on the other end, cooing into her ear. She genuinely loved the fact that Seb and Rowan were so unabashedly happy, but their sappiness frequently made her feel queasy.

She couldn't imagine acting like that—being so intertwined, so in tune with another person. It just wasn't her.

Callie looked up when a hand touched her shoulder and saw Jim, the owner of the bar, smiling down at her. He bent to kiss one cheek and then the other, and when he was done she allowed his big fingers to hold her chin.

'Where have you been, hun?'

'Here and there.'

'We've missed you,' Jim stated.

Callie grinned. 'You've missed me starting tequila

shooter competitions which invariably turn into massive parties which lead to your till feeling very full at the end of the evening.'

'That too.' Jim dropped his hand and tipped his head, his expression enquiring. 'Listen, I've got guys at the bar wanting to buy you a drink. You up for company or must I tell them you're not interested?'

Callie didn't bother looking at the bar. She just wanted to talk to Rowan and, if she was lucky, say hi to Finn Banning again. She shook her head. 'I'm not in the mood, Jim—and, besides, I told Rowan that I'd keep a low profile tonight and behave myself.'

'Why do I suspect that that is very difficult for you to do?'

Callie heard the deep, dark voice and whipped her head around to look up and into Finn's face. Tired, she thought, but still oh, so sexy. Purple shadows were painted beneath his eyes and his face looked drawn and thinner. His back and shoulders were taut with tension and his mouth was a slash in his face. She wanted to kiss him and cuddle him at the same time. And she thought that he needed the cuddling a lot more than he needed the kissing.

The last couple of days had clearly put him through the wringer. Experiencing that kind of pain, Callie thought, being that miserable, was why she never got emotionally involved. She'd experienced emotional devastation once before and it wasn't something she ever wanted to deal with again.

However, despite looking like a love refugee, he still looked good. Sage and white striped shirt over faded blue jeans and flat-soled boots. Curls that looked wild from, she guessed, fingers constantly being shoved into them, and a four-day beard. Tough, hard, stoic—and more than a smidgeon miserable.

Yeah, there was that tingle, that bounce in her heart's

step, the womb-clench and the slowly bubbling blood. *This* was what pure attraction—lust—felt like, she remembered. This crazy, want-to-lick-you-silly feeling she'd been missing.

Jim melted away and Finn looked at her with those sexy light eyes. She felt her face flush, her breath hitch.

Sexy, hot, *sad* man. What she wouldn't do to make him smile—she *needed* to make him smile.

'Now, why would you think that?' Callie asked him, projecting as much innocence as she could.

He slapped his hands on his hips and narrowed his eyes at her and she hoped he couldn't tell that her heart was thumping in excitement. He pulled his lips up into a smile which tried but didn't quite make it to his eyes.

'The passage to the bathroom facilities is covered in framed photographs of the parties that have happened here. Not so strangely, you are in most of them—front and centre. Oh, yeah, you're just trouble looking for a place to happen.'

Callie batted her eyelashes at him, her eyes inviting him to laugh with her…at her. 'My daddy told me that talent shouldn't ever be wasted.'

'Your daddy is probably on Prozac.' The smile lifted higher and brushed his eyes.

Progress, she thought.

He shook his head, bemused. 'Trouble. With a capital T. In flashing neon lights.'

Callie left Rowan and Finn discussing the dissolution of all his wedding plans—his eyes had gone back to being flat and miserable, dammit!—and went to sit on a small table on the outside deck, overlooking the harbour. On the mountain behind her lights from the expensive houses twinkled and a cool breeze skittered over the sea, raising goosebumps on her bare arms.

She tucked herself into her favourite corner, out of sight of the bar patrons, and put her feet up on the railing. The sea swished below her feet.

The noise from the bar had increased in volume and, as Finn had observed earlier, usually she'd be in the thick of the action—calling for shots, cranking up the music, and dancing…on the floor, on a bar stool or on the bar itself.

Nobody could ever call her a wallflower, and if they had to then she'd be an exotic one—climbing the wall with her brightly coloured petals and holding a loud hailer.

Where had she gone, that perfect party girl, loud and fearless? She'd cultivated the persona after the car accident—after she'd made a promise to her father and brother to pull herself away from the edge of destruction. It was the only way she'd been able to find the attention she'd craved and she'd got it—especially from men.

She got a lot of attention from men. Apparently it was because, as a previous lover had once told her, men felt good when they were with her: stronger, bolder, more alpha.

Whatever.

But Rowan was wrong. She didn't need a man in her life. Her life was fine—perfect, almost. She had absolutely nothing to complain about. She loved her life, loved her job, the world was her oyster and her pearl and the whole damn treasure chest. She liked her life, liked being alone, being independent, answerable only to herself. Her life was super-shiny. It didn't need additional enhancement.

Besides, as she had learned along the way, to a lot of the men she dated she was a prize to be conquered, a body to possess, a will to be bent. They loved the thrill of the chase and then, because, she didn't do anything but casual, they ended up getting competitive—thought they could be the one to get her to settle down, to commit. That they were 'the man'—had the goods, the bigger set of balls.

They tried to get her to play the role of lover or girlfriend and she always refused. And when their attention became a bit too pointed—when they showed the first signs of jealousy and possessiveness—she backed off. All the way off.

She'd never met a man she couldn't live without, couldn't leave behind. And if she ever had the slightest inkling that she might feel something deeper for someone she was dating she called it quits. She told him that her life was too hectic, too crazy for a relationship, and that wasn't a lie. It just wasn't the whole truth.

She always left before she could be left. It was that simple and that complicated.

Thanks, Mother.

Callie rubbed her forehead with her fingertips, noticing that a headache that was brewing. *Too much thinking, Callie. Maybe you do need a good party after all.*

A brief touch on her shoulder had her jumping and she whirled around. *Finn.* She put her hand on her heart and managed a smile.

'Sorry, I didn't mean to frighten you—you were miles away.' He held a beer bottle loosely in his hand; his other was in the pocket of his jeans. He had a couple of masculine leather and bead bracelets on one wrist and a high-tech watch on the other.

'Hi.' Callie waved him to an empty chair at her table and looked past him into the restaurant. 'Where's Rowan?'

'She met someone she knew at the bar.' Finn yanked the chair out and sat down, stretching his longs legs out in front of him. 'You okay?'

'Shouldn't I be asking that of you?' Callie replied. She leaned forward and asked softly, gently, 'What happened with your fiancée?'

Pain flickered in and out of his eyes. 'You are the nosiest woman I've ever met,' he complained, after taking a long pull of his beer.

'I am—but that doesn't mean I'm not deeply sorry that it happened. Besides, men usually love talking about themselves,' Callie replied.

'Not this one,' Finn replied.

Okay. Back off now, Hollis. Give him some space. 'Can Rowan help you sort out the mess of cancelling the wedding?'

'Luckily, she can. I was just going through the final non-arrangements with her; people are sympathetic but they still need to be paid. Understandable, since pretty much everything that needed to be ordered has already been ordered.'

'I bet Rowan refused to be paid,' Callie said on a small smile. 'She has a heart as big as the sun.'

Finn nodded. 'She did, but she will be—just like everyone else. It's not her fault that things went pear-shaped.'

Pear-shaped? Callie lifted her eyebrows in surprise. Pretty tame word for being jilted. 'So, what happened?' she probed again. Yeah, she was nosy—but this man needed to talk...he needed a friend. Who wouldn't, in his situation? She might be nosy but she could also be a damn good listener.

Finn shook his head. 'I know that you use your eyes as weapons of interrogation, but I'm not going to go there with you.'

Fair enough, Callie thought. He had a right to his secrets. She just hoped that he had someone to talk to—to work this through with.

Finn rolled his head in an effort to release some of the tension in his shoulders. He tapped his index finger against his thigh. 'I *can* tell you that my biggest hassle is that I landed a pretty sweet gig—writing articles about the best honeymoon destinations in Southern Africa. Liz and I were going to spend three weeks travelling…a few days at each destination. My publisher is not going to be happy that I'm doing it solo.'

Callie leaned forward and made a performance of batting her eyelashes. 'Take me—I'll be your substitute wife.'

Finn managed a small grin. 'I'm violently allergic to the word "wife"—even a pretend one.'

'Well, at least you'd be miserable in comfort.'

'If I end up keeping the assignment—which I very well might not.' Finn ran his hands over his short hair and blew out his breath. 'So, tell me why you're sitting here in the dark instead of causing chaos in the bar?'

Callie could clearly see that he'd closed the door on any further discussion about his non-wedding. She looked down into her drink and wrinkled her nose. 'I'm not in the mood to be…'

'Hit on all night?'

'That too. And someone walked in about fifteen minutes ago who I kind of said I might call. We made plans to have supper, then I had to fly to Milan on short notice—'

'Fashion-buying emergency?'

Callie lifted her nose at him in response to his gentle sarcasm. 'Something like that. And I lost his number, and I'm…'

'Not that interested any more?'

She bit her lip. 'Yeah. Not that interested.' She looked out across the ocean to the silver moon that hung low in the sky. She saw the craters, picked out the shape of the rabbit, and sighed.

When she dropped her head her eyes met Finn's and impulsively she reached out and tangled her fingers in his. She ignored the flash of heat, the rocketing attraction. It wasn't the time or the place.

'I'm sorry you're hurting. I'm so sorry for whatever happened that's put such sadness in your eyes.'

Finn licked his lips before staring at the ocean. 'Well, it's not rocket science. I was supposed to be getting married in less than two weeks.'

Callie shook her head, knowing that whatever it was that had mashed up his heart it was more than just losing his ex. 'I think that getting over her will be a lot easier than getting over whatever else has happened.'

Finn's eyes widened and she was surprised when he managed a low, harsh chuckle. He picked at the label on his bottle, not meeting her eyes. 'We changed our minds, decided that marriage wasn't what we wanted—that's all that happened.'

No, it wasn't. But Callie wasn't going to argue with him. 'Well, I am so, so sorry—because it's hurt you badly.'

And for some strange reason the thought of you being hurt makes me feel physically ill.

Finn stood up abruptly and Callie turned to see Rowan approaching them. Finn surprised her when he bent down and kissed her cheek, taking a moment to whisper in her ear.

'Callie, you are part witch and part angel and all sexy. I'm leaving before I say or do anything stupid around you.'

Callie inhaled his aftershave and couldn't help rubbing her cheek against his stubble. 'Like…?'

'Like suggesting that you come home with me.'

His comment wasn't unexpected, and she knew men well enough to know that he was looking for a distraction—a way to step out of the nightmare he was currently experiencing.

Ah, dammit! She wanted to say yes, but she wasn't going to be any man's panacea for pain—even one as sexy as this. If they slept together she wanted it to be because he wanted her beyond all reason and not just to dull the pain, to forget, to step outside his life.

She had to be sensible and she forced the words out. 'Sorry, Finn, that's really not a good idea.'

Finn raked his hand through his hair. 'I know…' He held her eyes and shrugged. 'I really do know. Rowan, hi—I was just leaving…'

CHAPTER TWO

A HALF HOUR LATER Finn tossed down the keys to his house and stared at the coffee-coloured tiles beneath his feet for a moment. Blowing air into his cheeks, he walked through the hall and down the passage to the kitchen, yanked open the double-door fridge and pulled out a beer.

Looking over to the open-plan couch area, he saw the pillow and sheet he'd left on the oatmeal-coloured couch. He'd spent the last few nights on that couch, not sleeping. He couldn't sleep in the bedroom—and not only because he no longer had a mattress on the bed.

Finn rubbed his forehead with the base of the cold bottle, hoping to dispel the permanent headache that had lodged in his brain since last week. Tuesday.

Along with the headache, the same horror film ran on the big screen in his mind…

God, there had been so much blood. As long as he lived he'd remember that bright red puddle on the sheets, Liz grunting beside him, as white as a sheet. He remembered calling for an ambulance and that it had seemed to take for ever to come, remembered Liz sobbing, more blood. The white walls of the hospital, the worried face of the obstetrician. Being told that they had to get Liz into surgery to make sure they didn't lose her too.

It had taken a while for that statement to make sense, and when it had pain had ricocheted through his body and stopped at his heart. Their baby was gone. He also remembered their final conversation as he'd perched on a chair next to her bed, knowing that she was awake but not wanting to talk to him.

'I lost the baby,' she'd said eventually.

'Yeah. I'm so sorry.'

Liz had shrugged, her eyes sunken in her face. 'I feel… empty.' She'd turned her head to look at the flowers he'd bought for her in the hospital gift shop. 'I want to go home, Finn.'

'The doctors say in a day or two. They want to keep an eye on you. You lost a lot of blood. Then I'll take you home.'

Liz shook her head. 'I want to go home—back to Durban, to my folks. We didn't tell anyone I was pregnant so I don't need to explain.'

She fiddled with the tape holding a drip into her vein. When she wouldn't look at him—at all—he knew what she was about to say.

'I don't want to get married any more. We've lost the reason we were both prepared to risk it. We loved the baby but we don't love each other—not enough to get married.'

He rubbed his hands over his face. 'God, Liz. Why don't we take some time to think about that?'

'We don't have time, Finn. And you know that I'm right. If I hadn't fallen pregnant we would've split. You know it and I know it.'

'I'm sorry.'

'Me too.' Liz looked at him then, finally, with pain and sadness and, yes, relief vying for control of her expression. 'Can you cancel the wedding? Sort out the house?'

'Sure.' It was the least he could do.

'And, Finn? I don't want anyone to know that I lost the baby. Just say that we called it quits, okay?'

Now, four days later, he was sad and confused and, to

add hydrochloric acid to an open wound, stuck with all the bills for a wedding that wouldn't happen.

Finn wrestled with the dodgy lock of the door that led out to the balcony and stepped out onto the huge outdoor area. He loved this house—mostly for the tremendous view. From most rooms he had endless views of False Bay, the wildness of the Peninsular, the rocking, rolling Atlantic Ocean. Out here on the balcony he felt he could breathe.

Liz loved the house too, and because she'd spent more time here than he had it seemed as if it was more hers than his. His name might be on the mortgage agreement, but she'd furnished and decorated the place—filled it with the things that made it a home. He supposed that he'd have to go through the place and pack up her stuff—which was pretty much everything. The house would be empty. But to him it felt mostly empty anyway.

They'd tried so hard to play the part of a happy family, but innate honesty had him admitting that, while he was devastated at the loss of their child, he wasn't heartbroken about the wedding being called off. Losing Liz didn't feel like something that had derailed his world, and shouldn't it? Shouldn't he be feeling—*more*? More pain? More confusion? More broken-hearted?

Instead of mourning the loss of his lover he was mourning not being able to hold his child, not being a dad. Although most of his and Liz's conversations lately had revolved around the wedding, they had obviously talked about the birth. They'd been excited—well, *he'd* been excited, Liz had been less so. They'd talked about what type of birth she wanted, had tossed a couple of names around, and he'd been in the process of moving his gym equipment from the third bedroom to the garage so that they could use the room as a nursery.

He felt lousy—as if his world had been tipped upside down. Was it crazy to feel so crap over losing a half-formed, half-baked person to whom he'd contributed DNA but whom he'd never met? Was this normal? Was his grief reasonable? God, he just didn't know.

And how much of his grief was over the baby and how much of it was the residue of the pain he felt about losing James? It felt as if his heart was wrapped in a dull, grey, icy, soggy blanket. The only time he'd felt as if it had lifted—even a little bit—was earlier this evening, when he'd been talking to Callie. For some reason that crazy flirt had managed to lift his spirits. It had been a brief respite and one he'd badly needed.

Finn drank again, leaned his forearms on the railing and stared hard at his feet. He knew that most people thought that because he was a travel journalist that he was a free spirit—that he was a laid-back type of individual—but nothing could be further from the truth. He was a Third Dan black belt in Taekwondo, held a black belt in Jiu-jitsu and, like the other two, his Krav Maga also demanded immense amounts of control and discipline.

But no amount of control, self-discipline or philosophising could rationalise this pain away. Because he'd tried. He really had.

He needed time, he decided—a lot of it—to sort out his head and his heart. Time to think through all he'd recently lost. His baby, his dreams of a family, even his stepdad. He needed time to get back on his feet, to make solid decisions, to work through the emotion of the last couple of weeks, months, years.

And even though he'd been so tempted to ask Callie to come home with him—sleeping with her would have been the perfect way to step out of his head—he knew that he needed to be alone for a while, to keep women at a distance, to work through what had gone wrong with Liz and how.

Ten days, he told himself, and he would be on a plane

to Kruger National Park for the first leg of his Southern Africa trip. Ten days and he could get some distance from this house, from the memory of the blood, Liz's ashen face, from the craziness of cancelling the wedding. Ten days and he would have an excuse to avoid all the calls from his friends and family. He wouldn't have to open the door to any of his three brothers who were taking turns to check up on him, making sure that he was okay.

Finn sighed. Ten more days. A part of him wished he was hiring a kitted-out Land Rover with rooftop tents and heading out into wild, crazy Africa. But visiting upmarket honeymoon destinations wouldn't be a kick in the pants either.

As Callie had said, there was something to be said for licking his wounds in luxury.

If he actually got to keep the job.

The travel magazine had forked out a shedload of cash, and some of the hotels had sponsored his stay in exchange for an honest review of their honeymoon experience. He would be writing the story but he was supposed to take his wife's opinions into consideration as he did so…except now he didn't have a wife to take.

He had to talk to Mike, his editor—and sooner rather than later.

Tomorrow Rowan would send out a blanket email to the wedding guests on his behalf and Mike, as a guest, would receive said email and soon put two and two together. Finn scrunched up his face, annoyed that he hadn't contacted Mike sooner. Cape Town was a small city and he might even have heard already.

Finn glanced at his watch. Ten-thirty. A bit late to call, but that couldn't be helped. He pulled his mobile from his pocket and looked up Mike's number, sighing as he pushed the green button.

'I wondered when you'd get around to calling me,' Mike answered without any preamble.

Finn rubbed his forehead. 'Yeah, it's been a bit mad. I presume you've heard that the wedding is off?'

'Yeah. Sorry.'

Finn heard Mike clearing his throat and jumped in before he could speak again.

'I'd still like to do the assignment.'

'It's a bit pointless without a wife,' Mike said.

'Can't I leave the honeymoon bit out and just write on the lodges themselves?'

'It's scheduled to be part of the honeymoon issue, Finn, with honeymoon and wedding advertising. The article has to concentrate on the honeymoon aspect.'

Finn swore.

Mike's voice in his ear sounded worried and frustrated. 'Tell me about it. I'm in a Catch-22 situation. The publisher agreed to foot the bill, as did many of the hotels, because *you* were writing the article. One of the world's best adventure and travel journalists writing on honeymoons. They loved the idea. And the promo people have already started working on the edition. You're part of that.'

Finn swore again.

'Take me—I'll be your substitute wife.'

He almost smiled, remembering Callie's words from earlier.

Wait, hold on… What had she said?

'Take me—I'll be your substitute wife.'

Could that possibly be a solution? Taking Callie or someone else with him?

'Can I take someone else?' he asked Mike.

Mike's long pause strained Finn's patience. 'I don't see why not,' he said eventually. 'It's not like anyone is going to ask for your wedding certificate or proof that you're married. The two of you would just need to be seen to be having fun. Enjoying the experience. Got anyone in mind?'

He did, actually. Someone who was vivacious, charming, loud, flirtatious, possibly crazy. 'Yeah, I do.'

'Is she someone I know?' Mike asked slyly.

'Judging by the way she talks to everyone and anyone, you probably do.'

'Who is she?'

'Let me talk to her first and see if her coming with me is an option,' Finn said, cautious.

Instinctively he knew that taking Callie—inviting Callie—would be a very good move for him. He'd get to keep this plum assignment and he'd have the company of someone who was a bundle of fun. On that flight back from New York they hadn't stopped talking, and Finn could see why men dropped their tongues to the floor around her. She had a surfer's body—broad shoulders, toned arms, flat stomach and that long, curly blonde hair. But when you looked past the body and face to the brain beyond it you got the shock of your life—because the woman was bright, knowledgeable, and as sharp as a spear-tip.

At her core, she had a lust for life that was contagious. And best of all—unless something had radically changed recently—she had absolutely no interest in relationships and commitment and would be an entertaining companion. She'd be distracting enough to keep him from feeling too sorry for himself.

'Well, talk to her and come back to me. And if you don't take her you'll have to take someone else to complete the assignment,' Mike told him before disconnecting.

Finn slapped his mobile in his hand, considering all his options. He tried to be honest with himself. He had to admit that he was attracted to Callie. If they were spending time in close proximity to each other—he didn't think that honeymoon suites came with twin beds—he'd want to sleep with her. Hell, he wanted to sleep with her now. So sue him. His heart might be battered and bruised, but his junk was in perfectly good working order.

So *sleep with her. It's not like you haven't had flings before. She could be your rebound girl—your way to get over and through this bleak time.*

She wouldn't say yes…

How do you know unless you try?

Finn, thinking he might be going off his head, scrolled through his contacts on his mobile. Rowan would have her number and after sweet talking her out, he had Callie's mobile number. Taking a deep breath, he pushed the green phone icon.

'Hey, how do you feel about being my fake wife?'

The next morning Callie rushed around her apartment, trying to get ready. It was crazy that when she was travelling for work she was super-organised but when she was back home all her wheels fell off. This morning wasn't the first time she'd forgotten to set her alarm, and now she was late for work. So she'd be late? She worked long enough and hard enough that nobody would make a fuss.

Callie pulled a pale yellow dress over her head and scrambled in her cupboards for the pair of nude sandals she wanted to wear with it. Finding them eventually—she really needed to clean out her overflowing cupboards—she smiled as she remembered the very odd conversation she'd had with Finn last night about being his fake wife.

She'd always thought that the 'wife for hire' premise in romance novels was odd, because she couldn't conceive of a situation in the twenty-first century when a fake wife would ever be needed.

But gorgeous Finn needed a wife. She was sorry that she couldn't help him out, but thanks to the eye-watering mortgage she paid each month on this flat, her job—even when she wasn't crazy about it—always came first. Which was a shame, because she could totally see herself swanning around five-star resorts, drinking cocktails and snuggling up to her husband's hot bod—fake…real…who cared?

With her hair and make-up done, Callie headed to the kitchen. She pulled open her fridge door with more hope than expectation and twisted her lips at the bare shelves. There was absolutely nothing to eat and she was starving.

But she knew of a house where there would be blueberry muffins and a hot pot of coffee. The downside was that she'd be even later for work than normal, but maybe she'd take the morning off, or even the day. The house was only a couple of minutes away, and a large part of the reason why she'd bought this expensive flat in this gated community.

Awelfor, red-bricked and old, was her childhood home. In it were her favourite people; Seb, her brother, her best friend and almost sister-in-law Rowan, and Yasmeen, their housekeeper.

But she was so much more than a housekeeper, Callie thought ten minutes later, when she stood in the big, bright sunny kitchen at Awelfor, bending over to hug Yasmeen. This tiny, fiery Malay woman was her north star, her homing beacon. Awelfor would not be home without her.

Yasmeen pulled away and lifted her hand to Callie's face. Her black eyes narrowed. 'You're too skinny and you look tired. When are you going to spend more time on land than you do in the air? And when are you going to find a man and have some babies?'

Situation normal, Callie thought. It was fine for Yasmeen to be a spinster, but not her. *Do as I say and not as I do* was Yas's position on this subject.

Callie rolled her eyes and snagged a muffin—choc chip, not blueberry, yum!—from the plate in the middle of the wooden table that dominated the kitchen.

'Don't nag me—nag them,' Callie retorted, gesturing to Seb and Rowan who had walked into the kitchen, both of them wearing that just-had-spectacular-wake-up-sex look.

Lucky rats. Callie wrinkled her nose when Finn's gorgeous face flashed onto her eyeballs. She'd love to wake up to morning sex with *him.*

Seb crossed the kitchen to where she perched on the corner of the table, munching her muffin. As usual, he kissed her temple and gave her a quick hug. Her brilliant, nice brother. She was so happy that he'd found Ro—that they'd found each other.

It almost, but not quite, made her believe in true love. If it existed then Seb and Ro had the best chance of experiencing it.

Callie was startled out of her musings by Yasmeen's hand slapping her thigh. She yelped and looked at her accusingly. 'What?' she demanded.

'Have you *ever* been allowed to sit on the table instead of at it?' Yasmeen demanded, hands on her hips. 'That's what chairs are for.'

Callie pulled a face at Rowan, who was laughing at her, but jumped off the table and pulled a chair out to sit down. 'Yas...?' she wheedled, using her best little-girl voice.

'Yes, I know—you want a stuffed omelette,' Yasmeen replied, heading to the fridge.

'You know me so well,' Callie purred.

'I should. You've had me wrapped around your little finger since you were a baby,' Yas retorted, pulling items out of the fridge. 'Make yourself useful and grate some cheese.'

Seb poured them all some coffee and placed a cup on the table in front of Callie. 'Aren't you late for work?' he asked, glancing at his watch.

Callie shrugged. 'I let them know. Besides, I have so

much holiday time due to me that I can take a morning here and there.'

She unwrapped the cheese and placed it on the cutting board Yasmeen had placed in front of her. Yasmeen passed her a grater and Callie got to work.

'Hey, Ro?'

'Mmm?' Rowan looked up from her job of cutting red bell peppers. In Yas's kitchen everyone helped. Including Seb, who was dicing mushrooms.

'I had a call from the sexy Finn last night.'

'What sexy Finn?' Seb demanded. 'Is this another European man you're dating?'

Callie laughed. 'No, this is Ro's client Finn. The one we went to meet last night.'

Callie pinched some cheese and popped it into her mouth. After chewing, she told them about Finn's crazy be-my-fake-wife offer.

Rowan looked at her, bemused. 'Are you mad? Take him up on it!'

'I'm flying to Paris, Ro, I have a job.'

'You've just said that you have so much holiday time owed to you,' Ro argued.

'Stop encouraging her to act crazy, darling,' Seb told Rowan. 'And running off with a man she doesn't know would be crazy. Talking about crazy—Cal, we need to talk.'

The mood in the room instantly turned serious as Seb cleared his throat. Rowan frowned and bit her bottom lip. Yasmeen stopped beating the eggs and Seb stared down at his pile of fungi.

Something was up, and whatever it was she knew from their response that she wouldn't like it. 'What's going on?' she asked.

Seb sent Rowan a pleading look, but Rowan just shook her head. Seb looked at her, fear and worry and, strangely, a touch of excitement in his deep blue eyes. 'Cal, I have to tell you something.'

Callie shook her head, knowing instinctively that she didn't want to hear whatever he was going to say. She held up her hand. 'I don't want to know.'

'Laura is coming home.'

Crap. Dammit. Hell.

Laura. Her mother. *Their* mother. The woman, as Seb had told her a few months back, he had reconnected with. Oh, she'd always suspected that he'd kept track of her; he was a brilliant ethical hacker and there wasn't any information he couldn't find.

'I want to see her again and she's returning to Cape Town for a visit.'

Seb had a stubborn look on his face and she knew that his mind was made up.

'Are you paying for her to come home?' Callie demanded.

Seb's lack of an answer was confirmation that he was.

'If you bring her back to Awelfor I'll never forgive you,' Callie whispered, her stomach now in a knot, twisted with tension and long-ago suppressed hurt.

Her mother had walked out when she was seven. As far as Callie was concerned she'd had twenty years to come back home. It was way too late now.

'I wasn't planning to—not yet,' Seb said in a quiet voice. 'She's coming home for a three-week visit and we've agreed to meet. She wants to see you too.'

Callie shook her head wildly. 'Hell, no! No to the max. *No!*'

Seb held up his hands. 'I know that this is a shock, but…'

Callie pulled in a deep breath and pushed back the hurt, the feeling of abandonment, the constant ache for her mother. Her eyes turned cold and her face tightened.

'When is she due to land?' she asked quietly, thinking that this was what Rowan had started to tell her the other night. She had been trying to warn her about Laura's arrival—trying to get her head wrapped around the idea of Laura returning.

Sorry, Ro, not even marginally interested.

Seb checked his watch. 'Today is the eleventh; she's flying in on the nineteenth. Will you be back in town by then?'

Callie grabbed her mobile from her bag and quickly pulled up her diary app. She cursed when she saw that after Paris she didn't have any trips scheduled for a couple of weeks. Three, to be exact. It was the end of a three-month rotation—but why, oh, why did it have to be now?

She'd be home at exactly the same time as her mother would be in the city. That wouldn't do. That wouldn't do at all. She wouldn't risk running into her, having her arrive on her doorstep, popping into Awelfor and seeing her here. She wouldn't take the chance.

She'd endured twenty years of silence and Laura didn't just get to rock up now and make demands. She'd made her choice when she left—she had to live with it now.

'Will you try to be here?' Seb asked quietly, rephrasing his question.

Callie shook her head before yanking her bag off the chair and heading for the door. 'Hell, no. I don't have a mother—I haven't had one for twenty years. So Laura can just go back to wherever she came from and I don't want to talk about her again. *Ever!*'

'Cal—' Seb pleaded.

'Don't mention her name again, Seb,' Callie muttered, before stepping out of the door, blinking back tears. It had to be the bright sunlight making her cry because her mother—*Laura!*—wasn't worth a single one of her tears.

Looking down at her mobile in her hand, she thought

that she couldn't be in the country, breathing the same air as Laura. She'd rather do anything else, *be* anywhere else. Even—

'Finn? It's Callie. You called me last night? If you haven't married, proposed to or found anybody else to be your wife since we spoke last night I might be your girl.'

CHAPTER THREE

CALLIE LEFT AWELFOR and headed directly to Simon's Town, the pretty town to the east of the city of Cape Town. Her father had set up a branch of his sea kayaking tours there after handing over the family property business to Seb. Patch loved his life as a kayak guide and tour operator. Like her, he was vivacious and open; if she had any charm at all she'd inherited it all from him.

Callie sat on the low wall that separated the promenade from the beach and watched Patch converse with his customers while his assistants unloaded the kayaks from the trailer that he'd driven onto the beach. He was still tall and broad and handsome—quite a silver fox, Callie thought. Thank God he'd finally given up dating vapid and beautiful women—mostly younger than her—and was about to marry a woman his own age.

He and Annie seemed to be blissfully happy, and after what Laura and the crazy gold-diggers had put him through she was happy for him. He deserved to be loved and loved well. And, judging by the perpetual grin he was sporting lately, Annie loved him very well indeed.

Callie let out a whistle that Patch had taught her as a kid and Patch instantly turned, his fantastic smile lighting up his face. She might have had a screwed-up childhood, and maybe Patch hadn't been the perfect father, but it had been a very long time since she'd doubted that he loved her. He was one of her best friends and the strongest rope keeping the balloon that was her life tethered to the ground.

Patch bounded across the sand and immediately pulled her into his arms, warm and strong. She buried her head in his neck, sucked in the smell of him and felt her tilting world settle down. Patch ran a hand over her hair before kissing her temple and stepping away from her to sit on the wall next to her.

'Seb told you, huh?'

'Yeah.' She suddenly remembered that her mother had been his wife and wondered how *he* was handling the news. 'How do you feel about her returning?'

Patch shrugged. 'Doesn't mean much to me except for how it affects you and Seb.'

Callie sank her bare feet into the warm sand and wiggled her toes. She bit the side of her lip and stared out to sea. 'I'm running away…'

Patch cocked his head. 'You are? Where to?'

'Well, it's not quite settled, but there's this guy and he needs a—a friend to go on a trip with him.'

'Uh-huh?'

'He seems nice, and he's just gone through a rough time, and we seem to like each other…' Callie waved her hands in the air. 'Not as…you know…but I think we could be friends… He needs a friend.'

'Most of us do,' Patch agreed. 'And you want to avoid seeing Laura.'

Callie waited a beat before turning anxious eyes to his face. 'Am I wrong? Should I be meeting her?'

Patch ran his hand over his jaw. 'Honey, for the last ten years, ever since you totalled your car at a thousand miles an hour, I have trusted you to do the right thing—not for me but for yourself. I still trust you to do that.' He reached for her hand and held it. 'That thing we call intuition? That little voice? It's your soul talking. You can trust it.'

'My intuition is telling me to go on this trip with Finn.'

'Then do it,' Patch said, before frowning. 'Wait—is this Rowan's client? The travel writer?'

'Mmm.'

Patch smiled broadly. 'Tell him to come kayaking with me—maybe he'll do an article on the tours.'

Callie had to smile. Her dad was her rock, but he was never shy about putting himself forward. Ah, well, she thought as she sat with him in the morning sun, you don't get apples from orange trees.

Callie buzzed Finn through the gates of her complex in Camps Bay and walked onto the wide veranda that encompassed most of her second-storey luxury flat. She leaned her arms on the railing, watching as he steered his expensive SUV into her visitor's parking space. He left his vehicle and Callie watched as he stretched, his T-shirt riding up his abdomen to reveal a ridged stomach that had to be an eight or ten-pack and the hint of make-women-stupid obliques.

She did appreciate a fine-looking man, Callie thought, and they didn't come much finer than Finn Banning. Sexy, and also very successful She'd researched him and read that he had been an award-winning investigative journalist before switching to travel journalism, where he was raking in the praise.

What had really gone wrong with his engagement? Why had they called it off? Why would any woman walk away from that?

Maybe there was something about Finn Banning that she didn't know yet—and that worried her. Especially if she was considering spending three weeks in his company.

After she'd called him from Awelfor she'd spent ten minutes convincing him that she wasn't joking about being his 'wife' and avoiding his probing questions around why she'd changed her mind. She'd ended the conversation with the suggestion that if he still thought that taking her along was a good idea he should pop by for a drink at sunset.

And here he was—still hot, still sexy, still sad and still, apparently, wifeless.

He was her get-out-of-the-country card. Okay, the truth was that she didn't need him to go anywhere—she had enough cash at her disposal to go anywhere she wanted. But since she was taking a month's holiday at very short notice wherever she went she would be going alone. Normally she wouldn't mind being alone, but at the moment she needed a distraction from her thoughts—from thinking about Laura.

She'd thought she'd buried those feelings of betrayal and abandonment but apparently it only took the knowledge that Laura was heading home to pull them all back up to the surface.

If she went anywhere alone she'd think and wallow and feel sad and miserable. But if she went with Finn she'd have a sexy man to distract her; she'd have to be happy and flirty and...well, *herself*.

She could shove all thoughts of Laura back into the box they'd escaped from.

Finn pulled off his sporty sunglasses and held them in his hand as he looked around the complex, eventually seeing her number on the front wall. He rubbed the back of his neck as he stopped a couple of feet from her door—a gesture that told Callie he wasn't totally comfortable with this idea and was thinking of backing out.

'Finn...hi.' She leaned over the balcony to look down at him, not aware that she was giving him a super-excellent view of her hot pink lace-covered breasts. 'The door is open. Come on up the stairs and hang a left. It's too gorgeous an evening to be inside.'

Finn nodded and walked through the front door. She

heard the thud of the door closing behind him, and his rapid footsteps told her that he was jogging up the stairs. Through the wooden patio doors she saw him entering her lounge, looking around at the eclectic furniture and her wild, colourful abstract art. He dropped his glasses, mobile and keys on her coffee table and looked at her across the room.

His eyes caught hers and a small smile played on his lips. 'Hello, possible fake wife.'

Callie laughed, immediately at ease. What was it about him that instantly had her relaxing? She felt she'd known him a lot longer than she had.

She watched as Finn stopped, as everyone always did, at the wall of photo frames. She watched his eyes skim over the photographs, quickly taking in her history—her journey from being a daredevil kid to a daredevil teenager to who she was today, whoever *that* was.

Finn spent more time than people usually did staring at the photos, eventually turning to look at her, his eyebrows raised. 'You're up a tree.'

'I frequently was.'

He pointed to a frame. 'You look like you're about forty feet up.'

She grinned. 'Forty-two feet—my dad measured it after his heart restarted.' She shrugged and waved her wine glass around. 'They told me not to climb it, so I did.'

'How old were you?'

'Five? Six? Somewhere around there.'

'You must have been a handful.'

'You have no idea. I thought I was indestructible. I had zero sense of self-preservation and was willing to try anything once—or four times. And if my brother was giving something a whirl—well, I would too. Surfing, diving, climbing, skateboarding, cycling…'

'And I thought *I* was a hellraiser. Your mum must have pulled her hair out,' Finn said, walking towards her.

Callie swallowed and looked away. Her mum had let her run wild—not particularly worried that Callie might crack her head open or break a limb. She would just shake her head before disappearing into her bedroom and locking the door behind her.

Then one day, a couple of weeks after her seventh birthday, she'd disappeared for ever.

Finn stepped out onto the veranda, gratefully taking the beer she held out to him. She dropped into the corner of her fat couch and tucked her bare feet up and under her bottom, gesturing to Finn to take a seat. When he'd sat down in the chair next to her he looked out at the sea view and the dropping sun and sighed.

'Nice place. How long have you lived here?'

'I bought it about five years ago. I love it, but I'm seldom home,' Callie explained, picking up her wine glass and taking a sip. She turned and looked at his profile, strong in the fading light of the day.

'So what's happened that you're suddenly available to come travelling?' Finn asked. 'And why are your eyes red-rimmed and puffy?'

Damn, that cosmetics rep had *so* lied. The eye cream that had cost the equivalent of a small house did *not* suck away the bags of fluid left there by a massive crying jag.

Callie couldn't meet his eyes. Mostly because she felt her own prickling with tears again and she never cried in company—especially not around sexy, fit men. 'It's not important.'

Finn shook his head. 'I suspect it's very damn important to you.' Then he lifted one broad shoulder. 'But, since I hate people prying, I'll leave you with your secrets.'

Thank you, she thought sarcastically, a little put out that he hadn't pushed. Did that mean that she actually *wanted* to tell him her sad tale of maternal neglect? *Blergh*—she didn't do sob stories. Especially her own.

Callie pulled herself out of her funk and tilted her head. 'So, it turns out that I can be free for the next four weeks or so. Do you want to explain your crazy proposal to me again?'

Finn stretched out his long legs, which ended in a pair of battered trainers. 'As I explained, I landed an assignment to write an article on upmarket lodges, focusing on the honeymoon aspect of said lodges. The magazine is Europe-based, a leader in its field, it has a huge readership and it's a plum assignment.'

'Of course it is.'

Finn was hot property—he wouldn't be writing for just any old magazine.

'With the wedding imploding I either have to give up the assignment or find someone to go with me.'

'As your wife?'

'As my editor said, nobody is going to ask for proof of my marriage. If I take someone who looks reasonably happy to be there with me I think I can get by without having to explain that the wedding was called off two weeks before the big day,' Finn said, his voice even but his expression pensive. 'I really don't want to give up the opportunity to get my foot in the door with *Go Travel*; they have a bunch of staff writers and rarely issue assignments to freelancers.'

But they did to you.

As she'd thought: hot property, indeed. And not just as a writer. The man had a body that you could strike tinder off.

Callie resisted the urge to fan her face with her hand as a bead of sweat trickled down her spine. Yes, it was summer in Cape Town, but her hot flush had nothing to do with the evening heat and everything to do with imagining him naked above her, his fabulous eyes locked on hers as he pushed himself home. She'd be tight and he'd be big, and he'd reach that special spot deep inside and rock her to screaming…

'Callie?'

Finn's voice pulled her out of her side trip into fantasy land and she waved a hand in front of her face, knowing that her cheeks were fire-red. 'Wow, it's so hot out here.'

'Actually, a cool breeze has picked up and the temperature has dropped a couple of degrees,' Finn countered, sending her a knowing smile. At least she thought it was knowing—for all she knew he could be thinking that she was loopy.

She fumbled for her wine and downed half a glass before resting it on her cheek.

'You okay?'

Just peachy, trying to deal with the fact that you are the first man I can imagine sleeping with for far too long.

'Fine.'

Liar, liar, womb on fire….

'Anyway, back to your trip. When are you supposed to arrive at your first destination? Where *is* the first destination?'

'The Baobab and Buffalo Lodge, which is on a private concession next to the Kruger National Park. We're booked in for a few nights.'

Holy fishcakes—when they said 'upmarket' they meant *upmarket.* Callie knew that the Baobab and Buffalo Lodge was booked solidly for years at a time. It was a six-star safari experience all the way.

Callie leaned forward, her eyes uncharacteristically serious. 'Cards on the table, Finn. What exactly does it entail? What do you expect from me?'

A ghost of a smile flitted over Finn's face. 'All it entails is you hanging out at expensive lodges and hotels, taking part in some of the activities, eating yourself into a coma and drinking yourself under the table. All on my expense account.'

'And the cons?'

'You have to do all of that with me.' Finn placed his ankle on his knee and picked at the label of his beer bottle. 'I'd like someone I can talk to—someone I could have fun with…someone who I know is not going to go all hearts and flowers on me, thinking that this will be the start of something special. I am in no way, shape or form looking to extend this beyond the holiday, nor looking for anything more than a friendship.'

Okay, she could understand that. Everybody needed time to regroup after a break-up, and of course he didn't want to get involved. And she was perfect for that as she didn't go hearts and flowers on any man, ever. And she was fun.

Well, she hadn't been fun for a while, but that was going to change. She'd pull herself out of her funk and go back to being the old, crazy, happy, party-like Callie.

She needed to be that Callie again.

Callie cocked her head. Time to pull out the big guns. 'And this *fun*. Where does it stop? In other words, are you expecting sex out of this deal?'

Finn's light eyes bumped into hers. 'It would be a nice side benefit but not a deal-breaker.'

Callie heard the honesty in his words and tone but thought she should just make sure. 'So I could still go with you and not be pressurised into having sex with you?'

Honesty had her silently admitting that she probably would—old Callie wouldn't have hesitated!—but she'd prefer to have it out in the open.

'Making me repeat it in another way isn't going to make my words more true. But if it makes you happy…' Finn lifted that broad shoulder again. 'Sex—if it happens—

will be a bonus, not an expectation. And totally without strings.'

Callie nibbled the inside of her lip, desperately trying to be sensible. She couldn't believe that she was seriously considering his offer, but on the other hand how often did the opportunity to visit such wonderful places in luxury—for free!—fall into one's lap?

How often did a person get the chance to do something so different on someone else's dime? That would be *never.* She'd be a fool to pass this up.

But she wasn't an idiot. She had to be marginally sensible about this. She was thinking about going on holiday with a stranger—a man she'd met twice. If he turned out to be a psycho she would be at his mercy, neck-deep in a situation that might become very sticky, very fast.

But he didn't give off any creepy vibes, and she had pretty good intuition. *It's your soul talking...you can trust it.* She suspected he was exactly what he appeared to be: a guy who'd had the emotional carpet yanked from underneath his feet; battered, who was bruised and trying to find his feet, to regroup.

But was she prepared to risk her life on her intuition?

'I'll need character references.' she blurted out, hoping that he would understand that she needed to protect herself. 'Just to make sure that you aren't a weird psycho. I can give you references too, if you want.'

At that, Finn did smile—possibly the fullest and most genuine smile she'd yet to see from him. 'Nah, I'm good. I already know that you're slightly psycho,' he teased.

'Funny…' Callie muttered, although in truth he was. It was a relief to realise that behind that gruff, stoic exterior was an offbeat sense of humour. When you travelled with someone a GSOH was the minimum requirement.

Callie put down her glass of wine and linked her fingers around her bare knee. 'Are you sure about this, Finn?

You don't know me. After two days with me, you might want to shoot me.'

Finn lifted the beer bottle to his lips, took a long sip and swallowed. 'If we were at a resort and I had to say to you that I wanted some time alone, some quiet, what would you do?'

Callie thought for moment. 'I'd find something to do—go hang out by the pool, read my book, flirt with the barman. I'd give you your space.'

'And if I said let's go bungee jumping or white-water rafting?'

'I'd say go on your own,' Callie replied quickly. She held up her hand and looked at him askance. 'Is me being a thrill-seeker part of the requirement? Because if it is then I might have to bail now. You might be Indiana Jones, but I'm not a run-through-the-jungle-barefoot type of girl.'

She had been at one time. Right up until her late teens—until her car accident—she'd tried anything wild or woolly once…probably twice.

Finn's mouth twitched with amusement as he glanced towards the photos on the wall before looking back at her. 'Fair enough. You might change your mind.'

No, she wouldn't. He could take that to the bank.

'You have a better chance of falling pregnant,' Callie quipped before turning serious again. 'Look, Finn, I'm honoured and flattered that you've asked me to go with you, but this will only work if you feel you can be honest with me, that you can treat me like you were taking a mate with you.' Her brows pulled together. 'Why *aren't* you taking a friend with you? Surely you have someone you could ask?'

'You keep forgetting the honeymoon angle.' Finn pushed his hand through his short curls. 'The magazine is paying through the nose for me to do this, and there is no way they will allow me to go on my own or with a mate.

They were expecting me to go with my wife, at the very least my girlfriend, at the very, *very* least with a woman.' Finn placed his beer on the wooden coffee table between them. 'So what do you think? Yes? No? Hell, no?' Finn raised a solid black eyebrow.

Callie nodded. 'I think so.' She slowly answered him. 'Let me have a bit more of a think.'

Why was she hesitating, being coy about this? She wanted, *needed*, to get out of Cape Town, and Finn was offering her a brilliant way to do that. She found him easy to talk to, he seemed to like her, and she was attracted to him.

What was holding her back?

Exactly that, she realised. The fact that she was so immensely attracted to him. Nobody had ever created such an intense longing in her and that made her wary…a little scared. If she were less drawn to him she wouldn't have any doubts and she'd be packing her bags already.

You are so weird, Hollis, Callie told herself. *Fruitcake nuts.*

'I'd love to know what is going through that very sharp brain of yours, Callie.'

There was no chance of her telling him what she was thinking. *I know that you were about to be married, and that you're probably hurting and missing your fiancée, but I'd really like to have you leaning over me, sliding on home...*

She didn't think so.

On the other hand she really didn't want to be someone's backstop. If Finn was making love to her then she wanted him to be *with* her, thinking of her and not of the lover he'd lost. She wasn't prepared to be his escape, his emotional aspirin, a distraction from the pain. She'd be his friend, but if he made love to her then it would be because he wanted her.

While she was prepared to be a fake wife, she refused

to be a second choice or a substitute lover. Maybe if she knew why he was so suddenly single she would have a better idea of how emotionally battered he really was. And the only way to get that information was to ask.

'Why *did* your engagement blow up?'

Finn glared at her. 'You are like a dog with a freakin' bone. Do you ever give up?'

Innate honesty compelled her to speak. 'No.'

Callie stared at him with big eyes as he stood up, walked around the table and gripped the arms of her chair, caging her in. Callie sucked in air and along with it the masculine, indefinable essence of Finn. A kick of spice, a hint of citrus, a tiny bit of natural musk. The hair on her arms and on the back of her neck stood up and she felt her skin prickle as his eyes locked on hers.

'Are you always this stubborn?'

Callie shook her head. 'Sorry to tell you that I haven't even hit stubborn yet.'

'Crap. Well, let's see if a little distraction will work,' Finn replied, his voice silky. 'And if my kisses don't distract you at least they'll get you to shut the hell up...'

Callie sucked in her breath as his mouth brushed her lips. Harder, thinner, masculine lips that knew exactly what they were doing as he nipped and teased her mouth. His hand came up to clasp the side of her head and he tipped her face sideways. Then his kiss deepened and his mouth became more insistent, asking—no, *demanding*—more.

'Kiss me, Callie. Open up and let me taste you,' he muttered against her lips.

Callie couldn't do anything but obey—didn't have the thought processes to do anything but follow where he led.

Instead of plunging inside, forcing its way in, his smart tongue explored her bottom lip, teased the corners of her mouth, deliberately avoided tangling with hers.

Frustrated with his teasing, Callie pushed against his

chest and, keeping her mouth locked on his, found her way to her feet, looping her arms around his back and pushing into his hard frame. Breast against chest, stomach against his steel erection, mouth under his. Needing more, she pushed her tongue into his mouth, sliding it against his and taking the kiss from hot to steamy to erotic, from wild to crazy.

His hands raced down her back, palmed her butt and lifted her up and into him. Her legs automatically wound around him and she tipped her hips so that his erection could rub her clit as his kisses—God, was it possible?—got deeper and steamier.

She wanted more…she needed more… This was just sex, lust! Six months was far too damn long, Callie realised from a place way, way outside of herself. She needed him—Finn—now.

Her hands were sliding down the back of his shorts, trying to feel that magnificent ass she'd been fantasising about, when Finn pulled his mouth off hers. He lifted his hand from the inside of her bra and one arm kept her anchored in place. He brushed her hair off her cheek and tucked it behind her ears. He looked rueful.

Callie felt her feet touch the floor and she held on to his arm to make sure that she wouldn't topple over.

'Ah…um…what was that?'

'God knows. But, after that I guess sex is closer to being on the table than before.'

Finn stepped away from her, seemingly unconcerned that he still had a steel pipe in his pants.

His words dumped a figurative bucket of cold water over her head. What *was* it about him? He just had to touch her and she was under his spell, ready to go where he led. She never lost control in a sexual situation—her head was always in the game.

'That's why I'm wary,' Callie admitted eventually, unable to stop licking her bottom lip, hoping the taste of him lingered there.

Finn's black brows pulled together. 'Sorry—lost you. What?'

'We have a hectic attraction. It could blow up in our faces,' Callie explained. 'It could burn hot and die fast, and if that happens while we're on holiday then we'd be up the creek without a paddle.'

Finn jammed his hands in the pockets of his shorts. 'We'll be together for three weeks. Do you normally lose interest that quickly?'

Sometimes, Callie wanted to admit. But with him she was more worried about feeling something deeper than basic lust than finding herself bored. Bored, she could fake her way through, but he intrigued her; he was a puzzle she longed to solve and that rarely…okay, *never* happened to her. And if she was this attracted to him—physically and mentally—so soon, then spending twenty-four-seven with him might make her feel so much more.

Dangerous.

Callie stepped away and held up her palms. *Okay, get a grip and shut this down before it goes any further. Get you head in the game, Hollis. Someone has to be sensible here and it looks like you've drawn the short straw.*

'Finn, I get that you're hurting, that you need a distraction from your crappy life. You've just broken up with your fiancée and that's got to be seriously painful.'

And I'm using you to escape dealing with my mother.

Finn just folded his arms and kept his face blank.

'You should know that I never treat sex casually, that I am very selective about who I bring into my bed.'

'Okay. Good to know.'

Callie blew out her breath. 'And you should also know that I'm not going to be your means of escaping that pain.'

And, conversely, I'm not going to use you to escape my memories.

Finn frowned. 'Lost you. Explain.'

She waved her hand in the space between them. 'We obviously generate some heat between us, and I have no doubt that sleeping with you would be fun, but we can't ignore the fact that until recently you were in a highly committed relationship. That relationship came to a skidding halt and pretty much went over a cliff. Fair to say that?'

Finn shrugged. 'I suppose.'

'So, to carry on with that analogy, I'm not going to sleep with you until I am fully convinced that you have come out of that coma and are mostly recovered. I'm *not* a way to dull the pain.'

Finn stared at her for a long time, his green eyes speculative. Eventually, ever so slightly, his mouth lifted at the corners. 'This isn't all about me and my relationship, is it? You're also running from something—or *someone*.'

Maybe. Possibly. Okay, dammit, yes.

'And that's why you've been crying.' Finn rubbed his jaw with the palm of his hand. After a long silence he lifted his muscled shoulders in a weary shrug. 'Look, Callie, I'm probably not ever going to tell you about the mess that was my almost-marriage, but would you think I was spinning a line to get into your pants if I said that I'm not that heartbroken? That I'm sad but also relieved?'

She heard something that sounded like the ring of truth in his voice but she didn't know him well enough to trust him. 'Maybe you're just telling yourself that to make it easier to cope with. People love to lie to themselves.' She saw Finn's mouth open to start his protest but she shook her head to stop him. 'Look, Finn, let's just take it slow, okay? One day at a time, as friends and companions. Let's not force it, okay?'

He looked as if he wanted to argue, but then she saw him swallowing his words, saw his nod.

'Yeah, okay, I suppose that's sensible.'

Finn lifted his hand to brush her cheek with the backs of his fingers. Callie could only look at him, her blood roaring through her veins and pooling between her legs. If he didn't go soon she was going to forget any doubts she had and drag him to the floor.

'That being said, I'm going to go.'

Callie licked her lips as her brain tried to restart. 'Um…okay.' Him going would be a very good idea.

'You'll let me know your decision? As soon as possible? Like tomorrow?'

Callie handed him a blank look. 'Uh…what decision?'

Finn grinned. 'About being my fake wife?'

Callie blushed. God, her brains were fried. 'Sure, as soon as possible.'

She opened her mouth to add a blanket yes to whatever he wanted, wherever he wanted, as long as he would kiss her like that again. At the last minute her rationality kicked in and mentally slapped her to bring her to her senses.

'I'll see you out.'

'Don't bother.'

Finn stepped towards her, dropped a quick kiss on her temple before heading inside and picking up his wallet, keys and mobile. He turned and looked at her, and the corner of his mouth kicked up.

'Yeah, I think you and I could have some fun. And, Cal?'

'Mmm?'

'No more crying, okay?'

CHAPTER FOUR

FINN HEARD HIS doorbell ring and cursed as he lifted another box onto the tower of boxes he was creating in his hallway. God, Liz had a lot of stuff, he thought as he turned sideways to navigate through the thin aisle between boxes to get to the door.

It would be a brother again, holding a six-pack and a takeaway, coming to keep him company in his darkest hour. He appreciated the beer and the food, but instead of their sympathy he wished that they'd give him something useful, like help with shifting and packing boxes.

He rolled his eyes as the doorbell pealed again and reached out to yank the door open. 'You can only come in if you're prepared to work, you lazy—'

He blinked at the vision on his doorstep. Instead of one of his big, brawny, young stepbrothers Callie, dressed in a short sleeveless sundress, stood in front of him, her blonde hair pulled up into a tail and most of her face covered by huge dark sunglasses.

'Oh, sorry. Wasn't expecting you.'

Callie pushed her glasses up into her hair and smiled. 'I can see that, since you're shirtless and shoeless. Who *were* you expecting?'

'Ah, one or more of my brothers—stepbrothers. They pop in most evenings, usually around this time.'

'Coming to check up on you?'

'Yeah.'

Callie placed a hand on her heart. 'That's so sweet.'

Finn grimaced. 'I appreciate the sentiment but I wish they would just stop. Because I'm not talking they think that Liz is to blame and that I need comforting.'

'*Is* she to blame?'

'Mutual decision,' he replied quickly, seeing the trap and dodging it. 'Anyway, because not all men are Neanderthals, they've been worried about me because Liz and I were together for a long time. I have so many offers for beer or lunch or dinner I could scream.'

Callie didn't say anything and he, like a rookie, just kept on talking.

'So I drink the beers and eat the food and try to convince everyone that I'm okay.'

'Are you?'

Callie took his right hand and held it between hers. She looked up at him from beneath those ridiculously long lashes, her expression earnest and concerned. She wasn't just asking for form's sake, he suddenly realised, she genuinely seemed to care. And her empathy—not pity or sympathy—melted one of the many icicles attached to his heart.

Finn thought about her question for a minute and left his hand where it was, his fingers entangled with hers. 'Mostly. I will be a feeling a lot more relieved when you say yay or nay.'

'Yay,' Callie said as she dropped his hand.

Finn looked down at her, not sure that he'd heard her correctly. 'What?'

'Yes, I will be your fake wife.' Callie said, her eyes dancing. 'Thanks for asking me.'

Finn felt relief course through him and was surprised at the wave of—hell—*happiness* that followed. He was going to be able to complete this amazing assignment, get out of this house and step out of his life, thanks to this phenomenal woman.

'That's the best news I've heard all day. Thanks, Callie.'

'I should be thanking you; it's an amazing opportunity to see some places that I haven't seen before.'

'And to get out of Dodge as well.' Finn folded his arms and raised a brow. 'Want to tell me why?'

Callie didn't miss a beat. 'Want to tell me what really happened to stop the wedding?'

'Touché.'

He wasn't going to open up and neither was she. Better that way, Finn decided, even though he was damn curious.

'So, do you want to come inside?'

Finn thought that she was about to say no but then she straightened her spine and pushed her shoulders back, lifting those small breasts. 'Yeah, okay. There's a couple of things we need to chat about.'

'That sounds ominous.' Finn gestured her inside and noticed that she had no problem negotiating the boxes. 'Liz's stuff. I'm packing it up and shipping it home to her parents.'

'Ah.'

Callie moved away from the boxes and looked at the now stark living room. All the things that had made it a home were gone—the scatter cushions, the art, the ornaments, the photo frames.

'The furniture—hers or yours?'

Finn shrugged. 'The couches and the furniture are mine. I'm pretty much handing over the rest of the house. She bought most of it and there's nothing much I want to keep.'

'Nothing?'

Finn shook his head. 'I'm not sentimental when it comes to stuff.'

He'd used to be but wasn't any more. Only with a gun

to his head would he admit that he'd kept all the sonar scan pictures of his baby—the baby that hadn't made it past four and a half months. Finn swallowed and steeled himself against the wave of pain. Okay, maybe he was a little sentimental about some things.

He pulled in a deep, restorative breath and along with it Callie's sweet perfume. She smelled so sweet and fresh, and he realised that *he* had to smell as if he'd been working his tail off all day—which he had—so he backed away from her.

'There's some wine or beer in the fridge—glasses in the cupboard next to the fridge. Help yourself. I'm just going to take a quick shower, if that's okay.'

'Sure, take your time.' Callie grinned at him. 'It'll give me time to snoop.'

'Snoop away—you won't find anything interesting,' Finn told her, before belting up the stairs to the en-suite bathroom off the guest bedroom.

As per normal, he glanced at the closed door of the room on the left and sighed. He really should try to move back into the master bedroom again. But he still hadn't replaced the mattress on their—*his*—bed, so what was the point? Maybe after he came back from his 'honeymoon' he'd try again.

Maybe. Or maybe he'd just get a whole new bed.

She liked Finn's house, Callie decided, liked the openness and the space. And the view was one of the best she'd seen. But the lack of anything personal surprised her; Finn was a world traveller—surely he would have picked up a memento here and there? Art? Pottery? Photographs?

Nothing in the house suggested that he'd lived here on an ongoing and permanent basis with his fiancée. Which was weird—weren't houses supposed to be shared? Granted, she wasn't an expert on co-habiting, but shouldn't the house be a place of compromise? Shouldn't there be a photograph of his family…his brothers? A trophy? A flat screen TV? Books…? Something that suggested that this was his house as much as hers?

For Finn's sake she hoped that his ex hadn't been an 'everything that's mine is mine and what's yours is mine too' type of woman. Maybe his priorities were a big screen TV and an internet connection—she'd dated more than a few men like that. Or maybe he simply wasn't a sentimental, collect-mementos-along-the-way type of guy.

Callie turned when she heard his footsteps behind her and saw that Finn had showered and dressed in a pair of black athletic shorts and a plain red T-shirt.

He ran his hands over his wet curls and sent her a small smile. 'Did you get some wine?'

'I didn't get that far.' Callie followed him into the kitchen and stood on the other side of a granite counter as he opened a cupboard door to pull out a glass. 'You look very fit—do you go to the gym?

Finn pulled a face. 'No. Martial arts.' He opened the fridge and she saw that it held nothing but a bottle of unopened wine, a mouldy block of cheese and some eggs. Someone hadn't been cooking or had been living on take-out.

Not healthy.

'What type of martial arts?' she asked, resisting the urge to mention his lack of food. Even if she was going to be his 'wife', she wasn't in a position to nag him about eating properly and taking care of himself. But, damn, she wanted to.

'Pretty much everything, actually. But I concentrate on Taekwondo and jiu-jitsu, occasionally taking a side trip into Krav Maga—'

'Notoriously difficult—out of the Israeli army.' She saw

the surprise flicker in his eyes at her even knowing about Krav Maga—but, hey, she read. A lot. 'Are you ranked?'

'You are the nosiest woman I've ever met,' Finn complained—not for the first and, she knew, not for the last time.

'And—I'll say it again—you're one of the few men who don't like talking about themselves.'

'So why do you keep asking?'

''Cos you're *fascinating*,' Callie replied, shoving her tongue into her cheek.

'Flirt.'

Callie dropped into a quick curtsy. 'Thank you, sir. So, what's your rank?'

Same question, phrased another way. His quick smile and the elaborate roll of his eyes told her that he was enjoying their banter. It would do him good to laugh, to smile.

'I'm ranked highly.'

She sighed dramatically at his answer. 'Trying to get information out of you is like trying to get blood out of a stone.' Callie took her glass of wine and sipped. 'Why don't you buy mementos of the places you've been?'

He blinked at the change of subject as he twisted the top off a bottle of beer. 'What? Like tourist tat?'

Callie sent him a patient look. 'Come on, Finn. Like you, I travel a lot and I know what is tat and what is art. And *everybody* sees something along the way that calls to them. I picked up a stunning vase in Murano that I treasure, a piece of street art in Rome. What do *you* buy?' She gestured to the soulless house. 'This is your house—why isn't there anything of you in it?'

Finn took a long sip of beer. 'You're going to nag me until I tell you, aren't you?'

'Actually, if it's a touchy or personal subject I won't. I know that I'm relentless, and curious, but I do respect your right not to talk. Just say *pass* and we'll move on.'

Callie shook her head and caught his look of surprise. 'This agreement we have doesn't include sharing our secrets. Well, you're welcome to share yours but I'm not sharing mine.'

Finn raised the bottle to his lips again and shook his head looking bewildered. That was okay, Callie thought. Bewildered she could live with. Annoyed or bored would make her think that she'd overstepped the mark.

'So why is there nothing personal in your house?' Callie grinned at his exasperation. 'What? You didn't say pass!'

'You are going to drive me crazy—I can just tell.' Finn closed his eyes and scratched the spot between his eyebrows. 'When I bought the house Liz moved in. She travelled as well, but she spent six weeks away and then a month at home. Her schedule was set but I could be away for two months, home for a week and gone again. She asked me time and time again to help her decorate the house—but, hell, I'm a guy. I'd rather watch sport or…watch paint dry. So one day she dumped all my stuff and all her stuff in the middle of the lounge—right over there—in front of the TV. There was a rugby match I wanted to watch so we had to sort through it. The whole process made me realise…'

'Pray tell?' Callie's lips quirked when he paused for dramatic effect.

'…that I buy crap and shouldn't be allowed anywhere near art galleries or home décor shops. If it's cheap and nasty, tasteless and fake, I *will* buy it.'

Callie's laughed bounced off the walls, and she was still chuckling when Finn led the way to the veranda, where Callie took a seat on an antique bench that had been converted into a swing.

'It's really better for everyone if I just hand over my credit card. Nobody gets hurt that way.'

Finn took a seat on a cane chair and propped his feet

up on the coffee table. After a minute of comfortable silence he spoke again.

'So, you said that there were things we needed to discuss?'

'I did.' Callie kicked off her sandals and felt comfortable enough to tuck her feet under her bottom on the denim fabric of the swing. 'I put in for a month's holiday today, and I also managed to organise it so that I don't have to fly to Paris this week. So I am, in the most virginal sense, all yours until we go.'

'That makes it easier, because there are a couple of things we need to sort out before we go.'

'Like?'

'Like the lawyers for the magazine would like you to sign an indemnity form, and they'd also like you to go for a full medical—just to cover their legal asses.'

Callie wrinkled her nose. 'What a pain.'

'I use the same travel clinic all the time. I'll make an appointment for you.' Finn rested his beer bottle on his flat stomach. 'You'll need clothes that are suitable for five and six-star resorts—'

Callie looked down at her designer sundress and lifted her eyebrows. 'Finn, I am a fashion buyer—I think I have the clothes covered.'

'Glad *you* do,' Finn grumbled, looking frustrated and miserable. 'Because I sure don't. I keep thinking that I have to get my act together and I keep putting it off. I hate clothes-shopping.'

'You always looked okay to me.' Better than okay—mighty fine, in fact. And his clothes were nice, too. 'So, does your ineptitude with home decoration extend to your wardrobe?'

Finn tipped his bottle up to lips. 'Yep. In spring and autumn Liz would drag my ass to the shops. She'd choose and I'd pay.'

Callie's lips quirked. Shopping was something she *could* help him with. After taking a big sip of wine, she stood up and jerked her head, indicating that he should get up too. 'Let's go.'

'Where?'

'Up to your bedroom.'

When she saw his eyes widen and a gleam appear, she rolled her eyes and thought that she should explain—quickly.

'Since you're giving me an all-expenses-paid holiday, the least I can do is to help you out with your wardrobe. I'll go through your clothes, pick out what's suitable, and then we'll go shopping for what you need.'

Finn looked suddenly and momentarily panicked, but she put it down to the fact that no man—especially one as masculine as Finn—wanted to spend any part of his evening discussing clothes.

'Trust me...it'll be painless.'

'I don't think that having you in my bedroom is a very good idea,' Finn stated as he followed her through the house and up the stairs.

'We're taking it slow, one day at a time, and today is not *that* day, Banning,' Callie told him as they hit the top floor. 'Where's your bedroom?''

Finn gestured wordlessly to the closed door on their right. Callie opened it and walked into a white-on-cream, endlessly pale bedroom. Placing her hands on her hips, she lifted her eyebrows as she took in the cream and white striped walls, the deep beige curtains and the neutrally shaded pillows piled high on the floor.

She felt as if she'd stepped into a dairy.

'Wow...' she murmured.

'I hate this room,' Finn muttered, standing at the door, glaring.

'It's not that bad...it just needs some colour,' Callie

said, forcing herself to sound cheerful. She gestured to the bed—a white wood canopied monstrosity that dominated the room. 'You must also have hated the mattress.'

'What?' Finn barked.

'The mattress—it's gone.'

Finn shoved both hands into his hair and dropped his head, for a brief instant looking like a little boy who'd been slapped. Then his face changed and turned hard and determined.

'You know what? Let's not worry about checking what I have that I can take. I'll just buy a whole new wardrobe.'

Callie started to argue, but stopped when she saw the misery underneath the fury. 'That's an expensive exercise,' she said carefully, knowing that there was something fundamental that she was missing.

'I can afford it,' Finn said and gestured for her to leave the room.

Callie knew that it wasn't the right time to argue with him, to try and push his buttons. He wanted her out for some deeply private reason, so she left the bedroom and headed for the stairs. She waited until they were halfway down before speaking again.

'Still want me to help you shop for clothes?'

Finn's tension seemed to fade as he closed the door behind him. His white teeth flashed. 'Hell, yes. I might come back with one of those khaki vests with a hundred pockets and pants that unzip at the knees to become shorts.'

Callie shuddered at the thought, not entirely convinced he was joking. 'You *definitely* need help.'

Finn's broad hand, warm and exciting, encircled her neck as they walked down the stairs. 'In more ways than one. So, what are we ordering for supper?'

She loved spending other people's money, Callie thought, holding up two shirts for Finn that she really liked. And it was so much fun shopping for a guy. Finn didn't think so, but she did. They'd only been at it for a couple of hours and he was starting to wilt—the lightweight.

There was a pile of bags in Finn's SUV already, and with the clothes now on a low couch in this store she thought he would have everything he might need for the next couple of weeks—possibly years. She'd made him buy belts and shorts, designer tees and shirts, shoes and ties, and she'd had a blast.

'Anything else, Callie?'

You knew you were a professional shopper when the sales clerks knew you by name, Callie thought. 'No, I think that's it, Annie. If you'd like to start ringing that pile up, I'll take these to Finn so that he can try them on. We'll meet you at the counter in a few.'

'Sounds like a plan,' Annie agreed, and Callie left her to gather up the clothes while she walked into the three-cubicle dressing room, the shirts over her arm.

The first two were empty, and she skidded to a halt as she saw Finn's reflection in the third changing room mirror through a gap in the curtains.

She couldn't pull her gaze away from the perfection that was his body. He was wearing nothing more than a brief pair of pants, and his body rippled with muscle as he shoved a shirt back onto a hanger. His legs were long and muscled, his tanned shoulders broad, his butt round and tight. His broad chest and rippled stomach made all the saliva in her mouth disappear.

How was she supposed to go on holiday with him, knowing how much she wanted him? This gnawing need to know what he felt like, how he made love, how he would feel as he filled her, completed her, was unusual for her, and it scared her as nothing else ever had. Yes, she needed to explore his body—but she also wanted to dig below his cool, calm and controlled surface to see what was underneath.

That wasn't good. She always kept her distance from men who made her feel too much, who intrigued her. They were dangerous. They made her want more than sex, more than a brief affair, and nobody had made her want more like Finn did.

It didn't matter how much she wanted him, she reminded herself. She could want and wish and pray, but the people she needed to stick around never did. *Remember?*

That cold dose of reality didn't make her desire for Finn disappear. Her mind might realise that he was dangerous but her body still craved him.

She could never allow herself to risk getting to know him too well. She couldn't get emotionally attached to him. But she wanted to know his touch, his taste, how it felt to have that powerful body giving and receiving pleasure.

Finn's eyes met hers in the mirror and he just stared at her, half naked, his desire for her blazing from his face. She watched, fascinated, as his penis grew into an erection from nothing more than looking at her. Finn didn't try to hide his reaction. Instead he just kept his eyes locked on hers, his hands on his hips.

'Keeping my hands off you is going to be a problem,' he said, his voice low and slow. He turned to face her and yanked the curtains open.

Callie licked her lips and shook her head, trying to be sensible.

'I'm not thinking of my failed engagement or my ex. I promise that I am not thinking of anyone but you,' Finn growled.

She heard the frustration and the truth in his voice. He wanted her—possibly as much as she did him.

How was he able to look inside her head and see what she was thinking? He seemed to be able to intuit immediately and correctly what she was thinking without her saying a word.

Nobody had ever managed to do that before.

'Too soon,' Callie stated, sighing as she felt her panties dampen. 'It really is, Finn.'

An F-bomb shattered the loaded silence between them and then Finn's hand shot out and grabbed her wrist. Yanking her into the cubicle, he jerked the curtains shut and the shirts she held fell to the floor.

Finn took her chin in his hand and tipped her head up. 'Have you ever stood in front of a fire and wanted to be in the heart of it? Inside the colours…the heat? Yeah, you have—because that's how you were looking at me just now. Like I was the fire and you wanted to feel my heat. You want me…'

She wanted to deny it but she couldn't. Of course she wanted him—she'd been fantasising about him for months. But it was just lust and attraction and the fact that she hadn't had an orgasm in far too long.

Didn't she deserve to feast on him just a little?

'It's just lust. I haven't felt it for a while,' she told him.

'It's a crazy chemical reaction. But we can handle a little chemistry, can't we?'

Yes—no. Maybe… What did she know? Her brain had long since shut down.

'So let's test the theory. Kiss me, lose yourself in my mouth. Right here, right now. Let me taste all of your heat, your passion.'

How could she say no? A hot, no-holds-barred kiss? She wanted it as much as he did. Just to test the theory, of course. People had sex-based relationships all the time—hell, *she'd* had sex-based relationships all her adult life. What was so different about Finn? *Nothing,* she resolutely lied to herself. Yes, he was hot—yes, he set her nerve-endings on fire—yes, he made her lady bits squirm. But she'd had good-looking men before. She'd handled them and she'd handle Finn Banning.

She would—even if it killed her. And this was her chance to prove it.

Then Finn's mouth covered hers and she realised that she was right to be hesitant, right to be a little scared. Because she'd never been held like this, touched liked this—*God*, tasted like this.

His arms were strong, his hands tender, one on her hip, the other holding the back of her head, keeping her mouth to his. She could feel the heat of his bare chest as her breasts smashed against it, could feel his erection brushing her stomach, hard and wonderful. But his mouth…

She would never get enough of his taste, of the way he sipped and then suckled and then, to mix it up, swirled his tongue around hers. He gently bit her bottom lip, then soothed the sting away with a swipe of his tongue. And while his mouth was busy decimating hers his hand started to explore her body.

She felt his fingers moving over the bumps of her spine, drifting across her bottom, sneaking under her skirt to feel the backs of her thighs, tracing her thong where it disappeared between her butt cheeks. He skimmed her happy place, and when she wiggled against his hand slid his finger under the cotton to her entrance, slipping through the heat and wet to that tiny bundle of nerves.

Callie felt her knees buckle and Finn instantly tightened his arm around her back, plastering her to him as her legs widened, allowing him deeper access. One finger, then two, and his thumb was brushing her clitoris.

'You feel so amazing…' Finn muttered against her mouth, green eyes blazing.

'We should stop.'

'Hell, no,' Finn muttered. 'Just this once…don't think… just lose yourself.'

'We can't have sex in a changing room cubicle, Finn,' Callie protested, trying to being sensible.

'We're not going to make love. You're just going to come, and I'm going to watch you fall apart in my arms.'

'I can't—'

'Yeah, you can—and you will,' Finn told her, hooking a small stool with his foot and dragging it over to them.

Turning Callie around, he placed her hands on the mirror before lifting her right foot up onto the stool. Bunching her skirt in one hand, he lifted it slowly to reveal her lacy thong. He pulled it to one side and stared at her waxed strip, tracing it with one finger before sliding that finger into her folds. Callie watched, turned on, as he started to pleasure her, sliding his finger over her clitoris and into her vagina in a slow, steady, orgasm-building rhythm.

His other hand came up to undo the buttons of her shirt, leaving it to fall open and show a hint of her ivory bra. His tanned hand was dark against her lighter skin—and then it disappeared beneath the cup of her bra to cover her breast. Instantly her nipple swelled into his palm, demanding attention.

His fingers worked in tandem to devastate her control—fingers in her panties and fingers rubbing her nipple—and soon she couldn't help her harsh breathing as she climbed up and up, reaching for that ultimate release, that burst of concentrated pleasure that she hadn't experienced in far too long…

'Look at you…so hot, so close,' Finn growled in her ear. 'See how beautiful you are.'

Callie almost didn't recognise the woman in the mirror—the one standing in Finn's arms. Her hair was messy, her face flushed, and her eyes were a deep, dark mesmerising blue. She looked wild and out of control.

'You're so frickin' hot I could come just looking at you.'

Finn pushed another finger into her channel and flicked her clit with his thumb. Callie shuddered in his arms.

'Come for me. Right now.'

At his command Callie fell apart in his arms, instinctively bucking against his fingers as she milked every last sensation from the experience. From a place far away, where fireworks were exploding inside her brain, she felt Finn stiffen against her, his erection against her back. She heard his low moan and then felt the hand that was on her breast leave her to grab himself, covering his penis as he turned away and came into the palm of his hand.

In a shop's dressing room. In the middle of the day. *Dear God.*

His muttered curse bounced off the walls of the dressing room and pulled her back from that happy place.

'I haven't done that since I was a horny teenager.' He sent her a hot, frustrated, embarrassed look. 'Apparently I have absolutely no control around you.'

Ditto, Callie thought. She rested her head against the mirror as he backed away from her, aftershocks still skittering through her body. The fact that they—two people who'd been around the block, the world—had no 'off' button when they touched was a huge warning that they should keep their distance.

She couldn't handle him—this. This nuclear reaction couldn't be controlled so it should be contained, and the only way to contain it was not to light the fuse.

She needed control. Control made her feel safe and secure. Control meant that her mind and emotions could stand apart and let her body have its fun. If all three got in on the action, as they had minutes before, then she was toast.

Finn quickly shucked his underwear, giving her a quick peek at a black thatch of hair and his still mostly erect penis. He swore as he used his underwear to clean up. 'That was *not* supposed to happen.'

'I don't think any of it was,' Callie said, closing her eyes.

She heard him stepping into his jeans, the rasp of the zip, a long sigh.

'Are you okay?'

Callie opened her eyes and stepped away from the mirror. She smoothed down her skirt as Finn pulled on his T-shirt.

Finn sent her a long, concerned look as he repeated his question. 'Callie, talk to me. Are you okay?'

Callie looked up at the ceiling. 'Yeah. Wow. Yes. But I think that we should get going. They're going to come looking for us soon.'

On cue, Annie's hesitant voice drifted from the entrance of the fitting rooms. 'Callie? Everything all right?'

Callie's lips twitched as she replied. 'We're coming!'

Finn started to grin. and Callie slapped his shoulder in warning. 'If you say *Been there, done that* I swear I will slap you!'

CHAPTER FIVE

FINN STEERED HIS SUV into the empty parking space in front of Callie's front door and frowned when he saw the tall blond guy sitting on her front step.

'I thought you said you were single,' he said to her bent head. He didn't like the fact that white-hot jealousy speared through him. The thought of any other man having her, being with her, while the delicious scent of her was still on his fingers, the memory of her falling apart in his arms was still so fresh, made him feel ill.

Callie picked up her head and frowned. 'I am. Why?'

He glared at the man—who just looked at them, waiting for them to leave the car. 'Pissed off male sitting on your steps.'

Callie looked out through the front windshield and pursed her lips. 'Older brother.'

Ah. Relief—which was bizarre, because he had no claim to this woman. 'Can he wait five minutes? We need to talk.'

Callie sat back and nodded. Finn ignored her brother's thundercloud face and turned in his seat to face her, making sure that the windows were up so no part of this conversation could leak from the car.

He thought about how to start, what exactly he wanted to say. They hadn't spoken since leaving the shopping mall and he thought that they needed to clear the air before this went any further.

'So, a little chemistry, huh?'

Callie broke the tense silence, verbalising his thoughts. How did she manage to do that?

'If you can call that explosion "a little chemistry",' Finn muttered, wanting to bang his forehead against the steering wheel. 'That was crazy. I've never…' Finn swallowed his embarrassment. 'Never lost it like that before. We had hot sex in a changing room, Callie!'

'Well, it wasn't really…' Callie blew air into her cheeks. 'Yeah.'

Callie's tongue touched the centre of her top lip and he held back his groan and cursed the stirring in his pants.

'This was supposed to be a simple arrangement!' he muttered, more to himself than to her.

'It's still simple,' Callie argued. 'We're going on holiday together, I'm going to pretend to be your wife, and we're going to end up in bed sooner or later. And, judging by that craziness, probably sooner.'

'I'm old enough to know that explosive sex has a way of making stuff extraordinarily complicated.'

'We're also old enough to work our way around that,' she said.

Finn frowned at her as he stared at her profile. '*Whoah*… Let me get this straight. Are you saying that you are *happy* to have sex? You said you wanted to take it day by day.'

Callie blushed and threw her hands up in the air. 'I don't know what to think! I'm still in orgasm land! And I'm still wrapping my head around the fact that we did *that*, in a semi-public place, at noon, in a busy shop where I know the sales ladies.'

She buried her face in her hands.

'I'm never going to be able to go back in there. They *knew*, Finn!' Callie pushed her fingers into her hair as she lifted her head. 'We didn't give where we were and what we were doing a moment's thought, Finn. Hell, we didn't think *at all*!'

We didn't think at all... Her words made him push back into the seat, his breath hitching. That was it—exactly it. The biggest problem he had around this woman was that he didn't think. He just had to put his hands on that warm skin, had to kiss that luscious mouth, and his freaking brain switched off.

And he needed to think—needed time not only to work through the runaway fire that was currently his life but also why she had the ability to short circuit his thought processes. He needed to think about how he was going to handle this craziness between them so that neither of them ended up scalded.

Callie stared out of the window. 'Would you prefer that I didn't come with you?

'No! Where the hell did *that* come from?' Finn shot back, panicked at the thought of her backing out. And not only because he needed a 'wife' so he could do his job.

Finn let out a long stream of air. Dammit, it was his turn to be sensible, to take a step back from the situation and use his brain. His big brain.

He needed some distance from her; his body needed to get closer but *he* needed space to think.

'Maybe we should just get through the next couple of days, get on the road and, as you said, see what happens—okay?'

Since Callie looked relieved at this reprieve, he knew that it was the right decision, that he was on the right track.

'Okay.'

Callie nodded, but her next words surprised the hell out of him. Whatever else he'd expected her to say it wasn't this:

'And still no hearts and flowers at the end?'

Finn nodded his agreement. 'Definitely not.' He gestured to her brother, whose look had now passed pissed off and was on its way to furious. 'You'd better go—he's been waiting long enough.'

Callie wrinkled her nose. 'Yeah.' She opened the door and swung her legs out of the car. 'Hey, Seb.'

'Callie. Is that who you're running away with? Want to introduce us?'

Finn heard the whipped out words before Callie slammed the door behind her. Hitting the button to take down his electric window, he made a production of putting his seat belt on before starting the car.

'No, I am *not* going to introduce you. Why are you here?'

'We need to talk about Laura and why you're running off with some stranger to avoid seeing her,' the brother stated as Callie brushed past him to her front door.

Finn, not able to delay his departure any longer without being caught out, reversed and sent a last look at her.

Who was Laura and why was Callie running from her? And why was he so curious to find out all he could about her? And why did he hate the stricken look he'd seen on her face when her brother had mentioned Laura's name?

It was the journalist in him, he told himself as he accelerated away. It was his job to be curious—about people as well as places.

And apparently, he thought as he turned the corner, his job now also included deception and lying to himself as well.

Crazy.

In her lounge, Callie tossed her bag onto the couch and faced her brother, hands on her hips. 'I don't appreciate you rocking up on my doorstep unannounced and looking for a fight.'

Seb, tall and strong and looking as frustrated as she

felt, pushed his fists into the pockets of his jeans. 'When my sister storms out of her house—'

'*Your* house.'

Seb glared at her interruption. '*Her* house and refuses to take my calls for three days I am allowed to rock up here and have it out with you. We're all worried about you.'

'So I hear,' Callie retorted. 'Apparently my life is now too good and I am too independent. I remember a time when you thought the exact opposite. There's just no pleasing you, is there, big bro?'

'That happened a long time ago and it has no bearing on this situation. Look, Ro and I—'

Ro and I. It had used to be *Callie and Ro.* They'd used to be a team—best friends. Had Seb driven a wedge between her and her best friend? Had he surpassed her in importance? It was natural if he had, but Rowan had always been her rock, her sounding board, her port in a storm. Now she was Seb's.

Callie had never felt so alone in her life. Oh, wait, maybe she had. For the first couple of months after Laura had left. First couple of months, years, most of her life…

You're being silly and sentimental and emotional, Callie thought as she walked over to the doors to the veranda and yanked them open, looking for some air. It had been a crazy couple of days—culminating with a very hot, very sexy, very confusing encounter in that dressing room—and she was exhausted and played out. Ro was still Ro, and she still loved her, but it just didn't feel as if anyone was standing in *her* corner right now.

But that was okay. It was time to pull on her big girl panties and kick some ass. And her brother was a great target.

Callie leaned against the frame of the now open door and turned back to him. 'Look, Seb, I absolutely understand and respect your right to talk to your mother, and I'd appreciate it if you'd respect my right not to.'

'She's your mother too. Don't you at least want to know why she left?' Seb demanded.

So like Seb, Callie thought. Analytical and clear-thinking. If he understood the cause he could make sense of the problem. For her it was a lot more simple —cut and dried.

'She left you and me—bottom line. I don't care what her reason was. She left. When you have kids you put *them* first, not yourself.'

'In one of her letters she said that her life was overwhelming—that was why she retreated to her room, why she eventually left.'

Callie threw her hands up in the air in exasperation at his explanation. 'Overwhelming? God, Seb, she was a stay-at-home mother with a housekeeper and a rich husband who spoilt her rotten. That's a stupid excuse. There are millions of women all over the world who have a lot less, who live in terrible circumstances, and who don't walk out on their kids.'

Seb shrugged. 'I don't disagree with you, but I still think that I need to meet with her—that *you* need to meet with her. To hear her side and to find closure, if nothing else.'

'I don't need closure. I'm perfectly fine,' Callie said stubbornly.

'All your issues are rooted in Laura leaving,' Seb stated, still pushing.

Callie ground her teeth together, trying to keep a hold on her bubbling temper. 'I do *not* have issues!'

Seb snorted. 'Honey, you delude yourself. You're crazy independent because you refuse to rely on anyone in case they let you down. You're consistently single because you don't trust anyone to be there long-term.'

From the couch Callie heard the strident ring tone of

her mobile and she walked over to answer the call, grateful for the interruption and the opportunity to get hold of her temper before she slapped her brother.

She saw Rowan's name on the display and barked a tense greeting.

'My fiancé there?' Rowan asked, after saying hello.

Callie answered in the affirmative and Rowan ordered her to put her on speaker phone. Callie shrugged, did what she said and held up the mobile in her hand.

'Seb!' Rowan's voice sounded frustrated. 'What did I say to you?'

Seb grimaced. 'I know, but—'

'Leave your sister alone. If she doesn't want to meet Laura, then it's her decision—not yours.'

'But—'

Rowan didn't give him a chance to explain. 'We spoke about this. We agreed that you would leave her alone! *God!*'

'But—'

'Respect her right to make her own decisions, Hollis.'

After that bombshell Rowan told Callie to take her off speaker phone, and Callie lifted her phone to her ear, watching as her brother threw his hands up in the air.

'As per usual, you two have ganged up on me. I'm out of here,' Seb stated, before turning and heading for the front door.

'He's left and he's not happy,' Callie told Rowan, not feeling quite so alone as before.

Callie could imagine Rowan's shrug. 'So? I might love him to distraction, but he's still messing with my best friend and nobody—not even him—does that. I'm the only one with that privilege.'

Callie felt tears prick her eyes. 'I love you, you know.'

'I love you too, kiddo.' Rowan sighed. 'I just need to ask you one question.'

'Okay.'

'Do you know what you're doing, Cal?'

Callie sank into the corner of the couch and tipped her head back. 'I don't have the foggiest idea. Can you come over? I need you.'

'On my way.'

Maybe, Callie thought as she placed her mobile on the couch next to her, she wasn't quite as alone as she'd thought.

Callie, her bags in a pile next to the door, pulled open the front door and sucked in her breath as she caught sight of her fake husband. Finn was dressed for travelling in a pair of lightweight grey linen shorts and a black and white checked shirt over a snow-white T-shirt that skimmed his broad chest. His arms were muscled and tanned, and the only jewellery he wore was a high-tech watch that could probably launch spaceships.

His eyes widened when he saw her. 'You look fantastic, fake wife.'

Callie grinned at him. 'Thank you.'

Callie knew that she looked good in the pink-orchid-coloured swing dress with its copper leather belt and drawstring neck. She'd kept her accessories and make-up minimal, and she wore flat, gold sequinned sandals. She knew she looked the part of a stylish woman about to embark on her honeymoon.

Did she have everything for her bogus honeymoon? Clothes—check. Passport—check. Accessories and toiletries—check. Jewellery, simple, classy, to go with all her outfits—check.

Except for one glaringly obvious exception… Hell, she wasn't wearing a wedding ring!

Finn caught her expression and frowned. 'What's wrong?'

'Your fake wife needs a fake ring,' she said, lifting her arm and wiggling the fingers of her left hand.

Finn twisted his lips as he stepped into her hallway and wound his way around her bags. 'I didn't even think of that.' He looked at his watch and sighed his annoyance. 'Liz still has the engagement ring I bought her.'

Callie's mouth dropped open. 'I am *not* wearing your ex's ring!'

A shallow dimple appeared in Finn's cheek. 'You're pretty picky for a wife who isn't actually my wife!'

Callie lifted her nose. 'I still have standards—fake or not.'

Finn sighed. 'I suppose we could pick up something at the airport.'

Callie lifted her eyebrows. The only jewellery stores at the airport were high-end and very expensive, and she couldn't justify him splurging for a ring that she'd only wear for three weeks. She quickly did a mental stroll through her jewellery collection in the hope that she had something remotely engagement-ring-like. Then she remembered the large velvet jewellery box Seb had left with her just after he'd got engaged to Rowan.

'It's mostly Grandma's jewellery, with a couple of pieces our mother left behind,' he'd said. 'You should have them.'

Callie hadn't wanted to keep the box and she'd never bothered to look inside. It was still at the back of her lingerie drawer, where she'd shoved it a year or so ago.

She still didn't want to open it, but this was an emergency.

'How much time have we got before we have to leave?' she asked Finn as she turned towards the stairs.

'A half hour or so,' Finn replied. 'Why? Do you have some diamond rings stashed upstairs?'

'Maybe,' Callie replied, hearing Finn's footsteps behind

her. She turned, faced him, and for once they were eye to eye. 'It might be better if you stay down here.'

'Why?'

'My room. It's a bit messy.' *Catastrophic* was a better word, Callie thought.

'I've seen messy before,' Finn told her.

'Not like this, you haven't,' Callie assured him. Seeing the stubborn look on his face, she sighed and shrugged. 'Don't say I didn't warn you.'

Dear God! Finn looked around the master bedroom, his mouth open wide enough to catch flies. Who had so many clothes and why were they scattered everywhere?

When he managed to find his voice, he croaked the words out. 'Newsflash, Callie: clothes can be put back into cupboards as well as taken out.'

Callie stepped over a pile of shoes as she headed to her dresser. 'No point,' she said over her shoulder. 'While I was trying to decide what to pack I realised that I have far too many clothes—'

'Seriously? I would never have guessed that!' Finn said from the doorway, thinking that if he went in he might not find his way out. *Ever.*

Callie ignored his interruption. 'And I decided that I need to clean out my wardrobe. That pile is for Rowan, that pile is for the secondhand shop, and that pile is to be donated.' She waved her hands around the room.

Finn leaned a shoulder into the doorframe and crossed his arms. 'Damn…' he muttered again.

Callie yanked open a drawer in her dresser and Finn's mouth went dry as she tossed a pile of rainbow-coloured thongs and bras onto a chair. They were skimpy and frothy and ultra-feminine.

'I get samples from the designers I do business with,' Callie said, seemingly oblivious to the fact that he was mentally stripping her in an attempt to see what she wearing under that sexy, stylish dress.

It would probably be the same sexy deep pink, he decided. Callie was nothing if not colour co-ordinated.

'I can't remember when last I actually went to a store and bought clothes. That's why I had so much fun shopping for you.'

With difficulty Finn raised his eyes to her face and tried to look as if he had heard her. But he was a guy—distract him with sexy lingerie and his brain headed south. With his blood. And his hearing.

'Ah—got it.'

Finn watched as Callie pulled out a large jewellery box and, cradling it in both hands, walked back towards him. She skirted the bed and sat on the side closest to him, on top of a pile of jackets, putting the box down next to her. A wistful, sad, wary look passed across her face and he straightened, all thoughts of sex and lingerie gone. This box meant something to her, and he wasn't sure if it was a good or bad something. Probably a mixture of both.

Then, very surprisingly, she stood up, picked up the box and thrust it towards him. Finn caught it as it hit his chest and she dropped it from her grasp.

'Look in there and see if you can find something that I can wear. If there isn't anything then I'm afraid you're out of luck. I'll be downstairs.'

Finn frowned as she slipped past him and ran down the stairs. Putting the box on the bedside table, he switched on the light and flipped the lid. His breath caught at the blink of gold inside. It was a pirate's treasure box, he thought, bubbling with thick gold chains and bracelets and the occasional flash of a precious stone in a pendant.

Lifting up a handful of chains, silver and gold, some with pendants and some without, he saw that there were smaller boxes below and dumped the chains on the bed.

The first box held earrings—mostly old-fashioned, but there was a nice pair of diamond studs he could see Callie wearing. The next box held rings, and he pulled in his breath as he ran his fingers over the jewels.

Of the eight or so in the box there were at least four that would pass as engagement rings, and three had matching wedding bands. One ring fascinated him: it looked older than the others—a big diamond, with spikes of platinum radiating in another circle embedded with tiny diamonds. A thin band sat under the diamond and he presumed that was a wedding band.

Finn held it under the light and on the inside could just make out the date: June the sixth, 1909.

That'll do, he thought, tucking it into the pocket of his pants.

He quickly replaced the boxes he'd taken out and dumped the tangle of chains back inside the larger box. Snapping the lid shut, he walked across to the near empty cupboard, found a shoebox and tossed the shoes inside on to the floor. Sliding the jewellery box into the shoebox, he used his height to stretch up and hide the box behind another pile of shoeboxes.

He wondered why he was bothering. If any thieves broke in and found themselves in Callie's bedroom while she was away they'd think she'd been ransacked already and leave.

Finn tried to close the cupboard doors and wondered why Callie wouldn't deal with the box herself. Why would a woman who obviously loved clothes—and, he presumed, accessories—ignore a box full of such amazing jewellery? Why couldn't she even open it to look inside for a ring she needed?

Strange. But interesting. Curiosity, he reminded himself, and he didn't need to indulge it. Not where Callie was concerned.

Finn rubbed the back of his neck, thinking that she couldn't do the jewellery box and he couldn't do his bedroom. Maybe they deserved each other.

Finn left the room and jogged down the stairs. He found Callie sitting on a chair in her hallway, legs crossed and her foot jiggling.

She looked up at him with those amazing reticent eyes. 'Did you find something?'

'Lots of things,' Finn said, keeping his voice easy. 'That's quite a little treasure trove you've got there. That box should be in a safe, by the way.'

Callie lifted a bare shoulder. 'I wouldn't know. I've never looked inside.'

'Why not?' Finn asked the question although he knew that she wouldn't answer.

'It's complicated and I have my reasons.' Callie stood up and held out her hand. 'Let's see it.'

Finn pulled the two rings from his pocket and dropped them into her hand. He watched as she stared at them. She looked as though she was trying to place them, but after she'd given the tiniest shake to her head she picked the wedding ring up to take a closer look.

'It's really pretty.'

'It has a date in 1909 inscribed on the band,' Finn told her.

'It must be my great-grandmother's—Seb told me that some of the family pieces were in the box,' Callie replied, sliding both rings over the ring finger on her left hand. 'They fit. Yay.'

'Good.' Finn smiled lazily. 'That was easily sorted. Just promise me you'll get the box into a safe deposit box or just a safe. There were quite a few bigger and better diamonds and precious stones than that one.'

Callie shifted on her feet. 'Maybe.' She nudged a suitcase with her foot. 'Shall we go?'

'Yep.' Finn looked at the pile of suitcases on the floor and sighed. Okay, they were going for a while, but two large cases and a carry-on seemed a bit excessive. But judging by what had been left behind she probably thought that this was—what had she called it the other day?—a capsule wardrobe. He thought it looked like backache waiting for a place to happen.

'Okay, grab your stuff and I'll wait for you in the car,' he said, teasing her.

Callie looked surprised, then confused, and then her eyes cleared as he realised he was joking. 'Carry on like that and I'm going to cut you off from fake sex.'

Finn slung the tote bag over his shoulder and pulled the bigger of the two suitcases up onto its wheels. 'Fake married for two seconds,' he grumbled as she opened the front door for him, 'and I'm already on rations for sex I might not even get. This is a tough gig.'

'You were the one who wanted to get married,' Callie reminded him. 'Didn't I tell you that it was a bad idea? I'm sure I said something about it being a long stupidity...'

Six hours later Callie stood in the tasteful lobby of the Baobab and Buffalo, sipping a welcome glass of champagne while Finn took care of the details surrounding their stay at this first six-star resort.

According to their itinerary they would be staying in the honeymoon suite for one night before being moved to another room for the rest of their three-night stay. Since bookings at the Baobab and Buffalo were harder to come by than hen's teeth, and since this entire 'honeymoon' was sponsored—and fake—Callie knew that they were in no position to complain.

And, really, what was there to complain about? The resort was utterly fantastic. The main building was built in grey stone and lavishly but tastefully decorated. Judging by the discreet signs, there was a business room, a library, various lounges and dining rooms. Callie walked across the lobby, intrigued by the double-volume doors and the view beyond the glass.

Stepping onto the long veranda, she gasped at the endless view of bush beyond her. Wild and wondrous. There was a watering hole for wildlife at the bottom of the cliff below, and verdant green terraces led to an infinity pool that seemed to cling to the edge of the cliff.

Well, wow.

Callie turned at a touch on her shoulder. 'Mrs Banning?'

Callie turned and looked into the eyes of a gorgeous redhead. 'No. I'm Callie—' Then she remembered that she was supposed to be married and flushed with embarrassment. Her brain kicked up a gear as she tried to explain her gaffe. 'Sorry—I'm still operating on my own name.'

The redhead grinned. 'I absolutely understand; I'm recently married myself. I'm Clem—welcome to the Two B.'

Callie had read her fair share of celebrity magazines and instantly recognised this ex-model, who'd once been engaged to one of the world's most notorious musicians. From socialite to living on an upmarket game reserve. Now *that* was a life-change.

'Thank you. It's beautiful.'

Clem sighed. 'It really is. I'm still in awe of what Nick's managed to build here.'

Clem jammed her hands in her khaki shorts and gestured to a dark-haired man who stood at the other end of the veranda, talking to a man dressed in the same uniform of khaki shorts and navy polo shirt.

'That's Nick and his right-hand man, Jabu. They are the heart and soul of the Two B. Sorry, that's what we call this place. The Baobab and Buffalo is such a mouthful.'

Callie watched as Nick and his wife exchanged a look across the veranda that blazed with passion and lust. Callie felt as if she needed a fan or a long drink of water when they finally looked away from each other, but Clem turned back to Callie, acting as if she *hadn't* just eye-bonked her husband.

'What are you hoping to do here? Or are you just planning to hibernate in your room and…well, do what honeymooners do?'

How the hell was she supposed to answer that question? She didn't even know the answer to any of the questions *she* had with regard to her and Finn's relationship—the fake one or the real one!

Were they going to sleep with each other? *Duh.* That was a no-brainer—as soon as they had to share a bed they'd be all over each other…there was no way they'd be able to resist. And that would be the start of their three-week fling. It would be hot and sexy and rollercoaster-crazy and she had to remember to keep her emotional distance. *No spilling the secrets of your soul, Hollis!*

Callie frowned at the rogue thought. What was wrong with her? She had always been able to separate sex and emotion—why was she worried that she wouldn't be able to do it with Finn? *Because you like him,* Callie admitted reluctantly. *Because you'd like to be his friend, have him be yours.* And that meant taking a step away from being 'safe' and unattached; it would take her into uncharted territory…

'Callie?'

Callie blinked at her hostess. 'Sorry, I zoned out. Tired…'

Clem laughed and patted her arm again. 'No problem—I understand. I was so exhausted after my wedding day I could barely string a sentence together.'

Yeah, that wasn't it. Looking into Clem's beautiful, open, happy face, Callie felt the urge to spill her secrets.

Actually, I'm not really married. I'm running away from reconnecting with my long-absent mother.

And I want to sleep with Finn; he's exciting and intriguing and the first man in for ever who I can imagine myself falling for. But I'm scared that he's the one man that I will like more after I've slept with him—not less. I already like him more than I should. Hell, I knew that I liked him more than was wise on the plane home from JFK—and this is all very scary for me. And he's on the rebound and I never, repeat never, sleep with men I can fall for.

So I'm confused. And more than little terrified.

And I really don't like being either.

Callie suspected that Clem would understand.

Callie sighed her relief as she saw Finn walking towards them, a Two B butler two steps behind. She gathered her wits and made the introductions. 'Finn Banning—meet Clem. She and her husband own and run the Baobab and Buffalo.'

Clem's eyes narrowed slightly and her smile was a little cool. 'You're the journalist doing an article on us?'

Hmm, it seemed that the fiery redhead wasn't fond of journalists—then again, with her history with the profession Callie couldn't blame her.

'I am,' Finn said easily, his hand resting low on Callie's back, his fingers just above her butt cheek. It was a very possessive, familiar gesture—one perfectly suited to a newly married man.

'We don't normally allow reporters to write about the Two B; we're booked for years in advance and don't need the publicity. We're doing this as a favour to the owner of *Go Travel* who's a regular visitor.'

Clem kept the smile on her face but there was a note of protectiveness in her voice that was unmistakable. Finn's fingers flexed on Callie's back and Callie knew that he'd heard Clem's warning too.

Finn sent her an easy smile. 'I'm morally bound to write on my personal experiences and I already know that my experience here will be utterly fantastic. We're so lucky to start off our honeymoon here.'

Clem relaxed and Callie released her pent-up breath. Finn casually sipped from the glass of champagne he'd been handed on walking through the front door.

Clem nodded at the papers in his hand. 'I've tweaked your itinerary to showcase the best of what we can offer honeymooners—which is an utterly unique and memorable experience.' Clem pulled a face, humour back in her eyes. 'I'm sorry, it doesn't leave much time for long, lazy mornings spent in bed, but it will be exciting and amazing.'

Wow. If all the lodges were going to pull out the stops the way Clem was doing then Callie was in for one hell of a holiday.

'We're grateful for your personal touch,' said Mr Charmer at her side.

'Then Sarah, your personal butler, will take it from here. Enjoy your stay,' Clem said, before turning away to walk towards her husband.

Nick immediately opened his arms and Clem snuggled up into his side. Callie briefly wondered what it would feel like to love a man like that—to be loved like that. To feel so absolutely, utterly secure in yourself and in his love that you could slide into a conversation and into his arms without either of you missing a beat, as if it was the most natural action in the world.

Love, it seemed, could work for some. But Callie knew that she wasn't one of the lucky few. No, she was better off on her own, walking her own path.

That way she could be in control and could stop her heart from walking off the side of a cliff and splattering on the rocks below.

CHAPTER SIX

INSTEAD OF WALKING them to their room, as he'd expected, Sarah led Finn and Callie to an open game-viewing vehicle and invited them to climb inside. As he hoisted himself up into the vehicle he noticed that their luggage was neatly stowed in the back of the vehicle, just behind the second row of bench seats.

Finn settled himself next to Callie, conscious that the sun was starting to set and the temperature was falling; the day's heat was giving way to the chill of the first, unexpectedly early cold front, suggesting that autumn was just around the corner. Callie pulled out a shawl from her bag and wound it around her shoulders as Sarah accelerated away.

When they drove back through the impressive entrance Finn realised that they were leaving the security of the electric fenced estate and were heading into the reserve itself—wild and beautiful.

This is more like it, he thought, his eyes scanning the bush for signs of wildlife.

Within five hundred yards of the gate they saw a herd of springbok and a female warthog with her piglets. Then they saw a fish eagle in a tree, and Sarah pointed out a reclusive eland bull in a thicket of acacias.

This is Africa, he thought, breathing deeply. *The sounds and sights of the bush.*

A part of him wished that Sarah would dump them in a clearing and pull out a tent. He needed the solitude and peace of nature. After this crazy couple of weeks he wanted to wind down, and he couldn't think of a better way to do it than being alone in the bush. But because this was the Buffalo and Baobab he suspected that their idea of getting up close and personal with nature would be much better.

He'd barely finished that thought when Sarah veered off the dirt road onto a grassy track. Within a hundred metres she'd stopped in a clearing and Finn looked around.

They were on the edge of a cliff, and he could hear the muted sound of a river smacking on rocks below them. In one of the huge wild fig trees overlooking the river he could see a tree house, nestled into its strong branches. Except that it was less house and more platforms—three of them in all, staggered up the tree. The bottom platform looked to be a bathroom, complete with shower, the second held couches and a table, and the highest one, he presumed, would hold a bed. A bed that was open to the African sky and the elements.

Finn hopped out and slapped his hands on his hips, grinning wildly. 'Oh, this is so cool! But what happens if it rains?' he asked Sarah, taking a moment to be practical.

'Retractable roofs and screens. We monitor the weather pretty closely, and if there's a chance of rain we come down and secure the platforms. Tonight is clear, though,' Sarah said. 'Cool, but no rain.'

'Excellent,' Finn replied. He turned to look at Callie, who was looking at the tree house in horror. 'Callie…?'

'My room is up *there*?' she whispered, staring at the huge tree.

Oh, so this wasn't what she was expecting. Finn hoped that she wouldn't make a scene—not on their first night. Besides, thousands of people all over the world would give their right arm and a considerable portion of their bank account to sleep under the stars in a luxury tree house on an African game reserve.

'Problem, honey?'

Out of the corner of his eye he could see Sarah stiffening, her welcoming face turning wary. *Please don't turn out to be a city girl diva, Callie,* he silently begged her.

'Look, I think the idea of sleeping in a tree house is seriously wonderful, but—well, this is a game reserve, right? And game reserves have wild animals. And some of those animals—like leopards—like to climb trees! I do *not* want to be a leopard's breakfast!' Callie stated, with a touch of hysteria in her voice.

Sarah bit the inside of her lip to keep from smiling. 'The tree house is completely animal-proof, Mrs Banning.'

Whoah—*Mrs Banning*. That sounded weird.

But Callie didn't seem particularly fazed about what she was being called. She was still fixating on ending up on the local leopard's menu. 'You're sure?'

'Very. We would never put our guests at risk,' Sarah assured her. 'Obviously we ask you to confine your movements to the platforms. If you do so, you'll be absolutely safe. And I'll leave you with a radio and a mobile phone to call me if there is any problem at all.'

A hyena barked in the distance and Callie jumped.

Sarah looked around. 'That being said, I'd prefer that we get you into the tree house. It's not safe to hang around in the bush.'

Callie practically scampered off the seat to stand between Sarah and Finn. Finn took her cold hand in his and linked their fingers together. Sarah walked around to the back of the Land Rover and looked at their pile of luggage. Well, Callie's pile of luggage. He just had one suitcase.

'Let me see you inside and then I'll come back for the luggage.'

Finn shook his head. 'Nah, I'll help. Cal, do you need all these suitcases or can you get away with just one?'

Callie pointed to the smaller case and her tote bag. 'I just need those two.'

Sarah looked relieved as she reached for Callie's bag.

Finn leaned past her and snagged his suitcase and Callie's tote bag. 'I've got it,' he told Sarah, who had started to protest.

'I'll store your other bags at the lodge, Mrs Banning.'

Mrs Banning. Still weird.

'We've set out a picnic dinner for you, including some wine and beer. There is also a selection of spirits and mixers. If you are unhappy with our selection please just call Reception and we'll have someone deliver anything you require,' Sarah said as she led them to the tree house.

As they walked up the stairs Sarah secured a gate behind them, and Finn could see the unobtrusive but strong netting under the first platform that would prevent leopards or any other creatures from making a nocturnal visit. He pointed out the animal-proofing to Callie and watched her shoulders drop a half-inch. He allowed himself a small grin as Sarah showed them the facilities, which included a shower, his and hers basins, and a slipper bath on the edge of the platform that overlooked the river and the valley below.

The second floor held comfortable couches and chairs, a hammock strung between two branches, and a small dining table covered with cloche dishes and champagne bottles in ice buckets. There was a small chest freezer containing soft drinks and beer, and a steel wine rack holding five bottles of exceptional red wine.

How much did they expect them to drink in one night? Finn wondered.

'I'll leave you to explore the bedroom on your own,' Sarah told him, gesturing to the mobile and the radio on a side table. 'You'll hear lions and hyenas, typical bush noises, but do not hesitate to radio or call me if you are uncomfortable or encounter a problem. Nick will collect you at six a.m. for a guided tour—which is a pretty big deal because he rarely does them any more.'

'Why not?' Callie asked.

'Pretty wife in his bed…' Finn explained, and was enchanted by her blush.

'Also the fact that he has two kids under the age of three who are up and roaring around at that time,' Sarah added, before bidding them goodnight and leaving them to their night under the African stars.

Within minutes they heard the Land Rover pulling away and Finn turned to Callie and gestured to the view. 'So, what do you think?'

'Pretty shoddy digs…' Callie teased. 'They've gone to absolutely no trouble at all.'

Finn watched as she walked to the edge of the platform and placed her hands on the safety railing. 'Want some champagne?'

Callie looked at him over her shoulder and wrinkled her nose. 'No, thanks. Actually, I'd love a beer.'

Finn poured beer into a glass for her and brought it and his own bottle over to where she stood. In silence they scanned the river, saw a pod of hippos on the far bank, and watched as the sun tossed ribbons of gold over the treetops.

Finn saw her shiver as the temperature dropped further and allowed the backs of his fingers to drift over the bare skin of her shoulders. 'You're cold… This wind has a bite to it. Why don't you change into something warm and I'll start a fire in the pit?'

Callie looked around. 'Where are our bags?'

'Sarah took them to the bedroom area,' Finn replied.

'Ah, the bedroom area. Bet you it's a massive bed covered in white linen and a mosquito net, surrounded by candles.'

'That's a sucker bet,' Finn replied.

Callie took a nervous sip of her beer before lifting her eyes to Finn's. 'So, are we still paying it by ear?'

He'd never met a woman as direct as Callie before. He liked that—respected it. He didn't need to play games with her.

But she wasn't ready to share herself with him yet, Finn realised. He could see reluctance in the hitch of her shoulders, the slight shake of her fingers—although that might be from the cold—and in the worry in her eyes. She would share his bed one of these days—just not yet. And that was okay. He could wait until the time was right.

And, in the spirit of honesty, he knew the more time he had between his break-up and sleeping with her, the better handle he'd have on this entire situation. *Damn*, it would all be so much easier if he didn't like her quite so much—and if she didn't make his junk want to do a happy dance whenever she breathed.

So. Much. Easier.

Finn's expression turned serious. 'I have the sense that your flirty nature doesn't often translate into bedtime fun.'

Callie tipped her head. 'How do you figure?'

'Well, if it meant less to you then we'd have already ripped each other's clothes off.'

Callie looked out at the stygian darkness. 'It wasn't always like that. I was a lot more impetuous when I was younger.' She held up her hand to explain. 'I wasn't a slut—I just didn't take sex as seriously as I do now. It used to just be a romp…some slap and tickle…fun…'

'It still can be,' Finn said, his eyes locked on her face.

'I know, but these days I prefer to have a little bit of friendship with my sex. Just a smidgeon—I don't expect more than that—but liking is a prerequisite, respect is a bonus.'

'I like you.'

'I like you too, but...'

Finn quirked an eyebrow. 'But?'

'But...' Callie sighed. 'I'm just not—'

Callie stopped speaking and Finn waited for her to finish her thought. She just wasn't *what*?

Callie sighed. 'Ready. I'm just not ready.'

Yeah, and that was a lie. There was another reason why she was hesitating, why she was treading carefully. She wanted him—he knew that...had no doubts about that. So something else was causing her to hesitate. What was it and why was he so desperate to know?

Callie was waiting for his reply, buy there was nothing that he could say except, 'We won't be doing anything together until you are a hundred per cent comfortable with me, Cal. So try and relax, stop worrying, go and get warm. We can share a bed without me jumping you, I promise. Actually, tonight I'd love to sleep in this hammock. It looks super-comfortable and I've slept in far worse.' Finn took a long sip of his beer. 'Go and put something warm on, honey.'

Callie nodded, put her untouched beer on the table and walked to the stairs leading to the sleeping platform. Finn watched her gorgeous ass moving up the spiral staircase and felt the action in his pants.

All he had to do was follow her, start kissing her, and she'd be his. He knew that. God, it was tempting. But he didn't want to have to coerce her, tempt her, persuade her. When they made love it would be because it was a mutual decision.

It had something to do with the respect that Callie had been talking about earlier.

'Finn! This bedroom is *amazing*!' Callie called down

to him. 'Come up here and look at this place. It would be like having sex in the clouds—I mean, sleeping with you in the clouds—I mean... *Aaarrrgggh!* Dammit!'

Finn grinned, happy that he wasn't the only one who had his mind in the bedroom.

'Ignore me.' Callie's low voice drifted down to him.

Yeah, not easy to do, Finn silently assured her as he swallowed his chuckle.

Callie pushed her plate away and groaned as she leaned back in her chair. She'd expected a cold supper. She hadn't expected delicious prawns, spicy fish fillets and perfectly cooked steak. There'd also been a couscous salad and a watermelon, olive and feta salad, along with crusty bread and a variety of dips.

After the flight from Cape Town and two glasses of red wine she was feeling lazy and hazy and very sleepy. At nearly eight it was fully dark, and the soundtrack of the African bush had started to play. The crickets chirping was a familiar sound, and there was the power saw noise of the African cicada beetle. Occasionally a fish eagle would let rip with a *heee-ah, heeah-heeah*, and from somewhere that sounded far too close they heard the yelping, woofing and whining of what Finn said was a family of black-backed jackals.

It was noisy, Callie realised. *Very* noisy.

Finn, his strong features looking even more handsome in the low light of the paraffin lamps, looked at her across the table. 'There's chocolate mousse in the cool box.'

'I wish I could. I'm stuffed.'

Like her, Finn had pulled on jeans and a hooded sweatshirt against the cool night air. The blazing fire in the pit kept the worst of the chill off, but this was a place that invited you to have a warm shower and then to snuggle under the down duvet on the bed upstairs, warm in each other's arms.

It was an attractive proposition, Callie thought. But Finn had reiterated his wish to sleep in the double hammock. He'd found another down duvet in a storage cupboard on the bathroom platform and announced that he'd be super-warm wrapped up in it in the hammock.

'You look tired,' Finn commentated, lifting his glass of red to his lips.

'I am.' Callie leaned her arms on the table. 'It's been an interesting week.'

'You should've been in Paris by now.'

Tearing around the city, rushing from designer to designer, not having a moment to enjoy the city in the spring… Callie thought that she would much rather be here.

'You never told me what happened that you could suddenly take me up on my offer to be a fake wife.'

Could she tell him? Would he understand? Callie ran her finger around the rim of her full glass. He was treating her to three weeks in luxury—maybe he deserved an explanation. And, geez, they were going to be in each other's company for three weeks—they were going to *have* to talk! They were going to be friends whether they liked it or not. It was up to her to keep things casual.

'I'm running away—trying to avoid someone,' she said, looking into the fire pit. So much for keeping it casual!

'Yeah, I sort of realised that.' Finn stretched out his legs and rested his wine glass on his folded arm. 'So, who is Laura and why are you avoiding her?'

Callie jerked her head up. 'Where did you hear that name?'

'The other day, when you were arguing with your brother. Who is she?' Finn asked again.

Well, she'd started this conversation, she couldn't shut it down now.

'My mother,' Callie said, slouching down in her chair, crossing her feet at the ankles. 'She left us. We haven't heard from her since I was seven. Seb, my brother, has been tracking her movements around the world for years—he's a hacker and can do that—and they started exchanging emails. The result of which is that Laura is coming home for a three-week visit, landing—' Callie checked her watch '—in about an hour. She and Seb are going to reconnect, and everybody wants me to meet her too. Well, "everybody" being Seb.'

'And you made damn sure that there was no possibility of that happening by leaving the city with me? That's why you changed your mind about coming?' Finn said, his voice deep in the darkness.

'Yeah. I needed to leave and you gave me a damn good excuse.' Would he think she was a coward? That she was being immature? Why did it matter so much that he didn't judge her?

Finn pulled his legs in and sat up. 'So why don't you want to meet her? Why don't you want to hear why she left?'

That question again, Callie thought.

'Because it doesn't matter! Because nothing she can say—and, trust me, I've thought of every excuse she could come up with—would make me feel better, would make me understand. I was *seven*, Finn. Seven! I needed a mother. Especially since my dad dealt with my mother leaving by hooking up with younger and younger women. They were mostly after his money, and weren't interested in his little daughter hanging around. Seb was twelve, and he dealt with her leaving by withdrawing into his sports and computers.'

Callie heard her voice rise and made a conscious effort to remain calm.

'If it wasn't for Rowan, who lived next door, and Yasmeen—'

'Who is she?'

'Our housekeeper—and I suppose my real mother in every way that counted,' Callie explained. She pushed her hair off her forehead and shoulders. 'Look, I know I sound harsh, but I can't meet Laura. I don't want to…'

'Don't want to meet her, like her, risk being hurt by her again?'

'Yeah.'

He got it—he understood. *Damn.* There were those fuzzies in her tummy again. She could get used to those. *Not* a good idea.

Finn rested his forearms on his thighs and looked up at her, sparks from the fire reflected in his eyes. Callie, feeling as if he'd taken a peek into part of her soul, thought that he'd heard enough from her, so she turned the spotlight onto him.

'So, you mentioned your stepbrothers? How many do you have?'

Finn half smiled. 'Three. All younger. They're driving me nuts lately.'

'Why?'

'They were, to put it mildly, upset that the wedding was called off. As I said, because they know me, and know that I never go back on my word, they assumed that the break-up was Liz's idea. I haven't bought food for two weeks because someone always pitches up at my house with beer and take-out.'

'Nobody rocked up that night I had dinner at your house,' Callie pointed out.

'I sent them a group message while I was upstairs and told them I would kick their ass if they didn't give me a night on my own.' Finn pulled a face. 'The next night I had all three of them coming to check up on me and had to spend half the evening reassuring them that I was okay.'

'And are you?' Callie asked. 'Okay?'

'Mostly. I'm glad to still be on this assignment, working. Glad of the distraction that is you.'

Callie smiled at that. Whatever they had cooking it was, she had to admit, a hell of a distraction. 'It's surprising that your younger brothers are so protective of you.'

'We're protective of each other. They're my brothers. My mum married James when I was fourteen and he already had the boys. Mum died when I was seventeen, and James acted as my legal guardian for a while.'

'Where's your real dad?'

'Who the hell knows? Jail? Dead? In a gutter somewhere?' Finn said harshly.

He rubbed a hand over his face, and when he finally met her eyes she made sure that her face was impassive.

'Pretend I didn't say that, please? I never talk about him and I have no idea where that came from.'

Maybe their bottle of wine had contained some magic truth potion, because she'd had no intention of telling him about Laura. Or maybe it was the fact that they were absolutely, utterly alone under an African night sky…

Or maybe it was because they liked talking to each other.

And she thought that *she* had had a messed-up childhood. God, they were a pair, Callie thought.

Finn cleared his throat before speaking again. 'I've always protected my brothers—yanked them out of scrapes, had their back. I've been their rock, their calm in the storm. This break-up has been the first crisis I've had that they've witnessed and they want to be there for me.'

'And your stepdad? How does he feel about your break-up?'

Finn shrugged and kept his shoulders up around his ears. 'Dunno. He died about six months ago.'

'I'm so sorry, Finn. You two were close?'

'Yeah. He was the best man I ever knew…' Finn cleared his throat. 'I adored him.'

God. He had a waste-of-space father, a dead mother, and his stepdad, whom he'd loved, had recently passed away. He'd broken up with his fiancée two weeks before his wedding. Was there anything else that life could throw at the poor guy?

Enough now, she told the universe, annoyed on his behalf. *Seriously. Just enough, already.*

Callie leaned forward and touched his knee in silent support. He hadn't stopped grieving, she realised. Probably wouldn't for a while. Losing his fiancée had undoubtedly pulled all those old feelings of grief over losing his stepfather to the surface again.

Oh, yeah, there was far too much emotion swirling around for them to sleep together. Because there was no chance that sex would be about just sex after a conversation like this. For her it would all be tangled up with the urge to soothe, to comfort. And to him she would be just a distraction…

Thinking that it would be prudent, and smart, to close this conversation down, Callie pushed her chair back and stood up. 'I'd really like a shower. I feel grubby.'

Finn stared up at her for the longest time before lifting one broad shoulder. 'Sure.'

Callie looked at the stairs that led to the dark bathroom area below them and bit her lip. 'Is there a torch anywhere?'

Finn stood up. 'I'll go down and light some lamps for you. There's a big tub on the deck if you'd prefer a bath.'

A hyena whooped in the distance and Callie shivered. 'Not that brave. I'm not entirely sure if my standards of animal-proof are the same as the lodge's, so I'd rather not take the chance.'

'The bath is at least twenty foot off the ground, Hollis,' Finn told her, smiling.

'There might a genius leopard out there who has the situation sussed,' Callie suggested, only half joking.

'You're a nut,' Finn said with on a shake of his head and a grin. 'Go get your PJs while I sort out some light for you.'

'Thanks.' Callie bit her bottom lip. 'I don't suppose you'll stand guard, will you?'

Finn touched her bottom lip with the pad of his thumb. 'The only way that will happen is if I'm in the shower with you.' Finn dropped his thumb when she shook her head. 'No, I didn't think so.'

Snuggled down in the enormous bed on the top platform, Callie couldn't keep her eyes off the magnificent night sky. It looked as if God had taken a handful of diamonds and tossed them against a sticky backdrop, allowing them to hang there in a perpetual grip. She'd never seen stars like this before—she almost felt she could reach out and touch them.

She was beyond tired, Callie thought, and wished that sleep would come. But every time she closed her eyes she was jolted by another strange sound. The rustle of something in the tree—probably just the breeze, or a bird—had her constantly on edge. It was *not* the genius leopard, she kept telling herself. And just when she felt her eyelids starting to close those pesky jackals would start their yelping again, and then something would grunt and the hyena would laugh.

Callie was over her night under the African stars and was not finding anything remotely amusing. She was exhausted, slightly chilled, and—though she hated to admit it—a lot scared. She realised she *liked* having walls and windows between her and the night, locks and safety chains. She didn't like feeling as if she was a snack on the buffet of the African savannah, and it didn't matter how much Mr Cool downstairs reassured her: this was *not* natural! Or maybe it was *too* natural.

Again—walls, doors, windows! That was what God had created them for!

The sounds of the night dropped away and Callie felt her eyelids drooping. She was on that wonderful edge of sleep when she felt a rumbling in her chest, felt electricity charge the air. Instantly the night sounds ceased as a deep-throated grunt echoed across the bush. Oh, crap!

Callie scrambled up in bed and pulled the duvet over her head.

The grunt increased in intensity and she felt the sound invade her chest, skitter down to her nerve-endings. *Lion!* Callie sucked in her breath and wished that she could belt out of bed and run all the way back to Cape Town. The deep grunts tailed off and she bit her lip, waiting for the next sound. Just when she thought that the lion had stopped he let out a massive, deep-throated roar that raised every hair on her arms.

God—oh, God—oh, God. Finn had to call the lodge. There was a lion below them. Who could sleep with a lion below them?

'Finn!' she whispered.

Finn didn't reply.

Throwing back the covers, Callie grabbed all her courage and belted for the stairs. She cursed when she stubbed her big toe against a table. The roars were still reverberating through the night. In bare feet she scampered down the steps and by sheer chance located the radio and mobile on the table, where Sarah had left them. Her shaky hands fumbled with the unfamiliar device.

'Whatcha doing?' Finn's drowsy voice came from the direction of the hammock.

'Finn! There's a lion below us!' Callie hissed. 'We've got to call the lodge!'

'Um, okay. Why?'

'Because there's a *lion*!' Callie shouted. 'Below us!'

'Lions don't climb trees, Hollis, especially animal-proofed trees,' Finn drawled.

If she hadn't been so freaked out Callie would have heard the amusement in his voice.

Another roar rolled through the stygian darkness and Callie jumped, dropping the mobile which skittered away. She swore and peered down at the pitch-black floor. She couldn't see the phone so she swore again.

She was going to owe Rowan a lot of money after tonight.

'Cal, calm down, honey.' Finn's voice was low and steady, a beacon in the darkness. 'Leave the phone and head over here.'

Thinking that sounded like a very good plan, Callie inched her way over the deck to the bulky outline that was Finn lying in the hammock. When she stood next to him he lifted his hands and in one smooth movement lifted her, so that she lay on top of him. Rolling her off, he pulled the duvet out from under her and pulled her up so that her head rested on his shoulder.

'Uh…what are you doing?'

'Trying to get you to settle down so that we both can get some sleep,' he muttered.

His hand rested on her lower back and she snuggled up to his warmth.

'Now, listen to me, city girl. A lion's roar can be heard up to five miles away, and I promise you that lion is nowhere near us. Yeah, he sounds amazing, but he's not about to eat us—so calm down, okay?'

'I still think we should call the lodge,' Callie protested on a huge yawn.

'What would we tell them? A lion is roaring? *Yeah, that's what they do in the wild, Mr Banning.* They'll think that I have the tiniest pair of balls in creation,' Finn scoffed.

'I'll call them and tell them that *you* aren't scared but I am terrified.'

Finn's sigh brushed the top of her head. 'There's nothing to be frightened of. Listen. He's stopped.'

Callie lifted her head and, true enough, the grunts and roars had stopped. She was just starting to relax when another rumbling loud roar split the night. Callie yelped and buried her face in Finn's neck, plastered herself tightly against him, hoping to climb inside.

Finn sighed. 'Or maybe not.'

Finn's hand stroked her neck, her hair, her back. His voice was low and warm and calming. 'You're safe, Cal, I promise.'

Callie shivered in his arms.

'Breathe, angel,' he told her.

Callie pulled in long deep breaths, felt his warmth and his strength and breathed again. Then her eyelids started to close and she pulled in another deep breath.

In Finn's arms, fast asleep, feeling warm and safe, she didn't even hear the next roar that shattered the night.

CHAPTER SEVEN

THEY DINED OUTSIDE the following evening, at a beautifully laid table on the lawn of the lodge, under another magnificent star-heavy sky. In the distance they could see a storm, the lightning lighting up huge thunderclouds. They could taste the rain in the air but were assured that dinner would be long over before the storm hit, so they sat back to enjoy the exceptional food placed in front of them.

Finn noticed that the lead singer of a popular band sat with a pouty waif at the next table, and beyond them he recognised an English politician with a woman who was definitely not his wife. If he were a tabloid journalist he would be having a field-day right now; he might be feeling a bit sleazy but he'd be making a fortune, he thought.

He looked across at Callie, who was leaning back in her chair, holding her wine glass, her eyes fixed on the storm on the horizon. God, she was beautiful, he thought. He'd always thought that she was attractive, but now, after seeing her without make-up and dozy with sleep, or animated and thrilled while she bottle-fed two orphaned cheetah cubs, or pensive while watching a pride of lions take down a zebra, he was slowly realising that she was more than pretty and deeper than he'd thought.

He'd thought that he would be taking a bubbly flirt on holiday with him, but the woman he was with—even if he'd only spent two full days in her company—was less bubble, more substance. And sexier than he'd believed possible.

Finn dropped his hand and surreptitiously rearranged himself under the table, feeling as if his pants were suddenly a size too small. Since he'd woken up with her clinging to him like an octopus he'd been super-aware of her all day. The length of her legs, the freckles on her chest, her white-tipped fingernails. God, if he was noticing a woman's nails then he was in deep, *deep* crap.

He'd thought he was going on holiday with Flirty Callie but instead he found himself with Intriguing Callie, and he wasn't sure he could handle her. Flirty Callie he could brush off—ignore if he had to. This other Callie had him wanting to dig a little, to see what was below the surface.

Finn took a sip of his Cabernet and pushed his dessert plate away. Then he manoeuvred his chair so that he was sitting next to her, facing the storm. He could smell her perfume and feel the heat of her bare shoulder when he touched it with his.

He slid his hand under hers and linked her fingers with his. He saw the quick, searching look she sent him and ignored it. If she asked he'd say that this was what married people did—touched each other—but the truth was that he couldn't sit there and *not* touch her.

'Tell me about your jewellery box.'

There was so much else he wanted to know about her—he had a list of burning questions—but this topic seemed the safest, the most innocuous.

He heard her quick intake of breath, felt her eyes on his face.

He slowly turned his head and lifted his eyebrows. 'Why would a woman who loves clothes and shoes and accessories not wear some of that fabulous jewellery?'

Callie crossed one leg over the other and her swinging foot told him she was considering her response, choosing her words. He didn't want the bog standard answer she obviously wanted to hand him—he wanted the truth. He'd rather not know than have her spin him a line.

'Don't wrap the truth up in a pretty bow—give it to me straight.'

The foot stopped swinging and the sigh was louder this time. She took so long to say anything that Finn began to doubt that she would speak at all. When she did, her voice was low and tight with tension.

'That was the first time I'd seen the box for…oh, fifteen years. It lived on my mum's dressing table and as a little girl I'd spend hours playing with her bangles and necklaces. Her rings.'

Finn tried not to wince at the thought of little Callie playing with the two and three carat diamonds he'd seen.

'Some of the jewellery was my grandmother's—my father's mother's—passed down through the family. A lot of it is my mother's. My father constantly bought her jewellery in an attempt to make her happy.'

Ah, well… 'I take it that the buying of jewellery didn't work?'

'Not so much. Neither did the pretty clothes and the gym membership and the credit cards.' Callie shrugged. 'She didn't want to be a wife…a mother. To be chained to my dad, the house, us. She gave birth to the expected son and was horrified, I once heard, to find herself pregnant with me. She'd never really wanted children, and apparently finding herself pregnant with me was a disaster of magnificent proportions.'

'Who told you that?'

Callie crossed her legs and shuffled in her chair. 'People say that kids don't remember stuff, but I do. She screamed that during one of their fights.'

'I'm sorry.' It was all he could say—all he could think of to say. Finn removed his hand from hers and put his arm around her shoulder, leaning sideways to kiss her temple. 'But people do say stuff they don't mean in the heat of the moment.'

'Except that her leaving me—us—made that statement true.' Callie took a large, serious sip from her glass. 'Anyway, the jewellery—she left it behind. It meant nothing to her. So why should it mean anything to me?'

God. Imagine knowing that your mother was out there somewhere but not interested in knowing whether you were dead or alive, happy or sad. People should have to take a test before they were allowed to become parents, Finn thought. His father should head up the queue.

Callie turned her head and blinded him with a big smile, perfect teeth flashing. 'Now, don't you go all sympathetic on me, Banning. I had a father who adored me and spoilt me rotten, an older brother who adored me and spoilt me rotten, and a housekeeper-cum-nanny who—'

'Let me guess,' Finn interrupted, making sure that his tone was bone-dry. 'Who adored you and spoilt you rotten?'

Callie laughed. 'I have a fabulous life, and I'm on holiday with a nice man.'

'I prefer sexy.'

This time her smile was more genuine. 'So I have nothing to complain about!'

Being abandoned by your mum is a pretty big deal, Callie, Finn told her silently. *Even if you choose to think it isn't. The one person who is supposed to put you first, love you best, stand in your corner left you. That's got to cause some deep scars on your psyche.*

Feeling the need to banish the sadness from her eyes, Finn nudged her with his shoulder. 'Want to take a walk down to the lookout over the waterhole and see if any wildlife has come down for a drink?'

Callie immediately nodded and a sparkle returned to

her eyes. 'Yeah, let's do that.' She stood up and folded her arms. 'How come I find myself telling you stuff?'

Finn wanted to make a joke but he couldn't. 'I don't know, but rest assured you're not alone. I keep doing the same thing.'

Callie bit her lip. 'Maybe we should stop?'

Finn held out his hand. 'Yeah, maybe we should. The thing is, I don't know if we can.'

There was nobody in the lookout and nothing at the waterhole except for a lone bull elephant. They watched him and the storm for a while, but Callie's thoughts were miles away. On Finn and their bizarre situation, and on the fact that every time they drew a line in the sand they managed either to smudge it or step right over it.

Maybe it was time to draw a line that couldn't be removed, stepped over or just plain ignored. But how to do that?

Callie yawned and felt his arm come around her shoulders. Without thought she circled her arms around his trim waist and laid her cheek on his chest.

Smudging that line again, Hollis?

Callie felt Finn's kiss on her hair. 'Tired?'

'Mmm...'

Callie moved her hands to his abs and Finn sucked in his breath. In response she scraped her nails across his cotton-covered skin. A quick glance down and she realised, by the tenting of his pants, that he had a hair trigger response to her touch.

This wasn't smudging the line—this was obliterating it. Was she prepared to go there? She had about five seconds either to take this to the next level or to back away.

Callie knew herself well enough to know that she wasn't going to step away. She was facing a fire and for the first time in, God, so long she was going to jump right in. But this time she was going to be a little wiser and don a fire suit.

'Finn?'

'Yeah?' His voice was husky with desire and so sexy.

'That thing that happened in the dressing room…I keep thinking about it.'

She knew exactly when he stopped breathing, when he finally sucked in much needed air. 'Okay. Where are you going with this?'

'Our room only has one bed, and if I climb into it with you I'm going to be all over you.'

Callie forced herself to walk out of his grip, to pick up the bottle of beer he'd brought with him and take the last sip. To keep herself from jumping him, she held the bottle in a loose grip.

Finn groaned. 'Good to know. Want to get going, then?'

She smiled at the hopeful note in his voice before quietly murmuring, 'Holiday romances seldom work out.'

'That's what I've heard.'

'People tend to put on rose-coloured glasses and, because they know their time together is short, the experience can be intense, powerful.'

'I guess.'

Callie rolled the bottle between her palms. 'I'm at a bit of a crossroads in my life and I'm questioning so much. I'm not thinking as straight as I usually do, so don't let me get forget that this is a couple of weeks of pure fun, okay? Don't let me get seduced by the luxury and the romance and the fact that I like you.'

That was the line in the sand, she decided. They could chat and talk, share confidences and make incredible love, but she had to remember that this was going to end. It was too easy to forget who they were and why they were here. It was not real life. They were on a fake honeymoon—emphasis on the *fake*—surrounded by romance and luxury.

She could easily get swept away and inadvertently slip on a pair of those rose-coloured glasses.

They were two strangers who hardly knew each other—not a couple on their honeymoon. They could have fun, even sex, but they had to keep it real. She wasn't in a place to consider a relationship beyond the three weeks. Sure, it would be easy to fall for Finn, but it wouldn't last because it wasn't based on anything real.

She—*they*—had to keep their eyes open, their heads in the game. If she had sex with him she would finally know how he felt, tasted, moved. and then she could stop thinking about him—and sex—all the damn time.

Callie turned her head and sent him a direct look. 'We're on the same page?'

He rubbed his hand over his jaw before nodding briskly. 'Yeah. Just to be clear, are you saying that you'll sleep with me?'

The tip of her tongue touched her top lip and her skin flushed with anticipated pleasure. *Yeah, that was the plan.* Callie held his eyes.

'Well, sleep isn't what we'll be doing, exactly.' He made a move towards her but her lifted hand stopped him in his tracks. 'I don't want to be seduced, Finn.'

She saw a moment of confusion and then his face cleared. 'No hearts and flowers, no expectations.'

How did he seem to know without her having to explain? It was unsettling, but reassuring at the same time.

Finn touched her bottom lip with the pad of his thumb. 'Only in my bed, honey. I promise. Sex is on the table—everything else is off it.'

They could do this, Callie thought as they made their way out of the hide and across the lawns to their new room behind the main lodge. If they were smart and sensible, and if they kept their heads, they could have three weeks of fun and walk away unscathed.

They *had* to do this, Callie amended as Finn took her hand in his. They didn't have another option.

In their private chalet within the protected grounds of the lodge Finn took her hand and led her out onto a dark, private veranda, where moonlight glistened off the bubbles created by the hot tub that sat in one corner. Callie watched his face as he reached behind her and slid down the zip of her simple A-line dress, pulling the collar away from her neck and allowing the silky sage-green fabric to fall to the wooden deck. She stood in her violet strapless bra and matching panties, open to his appreciative gaze, watching his eyes as one index finger traced her collarbone, her shoulder, the top of her right breast.

He looked entranced, engrossed, fully involved in touching her, learning her shape, making her a memory. *Don't get fanciful,* she warned herself, closing her eyes as his finger touched her nipple and it tightened and peaked immediately.

'This is about sex, about pleasure, about a three-week affair,' Callie gabbled, closing her eyes at the intense pleasure his touch aroused in her.

'Shut up, Callie,' Finn murmured gently.

You've had these before, remember? she told herself. *You sleep with him until it stops being fun and then you stop. It's not rocket science.*

Except that Finn touching her didn't feel like just another sex act, just another pursuit of physical pleasure. It felt like something more. Deeper, more important.

Finn's mouth brushed her ear. 'Stop thinking,' he muttered. 'Just feel me touching you, enjoying your smooth skin, tasting you, smelling you. You do the same to me.'

His breath tickled her cheek and the touch of his finger on her skin had heat pooling between her thighs, causing a rush of moisture to her panties. He had barely even started and she was already ready for him to take her—*right now.* Oh, this was going to be amazing, incredible…

'I think you should kiss me,' Callie said against his cheekbone.

'I think I'll go up like a cracker,' was Finn's wry reply.

Callie dropped her gaze to his pants and sucked in her breath. Unable to stop herself, she ran her finger down the long, rock-hard length of him.

Finn grabbed her wrist and pulled her hand away. 'Yeah, also not a good idea.'

'I need you to—'

'Honey, I know exactly what you need.' Finn lifted his hand and tipped her chin up. Their eyes slammed together and held. 'Trust me to take care of you.'

'I do…'

'You sure?'

'If you can make me forget who I am in a semi-public dressing room, I have no doubt that you can do it now.'

Finn waited a beat before he shot his arm out, encircled her hips and slammed her into him. As her mound made contact with his erection his tongue swept into her mouth. He tasted and tormented her, swirling her away on a whirlpool of pleasure. His hand slid into the back of her panties and he palmed her butt with his broad hands, dipping lower, stretching the silk over his wrists so that he could touch her inner thighs and explore her feminine folds.

Callie shuddered as she fumbled for the buttons on his shirt, ripping off the last one in her haste to feel his broad chest and his hard, ribbed stomach.

'Want you…want you…want you…' she chanted, standing on her tiptoes to nibble his jaw, to swirl her tongue down his neck.

Finn pulled his hands out from her panties and with one deft flick her bra fell between them. Callie couldn't have cared less; her nipples were rubbing through the hair on his chest and if he didn't touch her soon, in all those important burning places, she was going to scream.

Loudly.

Unable to wait, she took one of Finn's hands and placed it on her breast, tried to direct his other hand to her crotch. But instead of taking her direction Finn stepped away from her and shook his head.

'No—you're saying *no*?' Callie cried, her fists on her hips. She couldn't believe that he was stepping away, that he was backing off.

Finn had the audacity to laugh at her before his eyes turned serious. 'I have a feeling that you normally call the shots in the bedroom, but this time—this first time—I'm running the show, angel.'

His thumb rubbed her cheekbone and she forgot her thought.

'You said that you trusted me. Take your panties off.'

Callie looked at him, her mouth drying at his command. She was always in the driving seat when it came to sex—she set the pace—and it felt strange and wildly intoxicating to relinquish control. Her heart was pumping at a mile a minute.

She licked her lips before hooking her thumbs in the band of her panties and shimmying them over her hips. Finn looked at her lightning-shaped strip of pubic hair and his lips twitched. When he lifted his eyes again the humour had been replaced by flat-out desire.

'That's new.'

'Shut up…' Callie growled. They could discuss her beautician's creative streak later.

'Go and sit on the edge of the hot tub—feet in the water, legs open.'

Callie turned her back to him, walked up the steps to the tub and stepped over the ledge, dropping her feet into the hot, gorgeous water. She sighed her pleasure and couldn't help wondering what was coming next.

'Yeah, keep your eyes closed,' Finn told her. 'This is about you—only you.'

God, could she stand it? Callie thought as she obeyed his instruction. Immediately her other senses were heightened: she could taste the approaching storm on her lips, could smell the citronella in the candles that she heard Finn lighting, could feel bubbles popping against her feet and her calves.

The crickets were in full chorus again, and she thought she heard the bark of a zebra.

Callie had no idea where Finn was. She had heard the rustle of his clothing as he undressed, but after that nothing more. He'd gone Ninja on her, but she couldn't open her eyes—not until he told her to.

'Open your legs, Cal.'

Callie shivered as his voice caressed her skin, causing goosebumps up and down her arms. 'Wider, honey. Yeah. So pretty. No, don't open your eyes. Let me look at you.'

Callie sat on the edge of the tub, her eyes closed, feeling wild and free and as much a part of this savage place as the predators and the prey. Time slowed and the seconds ticked over sluggishly. She was content just to sit there and let her about-to-be lover look at her.

An owl screeched, a candle spluttered, and Callie yelped as hard hands pulled her knees further apart and a dark head appeared between her thighs. Then his mouth, hot, wild and experienced, dropped onto her sex and she bucked against him, her cries blending into the sounds of the night.

Callie gripped the sides of the tub as Finn pleasured her with his lips, his tongue, slid first one finger into her, then two. She arched her back as her orgasm built, desperate for Finn to push her over the edge. But just as she crested he pulled back, and she keened her disappointment. He allowed her to fall, just a little, before building her up again.

He repeated the torture until he lifted his head, looked her straight in the eye and, with his fingers still inside her, issued another order. 'Come for me. *Now.*'

And Callie responded, just as he knew she would, instantly gushing over his hand, her inner muscles gripping his fingers and seeking all the pleasure he could give her. Finn kept his eyes locked on hers, thoroughly captivated by her uninhibited response.

When she finally stopped shaking he pulled his hand away and lifted his arm to grab her waist and pull her into the middle of the tub. She wound her legs around his hips and felt the divine friction as her clit rubbed against his penis, revving her up again. She rode him and felt vindicated, powerful, when his eyes crossed.

Taking him in her fist, she positioned him so that his tip was at her entrance. His bicep bulged with the effort of keeping from ramming himself inside her.

'No condom,' he muttered, his arms shaking.

'I'm on the pill,' she told him. 'And I'm clean. I haven't had sex for over six months and I had a medical three months ago. You?'

'Same. Clean. Trust me?'

Callie didn't bother to reply. She just slid onto him and smiled at his expression, which combined relief with pure, unadulterated pleasure.

'God, you feel so good.'

Finn lifted a wet hand and pushed her hair back from her face. 'You ready to go again?''

'*So* ready.'

He lunged up and into her, his arms a vice around her waist. 'Then hang on, baby.'

Callie managed to push herself away just enough to

look into his eyes. She touched his mouth with the tips of her fingers. 'Finn?'

'Yeah?'

'Come for me. *Now*.'

And, with a roar that was as wild as the bush around them, Finn did exactly as she commanded.

'In the nineteenth century the local tribe in the area knew it as Mosi-oa-Tunya. Translated, that means the smoke that thunders.'

Callie stood gripped the railing in front of her and watched, utterly fascinated, as millions and millions of gallons of water thundered over the edge of the falls into a gorge over one hundred metres below them.

'The Victoria Falls is known as the greatest curtain of falling water in the world,' Finn told her, his face wet from the droplets of spray. 'The spray can be seen from miles away at the height of the rainy season. Apparently more than five hundred million cubic metres of water per minute plummet over the edge, over a width of nearly two kilometres.'

'Thank you, guidebook Finn,' Callie said dryly.

Finn pushed his wet hair off his forehead. 'It *is* an incredible sight, though, isn't it?

'It so is,' Callie agreed.

Finn placed his forearms on the railing and lifted his head to squint up at her. 'I wish we were here in winter,' he said, with a pensive look on his face.

'Why? Apart from the fact that it would be about a hundred degrees cooler than at the height of summer?'

Callie felt as if she was walking around in hot soup and she was melting from the inside out. Africa in late summer, early autumn, was still furnace-hot, she thought. And the towns of Livingstone and Victoria Falls, situated next to the massive river, had killer humidity as well. They were, she'd decided, minutes after landing in Livingstone, Zambia, three hours ago, after a chartered flight from the Baobab and Buffalo, standing above the devil's boiler house.

'Well, in winter, when the water levels are low, you can walk along the lip of the falls. There are rock pools there, and one is called the Devil's Pool.'

That made sense, Callie thought. After stoking the fires of hell, Satan would want to cool down.

Then Finn's words sank in and her eyes widened. 'You can walk across….' she waved at the massive falls behind her '*…that*?'

'Well, there'd be a lot less water.'

'That's insane! People *do* this?' Callie cried, her stomach clenching at the thought.

'Sure. You walk across the rocks, swim through some pools, and then there's this other pool, right at the lip of the falls. The rock lip stops you from going over.'

'And you'd do that?' Callie asked in a squeaky voice.

Finn shrugged. 'Sure. It would be a kick.'

Callie closed her eyes. 'That's insane. It's official: I'm sleeping with a mad man.'

Finn straightened and pushed a long wet strand of hair out of her eyes, tucked it behind her ear. 'Talking of sleeping… This morning was so rushed we haven't had a moment alone for me to ask—are you okay?'

Callie frowned. 'Sure. Why wouldn't I be?'

'You said that it had been a while, and we did it a couple of times last night. You're not sore or tired or—?'

Callie grinned, touched by his concern. She was a little stiff, a little uncomfortable, but she wasn't about to admit that. 'Finn, I'm twenty-eight—not a hundred and eight.'

'Just checkin'.' Finn rubbed his thumb over her cheekbone. 'I had fun.'

Hoo-boy. So had she. 'Me too.'

'Want to do it again?'

Callie made sure that her tone was flippant, carefree. 'Sure—since you're *marginally* good at it.'

She put her tongue in her cheek to make sure that he knew that she was teasing.

In a flash Finn scooped her up into his arms and swung her towards the railing. 'Can you swim?' he asked, grinning down at her.

Callie wound her arms around his neck in a chokehold as she squealed hysterically. 'Put me down, you jerk!'

Finn swung her towards the railing again. 'Tell me I'm the greatest you've ever had.'

'The best ever!' Callie shouted in his ear, tightening her arms. 'I promise!'

Finn finally allowed her legs to drop to the ground, but Callie kept her arms around his neck, peeking out from over his arm. His hands were running up and down her spine.

'You were pretty spectacular yourself, Cal.'

Callie dropped her head back to look into his face. His eyes looked warm and tender, and his mouth—that wonderful mouth—was heading towards hers. She allowed him one brush, two, then a quick taste of her tongue before pulling back and stepping away. Sleeping with him was one thing, but the banter, the teasing, the outright affection had to be curtailed—or at the very least controlled. Or else they'd forget that their fake relationship was…well, fake, and they'd end up in all sorts of emotional trouble.

'I don't want a relationship,' she stated baldly.

He met her eyes. 'Me neither.'

She wanted to tell him that she *really* didn't. She couldn't allow her feelings to be engaged, couldn't hand her heart over and trust its well-being to the hands of another person. As a little girl she'd done that. Her mum had been her entire world and she'd left. Just left.

I can't and won't allow myself to break the habit of a

lifetime and fall for you in any way, shape or form, she told him silently.

She made herself smile at him. 'Just so that you know: I am going to use you and abuse you, then callously toss you aside at the end of three weeks.' *I'm going to treat you like just another short-term prospect...some bed-based fun,* she added silently. *And that means no digging into the past, sharing secrets or stories. It means being sensible and unemotional and playing it super-cool.*

Finn nodded. 'Use, abuse and toss away. Got it.' The corners of his eyes crinkled with laughter. 'You are the most honest woman I've ever met, angel.'

He'd called her that before, and it sounded so natural that she wondered if he even knew he was doing it. Short-term lovers shouldn't have nicknames, but she didn't have the guts to ask him to stop. She rather liked it.

Callie looked down the gorge to the river, to what looked like a tiny speck on the water. Her attention captivated, she leaned forward and immediately felt Finn's hand on her elbow, placed there for protection. She would have to be an idiot to lean far enough over to lose her balance and go headfirst down into the gorge, but Finn's protective instinct warmed her from the inside out.

Don't go there, Hollis. Use, abuse, toss.

'Is that a boat?' Callie asked, pointing to the river so very far below them.

'Yep. That's one of the white-water rafting boats.' Finn nodded. 'I want to do that tomorrow. Want to come with me?'

Callie twisted her lips. 'That would be a no.'

But there was a tug of excitement in her belly—a wish that she could say yes, that she could experience the thrill of riding those rapids. She hadn't done anything to make her adrenalin pound since she was a teenager who'd loved pushing the envelope.

And she wouldn't. She'd promised Seb and her dad. But, *damn*, she'd loved it.

'Aw, come on!' Finn placed a hand on her back to steer her down the path, away from their lookout point.

'You have more chance of being impregnated by a member of the zombie apocalypse.' She leaned her shoulder into his. 'You'd better not die. I'll be narked if my holiday and my recently revived sex life is interrupted by having to ship you home in a body bag.'

Finn grinned at her. 'No worries. It's safe.'

'It's madness!' Callie hissed.

But it wasn't—it really wasn't. It looked fun and exciting and thrilling, and she hoped Finn loved every second of it.

She knew that *she* would. Damn, she could just do it and they wouldn't even know. But she'd promised. And promises couldn't be broken, she reminded herself.

CHAPTER EIGHT

CALLIE, IN A teeny bikini, sat on the deep step of the tepid hotel pool, a virgin mojito by her elbow and her face shielded from the early-afternoon sun by an enormous straw hat. Finn, dressed in a pair of board shorts and holding a beer in his hand, sat next to her, reading a travel magazine.

'I should be working,' he muttered as he flipped a page.

'This *is* working,' Callie assured him. 'You're researching the hotel's facilities.'

Finn didn't lift his eyes from the page. 'I'll go with that. Jeez, what a crock!'

Callie leaned into his shoulder. Judging by the mighty mountains in the photograph, she realised that he was reading an article about the Himalayas.

'What's the problem?'

Finn flicked the magazine with his thumb. 'This journalist is writing about Durbar Square in Kathmandu and being factually incorrect—which annoys the hell out of me. If you're going to write about a foreign place be respectful and get your damn facts straight!'

Callie's lips twitched in amusement. 'I'll keep that in mind if I decide to make a career change.'

'Smart-ass,' Finn muttered, but she saw his quick smile before he refocused on the offending article.

Callie heard her mobile ring She reluctantly stood up

and went to her lounger to answer it. It would be Rowan, or Seb, or her dad calling to check up on her. She could, she thought with a smile, only tell Rowan that she was having fabulous sex…

'I'm fine…I'm happy…I haven't done anything stupid yet,' she said, her voice full of laughter.

'Hello, Calista.'

Callie stiffened and her heart started to pound. She recognised that voice—it was the voice she heard in her dreams. Callie checked the unfamiliar number on her display. 'Who *is* this?' she demanded, although she had no doubt.

'It's your mother.'

Callie shook her head. 'Funny, that—I don't *have* a mother. She left while I was in hospital, getting X-rays for my broken arm and cracked ribs.'

'You always were a challenging child.'

Like you'd know. 'Says the woman who sneaked out through the door and didn't come back.'

'I'm back now.'

'Twenty-plus years too late and I don't care. Who gave you my number? Seb?'

Silence answered that question. 'Tell him he sucks. Don't call me again, Laura, we have nothing to say to each other.'

'Calista—'

Callie pushed the button to disconnect the call and bit down on her lip, concentrating on that pain in an attempt to ignore the throbbing clenching of her heart. Laura sounded exactly the same: her voice low and melodious. She had a beautiful voice, Callie remembered. She'd loved to hear her sing.

God, she couldn't think about her—couldn't start to remember. She didn't want to remember—didn't want to open that Pandora's box. She'd always sung when she was happy…which hadn't been that often.

One phone call and a host of memories flooded back—her laughter, her scent. Callie banded her arms across her stomach, trying to keep the pain at bay. She didn't want to remember, to start thinking about her, about everything she'd lost…

She needed something to distract her—something to make her forget. Callie threw her mobile back into her tote bag and looked to Finn. *He* would make her forget. One touch of his hands on her skin and she would be taken away to a place where no thought was necessary. A place of pleasure and delight…

Callie dived into the pool and surfaced by the step. She tugged on Finn's big toe and when he looked at her lowered her eyelids in a gesture that she hoped was sexy and alluring. 'Want to go back to the cabana and play?' she asked.

Finn pulled his glasses off his face and folded them carefully. He looked at her for a full minute before asking, 'Who called you, Cal?'

Callie pulled in her top lip and shrugged. 'No one important.' Her hand slid up his leg and gripped his knee. 'Let's go and fool around.'

'Nope.'

Callie's mouth fell open in astonishment. The man hadn't been able to keep his hands off her last night and some of this morning and now he was saying *no*? When she most needed him?

'Excuse me?'

Finn held her eyes, his expression inscrutable. 'As tempting as that offer is…no, we're not going back to the room to fool around.'

'Why not?' Callie demanded, finding her feet in the pool.

'Tell me who was on the phone, Cal.'

She didn't want to discuss her mother—that was the point! She didn't want to go there. Didn't want to revisit her bad childhood and her mother issues.

Suddenly she craved the rush of adrenalin, the freedom of doing something extreme, something to get her out of herself. She wanted to be Wild Callie, Free Callie. So if she couldn't have sex in the middle of the day with her fake husband then she'd do something else to get her adrenalin pumping, to distract her.

A part of her knew that she was lapsing back into old childhood habits—as a child and teenager she'd tried every daredevil stunt she could, either to attract attention or to distract herself from her mother-free life. But, God knew, after hearing her mother's voice for the first time in over twenty years, she more than needed a distraction.

Patch and Seb would understand why she had to break her promise.

'Fine.' Callie tossed her head and glared at Finn. 'Then I'm going back to the room, getting dressed, and then I am going to go and bungee jump.'

'Yeah? No. You're not.'

Now he was presuming to tell her what to do? She didn't think so!

'Since I am an adult, and since I am not asking you to pay for it, how do you think you're going to stop me?'

Finn drained the rest of his beer and placed the empty bottle on the side of the pool. He folded his arms and she wished she could crawl into them, rest her head on his chest and allow the tears that she was holding back to slide down her face. But that was impossible. Because Callie Hollis was a tough party-girl. She didn't cry.

'Obviously I can't stop you, if that's what you're determined to do, but yesterday you said that you didn't want to bungee, to do white-water rafting or the microlight over the Falls experience. You said that extreme sports isn't something you do any more.'

'Changed my mind,' Callie retorted.

Please don't sound so concerned and worried. If you do, I might break down totally.

'I can see that. Want to tell me why?'

Callie shook her head. 'I changed my mind. I'm allowed to do that, Finn!'

'Stop treating me like an idiot, Callie! Ten minutes ago you were happy and relaxed and then you got a call. Now you're more wound up than a spinning top! Whoever called you has put you over the edge and now you're acting like a…' Finn's words trailed off.

'A lunatic? A crazy person? A bitch?' Callie asked. God knew she felt like all three. But she didn't owe him an explanation for changing her mind—why couldn't he respect that? She didn't owe anyone anything! Besides, in the past couple of days she'd spoken more about her past than she had in twenty years!

'Now you're putting words in my mouth.'

How was she supposed to fight with him, argue, when he was so calm, so controlled, so unfazed? It was like arguing with a pile of soil—incredibly frustrating.

'Did your mum call you? It was her, wasn't it?'

Oh, God, don't go there, Finn, please. 'I'm not discussing this.'

Finn rested his forearms on his knees and Callie could see the disappointment in his eyes, on his face.

'Okay, Callie, I give up. Go bungee-jumping—do whatever the hell you want.'

'All I wanted to do was make love with you!' Callie cried.

If he'd just said yes, like any normal man, they wouldn't be fighting, wouldn't be having this torturous conversation.

'No, you wanted to use me as a distraction from her call,

from whatever she said, what she made you feel,' Finn replied, his tone low. 'And while I'm happy to have you any time and anywhere, angel, might I remind you that you weren't prepared to be a means for *me* to escape the pain of my break-up? Well, ditto back at you, babe.'

Callie squeezed the rope of wet hair that hung over her shoulder. 'You couldn't even hear what I was saying, so you're jumping to some very big conclusions, Banning!'

Finn tapped his sunglasses against his leg. 'Am I wrong?'

Callie tried to lie—she did—but while her tongue formed the words she couldn't push them past her lips. Unable to hold Finn's stare, she looked up at the deep blue sky before whirling around and plunging back into the pool, allowing her tears to mix with the chlorinated water.

Damn him. All she'd wanted was some crazy sex to help her forget. Was that such a big ask?

Okay, so today had been weird, Finn thought, as he left their room at The Thunder, a small, luxurious boutique hotel situated on the banks of the mighty Zambezi River. He was heading for a huge deck suspended above the river, which offered—according to the pile of literature the manager had left for him to peruse—superb views of wildlife coming down to the river to drink and magnificent sunrises and sunsets.

Right now all he hoped was that it held a certain navy-eyed blonde who was currently avoiding him.

Finn ran his hand through his wet hair before jamming his hands into the pockets of his stone-coloured linen shorts. After their argument she'd swum lengths in the pool, only stopping forty-five minutes later, when her breath was laboured and her limbs were shaking. Her eyes had still been tight with tension, red-rimmed either from the chlorine or her tears, and her lips had been a thin line in her face.

Thinking that he'd pushed her enough, and that she needed some time to cool down, he'd avoided her for the afternoon, taking his laptop and notes and finding a secluded spot in the hotel's library to start work on his honeymoon article.

When he'd surfaced hours later it had been early evening, and when he'd returned to their room Callie's scattered clothes and her light fragrance in the air had told him that she'd already dressed and left for dinner.

She wasn't on the deck, he realised, looking over the tables. Twisting his lips, he walked to the bar area—and there she sat, at the end of the bar, a margarita in her hand, holding court. Two guys his age and an older man were hanging off her every word, tongues practically resting on the bar.

On the other side of the bar Finn leaned his shoulder into the wall and watched her, unnoticed by anyone but the barman. *Look at her,* he thought, *so bold, so attractive, such a fake.* This Callie, this consummate, charming flirt, wasn't who she really was. *All* of who she was.

The real Callie was softer, more vulnerable, a great deal deeper than the person currently charming the pants off her admirers. This woman was harder, phonier, a great deal more Hollywood.

But sexy—always so damn sexy.

The man in him—her lover—got a kick knowing that she would share his bed tonight, be with him tonight. He shrugged. That was his ego talking. It was normal to like the idea of men envying him his woman.

His woman. Wow. Yet for at least the next two weeks she was. Fake wife or not, they were sleeping together, and that allowed him a certain measure of possessiveness. It didn't mean anything serious.

Did it?

Irritated with himself, Finn peeled himself off the wall and walked up to the bar, deliberately placing a hand low on Callie's spine. He felt her stiffen and caught the wary look she tossed his way.

'Evening,' he said, making eye contact with each of her admirers. Being men, and obviously not stupid, they received his non-verbal *back-the-hell-away-from-her* message loud and clear. Within minutes they all had somewhere they needed to be, and he was soon alone with Callie.

He ordered a beer from the barman and looked into her lovely face, immediately clocking her sad eyes, her wariness.

'We still fighting?' he asked gently.

'I was fighting more with you than myself,' she admitted, twisting the wedding ring on her left hand.

'Okay,' Finn replied. He didn't understand, but as long as he was not knee-deep in the brown stuff he was good. 'Do you want to talk about it?'

'Not really.'

He should be happy at that answer, since talking always led them into uncharted, emotional territory, but he couldn't help feeling a little disappointed. He wanted to help her, to work through that brief conversation with her mother that had rocked her world this afternoon.

He was whipped, he decided on an internal sigh. He was feeling protective of her and possessive of her, acting affectionate around her and calling her *angel*. But he felt as if he'd known her for a lot longer than the few weeks he had, and in a sense he seemed to read her better than he ever had Liz. He knew her instinctively.

He was stepping into quicksand and he should back up before he found himself nose-deep in mud and struggling to breathe.

'Okay. The sun is about to go down and I think the sunset is going to be absolutely amazing. Let's go watch it.'

Callie jerked her head in a quick nod and slid off her stool, her long, sleeveless halterneck dress skimming her slim body. The indigo colour lightened her eyes and set off the tan she'd managed to acquire in a few short days. Her naturally curly hair was pulled into a messy plait.

She looked sensational and smelt even better.

Finn picked up her glass and his beer and watched her buttocks sway as she walked towards the open doors and onto the deck. He was pleased when she made her way to a vacant table perched on the end, right over the river and private.

He placed her drink on the table in front of her, pulled out a chair and waited until she was sitting down before settling himself into his own chair. He took a long swig of his beer. He was not going to ask what had gone wrong today.

Finn just sat there, happy to swat mosquitoes away as the sun finger-painted the evening sky with bold oranges and pinks.

A waiter replenished their drinks, brought them a snack of homemade chunky bread and flavoured olive oil to dunk the bread into, and Callie just looked out onto the dark river, her profile exquisite in the low light provided by lamps and citronella candles.

She slapped her bare arm and grimaced at the mess left by a bloodsucking mosquito. 'I'm being eaten alive,' she complained, and he was glad to break the silence—even if it meant discussing the mozzies, which were big enough to pick them up and carry them away.

Which reminded him… 'Did you take your anti-malaria pill?'

Callie winced. 'Dammit, I forgot.'

Finn shook his head. 'Jeez, Cal, you *can't* forget. Malaria is not fun. Take it when you get back to the room, okay?'

'Okay.' Callie agreed, leaning forward to rest her arms on the table between them. 'So, today was—'

Finn lifted an eyebrow.

'—difficult.'

Finn scratched the back of his neck. 'Difficult? No. Confusing? Hell, yeah.'

Callie broke off a piece of bread, dunked it in the oil and popped it into her mouth. Finn urged himself to be patient. She'd explain in her own time. Oh, wait—he wasn't supposed to be waiting for her explanation. *Remember the point about backing the hell up?*

'Oh, Finn, look! There's a massive bull elephant coming down to the river. Oh, he's a big boy.'

Okay, so she still wasn't ready to talk. Why did he want her to? Why did he want her to trust him with her mind, her feelings, as well as her body?

Callie leaned forward, her elbows on the table and her chin cupped in her hands. Finn couldn't resist picking up his mobile and aiming it in her direction, trying to capture the look of admiration on her face.

The flash went off, Callie blinked rapidly, and he looked down at the captured image.

Callie's eyes were scrunched closed and the image was blurry and out of focus. He deleted the image and shook his head. Well, what did he expect? It had been that type of day.

Then again, surely things could only get better from now on, he thought.

Finn leaned back in his chair and his attention was caught by a couple a short distance from them. She had a huge smile on her face and was gesticulating wildly. He just looked shocked. Fantastically happy but utterly shocked. Finn felt dread settle in his stomach. He knew what she was telling him.

The man's loud whoop and his bouncing out of his chair to lay his cheek on his partner's stomach was a pretty good clue. She was pregnant and he was excited. Finn swallowed when the guy kissed that still flat feminine stomach and then reached up to cover her mouth with his.

He understood that wave of love. He'd never loved Liz as much as he had when she'd told him he was going to be a father. He'd thought that she'd hung the moon and stars.

Unable to watch them any more, Finn turned his head and stared out onto the river, fighting the urge to tell them not to get too excited, that bad things could and did happen. Happiness could be fleeting.

Caught up in the business of the last week—the elephant rides and the game drives, the amazing sex—he'd managed to shove his grief aside. To forget, just for a little while, why he was here…with Callie. He'd managed to have a break from mourning the loss of his baby, the loss of his dream of having a family, his stepdad—all of it.

Grief, hard and sour, rolled over him and memories flashed on the big screen in his head. He saw his bedroom, the blood, Liz's white face.

He couldn't resist looking across the room again at the excited couple. He didn't know if he could ever be that excited again, ever trust in happiness like that again. Nothing compared to the joy he had felt about becoming a father, and to have it ripped away was an experience he never wanted to repeat.

Maybe in a couple of years, after a great deal of thought, he might be ready to think about another relationship, about trying to create a family with someone again, but not yet—not when he was so raw and his emotions were all over the place.

The waiter put the menu down in front of them and Finn

felt his stomach roil at the thought of food. He couldn't eat—not now. Right now he needed to be alone, to lose himself in his writing, maybe do a couple of chapters of the anecdotal travel guide he was busy compiling.

It was either that or lose himself in Callie's body. And he couldn't do that—not since he'd taken the moral high ground earlier in the day. Besides, maybe they needed a break from each other…from sex. God, did he *really* think that? Shoot him now! But he needed to step away from the quicksand and he couldn't use her as a crutch. She wouldn't be around in a couple of weeks and what would he do then? No, he had to backtrack, put some distance between them.

He was going to act like an adult now, not scuttle from the room because a random couple were expecting a baby. That was just stupidly ridiculous. He was going to sit here, enjoy the evening, the balmy night. He was with a gorgeous, entrancing woman who fascinated and frustrated him in equal measure. He was not going to fall into the vortex of grief—not tonight.

'Are you okay?' Callie asked, her eyes flashing concern.

'Sure.'

'You're not still mad at me because I acted like a looney tune today?'

'I was never mad at you.' Finn saw that she didn't buy that statement and he smiled. 'Okay, I was a little frustrated.'

'You had a right to be,' Callie admitted. She blew out a long sigh. 'I can be a very frustrating woman.'

He smiled at her self-deprecation. 'You're also a smart-ass and a flirt and as sexy as hell.'

The light dimmed in Callie's eyes. 'Yet you turned me down today?'

Finn covered her hand with his, linking their fingers. 'That wasn't because I didn't want you.'

Callie pushed her hair back with her hand. 'I know; I

was using sex as a distraction and that wasn't fair—to you or to me. I'm so sorry, Finn, it was wrong of me.'

He wanted to tell her that not five minutes ago he'd wanted to do the same thing to her, so he wasn't exactly a saint. He slid a glance to the expecting couple and sighed. God, he and Callie were a pair. Outwardly successful, talented, in the prime of their lives.

The truth was that they were both pretty screwed up in different ways.

Callie sent him a small smile. 'You keep shifting in that chair—it looks like you're uncomfortable. Why don't you move to this chair?'

Finn looked at the chair to her right and realised that it would put his back to the couple—just what he needed.

Shifting over, he settled his long length in the new chair and immediately felt more relaxed, a lot more comfortable.

Callie pushed her hand under his and slid her fingers between his. 'We're really bad talkers, aren't we? I'd rather literally spill my guts than do it emotionally, and I suspect you are the same.'

'Yeah.'

'That being said—and I know that I have absolutely no right to say this—I want you to know that if you want to talk I'll listen.'

Finn squeezed her hand, shocked at the thought that he was tempted to do just that. But they'd made a decision not to be sucked into anything deep, anything important—not to be seduced by the romance and the company and luxury.

No, he needed to put distance between them, and talking wouldn't help with that. It would just make him ache for more.

Finn squeezed her hand again. 'Back at you, angel.'

There he went again with the endearments. God, could he get *nothing* right tonight?

CHAPTER NINE

CALLIE, DRESSED IN a short terry robe, her hair wet from the shower, was curled up in the corner of a cane couch on their private veranda, a bowl of fruit salad in her hand. Finn was half perched on the railing, the riverbank vegetation below him and the mighty Zambezi river behind him, the early-morning sun beating down on his bare chest.

After their meal last night they'd both retreated to their respective corners by silent agreement. He'd gone out onto the balcony and hunched over his computer and she hadn't disturbed him. Instead she'd showered and gone to bed, taking a little time to catch up with her e-reader. She'd fallen asleep somewhere around midnight and hadn't heard Finn coming to bed, but she'd woken up curled up half on him. It had been an easy slide completely on to him and she'd sighed when he'd entered her, filling her.

It had been easy and languorous and sexy.

'Croc on the sandbank,' Finn told her, pointing so that she knew where to look.

Now or never, Hollis, Callie thought. *Are you going to back away and pretend that you didn't notice what you noticed last night? Leave the status quo? Or are you going to make this situation more complicated than it needs to be? And if you get him to open up, then he has a right to do the same to you. You ready for that? Getting to know him better will make it so much harder to walk away...*

Callie spooned up a strawberry and slowly chewed. She understood that she was taking a risk, but she knew that Finn needed someone to talk to about the horror of the last few weeks. Because it was eating him up.

When he thought she wasn't paying attention his eyes would reveal his sadness, his grief. His lower lip would tremble before he flattened it out and then he'd pull in a deep breath. Yeah, the man was in pain and he needed to talk. It was more important that he do that than it was for her to protect her heart.

Her wounds were old and mostly healed, but his were raw.

'Did you love your fiancée?'

Finn's laugh had absolutely no humour in it. 'You go straight for the jugular, don't you? I loved her, but probably not as much as I should have.'

Thought so. So, now are you going to ask the really hard question?

Yeah, she was.

'So, how far along was Liz when she miscarried?'

Finn wobbled and grabbed the railing to steady himself as the colour ran from his face. He stared at his bare feet for so long that Callie didn't think he'd ever answer her.

'Four and a half months,' Finn said finally, his voice rough. 'How did you know?'

Callie placed her bowl on the coffee table and wrapped her arms around her bent knees. 'I've always thought that there was something more to your break-up than—well, just a break-up. Then I saw your reaction to that couple last night. It was written all over your face.'

Finn grimaced. 'And I thought I hid my reaction so well.'

Callie pushed her unbrushed curls out of her eyes. 'Not so much. I take it that you really wanted the baby?'

Finn slowly nodded. 'I really did… I've always wanted to have a family—a wife, a couple of kids.'

'Because of your own dad?'

Finn took a long time to answer her. 'My dad was useless. That's the kindest word I can find to describe him. He'd come back, make these elaborate promises to us, siphon money off my mum and disappear again. It was always just Mum and I, and life was tough sometimes. I wanted a dad I could rely on.'

'James was that person for you?'

Finn nodded. 'He really was. He taught me about family.'

'And when Liz told you she was pregnant it was your chance to have the family you'd always craved?' Callie gently pushed. 'Tell me about losing your baby, Finn.'

Finn rubbed his jaw in agitation. 'She just started to bleed that night. We were at home. I've seen war—reported on war—seen some pretty horrendous stuff, but there was always a distance been me and the event. This was up close and personal. Blood…so much of it.'

That's why he got rid of the mattress, Callie realised. *Oh, Finn, honey.*

Callie knew that if she spoke, if she uttered a word of sympathy, she'd lose him.

'They took her to Theatre, did a D&C, what is that, anyway?'

'Basically, they just go in and…' Callie bit her lip '…clean everything out.'

Finn briefly closed his eyes. 'Anyway, when she came out of Theatre we had a discussion and she suggested that we break it off. She said that we were only together for the baby. That if she hadn't fallen pregnant then she doubted we would've been together any more.'

Callie's respect for Liz rose and she placed her hand on her heart. 'That was enormously brave.'

Finn frowned at her. 'What?'

Callie lifted her shoulder. 'She was brave, Finn. It would've been so much easier to go through with the wedding, to go home and pretend that you still loved each other, that you could love each other again like you should. Instead she chose the hard route—the one that took courage. Cancelling the wedding, exposing herself to gossip, to questions. In her most painful moment she looked for the truth—you've got to respect that.'

Finn stared at her. 'I never thought about it like that.'

'She deserves some credit for making a tough choice when she could've lied to herself *and* to you.' Callie smiled softly. 'You have great taste in women, Banning,' she teased.

The corner of his mouth lifted. 'Apparently so.'

'Could they tell whether your baby was a boy or a girl?'

Finn's broad shoulders rose and fell. 'I have no idea. To me it just felt right that he was a boy.'

Callie rested her chin on her kneecap. 'I bet you named him after your stepdad.'

Finn's mouth lifted at the corners in another reluctant smile. 'Witch. Yeah, I did. In my head I called him James—Jamie—same as my stepdad.'

You're still in mourning, honey, for both your stepdad and your lost little boy.

'Does anyone know, apart from me, about the baby? About what you lost?'

Finn shook his head. 'We hadn't told anyone that she was pregnant and Liz asked me to keep it like that. She's pretty private and her folks are conservative.'

'I think coping with all the questions about why you broke up so close to the wedding would be hard enough; having to explain about the miscarriage too would probably have sent her running into the night,' Callie said, empathising.

'You seem to understand her a lot better than I ever did,' Finn said, his voice sad.

'I'm a woman—and you feel bad because you wish you could've loved her more.'

Finn stared at the wild African bush that edged the opposite bank of the river and Callie sensed that it was time to be quiet, to leave him to his thoughts.

After a couple of minutes he spoke again. 'I feel stupid for mourning like this. God, I can't even call him a baby—he didn't get that far. He was an entity that I never met! That's what I've been battling with—the idea that I can be so devastated when I hadn't even met him yet.'

'Don't feel stupid. You *are* allowed to mourn losing him, Finn. It doesn't matter that his time with you was brief, or that he wasn't even fully formed yet. He was a soul and you loved him. If you lose love you are always entitled to mourn.'

'When my stepdad died—God, it was six months ago, but it still feels like it was yesterday—I lost my mentor, my rock, my best bud. Losing the baby made me feel like I'd lost him all over again.'

He might be slow to talk but, *dang*, he definitely needed to, Callie thought. This was heavy baggage to carry on your own.

Finn turned his back to her and gripped the railing with his hands, his head dropping to his chest. Callie knew that he was fighting tears and that he'd hate for her to see them.

Staying where she was, she asked another soft question. 'Did you bury your stepdad? Does he have a grave? A headstone?'

'No. He wanted his ashes scattered out at sea. Why?' Finn, now back in control, turned to face her but kept his white-knuckled grip on the railing behind him.

Callie shrugged. 'It's nice to have a place to go to remember, to cry if you need to. A place where you can think about your stepfather and your son.'

'It's a nice idea, but I don't.' Finn released the railing and walked over to the coffee table. He drained the half-glass of orange juice he'd left there earlier. 'Can we change the subject? I'm feeling a bit like a specimen under a microscope.'

Callie looked up at him and saw his shuttered eyes, his now implacable face. Yeah, he was done talking. And that was okay, she thought. She'd got a lot more out of him than she'd expected to.

And she'd given him something in return. She wasn't sure what. Maybe a little comfort, a little support. And that was more than okay—she had it and he needed it.

She was beginning to think that there wasn't much that she *wouldn't* give Finn.

Including, if she wasn't very, very careful, her heart.

After Livingstone they were sent back to South Africa and booked into a sprawling, Vegas-type casino on the outskirts of the country's capital. Callie had been looking forward to this portion of their trip the most, but instead of loving it, as she'd expected to do, she wanted to go back to easy summer days and hot summer nights—in bed as well as out.

She didn't want fancy rooms or air-conditioning. She wanted to hear the call of the fish eagles, to smell the electricity of a wild storm. She didn't want to hear the *ker-ching* of slot machines or the whoops of overdressed, over-perfumed people.

Callie leaned back in her chair in the restaurant section of a popular bar and hoped Finn wouldn't take his time fetching her wrap from their hotel room. Then again, their room was about a mile from the entertainment area, so she might only see him again in an hour or two.

Callie gave a man approaching her table a look that said *don't even think about trying to chat me up* and he halted in his tracks and turned away. Fishing her mobile out of her purse, she pushed a speed dial number and blocked her other ear so that she could hear when Rowan answered.

'Uh…Cal. I didn't expect you to call tonight.'

'Why?' Callie demanded, laughter in her voice. 'Are you out having fun with my wicked witch of a mother?'

The long silence that followed her comment was all the confirmation she needed. Callie felt her stomach cramp and she stared at the table, fighting the burning sensation in her eyes.

'Where are you?' she croaked out.

'Awelfor,' Rowan finally answered.

'He allowed her to come *home*?'

'Callie—'

Callie heard a familiar guffaw in the background and her clenching stomach launched up her throat. 'Is my dad there?'

'Yeah, Seb invited him and Annie round for dinner.'

'With *Laura*?' Callie clasped her neck with her hand. 'Am I the only one who still has a problem with the fact that she left for over twenty years and we haven't heard from her since? That she abandoned me—us? How can you all just sit there and laugh and drink and pretend what she did was okay?'

'Honey—'

'Don't *honey* me. God, you all suck…' Callie whispered into the phone, before jamming her finger against the red button.

Hauling in air, she looked around for a waiter but there wasn't one to be seen. She needed a drink and she needed it now. More than that, she needed to forget that her family—the people who were supposed to love her most—were laughing and drinking and eating with Laura as if she'd done no wrong. How could they just forget? Just forgive?

And her dad? How *could* he? He was supposed to be on her side.

She didn't want to think about her mother and she couldn't consider forgetting or forgiving. No, what she needed was a distraction. Something to take her mind off her mother, her family and the aching void in her heart.

Callie looked around and through the window to a pub, where she saw a group of well-dressed adults. They looked sophisticated and successful and badly in need of a party.

Well, *she* was their girl.

He'd lost his fake wife, Finn thought, bemused, holding her wrap in his hand and back in the restaurant where he'd left her. Finding Callie was going to be a nightmare. Was it asking too much for her to have stayed where he'd left her?

Hearing a loud chorus of male laughter from the adjacent pub, Finn had a sinking feeling that he'd find her wherever the action was—and it sounded as if the action was next door.

Heading that way, he walked through the frosted doors and there she was, standing behind the bar, a bottle of tequila in her hand, happily pouring shots into the grubby glasses lined up in front of her. The bartender next to her had two bottles in his hand and was filling up the glasses too.

A mound of lemon segments sat on the plate in front of the fifteen-strong crowd and Finn shook his head when he saw that there were women in the group as well. It seemed that Callie could charm members of her own sex into drinking competitions as well.

He'd only been gone an hour. How the hell had she get managed to get front and centre and drinking in sixty minutes? God, bartenders must love her. Finn shook his head as Callie licked salt off her hand, tossed back her drink and sucked on her lemon, pulling the inevitable 'tequila face'.

She was a handful, and a man would have to have steel balls to take her on.

You are not that man, he reminded himself. *You are not in a place where you can even think about getting emotionally involved with another woman; Callie is your rebound fling. It doesn't matter that she totally gets you about the miscarriage, that she understands how it feels to lose something you've never had, that she's fun and smart and so sexy.*

It was the wrong time and place. He'd thought long and hard about getting involved with Liz, longer and harder about Liz moving into his house, and here he was, after a few short weeks, thinking about taking on a girl with a wild streak.

It would be crazy. And yet a reckless part of him wanted to. He wondered what it would be like to love her, to be loved by her. To have her there when he came home, to think about her when he was away. And he knew that he *would* think about her when he was gone—he knew that he wouldn't be able to compartmentalise her as easily as he had Liz.

Callie would demand so much more from him than Liz—or any other woman he'd ever met.

He didn't have it in him—not now and not any time soon—to give her a quarter of what she wanted or expected. Or deserved. Callie deserved the world and he didn't have it in him to give it to her.

'Hey, hubby!' Callie waved the tequila bottle at him, her eyes slightly squinty.

Finn pushed through the crowd to stand directly opposite her. 'You're on the wrong side of the bar, wife. How did you get there?'

Callie smiled broadly and pointed to a sophisticated-looking couple. 'Kelvin and Neil are celebrating their anniversary and these are all their friends!'

'Uh-huh?'

'And I offered to buy them a drink—to toast them—and they said yes, and then we got talking about our favourite shooters, and I showed Grant here—' she laid a hand on the barmen's shoulder '—how to make a champagne shooter, and we had some of those. Now we're doing it old school.'

'Ah…' Finn winced at the thought of what she'd spent, throwing liquor down strangers' throats. Correction: what *he* was about to spend—because Callie, dressed in a slinky black cocktail dress, certainly didn't have a credit card tucked between her magnificent breasts or under the thin cord of her tiny, tiny thong. He knew this because—well, because he'd happily watched her climb into, and out of, and back into that dress hours earlier.

And he couldn't put the booze on his hotel bill—even *he* wouldn't get away with forty-plus shooters on his expense account.

One half of the anniversary couple stood up and held his hand out for Finn to shake. He looked more sober than the rest of his crew. 'Your wife is an absolute delight and such a hoot.'

'Thank you,' Finn replied, looking at his wife, who was leaning across the bar, squishing her boobs with her elbows and giving herself a hell of a cleavage. Even the gay boys seemed fascinated by the view. Her breasts might be spectacular, but he was distracted by the fact that her eyes were more violet than blue—a colour he'd come to associate with Callie being upset or sad.

'Something happen while I was gone, angel?' he asked quietly.

Her smile was bright and bold and perfectly suited to this fake place. 'Yeah, I started a party! I haven't done that for a while. I have my mojo back!'

Oh, yeah, something had happened. Another call from her mother? Maybe…

'Honey, you never lost it.' He jerked his head as he put his hand in his back pocket to pull out his wallet. 'Time to go, angel.' He flipped open his wallet and pulled out a credit card, which he handed to the amused barman.

'Awww, I don't wanna…' Callie whined.

'I have a surprise for you waiting in our room,' Finn lied.

He just had to get her to the room; he knew that as soon as Callie fell onto the bed she'd be dead to the world, and he doubted that she'd remember that he promised her a surprise. After all, tequila was well known for its coma-inducing and amnesiac qualities.

As he'd suspected Callie's eyes lit up, and she skipped around Grant to come over to his side of the bar. 'What is it?'

'You'll have to wait and see.' Finn took the credit card slip and his eyes widened at the total. Damn! How many shooters and how many bottles of champagne had they gone through?

The barman sent him a sympathetic look. 'Sorry, sir.'

'She's going to bankrupt me,' Finn muttered, taking back his card. 'Let's go before you do any more damage.'

'Got to say goodbye first,' Callie told him, and Finn waited while she kissed cheeks and exchanged hugs as if she was saying goodbye to her best friends. Good grief, she'd only met these people an hour or so ago.

'Be happy, people!' Callie yelled at them as he steered her towards the door.

Most of them—Callie included—were certainly not going to be happy in the morning.

Callie rolled over in the massive bed and feeling as if she had a bowling ball bouncing off the inside of her skull.

There was a time, she thought on an internal whimper, when she could party herself stupid and wake up the next morning raring to go.

That time had passed, she decided mournfully. Squinting, she sat up on her elbows and forced her eyes open to look at the gold and white garish suite. *Ack*. If her husband—real, that was—had brought her here for her honeymoon she'd have stabbed him between the eyes with a fork.

Talking about husbands—where was hers?

He'd slept with her—she had a recollection of him waking her up to swallow some aspirin some time close to dawn—but she didn't recall him leaving their bed. She needed him right now. Mostly to order coffee and to hand her some more aspirin.

Note to self: *I can no longer drink like a twenty-year-old.*

Second note to self: *tequila is nasty and no longer your friend.*

But her brother and her best friend and her father and soon-to-be stepmother had spent last night laughing and drinking and socialising with Laura.

She'd wanted a distraction, to forget, and it had worked for a while. But this morning she still felt hurt and betrayed and she had a hangover. Talk about adding fuel to the fire. Callie tucked her hand under her cheek, ignoring the trickle of tears leaking from her eyes.

Hurting, she wondered if she was being harsh in not wanting to engage with Laura. *Was* she just being stubborn? Unfair? Why was reconnecting with her so much easier for Seb than it was for her?

She closed her eyes and remembered those long nights sobbing in her room, her ten, fifteen, eighteen-year-old self wondering what had been so wrong with Laura's life—with *her*—that she'd had to leave. What had she and her dad and Seb done that was so wrong that she'd had to leave and never call or write? Was she sick…poor—dead?

She'd spent most of her nights worrying about Laura and her days pretending that she was fine, so that her father and Seb wouldn't worry about her.

It had taken all the emotional energy she had.

And now she was supposed to just wipe her past away because Laura had decided that it was time to reconnect? *No.*

Callie felt the bed dip behind her and Finn's warm, broad hand stroking her bare back. Within seconds she felt comforted, calmer, as if she could cope with whatever life threw at her. What was it about this man that made her feel both brave and safe at the same time?

Finn was on her side, totally in her corner, all hers. Just as she'd known he would be.

'Angel, why the tears?'

She couldn't not tell him. It was her turn to let him in.

Callie rolled over and rested her forearm over her eyes. 'Something happened last night.'

'I know. What did your mother do?'

He just *got it*, she thought on an internal sigh. He got *her*. 'Had dinner with my father and brother and my best friend in my childhood home.'

'And you're mad at her? And them?' Finn pulled her arm from her eyes before rubbing a thumb over her cheekbone. 'I brought you aspirin and coffee; take them and we'll talk.'

Callie groaned as she pulled herself up so that she was leaning back against the padded headboard, the sheet tucked up under her arms. She picked the tablets out of Finn's hand and chased them down with a glass of water. He passed her a large mug of coffee, which she gratefully took.

Finn sat next to her, calm and strong, and his strength

seemed to flow into her. She could start to rely on having him around, she thought, having his calm presence in her life.

'So, start from the beginning and tell me about Laura.'

'It's a long story.'

'Nowhere else I need to be. No one else more important than you right now.'

She could see that truth in his eyes. Right now, right here, she was the most important person in his life and she loved it. Oh, dear God, if she wasn't careful she could love him.

Callie looked at his hand, big and tanned on her thigh. She took another sip of coffee before placing it on the bedside table. *Park any thoughts about love and for ever and talk to him,* Callie told herself. *You need to talk to someone.*

Pushing her curls behind her ears, she started trying to explain. 'I told you that I was a hell-on-wheels child. I tried anything once. And I mean anything, I had absolutely no sense of self-preservation. The highest tree, the tallest rock, the fastest bike, the biggest wave. Unfortunately I always bit off more than I could chew. The nurses and doctors at our nearest casualty department knew me by name.'

Callie drew invisible patterns on the sheet with her index finger.

'It was after another visit to Casualty, when my dad brought me home—with a broken arm and two cracked ribs—that we found out that that Laura had left us. For good.'

Finn held her thigh and his eyes encouraged her to go on. She'd never told anyone this before, but she felt safe with Finn.

'In my childish head I equated my being a wild child with her leaving. And, because I'm me, I thought, *What the hell? Let's make damn sure she had a good excuse for going.* I let it rip. I was wild, Finn. Crazy. I did stupid things, took incredible risks, put myself in danger. I went walking the streets at night, looking for trouble. I caught trains and buses into bad areas. I hitchhiked all over the place. I surfed huge waves, was a maniac on my skateboard and on my bike. Thank God that He protects the stupid.'

'Why did you do all of that?'

'Partly to justify her leaving—*Look how bad I am. I don't blame you for leaving*—and also because the adrenalin high was so damn good. I think I was also challenging my father's and brother's love. If they didn't walk away from me when I was so bad then they *did* love me. Crazy, huh?'

Finn stretched out beside her and rested his hand on her stomach. 'Not so much.'

'Anyway, the craziness got me out of my head, stopped me from feeling worthless and abandoned, and I craved it.' Callie stared at her hands. 'In my late teens that adrenalin high started to be more difficult to achieve and I started flirting with alcohol.'

She saw sympathy on his face, in his eyes, but not pity. She couldn't have handled pity.

'I got drunk and wrecked my car. I was damn lucky not to die.'

Finn swore. 'Angel…'

'Yeah. Well, that prompted my father and brother to tear me a new one and I was finally brought under control. I made a big deal of their authority and bossiness but secretly I loved it. I started to believe that they loved me and always would, and I promised them that I wouldn't do anything stupid again. So I cut out all the extreme stuff except the partying and grew up, I suppose.'

Finn looked puzzled. 'Yet that day in Livingstone you were prepared to break your promise to go bungee jumping? Oh, wait. It was a coping mechanism.'

'I needed to escape from myself. When she phoned I

didn't want to deal with all the old feelings that bubbled to the surface and I reverted to what worked. Sex with you or…' she pulled a face '…something else to make the adrenalin pump.'

Finn smiled. 'That's a hell of a backhanded compliment, Cal, but I'll take it.'

Callie couldn't smile—not just yet. 'God, it all sounds so stupid.' She pulled a face. 'It makes sense in my head.'

Finn's thumb stroked her knee. 'I'm not judging you, angel.'

Callie went on to explain how hurt she'd felt by her family having dinner with her mother and her need for distraction—which had prompted the party in the bar.

Finn took a sip of her coffee before asking, 'And you really don't want to see your mum? Meet her? Get an explanation?'

Callie shrugged. 'Do you think I should?' she asked.

His opinion was important to her; she respected and trusted it. And him. She trusted *him*. Dear God, she really did.

'I can't decide that for you, Cal. I can give you another perspective on it, but I would never presume to tell you what to do. First tell me why you're so against meeting her.'

Callie placed her hand on his and stared down at their linked hands. 'I haven't seen or heard from her in over twenty years. What's there to say? She missed out on every important day of my life and now she wants to make contact. Where was she when I needed a mother? Hotfooting it around the world! She chose to leave. I'm choosing not to acknowledge her return.' Callie lifted worried eyes to his. 'Am I wrong, Finn? Should I be able to just forgive her?'

'Again, no judging.' Finn lifted her hand and placed a kiss on her knuckles. 'Cal, my father is a shocking father and I have no freaking clue where he is. I worry about him, and sometimes I wish I could just talk to him, know that he's okay and find out why he made the choices he did. I'm not saying that I'd accept or forgive those choices—I'd just like to understand why he made them. And my two real parents are dead. I'd do anything to spend some more time with *them*.'

Finn spoke quietly but his voice was full of conviction and Callie listened carefully, soaking in his words.

'The other thing to consider is what if Laura chooses to stay in Cape Town? If she becomes part of your brother's life again? What then?'

Callie looked horrified. 'Oh, God, I never considered that possibility. I'm so close to Seb and Rowan… I would have to see her at family functions…' Callie closed her eyes. 'It would be horrible if we couldn't speak to one another. Oh, God, maybe I should just meet her.'

'Take a breath, honey. It's just something to consider. Cross one bridge at a time,' Finn told her, squeezing her hand to reassure her. 'You don't need to make any rash decisions—you just need to think it all through. You need to try and separate your emotions from your decision.'

'I don't know if I can.'

Finn kissed her bare shoulder. 'I believe in you. I believe that you can move mountains if you want to. You are one of the strongest women I have ever met.' He smiled into her skin. 'Crazy as a loon, but strong as hell.'

At his words Callie fell a little deeper, a little harder. This man might be exactly what she needed.

'How is your head?'

'Better.' Callie lifted her hand to her head and nodded. 'Yeah, definitely better.' She also felt lighter, because Finn had just listened without judgement. Acceptance, Callie thought. It was such a rare and beautiful thing.

'You hungry?'

'Starving!' Callie replied.

'Room Service? Or do you want to brave the hordes downstairs?' Finn asked.

Callie winced. 'Room Service, please.'

Finn nodded, his dimple flashing. He leaned back, his hands spread out on the covers, and cocked his head at her. 'So...how hungry are you really? Can breakfast wait?'

Callie tipped her head at his playful expression. 'Why?'

'I just thought that maybe you needed a rush of adrenalin? Please say yes.'

Callie's smile made her eyes crinkle and she placed a hand over them. 'Oh, God, I'm *so* going to regret telling you that.'

Finn placed his hands on her shoulders and pushed her onto her back. 'That wasn't a no. I didn't hear a no, so I'm going to take that as a yes.'

Callie sighed theatrically as she linked her hands around his neck and pulled his mouth down to hers. 'If you must...'

CHAPTER TEN

BUSH AND BEACH, Callie thought, digging her toes into the white sands of the Mozambique coastline. This was, hands-down, the best holiday of her life. And five days at the exceptionally luxurious, remote Manta Ray Lodge, on the Bazaruto Archipelago, was the best way to end their trip.

Callie sat up on her elbows and watched Finn walk out of the gentle surf, heading towards her after snorkelling above the reef just behind the breakers. He loved the sea, she realised. From scuba-diving to deep-sea fishing, to snorkelling, to kite-surfing—he wanted to do it all. She could easily see why he was so good at his job as a travel writer. He threw himself into every experience he was offered, wringing every drop of pleasure he could from the situation.

He was so gorgeous, she thought, watching as he walked up the beach to where she was lying on a towel in the sand. Tall, ripped, in peak physical condition. Hair pushed off his face and red board shorts clinging to those strong thighs. So drool-worthy.

She knew that body intimately—knew every toned muscle, every scar, the fact that one of his little toes was crooked. She knew that scraping her nails across his abs made him shiver and that he hated her blowing in his ear. She knew that he didn't have a favourite sexual position, that he liked to mix it up, and that he loved oral sex. That he could kiss her for hours without taking it further, that he always slept on his stomach, and that he needed to run or do a workout and have at least two cups of coffee in the morning before he could string a sentence together.

She knew he was loyal and responsible and that he loved his stepbrothers, and that he was mentally and physically tough. She also knew that she was on the very slippery slope to falling in love—if she wasn't there already. He was what she hadn't known she was looking for.

And he didn't want her—not like that. It wasn't part of the arrangement…the deal. *No hearts and flowers,* she'd said. How often had she said that? Along with *Don't let me be seduced, This is short-term, This is going to end.*

Use, abuse and toss.

She'd broken every rule they'd laid out from the beginning. She'd been so arrogant, thinking that she could control herself, control the situation, control her response to him. Life was rolling on the floor, laughing its ass off at her.

Even though she knew they couldn't be anything more she wanted to dream about a future with him. But there wasn't one—couldn't be one. Their jobs kept them both buzzing around the world, and she didn't need a man complicating her life—especially now. She had a mother who, after being absent for most of her life, was doing a very good job of that all by herself.

Was she just being seduced by the holiday? The romance of their surroundings? This wasn't real life. Real life had bills and work and family and jobs to complicate the situation. There was a reason holiday romances never worked out.

There wasn't any future for them. *Was there?*

Callie lifted her head as Finn approached her and sighed when his lips brushed hers in a gesture that felt so natural, so right. *Holiday romance,* she reminded herself, *not going to last.*

'I saw a scorpion fish and a small manta ray.'

'Cool…' Callie murmured as he dropped onto the hot sand next to her.

Finn looked around, catching the eye of a hovering waiter who walked over to them. Finn ordered a beer and Callie ordered a bottle of water.

'This is the life,' Finn stated, reaching for his sunglasses, which he'd left on top of her beach bag. He slipped them on and leaned back on his elbows, stretching like a cat in the sun.

Those sleek muscles rippled under tanned skin and Callie couldn't believe that her libido was buzzing again. She swallowed the urge to suggest they head back to their private, practically-in-the-sea chalet, just fifty metres away from them, so that she could worship that body. Instead she half turned, stretched out, and rested the back of her head on Finn's thigh.

'Talk to me.'

Above his wraparound shades a dark eyebrow lifted. 'Okay. About what?'

Callie sat up, put her back to the sea and faced him. 'Do you ever think of Liz? Do you miss her?' she asked, eyes down, wiggling in the sand.

'We were together for five years, Cal…so, yeah. I do.' Finn replied, his voice low. 'I was supposed to be sharing all this with her.'

Damn, that was a knife to her heart. 'I know. I'm sorry.'

'I'm not.'

Callie's head shot up and she met his rueful eyes. 'I don't understand.'

'She was right to call it quits. We'd stopped loving each other. Our marriage would never have lasted.' Finn pushed his hand through his hair, his eyes still on the sea. 'Getting married seemed like a good idea at the time. We'd talked about it and we'd been together for a long time. When she fell pregnant it seemed like the next step to take—a natural progression,' Finn explained. 'Then she lost the baby, and our last reason to be together was removed.'

'Do you see yourself in a relationship again?'

Finn took a long time to answer. 'I think I need to be on my own for a while.'

No surprised there, Callie thought.

'I never jump into situations with my eyes closed, Callie. I think everything through. I don't do quick and impulsive and crazy. Relationships that are meant to last take time and are hard work.'

His words rumbled over her and she could hear the conviction in his tone.

'I'm pretty sure that I don't want a long-distance relationship again, but that's all I can have until I give up my job and find something else to do. And that's not going to happen any time soon.'

You, me, us—we're not going to happen either. Callie heard his unspoken words. *That wasn't the deal.*

Callie stretched out her legs and dug her toes into the sand, her eyes burning behind her dark glasses. 'I'm really glad that I was able to be your rebound girl, Finn.'

Finn linked her hand in his. 'Maybe you should try being in a relationship some time, Cal.'

She forced herself to sound jovial, carefree. 'How come you get to be footloose and fancy-free but I should settle down?' she asked, making sure that she had a small smile on her face.

'Because you've only *ever* been footloose and fancy-free. I think that you would be a brilliant partner: you're fun, intelligent, and crazy good in the sack.'

Finn pushed his sunglasses into his hair and she caught her breath at the passion and...*affection?*...she saw in his eyes.

'And you'd be a stunning mum one day.'

Callie instinctively shook her head. 'Yeah, *that's* not going to happen.'

'Why not?' Finn asked gently.

Callie folded her arms against her chest and shook her head. 'I'm never putting any child through what my mother did to me!'

Finn grabbed her chin and tipped her head up, making her meet his eyes. 'Honey, you would never do to your kid what your mum did to you. No way, no how.'

Callie swallowed the lump in her throat. 'How do you know? I'm selfish, I bounce around the world, I'm totally self-involved.'

'No, you're not. That's who you pretend to be.' Finn cupped the side of her face in his broad palm. 'When you decide that you're strong enough to be brave, when you find someone you love enough to risk your heart, you'll hand it over because you're so damn generous. And when you bring a kid into the world you'll be incredible at that—because you know how not having a mum affected *you*.'

'I don't know if I can do either—hand my heart over *or* have a kid,' Callie admitted.

'One day…' Finn said, lying back in the sand and placing a forearm over his eyes. 'I can almost guarantee it.'

Except that right now, holiday romance or not, Callie thought bitterly, *I can't imagine doing that with anyone else but you.*

Stupid girl, she thought, standing up and walking to the super-clear water. She waded in, waiting for it to become deep enough so that she could dive. *That's why you shouldn't have deep conversations with Finn…why you should keep it light and frothy.*

Because deep conversations raised possibilities that she wasn't ready to think about or deal with. Deep conversations gave birth to dreams that would never come true, possibilities that would never be realised.

Wishes that would never be fulfilled.

After a light lunch of freshly caught prawns and garden salad, accompanied by a glass of dry white wine, Finn and Callie headed back to their room to escape the intensity of the midday sun. The private villa, tucked away into the palm trees just off the beach, was incredibly private—perfect for a honeymoon couple.

Except they weren't on honeymoon, Finn reminded himself again. She was his fake wife and they were having a very temporary affair. But for a moment just now on the beach he'd been tempted to suggest that he and Callie try and extend it into real life.

Then he'd pulled himself back to reality. Callie was a stunning travelling companion: easy to look at, fun to talk to, great in bed.

The end.

Despite sharing their secrets, the mental and physical connection they had, she'd never once hinted at wanting anything more from him, wanting to change the rules. *She* knew that this was a holiday romance, so why was he suddenly doubting it? What the hell was he thinking?

Finn closed his eyes and shook his head. Goddammit, he was losing his mind. This trip was not real life—this was an aberration, a step out of time. It wouldn't be like this every trip. It was usually hectic: a combination of stunning sights and experiences interrupted by long periods of boredom spent in hotel rooms and airport lounges.

It wasn't a life to build a relationship on. As for another long-distance one? Well, that hadn't worked out so well the last time he'd tried it, and Callie wasn't the type of girl he'd be able to stay away from for long.

Finn walked over to the small fridge in the corner of the

lounge area and took out a bottle of water. Cracking the lid, he took a long drink and watched Callie as she pulled her T-shirt up and over her head, revealing the top half of the pink and orange bikini she was wearing. A vision of her, round and bursting with life with his child, flashed across his retina and he groaned. No, he wasn't going to think of her in terms of for ever, in terms of creating a family with her.

Or being the man she fell in love with.

He wanted to be single, to get his bearings, and she was even more wary of commitment than he was. Why did he want to put his fist through that glass door at the thought of her loving and living with someone else? Handing over that very fragile heart to another man?

He was just projecting, influenced by the incredibleness of these past two weeks. This wasn't reality.

Get a grip, Banning. She's fun, good company and brilliant in the sack. That's it. You have less than a week left of this—of her—so get your head out of your ass, stop obsessing, and catch a clue. Instead of standing here, staring at her like a moonstruck whipped boy, do something!

So he would do what he…they…did best. Lose themselves in each other…

He gestured with his water bottle. 'Carry on,' he told her.

Callie lifted her eyebrows at him. 'Sorry?'

Her voice was prissy, but her sexy smile told him that she knew where he wanted to go and was happy to tag along.

'Shorts off.'

Callie's eyes deepened with passion as she slowly pulled down the zip to her brief denim shorts and shimmied them over her hips. When they dropped to the floor he looked at her standing there in the shadows, the shades drawn to keep the heat out.

'Top off,' he said in a croaky voice, and took another sip of water to moisten his mouth.

Callie reached behind her back and pulled one of the ties holding her top together before reaching for the other one around her neck. The two triangles joined her shorts on the floor and she placed her fists on her hips and stared at him.

He was rock-hard and ready to spring out of his pants—and he hadn't even touched her yet. Surely after so much sex he should be able to temper his reaction to her by now? But it took just one look into those amazing eyes for him to be ready to roll. Surely he should have more control?

Then Callie stepped out of her bikini panties and he knew that, with her, he had absolutely no control at all.

As he reached for her he wondered how he was supposed to walk away from her. From the amazing sex but also, even harder, from her sharp mind, her dirty sense of humour and the vulnerable, soft soul beneath that vivacious personality?

How?

It was past eleven at night when their plane finally landed in Cape Town, and nearly midnight when Finn swung his SUV into the driveway in front of her closed-up house. This was unlike any homecoming she'd ever experienced, Callie thought, staring at her tightly laced hands in her lap. She didn't want to be here, back in the city. She didn't want to go back to real life, to work, to a life without Finn to wake up to, to make love with, to snuggle up to at night.

She wanted to be back in Kruger, in the sweltering heat of Livingstone, on that white sand beach. Anywhere with Finn…everywhere with Finn.

Finn's white-knuckled hands gripped the steering wheel. 'So, this is it.'

Callie sucked in her top lip. 'Yep.'

'How long are you in the country for?' Finn asked, his voice low.

'I think I have a quick trip scheduled to Milan for next week. You?'

'Not sure. I have to get this article in and accepted, then I can choose between a dude ranch in Montana or the northern lights in Alaska.'

Callie made herself pat his shoulder. 'Poor guy. I'm sure both will be terrible,' she teased, and felt proud of herself. She wouldn't make this goodbye difficult by weeping and wailing. She would hold her head up high and go out on a huge smile.

Finn turned his head to look at her. 'They won't be as much fun without you.'

Callie felt the tears well. 'You can't say that. I'm trying to be brave, here,' she protested.

'Me too.' Finn blew out a long sigh before dropping his head back onto the headrest. He rolled his head to look at her. His eyes, deep with regret, caught and held hers. 'I still want you.'

Callie swallowed and her hand instinctively reached out to grip his thigh. 'I know. I want you too.'

'Last time for the road?'

'It's a really bad idea, Finn.'

'I know, but let's do it anyway. I need to burn you into my memory one last time.'

The next morning, for the first time in weeks, Callie didn't wake up to Finn laying hot, wet kisses down her back, or a hard, heavy arm across her waist, or warm male breath tickling her ear.

She was alone and she really didn't like it.

Rolling over, she looked at the dent his head had left on the pillow and, inexplicably, felt tears burn her eyes. How was she supposed to live without him? Be without him?

Exist without him? How was she supposed to love him if he wasn't even around?

Love? Was she in love? Could she be?

This was insane. Nobody fell in love after a month—especially her, a girl who didn't believe in love and happily-ever-after. But she couldn't deny it any more. She loved Finn—absolutely, utterly, probably catastrophically.

Callie sat up in bed and rested her head on her bent knees. This was *so* not a clever thing to have done. Finn was on the rebound—he didn't want a relationship, wasn't interested. She knew all this, but *she* was.

Should she tell him? A part of her wanted to, needed to. Callie had loved too few people in her life, had been loved by too few, to bury or ignore this amazing sensation when it came her way. It was what it was and it demanded to be expressed—to be validated, to be acknowledged. But she'd also told him that there would be no hearts and flowers, no demands for anything more, no complications. Was telling him that she loved him more important than keeping her promise? Especially since she knew that he didn't feel the same way about her?

What should she do?

Callie lifted her head when she heard footsteps outside her door and made herself look at him as he stepped into her bedroom. She had to look at him because she didn't know when she would again.

If she would again…

Love was love, but that didn't automatically translate into happily-ever-after. She knew that now. Her mother had said she loved her but she hadn't stayed; she loved Finn, and even if by some miracle he felt the same they had so many obstacles in their way. They both travelled extensively. How could they mesh their schedules so that they could build a relationship? Maintain it?

But she was getting way ahead of herself. She still had to decide whether to tell him or not.

'Hey, you're awake,' Finn said, handing her a cup of coffee.

'I am. Thanks.' Callie took the coffee and took a grateful sip, thankful for a reason not to talk.

'I brought your bags in,' Finn said, moving to look out of her window to the view of the sea.

Callie cocked her head at his quiet voice and knew that he was trying to ease his way out of her bedroom and her life. His fists were bunched in his pockets and his lips were pulled tight.

'I checked my email while you were sleeping. I'm heading for Alaska.'

Callie felt as if the coffee was threatening to come up her throat again. 'When?' she asked, her throat hoarse.

'Within a day or two.'

'That soon, huh?'

Callie carefully placed her coffee cup on the side table and swung her legs out of bed. Reaching for a robe that hung over the back of her chair, she pulled it on. Her hands were shaky as she tied it at the waist.

'So this is definitely goodbye?'

Finn turned and sat on the open windowsill. 'It should have been goodbye last night. We just make it harder the longer we draw this out.' His voice was low, but resolute.

He had no idea how hard it could be, Callie thought. He wasn't in love with her but she was with him.

'Do you think you'll ever fall in love again?' she asked, as a way to test these very turbulent waters. Just to make sure…

Finn's head snapped up in surprise at the question. 'I'm not sure I was in the first place.' He raked a hand through his hair. 'I don't know… I don't think so. If I was so inclined then it would've been with you, during this last month.'

Callie struggled to keep him from seeing how those words pierced her soul. She used every acting skill she had to make her voice sound light and flirty.

'So you're not in love with me, then?' she asked him, deliberately batting her eyelashes.

'Nope. Why? Are you in love with me?' Finn teased back, and she was faced with the do or die question.

Did she admit it and have their relationship end on an awkward, weird note—or did she let him leave her life thinking she was unaffected?

Never had a choice been so hard.

She tipped her head and dredged up a big, bold smile. 'What would you say if I told you I was?'

Finn took his time answering. 'I'd tell you what I've been telling myself: that we're blinded by the passion between us, that we stepped out of the reality of daily life and the romantic settings and the warm weather and the luxury changed the way we behaved. That we can't trust out judgement.'

Callie nodded. She'd thought about all of that, but none of it had changed her mind or her knowledge of what *was*. She loved him. Simply. Crazily. For ever.

He didn't love her. Oh, she knew that he loved her body, loved sex with her, but it wasn't the same thing. Callie rubbed her forehead with her fingers as her mind operated at warp speed, trying to decide what to do.

Then Finn took the decision out of her hands by walking over to her and kissing her gently on the lips before folding her into his strong arms.

'We agreed to walk away, Cal.'

Callie looked up at him, feeling so safe in the circle of his arms. Arms that would soon be gone. 'Guess it's time to rip off those rose-coloured glasses and get back to real life, huh?'

'In a couple of days…weeks…we'll settle down into that real life and this will feel like a dream.'

Callie buried her face in his neck. 'So I'll always be your dream girl?'

'You bet.' Finn stroked her hair. His long sigh blew into her curls. 'This wasn't supposed to get this tangled, this complicated.'

Still no *I love you.*

Callie tried to swallow the golf ball that was lodged in her throat. 'I'll miss you. Thanks for a brilliant time.'

'I'll miss you too. Thanks for being a brilliant fake wife.' Finn kissed the top of her head—the brush-off kiss for any man—and stepped away from her. 'Take care, Callie. And think about what I said about your mother.'

'Yeah.'

In her eagerness to avoid the first person who'd broken her heart she'd run away with a second person who'd just rebroken it. She had the intelligence of a pot plant, Callie thought, watching him walk across her lounge to the front door.

'Bye, angel.'

It took every iota of willpower she had, and then some, not to throw her arms around his knees and beg him not to go.

'Bye.'

Then the door snicked closed behind him and she felt her heart cleave in two. Overwhelmed, she sank to the floor and wrapped her arms around her head, trying to shield herself from the burning miasma of pain that engulfed her.

It didn't help, she realised. Nothing would—not for a while. She knew this. She'd been here before.

CHAPTER ELEVEN

CALLIE MADE HERSELF get up the next morning, forced herself to put on a pretty dress, curl her hair and do her make-up. Her world might be falling apart but there was no reason for people to know that she was too. Besides, if she pretended hard enough and long enough that everything was fine then maybe it would be. Eventually.

She was making herself a smoothie, in an effort to start losing the pounds she'd picked up drinking cocktails on the beach with he-whose-name-could-not-be-mentioned, when her doorbell rang. She considered ignoring it and had just decided to do that when it pealed again.

Dammit! Thinking that she wasn't in the mood to see anyone, to explain anything, she stomped through to the front door and looked through the peephole at the distorted image of a tall blonde woman. It took her a minute to recognise the blue, blue eyes of Laura, the tall frame, the long face.

She looked older, Callie thought, her heart accelerating. An older, harder, tougher *me*. Even through the peephole she could see that she looked as if she'd lived a hard life—too much sun, booze, too many cigarettes. Callie wanted to tell her to go away, that she didn't want to see her, but she couldn't push any words past her thick tongue.

'Cal-belle? Honey?'

Callie could hear her voice clearly through the wooden door.

'I know that you're there. I heard your footsteps.'

Cal-Belle. God, she hadn't heard that in over twenty years. Her mum's pet name for her—Laura's pet name for her.

'Callie, I know that you don't want to see me, and I understand why. I do—I really do. But I just couldn't leave, fly back to Sao Paulo, without trying at least once.'

Callie kept silent but let Laura speak. She wanted to be strong enough to walk away but she couldn't—not yet.

'There's so much I want to say to you, so much I want to explain.'

Callie, feeling drained and very, very vulnerable, didn't even realise that hot, thick tears were rolling down her face. All she could think was that she wanted Finn… needed Finn. She needed his strong arms to hold her up, his voice in her ear telling her that she was okay, that she would always be okay, that she could do this.

But he wasn't here. Like her mother, when she needed him most he was AWOL. The people she loved most had the ability to let her down the hardest.

Hardening her heart, she finally managed to speak. 'I'm not ready to talk to you, Laura. I don't know if I'll ever be ready.'

She didn't think she could even open the door.

'I've made a lot of mistakes, Callie, but the biggest one was walking out on you and your brother.'

You think?

'I want to tell you that I'm sorry, and if this is the only way I get to do it—through a closed door—then this is how I'll do it.'

Callie slipped off her shoes and quickly moved to the right, to the thin sliver of tinted glass that allowed her to see out but kept visitors from looking in. Laura was looking at her fingernails and her foot was tapping on the terracotta tiles. She looked bone-deep scared.

Callie remembered what she'd said to Finn about Liz, about how courageous her decision to end their relationship had been. Wasn't it equally courageous of Laura to face her, to ask for forgiveness after so long? She had to know that it wouldn't be easy, that she might not get it, but she was still willing to try.

Her mother was standing there offering an explanation—something that Finn desperately wanted from his own father. And she was alive. Finn's parents weren't. If she turned Laura away now, would she regret it for the rest of her life?

'Callie?'

'Can you hang on a sec? I just need a moment.'

Callie paced the small area of her hallway—the place where Finn had made love to her the night before. *Finn...* He'd made her better, she realised. Stronger. He'd left behind a little of his strength and a lot of his wisdom.

She could almost hear his deep voice in her ear. 'You don't have to accept or forgive her choices—just understand why she made them.'

Not now, she thought. *I'm still reeling because you're not here.*

'You can move mountains. You don't need her to be happy. And I'm still with you.'

He was, Callie realised. Oh, she missed him desperately, but he'd left a part of himself with her. His belief in her. She *could* move mountains, she *could* be happy—one day, maybe. She was stronger than she thought.

She could choose either to hang on to her bitterness towards her mother or she could set herself, and her mother free. She could listen to what she had to say and then decide whether she wanted Laura back in her life—*wanted*, not needed!

She might not be able to make a certain travel reporter

love her, but, by God, she could do this, she could face her mother.

Callie turned back to the door and wrenched it open. 'Come in and talk, but I'm making no promises beyond this meeting.'

Laura bit her lip as she stepped into the hall. 'I understand.' She glanced down, transfixed by the rings on Callie's hand. 'Oh, my goodness. You're wearing them! And on your wedding finger!'

'I'm not married,' Callie hastened to explain, lifting her hand. 'You *know* these rings?' she asked, confused.

'Sure. Your father bought them for me from an antique store to celebrate your birth.' Laura placed the tip of her finger on the raised stone. 'They were the only rings I ever wore.'

Callie looked up at the ceiling and let out a deep breath. Of course they were. Because this was her life and nothing could be simple.

It wasn't a surprise that Alaska in the dead of winter was cold, Finn thought, looking out from his hotel window into the weird light that was supposed to signal dusk—at two in the afternoon! In an hour or so it would be pitch-dark and the sun had only appeared four hours earlier. Crazy place, crazy life.

Fairbanks, Alaska, in the dead of winter and he was alone. Oh, the Northern Lights were amazing, awe-inspiring, incredible—all the adjectives so many writers before him had used and the ones he intended to avoid when he finally got around to writing his article. But his was a strange life, and one he wasn't sure he wanted any more.

He still hadn't turned in his honeymoon article and he wasn't sure when he would. Writing—always so easy—had become a task of herculean proportions. *Why?* His life, apart from no longer having a fiancée he seldom saw in it, was pretty much back to normal. He was back on the road, he had an editor squawking at him, and he was alone. So what was the problem?

He *liked* being alone, he reminded himself. Apart from his three weeks with Callie he'd always travelled alone and he was used to it. He didn't have to think of anyone, could jump into his work without distractions, didn't have to worry that he was neglecting anyone.

So, Einstein, if you like it so much then why are you feeling so damn miserable? Okay, he got that it was okay to miss Callie. They'd spent practically every minute together for most of the past month, so that was to be expected, wasn't it? He was allowed to miss her laugh, her piggy snores, waking up and realising that she was wrapped around him like a vine. And naturally he missed the sex. That was normal, right?

What *wasn't* normal was the crater-sized hole he felt in his heart at not seeing her again, not hearing that laugh, that piggy snore, not waking up to the feeling that he was being smothered.

This was the way he should have felt when he and Liz broke up, he thought. Wretched—as if the world had no colour, as if he was just going through the motions. Everything he should have experienced after losing his fiancée he was now experiencing in this cold, cold place on the other side of the world.

Was it just delayed reaction? Was he transferring his feelings for Liz on to Callie? He wished he was—it would help this crazy situation make a whole lot more sense. Unfortunately it had nothing to do with Liz and everything to do with that commitment-phobic wild-child woman he'd left behind in Cape Town.

He missed her…he wanted her. In his bed and in his life. Now and for ever.

That complicated and that simple.

He'd thought he could just walk away with a casual goodbye, with heartfelt thanks for helping him out of a jam and giving him the best short-term fling of his life. God, he was such a moron.

'What would you say if I said I was in love with you?'

Her memory drifted across his mind and he frowned, looking out into the nearly dark afternoon. Had she been trying to tell him something? Something crucial? At the time he'd just dismissed her cocky question as Callie being Callie, trying to push his buttons, teasing him as she often did. Then he remembered her serious eyes, the trepidation on her face that he'd ignored. Had he, in his quest to leave, to get back to normal, missed that she was trying to tell him that she loved him? That she wanted more?

In the dark, Finn moved to his laptop and moved his finger across the mouse pad, pulling up the folder named 'Angel'. Her face appeared on the screen and he stared at the images of her that changed every few seconds. Every photo he'd taken of her was filled with sunlight, with happiness, with joy. Everything his life didn't have now.

Finn shook his head. She was anti-commitment—she readily admitted to it. She thought that commitment and long-term were the emotional equivalent of the rabies virus. But she was also the woman who had resisted falling into bed with him, had tried to keep her distance because she'd said that she had the potential to fall for him. *Had* she? Fallen for him as he had for her?

Finn thought back on their relationship—to the glossy, sophisticated woman he'd first met and how her walls had slowly started to crumble. She'd begun to open herself up to him, to let him see glimpses of the lost little girl behind the charming, flirty façade. Finn knew that she wouldn't have done that for just any man, for just anyone. He'd got to her and she'd trusted him, let him look inside.

Trust was a very big deal for Callie…

Trust was a short degree of separation from love. For her and for him.

When Callie loved and trusted and decided to commit she'd do it with everything she had. He knew that without any hesitation. She'd toss her hat and every other of item of clothing she wore into the ring and go all out to make it work. She wouldn't cheat, she wouldn't run away, she wouldn't play games. She'd been hurt by love and she wouldn't want to hurt anyone *she* loved.

He remembered her question again. *What would you say if I said I was in love with you?*

I'd say I'm in love with you too, Cal, and call myself a million types of an idiot for not realising what you were trying to say earlier. I'd say my life without you isn't a life—it's just a random set of happenings that mean little.

I'd say I'm in love with you too...

Callie cursed Finn's lack of gardening skills as her shovel bounced off the hard soil in the corner of what had used to be a flowerbed. Didn't the man know that a garden required water? Pushing her hair off her sweaty forehead with the back of her hand, she looked at the shallow dent she'd made and sighed despondently.

This wasn't going to work. Oh, the bench looked stunning—a wooden three-seater, with a brass inscription screwed onto the back strut. Expensive, but worth the price—as was the case of beer she'd paid Finn's youngest stepbrother Michael so he'd let her onto the property and help her lug the bench into its position in the corner of Finn's yard overlooking the ocean.

To his credit, Michael had taken the crazy request from a strange woman in his stride and had refrained from asking too many questions. The ones he had asked she'd managed to fudge her way through.

Callie stood up and glared at the ground. She'd planned

to plant two rosebushes on either side of the bench, but now she thought she might take them away with her. There was no way they'd survive Finn's black thumb. Or lack of skill with a hose or a watering can.

Maybe she'd take them home and plant them in pots on her veranda—a reminder of the only man she'd ever loved.

She dropped the shovel to the hard soil and sat on the bench, resting her elbows on her thighs, thinking of Finn.

She could stay here for a while…hang out in his garden. After all, as she'd confirmed with Michael, he was still in Alaska and wasn't due home for a week or so. Then he was off to Patagonia—or was it Pakistan? She couldn't remember. But it didn't matter. He was away and she had time to deliver the bench, to plant the rose bushes—or *not* plant them as seemed to be the case.

God, she missed him. Missed everything about him.

They'd been apart two weeks and she still felt as if she was operating on only one cylinder, as if she was walking a tight wire. She'd tried to get back into the swing of things at work, taken a four-day trip to Milan, and had hated every second of it. Callie dropped her head and stared at the hard ground beneath her flip-flops. If her work didn't distract her from missing Finn then what was she going to do?

Go slowly mad? It was a very distinct possibility.

Man, life was just rolling on the floor laughing at her. Callie Hollis, party-girl and commitment-phobe, sitting on a bench, trespassing on her fake husband's—now *ex*-fake-husband's—property and trying to keep from falling apart because she was ass-over-kettle in love with a man she'd promised not to fall in love with.

Yeah, life was such a joke.

Callie felt a tear drop off her chin and land on the hard-as-concrete soil below. Well, that was a hell of a way to get the ground wet. Finn had turned her into a crier—she'd never cried before he came along.

'Bastard…' she muttered, feeling as if that was the final insult.

'Sorry?'

At the deep, familiar voice Callie jerked her head up and whirled around. And there he was, standing a couple of feet behind her, dressed in board shorts and an old T-shirt, a four-day-old beard on his jaw. God, he looked good. *So* good.

'What are you doing here?' she demanded in a thready voice.

Finn's mouth kicked up, just a little, at the corners. 'I live here. What's your excuse? And why do I have a bench at the end of my garden?'

Suddenly Callie didn't know how to explain. Would he think she was sentimental? Sappy? That it was a stupid idea?

As he walked towards her she leaned back so that her shoulder was covering the plaque on the back of the bench. Would he think that she'd overstepped the mark? That she was being too presumptuous?

'Why the bench, Cal?'

'A view like this needs a bench,' Callie muttered, unable to meet his eye. He was now standing close enough for her to smell his aftershave, to feel the heat from his amazing body. She closed her eyes and told herself that she couldn't stand up and fold herself into his arms any more, that she didn't have the right to do that.

'There are chairs on the veranda with the same view,' Finn said, and Callie opened her eyes to see his strong hand—the same hand that had loved her with such skill—stroke the arm of the bench.

She wished he was stroking her. She'd reached a new low. She was jealous of an inanimate object.

'It's beautifully made. Hand-crafted?'

'Yeah.' Callie wished he'd take off his sunglasses. She needed to see his eyes because he had that implacable expression on his face. 'You needed a bench…'

'So you bought me one? OK.'

Finn walked around the bench and squatted in front of her. He shoved his glasses up into his hair and Callie sighed when her eyes met his. They were liquid and full of heat. God, she could look into those eyes for ever.

Finn lifted his hand and his thumb stroked her chin. 'You're filthy. Were you trying to plant these rosebushes?'

'You should water your garden more often,' Callie complained.

'I should.' Finn placed his hands on her knees and stared into her face, his eyes no longer playful. Instead they looked serious and intense. 'What are you doing here, Cal? Really?'

Callie hauled in air and scooted down the bench so that he could see the brass inscription. 'I wanted to do this for you. I thought you needed a place…somewhere to think about them.'

Finn looked at the inscription and Callie saw his Adam's apple bob.

'"In memory of James, big and small".' Finn read aloud.

He rubbed his hands over his face before staring at the plaque again. She couldn't tell what he was thinking and she needed to.

'If I've been too presumptuous or if you don't like it no harm, no foul. I'll take it away again,' Callie gabbled. 'I just wanted to give you some place where you could… I don't know…'

'Think about them? Remember them?'

'Yes…' Callie whispered.

'Thank you, angel.' Finn's voice was barely above a

whisper itself. 'It's spectacular. A little overwhelming, but spectacular.'

Finn reached out to rest his fingers on the inscription, his chest heaving under that ratty T-shirt.

After a little while, he looked at her again. 'How did you get in here? How did you get on to the property?'

Callie lifted a shoulder. 'Rowan had the email addresses for all your stepbrothers. Michael agreed to help me. He left about a half hour ago. He asked me to explain the "James, big and small" but I told him to ask you. That it was your story to tell. He said he would.'

'And he will. My brothers are insatiably curious.'

Callie winced. 'I'm sorry. I shouldn't have. I was out of line. I shouldn't have done this.'

Finn rested his hand on her knee and squeezed. 'No—thank you. It's an awesome gift. I'm at a loss for words, actually.'

Callie, thinking that this was a great time to go, abruptly stood up. The rosebushes would have to stay, she thought. Maybe Finn would plant them, maybe he wouldn't. She'd done all she could. It was past time for her to leave—before she broke down and begged him to let her stay.

Finn allowed her to stand up and watched her walk away, each step pulling her heart closer to breaking again. Why did he have to be here? Why couldn't she have done this without seeing him? It was taking every bit of willpower she had to put one foot in front of the other.

She was on the other side of the pool when he spoke again. 'Where are you going, Hollis?'

Callie turned back to look at him, standing tall and strong in the midday sunshine. She gestured to the house and shrugged. 'Home, I guess.'

'You guess wrong,' Finn told her, arms crossed. 'You're not going anywhere.'

She couldn't help the bloom of hope in her heart or the lifting of her chin at his arrogant words. 'Excuse me?'

'The only place you're going is into a shower. With me.'

Callie reached out and grabbed the back of a pool lounger to keep her balance, hope draining away. No, she couldn't do this. She wasn't going back to an affair, to crazy sex in the shower and then going home alone. She wanted more—she needed more. As much as she wanted Finn, settling for a no-strings, only-when-they-were-in-town-together fling would kill her.

Because she loved him so damn much.

'We can't go back, Finn.' She managed to croak the words out. 'I can't do it again.'

'Do what?'

'Have an affair with you!' Callie cried. 'I just can't—not again. Not feeling like this.'

Finn took two strides to reach her, and when he did he held her face in her hands. 'What are you feeling, angel? Tell me.'

'Why? What does it matter?' Callie flung the words into his face.

'It matters, darling Cal, because *you* matter.'

Finn brushed his lips against hers gently, briefly, before picking his head up and looking back into her shocked face. 'Okay, then, I'll tell you what *I'm* feeling. I saw you and my world settled down. I feel complete. Seeing you here makes me feel like I'm home. Normal.'

'Wha—at?' Callie frowned, confused.

'I came home from the gym, kicked off my trainers and walked onto my veranda—and I saw and heard you, cursing me for not watering my garden. And my world, for the first time in weeks, was the right way up. Me coming home, seeing you, made sense.'

'Um...what are you saying, Finn?'

Finn's smile warmed her from her toes up.

'I'm saying that I'm in love with you. Fathoms deep in love with you.'

'Oh.'

Finn's mouth twitched. 'That's all you've got?'

Callie held up her hand, trying to process what he'd just told her. 'You're in love with me?' she asked, just to clarify, not sure she'd heard him properly.

'Seems that way.'

Callie rested her forehead on his chest. 'Okay…wow.'

Finn's hand drifted down her spine. 'Still not the response I was waiting to hear. Any chance of *I love you, too, Finn*?'

Callie lifted her head and frowned at him. 'Of course I love you. How could you think for one moment that I don't?'

'Oh, let me think… Maybe it's the fact that you told me that you were going to use, abuse and toss me. That you aren't interested in commitment, that you don't believe in love, that I was allowed to seduce your body but not your mind.'

Finn rested his hands on Callie's hips and his forehead on hers.

'Might I remind you that you left me with that "Thanks for being a brilliant fake wife" comment?' Callie replied tartly.

Finn brushed his mouth across hers, sighed, and did it again. 'Okay, I admit it—we are equally bad at falling in love. Admitting we are in love. But I *do* love you. So much.'

Callie linked her arms around his neck and reached up to rest her mouth against his. 'I love you too.' She tipped her head back and her eyes laughed. 'So…what do we do now?'

Finn shrugged, his hand resting on her bottom. 'Haven't

the foggiest idea except that we go back to my original plan.'

'Which was…?'

His grin was pure mischief. 'You and me in the shower. Naked.'

Callie, her heart about to explode from happiness, thought that sounded like a marvellous idea and led him into the house.

The next morning Callie, dressed only in one of Finn's T-shirts, followed him through the garden to the bench, a cup of coffee in her wobbly hand.

Was this real? Any of it? Had they really made love all night long? Soft and sure, tender and wild, they'd lost themselves in each other's bodies, safe and secure in their love and their need for each other.

But what now? Where did they go from here?

Take a breath, Callie, she told herself. *Take it minute by minute, hour by hour. You don't need to have it all worked out right now. Right now you need to sit next to your man, on this bench, and watch the sea dance beneath the mid-morning sun.*

Callie leaned back against the arm of the bench and draped her legs across Finn's lap. He drew patterns on her bare thighs with his fingertips, his relaxed face lifted up to the sun. He was beautiful and he was hers.

'I spoke to my…to Laura,' she told him after watching him for a while.

Finn turned his head to smile at her. 'Yeah? And…?'

Callie shrugged. 'Old story. Married at eighteen, feeling like life had passed her by. Needed to leave to "find herself".' Callie lifted her cup to her lips. 'I don't know if we're ever going to have a mother-daughter relationship but I can be civil to her. *You* got me through that conversation, by the way.'

'I did? All the way from Alaska?'

'I heard you telling me you believed in me, that I could move mountains. You gave me your courage.'

Finn pulled a face. 'If I had any courage I wouldn't have left you and put us both through hell.'

'Maybe. But at least we realised that real life sucked without each other.' Callie put her cup on the arm of her chair. 'Talking about real life… How are we going to make this work? How are we going to be together? I know you don't want a long-distance relationship and neither do I.'

'Are you willing to give up your job?'

God, that was a big ask, but she would if she had to, as she told him. 'I love my job—I do. I wasn't sure I did six weeks ago, but having you in my life just makes everything seem exciting again.'

Finn's hand tightened on her knee. 'I would give up mine too, if it meant spending more time with you. So how about neither of us giving up anything?'

Callie's brows lifted. 'And how do we do that?'

'We travel together. If you're in London or Europe, I'll write about something in London or Europe. If you're in the States, the same thing. We spend most nights together. If there's an assignment I feel like I really need to take then it had better not take longer than a week—because that's my limit. That will always be my limit to the amount of time I can be away from you.'

Callie looked at him, astounded. 'Are you sure?'

'Hell, yes. What do you say?'

Callie bit her lip. 'What happens if one of us gets sick of travelling? What if I want to stay at home and—?'

Finn's eyes sharpened. 'And…?'

'Work in the garden? Redecorate the house?' Callie's voice dropped. 'Have a baby?'

Finn cupped her face with his hand. 'Then we both quit

and do something else. There'll always be something else, angel, but there's only one you and me.'

Callie took his hand and kissed the centre of his palm. 'There's only you for me.'

'Good to know.'

Finn glanced at her left hand and after Callie had explained why her dad had given the rings to her mother played with the rings with his fingers.

'You haven't taken them off.'

Callie felt her heart speed up. 'Should I?'

'Since I intend to change your status from fake wife to real wife as soon as possible, don't bother on my account,' Finn told her, his eyes blazing with love and passion. 'Proper proposal and new engagement ring to follow in due course.'

Callie gurgled with laughter. 'Just as long as you remember that I am trouble with a capital T. In neon letters.'

Finn sent her an amused look. 'I wouldn't have it any other way. Talent, as you once told me, shouldn't be wasted.'

* * * * *

In the darkness of the bar, with the slow, sexy beat of the music in the background, Jack was looking... *delicious*.

He saw her and smiled, and she steeled herself against the anxious flutter in her chest.

Don't look at his smile...look at his teeth. White, straight—perfect. No, not helping. Look away.

His hair. Look up.

It looked thick and wavy and it was being held up over his forehead. Very nice hair.

Don't look at his hair.

His eyes. Dark and velvety. Chocolaty. Sexy. Bedroom eyes.

Definitely don't look there.

A lazy layer of dark stubble sat on his jaw. It made him look a little rougher, a little more manly—maybe even a little dirty.

Brooke swallowed hard and pulled at the collar of her shirt. She'd wanted to look sophisticated, in charge and in control. But now all she felt was exposed. She tried to cover herself up a little before pushing her lips into a wide smile and attempting to saunter towards him.

He smiled and said, 'You look incredibly sexy tonight. Hot date?'

Dear Reader

Something that has always fascinated me is finding out why people make the choices they do and where their emotions stem from. Reality TV is supposed to be a fly-on-the-wall interpretation of real life, but often it's not. It's manipulated to increase drama and sex appeal.

This thought led me on to social media, and the way people use that to manipulate the way people interpret life. Often it's through a filter, and supposedly there are only 'good hair' days. Modern dating has become an exciting but scary place. All it takes is a 'like' on Instagram and a couple of Snapchats and next thing you're tearing each other's clothes off on the floor. *Before* you get to know each other. *Before* you consider the realities of spending time with that person.

We live in an age of filtered reality—and it ain't changing any time soon. But I'm old school. I'd rather meet someone *in person* and find out whether they're a sandwich short of a picnic or if they exude a strange smell, rather than 'like' them on social media and think later.

Brooke and Jack's involvement in a reality TV show skews the way they look at life, love and each other. It takes time spent alone with each other for them to realise that the only way to fall in love—*really* fall in love—is to switch off, push aside pre-judgements and filtered realities and reach deep into each other's souls. Love is *not* a filtered reality. It's dirty and messy, heartbreaking and exhilarating. But when Jack and Brooke realise they need to experience it to feel it their lives can really begin.

Jennifer Rae x

www.jenniferraeromance.com

WHO'S CALLING THE SHOTS?

BY

JENNIFER RAE

MILLS & BOON

Published in Great Britain 2015
by Mills & Boon, an imprint of Harlequin (UK) Limited,
Eton House, 18-24 Paradise Road, Richmond, Surrey, TW9 1SR

ISBN: 978-0-263-25394-8

Harlequin (UK) Limited's policy is to use papers that are natural, renewable and recyclable products and made from wood grown in sustainable forests. The logging and manufacturing processes conform to the legal environmental regulations of the country of origin.

Printed and bound in Spain
by CPI, Barcelona

Jennifer Rae was raised on a farm in Australia by salt-of-the-earth farming parents. There were two career options for girls like her—become a teacher or a nurse. Rather disappointingly for her dear old dad, she became neither.

All she'd ever wanted to do was write, but she didn't have the confidence to share her stories with the world. So instead she forged a career in marketing and PR—after all, marketing and PR professionals are the greatest storytellers of our time!

But following an early mid-life crisis several years ago Jennifer decided to retrain and become a journalist. She rediscovered the joy of writing and became a freelance writer for some of Australia's leading lifestyle magazines. When she received a commission to interview a couple of romance-writers for a feature article Jennifer met two incredible Australian authors whose compelling stories and beautiful writing touched her cold, cynical heart.

Finally the characters who had been milling around Jennifer's head since her long years on the farm made sense. Jennifer realised romance was the genre she had to write. So, with little more than a guidebook borrowed from the local library and a you-can-do-this attitude, Jennifer sat down to release her characters and write her first romance novel.

When she's not ferrying her three children to their various sports, musical endeavours and birthday parties, you can find Jennifer at the boxing gym, out to dinner with her friends or at home devouring books.

Jennifer has lived in New Orleans, London and Sydney, but now calls country New South Wales home.

Other Modern Tempted™ titles by Jennifer Rae:

SEX, LIES & HER IMPOSSIBLE BOSS
CONFESSIONS OF A BAD BRIDESMAID

This and other titles by Jennifer Rae are available in eBook format from www.millsandboon.co.uk

To my sisters from other misters:
Sonja Screpis, Carla Poole, Tiffany Steel
and Julie Whittington.
Without you I'd understand nothing
and laugh a lot less.
Massive love, my beautiful friends. x

CHAPTER ONE

Twelve pairs of long eyelashes blinked at Jack Douglas. Some of the women were smiling, and some looked as if they were about to burst into a blubbering mess of tears. It was time.

'Congratulations, ladies. You've all made it.'

Squeals, screams and loud relieved sighs followed his announcement.

This day had started like the previous seven. A hundred women at his door, all wanting the same thing. A chance to meet their *Perfect Match*.

'Excuse me.'

The squeals were subsiding and being replaced by excited chatter. Jack watched as the women—virtual strangers this morning—hugged each other. How did women *do* that? Go from open disdain to long-lost best friends in hours? He had known people for years without knowing their last name, let alone throwing his arms around them.

One of the lip-chewing women was in front of him, not hugging anyone. She was standing too close. He looked down. She was a petite woman—tiny, actually. So small he could possibly pick her up and carry her under one arm. Pretty. With a hopeful look in her big green eyes. He swallowed and gave himself a mental uppercut. *Not your problem.*

'Yes?'

He waited for it—the feeling of her tiny little arms around him. He took a step back. She stepped closer. Not only was she going to touch him without permission, she was a close talker. He folded his arms and lifted his chin. Message couldn't be clearer.

'I think there's been a mistake. I shouldn't be here. I should be in one of the other rooms, with the losers.'

She batted her long eyelashes and pulled her lips back into a thin line. She had a wide mouth with full lips, so it looked strange all puckered like that. Jack let his forehead furrow.

'There's no mistake. You've been chosen as a contestant. You're one of the lucky ones.' He smiled, hoping that would satisfy her and she'd step away.

She smiled and a deep dimple formed in her cheek.

'The thing is, I only came here for my sister. She was the one who wanted to get on the show. I'm only here for...support. You should probably check your list. Her name is Madeline Wright—not Brooke Wright.'

Her hands waved as she spoke, and because she was so close the hand holding her phone hit him on the arm. He flinched, but refrained from letting it show on his face.

'The names are correct. Everyone in this room is a winner.'

'But I don't want to *be* here!'

Jack's eyebrows shot up at her fierce announcement. She didn't want to be here? Jack let his eyes run the length of her body. She was dressed in a crisp white shirt and a black skirt to her knees. Clearly she was trying to look professional, but her slightly messy hair and killer body made her look anything but. She looked sexy. Tanned and athletic. As if she didn't belong in those constricting clothes but outside in the sunshine.

Which was where he'd rather be right now. But he was here, trying to get this show off the ground. He wished he was more excited about it. He needed to be—this show was his ticket out—but something was niggling at him. Something he couldn't put his finger on.

It wasn't the format: twelve women competing in a number of challenges in order to win the chance to go on a date with one of the twelve men who had been chosen to match them perfectly. The more challenges they won the more dates they went on. By the end the audience would find out if the man chosen to be their match was the man who had been pegged as their *Perfect Match*. It was fun and interesting and fairly straightforward.

And it wasn't the contestants that bothered him. He'd hand-chosen them all. Even this one. The woman who didn't want to be here. He remembered her audition tape. She'd seemed funny and smart, and he remembered her eyes. A strange dark green. He remembered choosing her. Her eyes had attracted him, but it was her smile that he remembered. A smile that was definitely not present on her face now.

'Did you sign the contract that all the ladies signed before being interviewed by our producers?'

'Well…yes.' The dimple disappeared and colour slashed across her cheeks. 'But…'

'Then you're on the show. We start filming the day after tomorrow.'

Jack pushed a foot back. She was too close and he didn't like close. But she was quick. She reached out and grabbed at his forearm. He stilled. His whole body stiffened. She was touching him and it felt intimate. Wrong. Too personal. His body remained still as the warmth from her fingers spread across his forearm and up past his elbow. Warm and soft, with a firm grip. The back of his neck prickled with heat.

'No,' she said, those eyes of hers narrowing. 'There's been a mistake. I can't go on the show. I'm only here as a reserve. I would be hopeless. I'm not even looking for a husband. I'm marriage-averse. Like, *really* averse. I'd rather chew my own arm off than walk down the aisle.'

Jack tried to move, but her arm was still on his arm and it was all he could think about. He forced his mind into gear. Slowly, carefully, he reached over and gripped her hand. It was as small as the rest of her. Dainty. Slight. But her grip was firm. He prised her fingers clear of his arm and relief swam across his shoulders immediately.

Her eyes opened wide. She was clearly not appreciating being manhandled. But he pushed her hand away and stepped back. Her big green eyes stared at him. Her head cocked to one side and something in her gaze changed. First to confusion, then something else. Something more smug.

'Is my hand bothering you?'

'No.' He smiled. *Charm*. Time to turn on the charm. It always worked. 'As much as I appreciate a beautiful woman touching me, I'm afraid I'm going to have to leave you for your perfect match. After all—that's what you're here for. *Perfect Match*—the only show on TV where we make sure the man you marry is the man of your dreams!'

His marketing team would be proud of that speech.

Jack pulled his face into a wide grin flashing the set of teeth his father had paid thousands of dollars to fix. And reminded him about frequently.

Her hands folded tightly across her chest. 'Look… Jack, is it?'

He nodded tightly. They were definitely not on a first-name basis, but he had to keep the peace here. Nothing could go wrong this time.

'Jack...' Her smile changed. Dimples formed in her cheeks and she fluttered her eyelashes.

She was good. But she wasn't that good. She was trying to use her looks and her charm to get her own way—that much was obvious. Little did this twittering sparrow know that he'd written the book on that game.

'I understand that it's probably a pain to change things now, but I have to tell you I really can't do this. I'm not great around cameras and I'm quite shy—and to be honest there's not really much interesting about me. I'm dull. I'll send your viewers to sleep. Wouldn't it be better to give the spot to someone more exciting? My sister Maddy ticks all those boxes. Seriously—you really should reconsider.'

Jack blinked. Her speech had been a passionate one. His mind wandered back to that audition tape. She'd made fun of herself, pulled faces, clearly not taking it too seriously. She'd smiled that amazing smile a lot on the tape, but she wasn't smiling today.

Mick had said no to her straight up—said she'd be trouble. But there had been something about her...something that had caught his eye. Something that had made him keep watching. She said the viewers wouldn't want to watch her, that she was dull, but he couldn't disagree more. Those eyes, that smile...that body. She'd make perfect viewing. Especially now he knew she didn't want to be here. People out of their comfort zone always made excellent reality TV.

'Our decisions have been made and I don't think you give yourself enough credit. You don't seem dull at all. A little pushy—but definitely not dull.'

Her brows furrowed. 'Pushy? I'm not *pushy*. I'm just telling you the facts.'

'Then let me tell you some facts. You're on the show. You signed a contract. We'll see you back here at nine a.m. the day after tomorrow.'

She didn't say anything, but he watched her chest rise and fall as she breathed deeply.

'I don't think you understand—I can't go on this show.'

'Then perhaps you should have thought of that before you applied.' Her eyes were big and her shoulders slumped. He felt himself falter. *No*. He couldn't do that again. He couldn't feel sorry for her. This was her problem—not his. His job was to make this show a success—not to get her out of the hole she'd dug for herself.

'Think of this as an opportunity. What do you need? Publicity? Money? Hell—you may even meet your perfect match. What woman doesn't want that?'

As soon as he'd said it he knew it had been the wrong thing to say. Her cheeks pinked. Her mouth opened, then closed. Her arms unfolded and she stood with feet shoulder-width apart, fists clenched.

'That's not what I'm here for,' she said tightly, clearly trying to stay controlled. 'I don't want to be here. My sister can take my place; she's the one who wants to be here. She's the one who's looking for love. She's wanted to marry since she was five years old. Trust me, you don't want me. Like I said before—I would *not* make very good viewing.'

'You're making good viewing right now, beautiful.'

Jack let his eyes sweep over her. A compliment always calmed the savage beast. Compliments rolled off his tongue easily, but this time there was a bit of truth in his hollow words. She was a beautiful woman. A nice heart-shaped face, and those perfectly placed big green eyes. She looked healthy, tanned and fun, and she was making his body stand still and take notice. Their male audience would love her.

He shifted his feet. Something grabbed at him. A strange, quiet pull inside him that he recognised immediately but pushed aside. No. He couldn't feel anything. Not for her or anyone else. He couldn't think of any of these women as different from each other. They were all the same. And none of them was anything to him—nor would they ever be. Especially not her.

The way she looked up at him was starting to make something else shift. She stepped forward until her breasts were almost touching his still folded arms. Heat radiated from her but he didn't step back. The scent of her perfume touched his nose and kept him still. Something rumbled inside him. He pushed it down. *No.* Not his problem. Not his anything.

'I'm not here for your viewing pleasure. I'm not here for *anyone's* viewing pleasure. And I'm not going on your stupid show.'

Jack felt his smile falter; she was getting serious now and it was time he did too. She needed to know the rules of this game, and she needed to play by those rules.

'Let me tell you a little about the TV business, darlin'.'

She flinched when he called her *darlin'*, just as he'd thought she would. She didn't like to be patronised—that much was clear. Smart woman. Smart women were much harder to deal with, but he'd done it before. He could deal with her.

'When you sign a contract, your soul belongs to me.' That was a lesson he'd learned years ago. When he'd first sold his own soul.

'I beg your pardon?'

Her voice changed. It became clipped, professional. The voice of a woman who could turn herself into someone else quickly. She straightened her spine and ran a hand over her hair, smoothing it as if trying to take the mess out of it and make it look neater and more business-like. It didn't work. She still looked young and fun and as if she belonged on a beach somewhere in a skimpy bikini.

Jack's producer's mind kicked in. The beach. Perfect for the first episode. And no wetsuits—he'd make the girls dress in bikinis—what a first great ep. He'd open with a faux *Baywatch* running sequence. The girls running along the beach…chasing the men! Gold! It would rate its butt off.

Her voice brought him back to the moment. It was tight and high and way too loud.

'My soul does not—nor will it ever—belong to you. I signed a contract, yes. But now I choose to break that contract. What do I need to do? Pay you some money? Fine. But don't assume that you own me—or that I won't fight you to get what I want.'

Jack's cheeks heated. Her fire was surprisingly sexy. She'd gone from twittering sparrow to swooping eagle in seconds, but those green eyes remained the same. Strong, wide, green as an open ocean and beautiful.

Jack shook it off. He couldn't think of her as beautiful. He couldn't think about her at all. That was when things got complicated and he got into trouble. This woman was definitely one who could cause trouble. Too smart. Too pretty. And she knew what she was worth, which made her dangerous. He didn't need dangerous. He needed this show to be a hit.

Maybe Mick was right and she would be too much trouble. But, then again, that was exactly what the show needed. She was perfect. Bad-tempered, unwilling and impossible to control. That was what this show was lacking. He knew she was a risk, but he needed to take some risks. If he didn't he'd continue to be the man who'd got his job through nepotism rather than because he deserved it. He should leave. Get a job as a garbage man. Far away from his father and far away from all the talk of him not deserving his job. But the truth was this station—and by extension his father—owned him. Until he proved he could finally produce a hit show he was stuck. And so was she. And as long as he didn't get sucked in to her sob story he was out of danger.

She stepped forward and he stepped back—away from her—but she managed to step forward again.

'Don't you run away from me. I need this sorted. I cannot stay.'

Jack felt the air thicken and his breath shorten. Her eyes sparked and he felt it deep in his core. Her pretty eyes were ready for a fight. She might be small, but this one didn't need his protection. She was doing a good job of protecting herself.

He let out a breath and sucked in another big one. He could read the way she felt on her face. *Trapped.* He knew the feeling well. But, like him, she would have to figure it out for herself. Like him, she was on her own. A strange feeling of solidarity with this woman crept over him. Two independent souls. Two people who could take care of themselves. Two people who came up swinging no matter how many times they were knocked down.

'I'm afraid you have no choice, Ms Wright. You are now a lucky contestant on *Perfect Match*!'

'Are you kidding me? This is *great* news!'

Brooke stared at her boss, who was also her sister. Her mad sister. Who had convinced her to join in with this ridiculous, absurd scheme. A scheme that was so bonkers Brooke wondered if she'd actually lost all sense of reality for a moment.

'Brooky—it's perfect. I wanted to go on the show because I'm sick of meeting losers. I wanted to meet Mr Right—someone who's been interviewed and vetted so I didn't have to do all the hard work. Which, when you think about it, is a silly reason to go on the show. Interviewing and vetting men is the fun part! But you—you're not there to find love. You're there with your head screwed on—which makes you an even better candidate than me.'

'Maddy—I really don't think it's a great idea...'

Caution shot through Brooke. Maddy always made sense. She was the eldest of the Wright clan, and the most sensible sister. Brooke looked to Maddy whenever she needed advice. But right now Maddy was acting more like Melody, the youngest and loopiest sister.

This scheme to gain promotion for their business was mad. It had been mad when Maddy had thought it up a month ago. It had been mad when Maddy had suggested she come along as 'back-up', and it was even madder now that Brooke was going to have to make a fool of herself in front of the entire country just to sell some gym gear.

'It makes perfect sense, Brooky! I would have been too emotional. I would have been distracted. But you will be perfect! Sensible, straightforward, practical Brooky.' Maddy's animated face softened and she came out from behind her desk to put her arms out. 'Think about it. How much would we have to pay to advertise on prime time TV every night for three months?'

Brooke didn't care about the free advertising this show would expose their gym gear to. She couldn't think about marketing opportunities and how well-known their brand might be if she managed to get their products on the screen. All she could think of was the potential humiliation. When all those millions of people watching realised how bad she was at relationships and love and flirting and all the other rubbish that was sure to happen on this ridiculous show.

Brooke breathed in, then out. That familiar feeling crept over her. She knew what it was and she breathed through it, just as Maddy had taught her all those years ago. She wasn't going to get angry. She was going to explain herself rationally and clearly. Brooke released the fist her hand had formed. Her palm hurt where her fingernails had dug in.

'Thousands, Brooky!'

Maddy threw her arms around her sister and hugged her hard. The hug helped. Brooke felt her sister's love as she let go and held on to Brooke's shoulders.

'You know that because we checked. And we checked because the brand needs help, Brooke. *Major* help. Think about how many people will be watching you. Think about all those lonely, desperate women out there, watching you night after night as a handsome man falls in love with you. They'll be listening to every word you say—and looking at everything you wear. *Everything.* Including your clothes. They'll want to be like you, work out like you, dress like you so they can find the man of their dreams too.'

Maddy was doing what she always did to calm Brooke down. Giving her rational arguments. Explaining things. Talking to her until Brooke started to breathe normally again.

'Maddy…' Brooke started, her voice normal again. 'You're crazy. That's an awfully long shot.'

'It's perfect PR—you even said it yourself at the marketing pow-wow last month. You don't have to tell anyone to buy our products—you just show them how fabulous they look and how well they work and be your amazing self and they will sell themselves.'

Maddy was really working overtime. Brooke could tell she was passionate about this, and she could also tell her sister was working hard to get her excited. But Brooke wasn't buying it.

'Maddy! Listen to yourself. This is ridiculous!'

'No, it's not.' Maddy said, her voice calm, strong and matter-of-fact. 'It's genius. *I'm* a genius. Wright Sports is poised for world domination, little sister.'

'You're not a genius—you're a madwoman. First of all, if you want someone to model the clothes to make women aspire to be like them, you should have chosen Melissa. She's the long-legged, big-boobed beauty in the family. Or even Melody—she's cute and perky and blonde and fun! I'm short and I have a forgettable face and my mouth is too wide.'

Maddy attempted to interject but Brooke held up a hand.

'I don't need you to compliment me, Maddy, which I know you were going to do. I'm just stating facts here. And reason number two why this plan is absolutely bonkers: women will only aspire to be like me if I successfully seduce a man. Which I won't. I can't flirt, I'm awkward and boring, and I am *really* bad at competing. I'm the only one in this family who hasn't won a gold medal in something. And even if I don't fail every challenge I'm sure my appointed "perfect match" will probably kill me in my sleep. You've got the wrong girl, Maddy. Me being me will do more damage to the brand than good.'

'Why do you do that, Brooky?' Maddy asked gently.

Brook bristled. 'I'm not doing anything besides telling you what a terrible idea this is.'

'Brooke, you're beautiful and talented and fabulous. You'll win every challenge and your perfect match will fall for you—just like the entire country will when they see you on the telly. You're exactly the right girl. I *knew* you'd get it—why do you think I made you come along with me?'

'Maddy, I don't need any of your motivational nonsense right now.'

'It's not motivational nonsense. As a matter of fact…' Maddy moved away to go back behind her desk. She drew herself up to her full five foot nine and stared straight at her little sister. 'I think this will be good for you. You need to put yourself out there. It's time you got yourself a man.'

Brooke rolled her eyes. This wasn't the first time she'd heard this lecture. Her four sisters were always telling her she needed to go out more, be more social—meet new people. But the truth was she liked being alone. It was safer that way. She liked her quiet nights in and she didn't need a man bothering her with his opinions and demands…and his lies and broken promises.

'I don't want a man, Maddy.'

'Brooke. It's time you got over Mitch. It's been twelve months.'

Brooke felt the familiar burn of tears in the backs of her eyes. *Mitch.* Even the sound of his name felt like sandpaper rubbing on foam.

'I'm over him, Maddy.' She heard her voice go quiet. She wished it hadn't. She didn't want her sisters to worry about her. She was over Mitch. Of course she was. Why wouldn't she be? Like Maddy said—it had been twelve months.

Something caught in Brooke's throat. Twelve months since she'd decided not to put up with another one of his lies. Twelve months of thinking about all the things she'd say to him if she ever saw him. Something hurt in Brooke's chest. She wasn't in love with Mitch any more, but the anger about what he'd done was still there. She'd tried everything—yoga, meditation, drinking some disgusting concoction Melody called 'calm juice'—but the feeling was still there. A hard ball of anger she couldn't seem to shake.

'It's clear you're not, Brooke. You don't go out; you don't want to meet anyone new. You just sit at home listening to sad music or working out like a demon. Honestly, babe, we're worried about you. You need this. More than me. More than the brand. You need to do something to break you out of this rut.'

Brooke breathed out heavily. She *was* in a rut. It was true. But she was happy in her rut. Happy to push herself to her limits at the family-owned gym and happy to work herself ragged as marketing manager for her family's company.

She excelled at her job. It was the only time she'd ever been close to competing with her sisters. Micky, the second oldest, was the country's leading female equestrian at only twenty, Melody was in line to join their sister Melissa at the next Commonwealth Games, while Maddy, the most successful of all, was a former gold medallist.

Brooke had just achieved her personal best number of pull-ups in a row at the gym. Five. Pathetic. At only four foot nine, and barely fifty-two kilograms, Brooke was smaller, weaker and so much less remarkable than her sisters. But she was very good at data and statistics and predicting trends.

Since leaving school six years ago she'd managed to

help Maddy take their company from a fledgling gym and activewear business to an award-winning national brand, with seventeen retail stores across the country and a dozen new lines ranging from home workout gear to protein powders. But times were tough. Money was tight. And to move to the next level—which they'd all decided it was time for—they needed to up their game.

Publicity. Recognition. That was what they needed. Brooke knew it. But they'd planned for *Maddy* to get on to this stupid TV programme—Brooke had gone there for moral support and some sort of pathetic back-up on the off-chance Maddy didn't get it. Brooke hadn't doubted for a second that Maddy would get in. Maddy always won everything… Except this time.

And now, in some cruel, unexpected twist of fate, Brooke was expected to expose herself on a reality show based on the ridiculous premise that there was a *Perfect Match* out there for everyone. But Brooke knew what she had to do. She had no choice. This was her family's future and it was in her hands. Every team she'd ever been on had dumped her, due to her pathetic athletic ability, but her sisters never had. They'd always been there for her. From that first day.

'OK, I'll do it.'

Maddy came around the desk to throw herself at Brooke, but Brooke held her back with an arm.

'I'm going to hate every second, I'm going to regret this with every atom in my tiny body, but I'll do it. For you. And Micky and M'Liss and Melody.'

Maddy smiled her brilliant white smile and pulled her in for a giant hug. 'You might be surprised, little sister—you might end up loving every minute.'

Brooke pulled her face into a massive frown as she was squashed into Maddy's chest, knowing deep, deep down that there was no way in hell she was going to enjoy *any* minute of this humiliating and utterly absurd experience.

CHAPTER TWO

JACK SCHOOLED HIS features into something more gentlemanly. His father's face beamed at him from the big screen TV.

'He's a quality unit, Jack. He can make a hit out of anything. I want you to do anything you can to help him out.'

The hairs on the back of Jack's neck stood erect. It was happening again. Just like last time. Just like every damn time. And, just like last time, he wanted to hit someone. Preferably his father. But since his father was on the screen, not there in person, he'd do more damage to himself and probably have to fork out for a new TV. Not smart.

'I've got it sorted, Max. I don't need any help.' He kept his tone low and calm.

'Now, don't go getting your knickers in a knot, Jacko. Rob Gunn is not there to take over. He's a hit-maker—you should be relieved he's coming on board.'

His father never kept his voice low and calm. When Jack was younger, he'd thought of his father as some kind of god-like Santa Claus. He was big and loud and jolly, and he would fly back home laden with gifts for his only child. He hadn't seen him often, so when he had Jack would hang on every word and lap up any attention he could get. But Jack wasn't a child any more, and he could see his father for what he was. And he no longer believed in Santa Claus.

'Mick and I have this under control. Anyone else joining would just make it messy…'

Jack's father held up a big, beefy sun-reddened hand. 'Like you and Mick had it "under control" last time? We can't afford another stuff-up like that, Jack. I've told you—'

Jack knew his father hated being interrupted. It was one of the few things they had in common. Which was why Jack did it. That, and the fact that his father was moving into uncomfortable territory.

'Max, I told *you* it's under control. I don't need your hotshot. What happened last time won't happen again. Trust me.'

Jack watched as his father's face turned redder, which made his grey hair burn even brighter. Not for the first time during this conversation Jack noticed how old his father was looking. His normally round cheeks were drooping, his fleshy nose was covered in purple veins and his hair looked even thinner and greyer than normal. Jack felt an unusual flash of sympathy for the man. Something he hadn't felt in a long time. Not since he'd grown up and realised that this loud, full-of-life man was an overbearing bully. Jack shook it off. If his father had taught him anything it was to eradicate any emotions when you were talking business.

'You listen to me, boy. I've lined this bloke up to help you. It's all about *you*. Like everything I do—trying to keep your head above water. Trying to keep you afloat. Do you have any idea how much your last little mistake cost our company?'

Jack knew exactly how much it had cost. He'd been

at every meeting. He'd gone through every figure with the accountants and he'd earned back every penny. But there was no use telling his father that. From the look on his face Jack knew the steam train had already left the station. The old man was about to blow and Jack was going to cop it—big-time.

'I started from nothing to build this company, boy. *Nothing.* You have no idea of the things I did to make this company what it is today. And I did it for you. So you would be left with something rather than nothing—like I was.'

Jack leaned back in his chair. He was going to be there a long time. He'd heard this story so many times he could predict what his father was going to say next.

'And what have you done to repay me? Drugs. Women. Wild parties. Deadbeat mates. You haven't appreciated *anything.* I gave you the best of everything—the greatest opportunities. Any kid would gnaw off their right arm to be handed the position of Executive Producer for all our media, the way you were, and what have you done to repay me?'

Jack mouthed the words along with him, knowing full well his father was too blind with his own indignation to notice.

'You've produced a string of reality shows that have ended in fights and lawsuits and disaster. I can tell you now, boy, that's *not* going to happen again. Not on my watch. This time you'd better get it right or you can kiss your inheritance goodbye.'

Jack sighed. 'Like I've said to you a thousand times, Dad—I don't want your money. I don't need your money.'

His father's heavy breaths could be heard through the speakers. Jack saw him knock against the computer he was speaking into, losing his balance a little. Max's lips pursed and released, then pursed and released again. He was thinking. Jack could practically see the old man's mind ticking behind his eyes.

'Maybe not, Jacko. Maybe you would be able to make a few measly bucks on your own. But how 'bout your mother? What would happen to *her*, Jack, if I were to shut up shop, take my money and run?'

And there was the stinger. It pierced Jack's gut and lodged there. Jack's father only had one weapon left to use against Jack. His mother. Who was still in love with his father, for some reason Jack couldn't understand. His mother—who would be devastated if she found out how much Max *didn't* care for her any more.

Jack knew exactly what his father meant. At the moment everything Max had—everything he knew about, anyway—was fifty per cent owned by Jack's mother. But when Jack had discovered his father was having an affair fifteen years ago and threatened to tell his mother Max had told him he'd leave his mother with nothing if he did. He'd made Jack realise how powerless he was and then produced a contract saying he had to stay with the media arm of his father's company until he earned enough money to buy his way out of it.

At nineteen, he'd thought it would be easy. But after station cutbacks, a fall in the economy and a cultural shift towards reality TV, Jack had barely covered costs each year. *Perfect Match* was his chance. It had trialled well in market research and the time was right. Dating shows were rating through the roof, and he'd already had a few bites to syndicate it in the US, the UK and India. This show was his ticket out of here—away from his father and the hold he had over him. But until then his father owned him, and he knew it.

'What's that, Jack? Your smart mouth can't come up with anything intelligent to say?'

Jack's blood sizzled but he held his face steady. He was getting too old for this. He needed to take control—one way or another. He needed to get his father out of his life, and today was going to be the start.

'I'm running this company. I'm in charge. Not you. Goodbye, Max.'

Jack pressed the button that would end the video call. His father's face disappeared. This show would be a hit. And when it was he'd pay his father his money and he'd never look back. And when he'd made his own money his mother wouldn't need his father either. They could both escape from his cage.

'Mick, I need you in here, my friend.' Jack spoke into his phone, his voice back to its low, calm tone.

Mick didn't need to know about that conversation. The crew were jumpy enough as it was, with all the rumours flying around about Max pulling their funding. He didn't need them thinking there would be any changes in management. He needed to keep this ship sailing steady.

'How'd it go with Max, boss?' Mick was a man of few words, but he had an eye for entertainment and was one of the best editors in the business. For a man of such little drama, he knew how to produce one.

'Excellent. Couldn't have gone better,' Jack lied. 'But I've been thinking about the format for the show. I know we were going to introduce the men later in the show, once the girls have had a chance to get to know each other, but I think we should move it forward.'

Mick remained silent.

'Bring the men in and have them decide what challenges they want the girls to do. Have them call the shots so they can decide which girls they want to take on dates.

And I think we should cut it back to only four men. That way the girls will have to fight for a chance to meet their perfect match.'

Mick looked thoughtful. He stood still, moving only his head to stare out of the window behind Jack. Jack was used to him by now. He knew what he was doing. Thinking. He gave him a few minutes.

'Female audience are not gonna like it,' Mick finally said in his quiet voice.

'Exactly. They'll hate it. They'll rage and be indignant and it'll be all over social media. It's a genius idea.'

Jack knew the female audience would hate it. He wasn't even sure if it was a great idea. But he needed this show to be a hit. He needed it to work and work quickly—he couldn't afford for anything to happen like last time. This time he was going to be brutal. He was going to call the shots. He was going to create a drama-filled show that had people tuning in every week. This show was about ratings—not about the people on the show. He had to remember that.

Slowly Mick faced Jack and a stern furrow formed on his weathered forehead. 'They'll kill you.'

They would. They'd slam him in the media. They'd call him a misogynist pig. He wondered how the contestants would react to the change. It was within his rights to change the format. He'd written it into the contract. Reality TV was like that—it needed to be fluid and reactive.

And the girls might not understand—they might have questions. He'd go and see them after this. He was sure he'd be able to win them over—he'd deliberately chosen women he could mould and shape. Except *that* one. Ms Wright. She hadn't seemed very malleable. Gorgeous. Great mouth. Insane body. But not malleable. No, if anyone was going to jack up about this new twist it would be her.

'That little firecracker won't like it,' Jack admitted.

Mick grunted. 'I told you not to put her on the show. I knew she'd be trouble.'

Brooke Wright was the only contestant Mick had objected to. He'd said she'd be trouble, would cause problems and make their job harder. And he had been right. She'd protested from the beginning—not wanting to be on the show, then grumbling when he'd informed them they wouldn't have any contact with their friends and families during the entire six weeks of taping. But she was nothing he couldn't handle. He had learned how to charm women years ago. His father had been his mentor.

'Tell 'em what they want to hear,' his father would say. 'Then do whatever the hell you want anyway!'

He'd always laugh after that. Jack never had. Not when it came to his mother. But after a few awkward 'falling in love with a girl who didn't love him' moments back in high school he'd started to use his father's tactics. And it had worked. Since then he'd been able to get women to do what he wanted—mostly.

Ms Wright, however, might prove to be a bit of a challenge. She tended to get into his personal space. She was a little too confrontational. To be honest, she made him a little uncomfortable. But she wasn't there for him. She was there for the show—to make it a hit. Maybe this would be perfect. This new twist would send her into a new flutter and he'd catch it all on camera. It would be just what he needed.

He pushed down the small flutter of guilt that settled in his chest. He needed to work out the details and amend their choice of men. But first he had to supervise the taping of the first challenge. This time he was going to be there for everything. All the on-camera highlights as well as the off-camera drama. This time he wasn't missing a thing—because this time was his last.

'Tell Gaz to bring the car around, Mick—we're going to see the ladies.'

She could do this. She knew she could do this. It was like lifting heavy weights. Ninety per cent mental, ten per cent physical. All she had to do was believe she could paddle out past the crashing waves, stand up on a thin piece of timber and balance while avoiding sharks and the tumble of the constantly moving water, all the while making sure she kept a smile on her face and her bikini top up—because at least eight cameras were set up on the beach and on jet skis to capture every fall, every failure and every embarrassing facial expression.

Yep, she could do this. For sure. Absolutely. Brooke hitched up the strap of her candy-red Wright Sports bikini and pushed a large ball of nervous energy back down her throat.

She'd never been surfing. It seemed like just another sport to fail at, and her balance wasn't great even on solid ground, so she'd never been tempted to try. But now she had to go out there. Because her crazy sisters thought her coming on this show was their most cunning scheme ever.

'It'll be so good for you, Brooky.'

'It'll help you come out of your shell.'

'People will love you.'

'Imagine what it will do for the brand!'

And the last and most irritating comment of all: 'You might meet your Mr Right.'

She wasn't interested in meeting Mr Right. Or Mr Wrong. She was interested in meeting this month's sales targets. And besides, if Mr Right were out there she was pretty sure he wouldn't be on a surfboard. She had always been more into quiet, sensitive, musician-types. They *got* her. Those carefree athletic types were way too into themselves even to attempt to get her.

'OK, ladies. On your boards.'

The tall, broad-shouldered instructor was hurling instructions at the twelve women lined up on the beach. At least *he* got to wear a wetsuit. Brooke pulled the skimpy fabric to cover up more of her breasts. She'd already argued with the producer over this. Why were they lined up like sheep at a sale yard? Why couldn't they wear wetsuits? Wright Sports made an amazing one, lined with the highest quality Neoprene.

But the producer, Jack Douglas, had done what he always did. Smiled. Turned on his deep, calm voice. His 'you're crazy and I need to calm you down' voice. Stepped back, away from her, and brushed her off.

She was sure she'd got a little red-faced when she'd argued with him about it, but he'd ignored her concerns. Told her that viewers wanted the full beach scene. And then he'd had the hide to tell her she had an amazing body and she should be proud to show it off. Which was totally not the point.

But arguing had been useless. Before too much longer he'd pulled out the old 'you're under contract, sweetheart' card and walked away. So she'd lost. Again. And now she was lined up like a horse in the ring at the Melbourne Cup, awkwardly turning away every time she noticed a camera swivelling towards her butt cheeks.

Most of the other girls didn't seem to care a fig. They were on their boards, laughing, joking—jumping up and down so their bountiful breasts bounced in the sunlight. Brooke's breasts didn't bounce—they were way too small for that—but she did try to smile. For her sisters. For the brand. For her family's business. For the most important people in her life.

That was why she was here, she reminded herself as she heaved the huge board up under her arm and wrapped her fingers tightly around the edge.

Brooke grimaced to the girl on her left—Katy, she remembered. Katy the Lawyer, with her long shiny dark hair and big soulful eyes.

'Let's hope the lifeguards are on duty,' she quipped.

Katy smiled back. 'Hopefully they'll be cute, because I'm sure I'll end up face-down in the sand.'

Brooke felt her shoulders relax. At least most of the other girls were friendly. Something about having to go through this all together had bonded them. That and the fact that the annoying producer had forced them to all live together in a Manly penthouse. As if they were a bevy of pets from the seventies and he was hoping for a little girl-on-girl action.

Brooke felt the steam rise again. At the fact that she was being filmed in a bikini on the beach, doing something she knew she was going to fail at. At the idea of being forced to compete with other women for the chance to go on a date with a man she hadn't even met yet and was sure she wouldn't like anyway. But mostly she fumed at the producer. Jack Douglas.

She knew all about Jack Douglas. After their first disastrous meeting she'd looked him up. The man had only got where he was because of his dear old dad. Although, to be honest, she was in *her* job because of her family, too. But that was different. Jack Douglas was, by all accounts, a womaniser, a publicity whore, a charming pig. And from what she'd seen all of that was true.

Because—seriously—what type of man encouraged this type of sexist, voyeuristic television?

But what annoyed her the most about Jack Douglas was that every time she looked at him she moved. Inside. Deep down. Where she didn't want to move. Especially not for him. But his jaw was so square and his eyes were so dark, and when he crossed his arms he stood tall and strong and so incredibly sexy…it moved her. And she couldn't control it. And that annoyed her. She was so good at controlling herself. She'd taught herself how to control her temper a long time ago. She was now quiet and easygoing and Zen. But Jack Douglas was doing his best to upset her Zen.

'Ladies! Looking beautiful, as always.'

And there he was. Tall, athletic, self-centred, small-minded. The exact opposite of her type. Brooke hadn't had a drink all day, but right then she felt drunk. Drunk on her own indignation. Drunk on humiliation and drunk on the idea that there was no way she was getting out of this mess now she was in it.

'We look stupid. We should be in wetsuits,' Brooke fumed. *Zen*, she reminded herself, breathing deeply the way Maddy had taught her when she was young. *Stay Zen.*

Jack stopped and turned to her, looking at her as if he was surprised she was even there. Arrogant. Self-important. And he still managed to move her…*again*. Annoying.

'Nonsense. It's a beautiful, summer's day in Manly. What you're wearing is perfect. And you all look so good—why would you want to cover that up?'

Jack's eyes were almost black in the sun. His hair was thick, with a slight wave at the front where it swept over as if he'd just run a hand through it. His cheekbones were high and his jaw was strong, but that wasn't what made him sexy. It was the way he looked at her. His chin tilted up, his eyebrows slightly furrowed, his full lips together. Arrogant. Entitled. Confident. As if he was thinking about having sex with her right now.

He stood like a man who was aware of his own presence. He was physically intimidating and he knew it. And he was using that now. Despite the various…*annoying*… movements in her core, Brooke was aware of what he was doing and she wasn't buying into it. He could stand there, all pouty and sexy and as manly as he wanted, but right now all Brooke saw was a snout and two piggy eyes.

'Are you serious? I mean—did you actually *say* that?' Heat rose up the back of Brooke's neck and fizzed in her ears. She turned to the cameraman who was now getting closer to Katy's breasts. 'Did you get that? I mean—on film? Did you get that sexist, disgusting comment on tape?'

She turned back to Jack, who was standing with his hands in his pockets, his face blankly staring at her as if he had no idea what she was talking about.

'Because that's what the Australian public need to see. The extent of this man's sexism and arrogance and…and piggishness.'

Her voice was getting higher. Her fists were in balls. She wasn't even sure what she was saying. But a thought was forming in her head. *That's it!* That was all she had to do! He wouldn't put her on the telly if she was insulting and rude and…and honest! But then if he didn't put her on the telly where would that leave Wright Sports?

Brooke tried to breathe. She tried to think. But her tongue had other ideas. 'This whole show is a vulgar attempt to make women appear shallow and stupid and competitive. A way to prove this man's theory that women are second-class citizens. Well—I won't do it!'

Brooke dropped her surfboard and it made a satisfying thud in the sand.

'And nor will anyone else. Will we, girls?'

Brooke turned to her fellow contestants. Her peeps. Her sisters from other misters. She expected them to crowd around her, fists raised, a cry of *I am woman, hear me roar* on their lips. Just as her real sisters would have. But instead eleven sets of long eyelashes blinked. A seagull swooped and made Contestant Number Four swat above her head. Someone coughed.

'Right, girls?'

The girls were still blinking at her.

'C'mon. We're not going to let him get away with this, are we?'

Someone shuffled in the sand. Katy moved her surfboard from one side to the other.

'We aren't here to be ogled…' Katy said quietly, hesitantly.

'Yes! Exactly!' Brooke let out a yell and pointed at Katy before turning back to Jack. 'We're not here to be ogled. Our *Perfect Match* won't care what we look like. Not if he's truly our perfect match. He won't be attracted to big boobs or a small bum or be interested in the size of our thigh-gap. Love is more chemical than that. Love is more intuitive than that. Our perfect match will see through all that. He'll be attracted to us because of our thoughts, our opinions… That's what we should be showing. Our minds—not our butt cheeks.'

Jack nodded slowly. He pushed his lips together and his mouth turned down at the corners.

'Is that right?' He raised his eyebrows.

'Yes!'

Brooke left her position to move and throw an arm around Katy. Katy was quite a bit taller than Brooke, so putting her arm around her was a little awkward, but they were banding together for a common good. There was nothing awkward about that.

'That's right—isn't it, Katy?'

Katy didn't speak, but she nodded. Slowly. Tentatively. But she definitely nodded.

Brooke squeezed her shoulder. 'We won't be paraded like cattle,' Brooke said firmly.

'Actually…'

Brooke's head swivelled to face Alissa, a blonde-haired, big-boobed beauty who stood behind her.

'I don't mind being in a bikini. I mean—yes—I want my perfect match to want me for who I am, but I mean—a man's got to have a little incentive.' Alissa jiggled her boobs and giggled. 'He i*s* a man, after all.'

Brooke watched as the evolution of woman stepped back at least forty years.

'She's right…' another big-bosomed beauty piped up. 'We have to use what we have to attract them in the first place.'

'You don't want a man who's attracted to you just for your looks!' Brooke insisted.

'No,' said someone else. 'But men are men, Brooke. They're visual creatures. They have to like what they see.'

'You're missing the point.' Brooke was feeling hot, and she knew she should probably stop but she couldn't. She needed to say what she had to say. 'Your perfect match will be attracted to *you*. To *your* face and *your* body and *your* eyes—and *your* bum. Not because it's perfect, and not because it's out on display. Think about it—when you're attracted to someone you just *are*. You can't help it. And it doesn't matter if they have a crooked nose or thinning hair. When that chemical attraction takes hold all their imperfections are gorgeous. They make them who they are. You don't see them as negatives—you see everything about them as gorgeous.'

'That's true, Brooke, and I'm not saying we're all perfect. I'm saying that it doesn't hurt to introduce the men to some of our…imperfections.'

Alissa smiled, but Brooke didn't. She turned back to smug Jack Douglas and realised her mistake immediately. He was rocking on his heels with his hands in his pockets. Satisfied. Triumphant.

'And, *cut*!'

Horrified, Brooke turned to face the camera now on her face. Jack sauntered towards her and came in closer than he ever had before, the heat of his skin making her cheeks burn.

'Ratings gold.'

That deep, calm voice didn't calm her this time. But it did make her whole body break out in a rash.

'Good Job, Ms Wright.'

Then he moved back, smiled wide, turned and walked away—while eleven girls stood silently behind her and a lone camera beeped to indicate that it was back on and recording.

CHAPTER THREE

JACK'S HEAD WAS beating incessantly. Over and over. It had started with a throbbing in the back of his head and had now moved to right behind his temple. He resisted the urge to rub at it. All eyes were on him. Now wasn't the time to show any weakness.

'Keep rolling.'

'But, Jack…'

'Keep rolling.'

Jack's calm was slipping. As a matter of fact it was now sliding right out of him and creeping into the ocean, where Contestant Number Three was being hauled up into a lifeboat by three lifeguards. She couldn't swim. A fact she'd failed to mention when they'd told the women they'd be surfing today. So desperate to find her 'perfect match', the crazy woman would rather drown than lose the opportunity to go on a date with a man she'd never met.

Jack tried to relax. The lifeguards had this. But his shoulders stayed tense. He wasn't sure why he was so anxious. Maybe it was the fact that these twelve women were his responsibility. All of them. For the entire six weeks of taping. No matter how much he wanted to stay out of it, the truth was he had to make sure they were safe, make sure they were happy, and make sure they all stayed right where he needed them—in front of the cameras.

Most of them were proving to be easy to manage—except Stephanie Rice, out there, and Ms Wright. The petite blonde. The fiery woman with the sparkling eyes. The woman he couldn't get out of his mind and he suspected the reason his shoulders remained tight even as the lifeguard pulled the flailing contestant out of the water.

Her rousing speech kept going through his mind. Her pink cheeks, her clenched fists. She hadn't just been spouting words back there—she'd felt it. *'When you're attracted to someone you just* are. *You can't help it.'*

He didn't want her to be right about that. She *couldn't* be right about that. It was his responsibility to find perfect matches for these women. But what if she was right?

Attraction *didn't* make sense. It *wasn't* logical. A questionnaire could tell you about likes and dislikes, but it couldn't predict that physical blow right in your chest when you met someone and they blew you away. Not just because of their body or their looks, but because of something else. Something you couldn't explain. Something he was becoming very afraid he felt when he looked at Brooke Wright.

She was a beautiful woman, that was obvious—but it wasn't her beauty that made his heart beat faster when she was around. It was something else. A look she gave him when she was standing up for what she believed in. Attraction was purely physical, wasn't it? Why couldn't he just think about one of the other women? They were beautiful. And they all looked magnificent in a bikini.

But every time he tried to think of another woman his thoughts wandered back to Brooke. To *her* body in that tiny red bikini. To the way she'd tried to rouse the girls. To the way her eyes had glowed brighter and her hair had moved as she'd bounced around, encouraging the girls to fight. Holding her sword aloft against the fire-breathing dragon to protect her people. She was brave and strong and smart and perfect.

But of course she wasn't perfect. She was argumentative and difficult—and if he was honest her mouth was too wide for her face. But somehow that just made him want to look at her even more. He wanted to stare at her and he had to force himself to look away. He was sure he was becoming obvious.

Sex. Lust. That was all it was. Physical attraction. It wasn't as if he hadn't felt it before. He just had to push the feeling down. Easy. He did it all the time. It was just a stupid crush. But somehow it felt different, and that irritated him. She *wasn't* different. She'd be like all the others—after something. His money, his influence, his name. He'd not met anyone yet who liked him for *him*. It was what his father had always warned him about and unfortunately the old man had been right. Every damn time.

He couldn't trust anyone—he knew that. And he definitely couldn't trust Brooke Wright. And not just because he hadn't figured her angle out yet—because she was beginning to occupy his mind a little more than he was comfortable with. And right now he needed to focus on the show. On his father's threats and the executive producer his father was pushing him to take on. And on the contestant they were now struggling to get on an inflatable rescue boat.

He needed to concentrate on how he was going to introduce more twists and turns to keep viewers tuned in. But every time he thought of something he also thought of Brooke's reaction and what she would say. And he wasn't sure why. Why did it even *matter* what she said or did? He barely knew her. She was just another contestant. But the way she'd spoken about the way the show was representing women stuck in his chest. It forced him to think of his mother and the way his father treated her. How he lied to her, cheated on her, threatened her, bullied her. He hated it. He hated seeing the look in her eyes when his father said something cruel or thoughtless or failed to turn up again.

This was nothing like that. This was just a game—just a TV show—surely she could see that? It wasn't real.

But Brooke had no idea. She was too sincere. Too ethical.

Jack ran a hand through his hair. Nothing came easy. Between ensuring this show became a hit, protecting his mother from the truth about his father and trying to earn enough money to buy himself out of his contact, he was wondering when it would let up. When he'd get a break. And now Brooke Wright had come along and embedded herself under his skin. Questioned him. Argued with him. He didn't need that, and he definitely didn't need to feel attracted to her.

He wondered for a minute how someone so small could be so much trouble. And *why* was she so much trouble? The woman seemed constantly angry. Why?

He'd thought he knew all about her. Just as he'd had all the other contestants researched, he'd had *her* researched. Marketing Manager of a family-owned company, one of five sisters. Seemed to have had a comfortable upbringing. Seemed to get along with everyone. No enemies anyone could find. No psycho ex-boyfriends. Currently single. Financially stable.

She had every reason to be perfectly happy, yet clearly she wasn't. At least she wasn't when he was around. Maybe something about *him* made her mad? Maybe he reminded her of an ex-boyfriend or someone else who had annoyed her?

From experience he knew that the way people reacted to each other almost never reflected how they felt about that person—it was more about what was happening in their head. The story they'd made up or the conclusion they'd come to almost never had any bearing on reality. Women were experts at it.

He made a conscious effort to work with facts. Not to read too far into things, to take each moment for what it was. *Don't look forward and don't look back.* So far that approach was working for him, and every time he found himself reflecting or looking forward to something he pushed those feelings right back down where they belonged. Out of sight and out of mind.

Some people called him cold. Distant. One particularly upset woman had called him soulless. But that wasn't true. The truth was everyone had an ulterior motive and you couldn't trust anyone. He was just protecting himself.

The lifeguards' boat had reached the woman in the waves. She was still afloat, waving her arms. Her calls could be heard faintly billowing on the wind as it blew towards shore. His shoulders hurt from holding them so tight but he didn't move his eyes. They had to keep rolling.

He had their number—these women on the show. He knew the ones who were doing it just to get famous, the ones who were looking for true love and the ones who were hoping it would change their lives.

His mind turned back to the Tiny Terror. He wasn't sure what her angle was yet. She seemed sincere when she spoke, but she could just be a very good actress—most women were. She also seemed determined not to spend too much time on-camera. She'd come in, see the camera, smile awkwardly and move towards it, then she'd seem to change her mind and hightail it out of the room, or—more often—give him a tongue-lashing and then leave.

He hadn't figured her out yet, but he would. He always did. Everyone had an angle, and sooner or later they slipped up—giving him the perfect opportunity to see them for what they really were.

'Aren't you going to do anything?'

Jack turned to see the woman he'd just been thinking of. Dripping wet in that small red bikini. It was a *very* small bikini. A bikini that was in danger of exposing even more than it already was. He stood, transfixed. Not by her face but by her body. Her petite but muscular body. It was perfect. It curved in where it should and was soft where there should be softness. But where there was no softness it was hard, glistening with sea water when the sun hit her. His throat went dry and his eyebrows felt heavy.

'She's drowning!'

Her manic cry snapped his head back up to her face. Her forehead was creased and her wide mouth was hanging open. He watched as she drew her bottom lip in and held it against her teeth. His already tense shoulders seized up. She was angry again. Getting ready to tell him off. But rather than annoying him right then it was turning him on.

Not many women argued with him. Not many people in general argued with him. And when they did he could normally talk them down, make a joke and defuse the situation, but she seemed determined to disagree with him. It should annoy the hell out of him, but it didn't. Nothing about her was turning him off right now.

Lust. Physical attraction. That was all this was.

'What?' he asked absently as her lip bounced out from between her teeth again.

'Alissa! She's drowning out there and all you can do is stand and watch.'

Jack's face moved back to the ocean. He remembered Contestant Number Three and the action that was unfolding out on the sapphire-blue water among the white tips of the waves that were crashing relentlessly to the shore.

'She's fine. The lifeguards have her.'

No point panicking. She was in good hands. He hoped she hadn't swallowed too much water. She was a long way out but he could see her moving into the boat. She was flailing about a lot. So much so that one of the lifeguards had just received a nice hefty slap up the side of his head. She was fine.

His shoulders relaxed a little and he allowed a smile to lift one side of his mouth.

'You think this is *funny*?'

Jack felt Brooke move closer. He didn't move a muscle.

'This isn't funny! She could have drowned. She could have died. All for the chance to meet some man she doesn't even know if she's going to like! Don't you see how crazy this is?'

She'd moved now and was standing in front of him. He wished she wasn't. She was angry—that was obvious. He wanted to listen to her and calm her down, but it was hard when she stood dripping in front of him. Her breasts peeped out of her brief bikini top—so much so he was sure that if she just moved a little more he'd be able to see the darkness of her nipple.

'Are you looking at my breasts?'

Busted.

'Yes.' He met her eyes. No point in lying. She'd caught him—and why *wouldn't* he look? They were lovely, and she wasn't exactly trying to cover them up. For someone who had spent an hour arguing about why they should be wearing wetsuits instead of bikinis earlier that morning, she'd chosen herself one of the briefest and sexiest ones he'd ever seen.

'You make me sick.'

'Well, clearly I make you *something…*' He nodded towards her breasts, where her nipples now stood to attention. She was either excited or cold and he didn't mind which. There was something incredibly hot about hard nipples showing through a bikini.

She folded her arms across her chest. 'That—' her voice was practically a hiss '—was caused by extreme anger. At you and your disgusting attitude.'

'In my experience that reaction is usually due to excitement—not anger.'

Her eyes opened wide at that comment, as he'd expected them to do. He was finding annoying her strangely pleasant.

'I can assure you that you *don't* excite me. Quite the opposite. You make me feel…'

She paused and he cocked his head, removing his hands from his pockets to fold them across his chest. How *did* he make her feel? He wanted to know—because right now she was making *him* feel something he hadn't felt in a long time: playful. And interested in what she had to say next.

'I make you feel…what?'

'You make me feel…' Her lips moved as if she was about to say something but nothing came out. 'You make me feel….indignant.'

'Indignant?'

'Yes. And offended and outraged and angry and… and…furious.'

'You seem to be quite an angry person. What's the matter—some old boyfriend do you wrong?'

He could practically light a cigarette with the steam coming out of her ears.

'I am *not* an angry person. I'm actually quite calm and quiet. But you have a way of ruining my Zen.'

'Zen is about inner peace. You need to be at peace with *yourself* to have Zen. It shouldn't matter what other people say and do—other people can't ruin your Zen… only you can do that.'

'Well, apparently you can.'

'I'd love to know what it is exactly that you find so offensive about me. It can't be my looks—I've been told I'm unusually handsome.'

She sniffed and folded her arms, which just resulted in him getting a better view of her breasts. He shifted his eyes quickly.

'And it can't be my personality because—let's face it—I'm charming.' He smiled. She'd laugh at that. Surely? He hadn't seen her laugh and something inside him ached to see her laugh.

But she didn't.

'I find you offensive because you're an insensitive bully who couldn't give a toss about what anyone else thinks.'

For some reason that comment caught in his chest. She'd called him a bully. He *wasn't* a bully. His father was a bully. He wasn't.

'Well, you're an opinionated troublemaker who speaks before thinking. What's the matter—didn't get a say when you were a kid? Picked on by your sisters? Left out? There's got to be a reason you feel this need to stand up for everyone.'

To his surprise, she stopped. Her big eyes widened.

He recognised that look immediately and a foul taste rose in his mouth.

'You really *are* a piece of work, Jack Douglas. You don't care about anyone but yourself, do you? Alissa could have drowned out there and all you can do is stand here on the sand and pass judgement on me when you have no idea who I am.'

Jack sucked in a breath and swallowed.

That look. That was the look his mother's face had when his father let rip with one of his insults. He knew that look and he'd never thought he'd be the one to cause it. He wanted to take it back. He wanted to rewind the tape and start again. But he couldn't, and she was standing there all hurt and confused.

What had he done?

'Brooke…I'm…'

'No.' She stepped back. 'Forget it. I shouldn't have said anything about anything. I shouldn't have expected you of all people to understand what I was trying to say.'

He wanted to stop her from leaving, explain himself, but they were hauling Alissa onto the sand and all he could do was follow Brooke to where the woman lay.

Brooke's body buzzed. Jack Douglas was standing closer to her than he ever had before. Tall and big and confrontational. He was behind her and her breath was coming in short bursts.

What the hell was she *doing*? Why was she getting so emotional? She barely knew this man, but for some reason everything he said seemed to touch her deep down. She wasn't sure what the hell was going on with her lately. She didn't have a bad temper. Not any more. Not for years. Not since she'd been loved and felt loved and had come to realise what it meant to care about people.

She certainly didn't normally lecture people. She was usually the one who stayed well in the background, forced herself to stay in the background—but since she'd been here and since she'd met him she'd felt compelled to stand up. For herself, for the other women, and strangely for all of womankind.

Brooke classed herself as a feminist—surely all self-respecting women did. She believed in equality and didn't appreciate women being treated badly. But she'd never so aggressively attacked someone about their sexism before. But then, she'd never met anyone quite like Jack Douglas. Charming, handsome. A man who took no prisoners. Who used people and spat them out.

Her internet research had proved her suspicions that Jack Douglas was a womanising, partying, poor little rich boy. He worked for his father—had done since leaving his exclusive private school. But what she hadn't found out was any private information. There were plenty of photos of Jack at parties, standing with yet another glamorous woman, but as far as friends or pastimes went the man was impenetrable. It seemed as if he lived alone and was close to no one.

She hated him—she was sure of that. Hated everything he stood for. There really was nothing to like about him. But for some reason her stupid body and her ridiculous mind and her outrageously misinformed heart wouldn't listen.

Lust. Sex. Physical attraction. That was all this was, she reminded herself. Nothing else. He wasn't different from any other handsome man. But somehow it felt different. Awful, dangerous…*different*.

'Ohhh, help me!'

The moan from Alissa brought Brooke back to the moment.

Alissa was coughing and crying and calling out. Her hair was plastered to her face and her bikini was barely staying on her body. She was trying to get up out of the boat, clinging to the shoulders of a lifeguard who was trying to get an oxygen mask on her. But she wouldn't let him.

'I went under…I was drowning…' Her tears were manic, which was clearly making breathing more difficult. She gasped for air and the lifeguard tried to haul her backwards, but she was strong and fought him off, her arms reaching for Jack as he moved past Brooke and knelt at Alissa's side.

'I was going to die out there. I couldn't breathe. I didn't know how to get up!'

Her eyes were wide and tracks of red made them look almost mad. Her hands clawed at Jack's shoulders, soaking his shirt. Brooke saw Jack tense. Something about people touching him clearly made Jack uncomfortable. But he didn't move. He was solid, allowing Alissa to claw at him.

Brooke heard the deep tenor of his voice before she heard his words. Alissa was looking straight into his face, her eyes not moving but her hands still clawing at his shirt.

'You're safe now, Alissa, we have you. You're OK.'

Jack's words were delivered calmly and they reverberated with a sincerity Brooke hadn't heard before.

'C'mon, now, love—you need to lie back. We have to put the mask on.'

'No! No!' Alissa started to move again, away from the lifeguard and closer to Jack and his deep voice.

'It's all right, Alissa. We have you. *I* have you. Just look at me. Look at *me*.'

Alissa turned at his voice and stared into his eyes

again, her gaze shifting from one of his eyes to the other. 'I couldn't breathe.' Tears were falling fast down her face.

Jack let his hand rub from her forehead down the back of her head. 'You're OK now, Alissa. You're safe.'

His calm, steady voice and the way he stroked her head over and over again as his other hand held hers on his shoulder was clearly making Alissa breathe deeply and more steadily. He kept repeating himself, reassuring her, letting her hands claw him until they stilled and her head fell onto his shoulder.

Again Jack tensed. Brooke watched the muscles in his back through the now wet shirt. He didn't move from where he was perched on the sand in front of Alissa. His eyes never left her face.

This was a Jack Brooke hadn't seen before. She hadn't expected it. She hadn't expected the calm with which he handled the situation or the tenderness as he stroked Alissa's head. Jack didn't seem to her to be a sympathetic man. She wondered if he was doing it just for the cameras, but when she looked around the cameras were switched off. This wasn't for TV— this was just him. Calming Alissa down. Making her feel safe.

But of course he was. Anyone would do that in this situation. No one could see a panicked woman and ignore her. He wasn't special. He wasn't doing anything a normal person wouldn't do. Not that she thought him a normal person. But right now, on the beach in the sand, with a woman who'd thought she was going to die, Brooke saw a man. Just a man. Trying to help.

She shook her head. He was the enemy. The man who was trying to make her look like a fool. The man who didn't care about the women on this show. She was just shocked that he was a normal human being, that was all. He definitely wasn't different.

The lifeguard managed to lie Alissa down with Jack's help, but she wouldn't let Jack's hand go. He had to walk to the ambulance with her.

'Please come with me,' begged Alissa, her eyes still red and her chest still heaving.

An ample chest, Brooke noticed. Alissa's breasts were spilling out of her bikini top. Brooke managed to locate a blanket and threw it over Alissa. To keep her warm and protect her modesty. Definitely not because she didn't want Jack to see her breasts. She didn't care whose breasts Jack ogled.

'Of course I will. Brooke—you jump in too.' Jack turned to her for the first time since they'd met Alissa on the beach.

'Me? What for? There's not enough room.' It wasn't that she didn't want to go with Alissa. She just didn't like to be ordered about by him. And she noticed the cameras had been turned on again.

'Because I shouldn't be in the shots and she needs someone to be with her the whole time. You'll have to sit next to her so it looks like you're taking her to the hospital.'

Brooke wanted to argue. She wanted to tell him that it wasn't reality TV if he dictated who went where and sat where and said what—where was the reality in that? But the truth was she was worried about Alissa and she knew Alissa wouldn't let him go. And she knew he'd keep insisting and she just wanted to fix this.

So she hauled herself up into the ambulance, knowing the camera was on her face and knowing it would look as if she was the one who was comforting Alissa when it was really Jack.

But then she remembered her tiny red bikini. And how good it would look if she were the heroine, helping someone in her Wright Sports bikini. And she thought of her sisters, and she sat in the ambulance and held Alissa's hand while Jack sat on the other side, just out of camera view, doing all the comforting work.

CHAPTER FOUR

THE OXYGEN AND whatever else the lifeguards and the paramedics had mixed into Alissa's mask was calming her down. They'd checked her out and there didn't seem to be anything very wrong with her. Her lungs had taken in a lot of water and she was in shock, but otherwise she was well. No cuts or bruises or dangerous internal injuries.

Alissa's hand relaxed in Brooke's. Her eyes rolled back and forth between Brooke and Jack.

'You saved me,' she said to Jack, who was off-camera.

He smiled at her. Brooke watched his face as the sincere smile softened it. Lines appeared at his eyes. He looked older, gentler. More real. He didn't say anything but flicked his eyes suddenly to Brooke and raised his eyebrows—nodding as if to tell her to say something in response because he wasn't supposed to be there.

'Oh, you're...you're safe now, Alissa.'

Alissa's head lolled back to Brooke. 'Brooke, you're here too?' She was smiling.

Brooke smiled back and squeezed the spaced-out Alissa's hand. 'I'm here too.'

'You're here... You're always here. Fighting for us and sticking up for us and not taking any crap from anyone. Our big sister.'

Alissa squeezed Brooke's hand and tried to get up. Brooke rested her hand on Alissa's shoulder. Jack did the same on his side.

'You're so little, but you're so big—y'know? Angry. Loud. Opinionated.'

Alissa smiled at her and Brooke smiled tightly back. Brooke knew Alissa's drugs were starting to kick in, but her words had still managed to freeze Brooke's heart. Angry? Loud? Opinionated? *Her?* Was that what they thought of her? That *so* wasn't her. Quiet. Predictable. Dull. Easy. That was her. Happy. Alissa was just pumped up on something. She didn't know what she was talking about.

'I'm not loud…' Brooke's eyes flicked to Jack's and they met. He smiled with one side of his mouth and she understood. She was *always* loud with him. And angry and argumentative. This was bad. This show was changing her. She was becoming someone she wasn't and she didn't like it.

'We've been worried about you, Brooke…' Alissa was talking again—all slurred and sleepy. 'Who's going to be your perfect match? What man will want you? You'll frighten them all away with your angry women's lib speeches and all those little muscles you have. So *hard*, Brooke…' Alissa reached out and squeezed Brooke's bicep. 'Hard and angry.'

Brooke's smile froze. That was what the others thought of her? That wasn't her. She wasn't hard or angry. It was these cameras and Jack. Brooke looked up. *Him.* It was him who brought this out in her. This side of her personality she thought she'd buried years ago.

'You're pretty, though. You have a lovely smile. You should smile more. You'd look prettier. And you have some amazing clothes!' Alissa turned to Jack. 'She's pretty and nice and has nice clothes. You like her, don't you, Jack? *He* likes you Brooke. Can't stop looking at you. Can you, Jack? Maybe *he's* your perfect match!'

Brooke knew it was the drugs talking. She knew Alissa had no idea what she was saying. But still her words made her stop still. Jack *looked* at her? No, he didn't. Not like that. He thought she was a troublemaker. Someone who spoke without thinking. He didn't like her.

A lump caught in Brooke's chest. She'd thought her temper was gone. Her sisters had made sure of that. They'd loved her despite her temper. But her parents hadn't been able to tolerate it. She hadn't been good enough for them.

The thought flew into her head unexpectedly. She hadn't thought like that in years. Her sisters had made sure those thoughts stayed out of her head. But her sisters weren't here. She hadn't seen them or talked to them in almost a week and she just wasn't herself without them. She was angry and volatile and now she was pathetic and feeling sorry for herself.

Right now, as she held Alissa's hand and let the drugged woman's words swirl in her head, all she wanted to do was call her sisters. But Jack's rules stated that there was to be no contact with the outside world. The only people they could talk to were people on the show.

Jack had provided counsellors, and a couple of the girls had already spoken to them. But Brooke just wanted her sisters. The women who loved her and cared about her and wanted the best for her. The people who would tell her when she was being difficult, let her know when her dress was too short and hold her when everything got too much. But they weren't here and the cameras were rolling and Alissa was still going on to Jack about how much he looked at Brooke.

'No one is looking at me, Alissa. You're right. I'm too loud and angry. But I'm not worried about me right now—how are *you* feeling?'

Alissa moved sluggishly. 'Oh, darling, you're not angry at me, are you?' Alissa turned to Jack. 'She's always angry at something and someone. Mainly you. Why is she so angry at you all the time? What have you done? Have you hurt her?' Alissa tried to get up again. 'Don't you hurt her—because she sticks up for us and she's good and kind and lovely and I don't *want* you to hurt her.'

Brooke's cheeks burned. Alissa's words were making it more and more awkward by the second. Her insistence that Jack felt something for her was ridiculous. And her insistence that Brooke was an angry person was even more humiliating. Angry was something she never wanted to be again.

Brooke couldn't look at Jack. She knew what she'd see. Horror. Denial. She had to get Alissa to stop talking about her because the cameras were rolling and she wouldn't shut up and she didn't want everyone in Australia hearing about all this stuff.

'You need to rest, Alissa. Stop talking and rest.'

Finally she looked at Jack. She dreaded his smug and patronising face. Or, worse, his pathetic sad face, feeling sorry for her. But when she looked at him his face was none of those things. He was looking at her, his eyes steady and his jaw set. He looked as if he wanted to say something, but he didn't. He just held her eyes as he held Alissa's hand.

Alissa spoke again, this time to Jack, but Brooke didn't hear. All she could focus on was Jack's direct look. It spoke of comfort and understanding and resolution. She wasn't sure why, but he was holding her gaze steady.

Brooke felt the thumping in her chest caused by Alissa's words starting to recede. Alissa was talking about something else now. Something about a zoo and the animals escaping. Her words made Brooke break Jack's gaze and she looked back just in time to see Alissa start to doze off.

The paramedics came then and checked her over, so Brooke moved away to the front of the ambulance. She watched as the camera followed the movements of the paramedics and Alissa, and didn't notice that Jack had moved and was now sitting next to her.

'I think she'll be OK.'

He didn't say anything about what Alissa had said. Good. She didn't want him to.

'You look at me?' *No, don't say that.*

'I…'

'You hate me.'

'I don't hate you, Brooke.'

'You said I was a troublemaker.'

'You are.'

'Then why do you look at me?' Brooke faced him, her fingers hurting as she gripped the seat. She really shouldn't be talking—shouldn't be asking him this. Why couldn't she just shut up?

His dark eyes held hers. Brooke's heart thumped. They weren't close. They weren't touching. But she could feel him. Feel him breathing and feel him near her. Big and strong and solid. She held her breath.

'I look at you because I find it hard to turn away.'

Brooke sat silently. She had nothing to say. No words formed on her tongue or in her head. Nothing.

Alissa started to talk again and the ambulance bounced heavily on the road. Brooke felt Jack's leg press against hers. Deliberately. It didn't move with the bumps. The muscles in his thigh were tense. He was keeping his leg right next to hers.

Again, he'd surprised her. What the hell was going on and why was her heart beating so fast? What did she care if he looked at her? If he couldn't turn away? She didn't want his attention. She didn't want *him*. So why did his words seep so quickly and violently into her dry, parched heart?

'I'm not normally angry. Or opinionated.'

Why had she said that? She didn't have to justify herself to him.

'It's OK to be angry sometimes. If you don't like something you should speak up. This situation you're in would make anyone angry.'

'I'm not me right now. You don't even know me.'

He smiled and the ambulance moved again, rocking her sideways. Although she wasn't entirely sure the ambulance had moved…

'You're right. I don't know you. But I do know you're more than angry. You're loyal and passionate and…you're gorgeous.'

'Gorgeous?'

She kept her eyes on him and his eyes remained on her. He held steady with every bump and every turn and she involuntarily leaned a little closer, mesmerised by the way he held her still.

'Stunning.'

His words were sincere and his voice was deep, and the way he said it—not looking away as his body held against her still—made something shake inside her. A feeling she knew lay dormant—something she didn't want to wake—stirred. She pushed it down, but it rattled her as he looked at her.

'What's so stunning about me?'

Her voice was quiet but she wanted to know. She really wanted to know what he could possibly find stunning about her. She wasn't that pretty. And since she'd met him she'd abused him and caused him trouble and been mean and rude and difficult and so angry. How did he find *that* stunning?

She waited for his answer. Not breathing, not moving—allowing the moment to last.

'Everything.'

His answer came just as the ambulance pulled up at the hospital. A mad rush meant everyone was pulled out of the ambulance and the cameras rushed to film their responses. Brooke was whisked away by one of the production staff and Jack remained at the ambulance.

Brooke's heart beat hard and fast. Adrenalin rushed through her. *Everything.* That was what he'd said. Everything? How could he say that? What did he mean? He didn't even know her. And what he did know wasn't very good. Why had he said that? Was it a line? He'd seemed so sincere.

Confusion rattled her brain and made her reactions slow.

'We've got to get you to the emergency beds, Brooke. We want you to go see Alissa.'

The production team rushed her to Alissa's side. Jack didn't reappear.

Brooke spent the afternoon getting ice and water and food for Alissa. She didn't see Jack again but she did think about him. *A lot.* He'd said that everything about her was stunning. Was that what he really thought?

Confusion made her tired. Alissa's demands made her tired. Until eventually she fell asleep on a hospital chair, dressed in nothing but a bikini and dreaming of drowning in a sea of crashing waves.

CHAPTER FIVE

BOTH THE GIRLS were asleep. Heavy breathing and the occasional snore coming from under the covers in the bed assured Jack that Alissa was sleeping soundly, and Brooke was on an armchair, her head bent right over to the arm, her legs twisted.

She looked uncomfortable, but she was asleep too. Deep, steady breaths came from her tiny body. She was still and quiet—two things he'd never associated with her. Brooke was a fireball of energy and opinions. She made him tense, but yesterday in the ambulance he'd seen something else in her. A vulnerability he'd not noticed before.

Alissa's words had shocked and upset her and he'd known exactly what Brooke was feeling. She hadn't had to tell him—he'd been able to see it in the way her shoulders had fallen forward. In the way her eyes had opened and she'd sucked the edge of her bottom lip in. Alissa had hurt her.

For a moment Brooke hadn't looked like a confident woman. She'd looked like a little girl bullied in the schoolyard. Unsure how to react. That was why he'd felt the need to come to her rescue. Feeling alone and picked on was a feeling he knew too well. He didn't deserve to feel that way and neither did Brooke.

He'd wanted to tell her that Alissa didn't know what she was talking about. He'd wanted her to know that having cameras pointed in her face and feeling out of control was normal—and so was her reaction. Getting angry wasn't a weakness—sometimes it was the right thing to do. But clearly she wasn't comfortable with that side of her personality. Something about losing control upset Brooke, and he wanted to find out why. He wanted to know more.

But he shouldn't have said what he had. Brooke might think things. She might imagine he wanted something he didn't and he didn't want her to do that. Because he didn't want anything. He couldn't allow anything to happen—and not only for the sake of the show. He knew that if he let Brooke in he would hurt her for sure.

Brooke was the kind of woman who threw herself into things. A defender of the universe. A superwoman. Strong and kind. But she was still a woman. She still got hurt. Alissa had hurt her. And he knew he would hurt her too. At the beach, he'd said things he didn't mean. As much as he tried to keep it at bay he knew deep down he was just like his father. A selfish bastard who was only out for himself.

Today he'd fix it. He'd let her know what he'd meant. She *was* gorgeous, of course—she was passionate and interesting and argumentative and challenging and a breath of fresh air. She'd be special to someone one day. Someone would see her and sweep her off her feet and they'd deserve her. But it wouldn't be him.

Brooke moved and moaned and shifted, and sleepily she opened her eyes. Rubbing them, she ran her fingers through her hair and yawned wide as she sat up, looking around. He could see she was a little confused and unsure where she was.

'Good morning, Sleeping Beauty.' Best to keep it light and flirty.

She turned to him with a start. 'Jack! What are you doing here?'

'Just checking on the patient.'

Her eyes darted behind him. They opened wide and narrowed. 'You brought the cameras?'

'Of course.' Brooke seemed constantly surprised by the appearance of the cameras. Didn't she know what she'd signed up for?

'Jack, Alissa is going to wake up and feel terrible. She's going to *look* terrible. She's not going to want the cameras here.'

Brooke was sitting up now. All quiet and peace was fast evaporating. Jack's shoulders tensed. Ready for a fight. Brooke liked to fight with him, it seemed. She did it so often. He wondered for a moment what she'd be like if she didn't want to fight. All soft and loving, lying in his bed after a wild session.

His mind wandered…he grew hard. Taming Brooke would be a fun task. She was certainly hot—and he was sure she'd be the type to demand she received her own pleasure in bed. He wasn't into those girls who just lay there—waiting for him to take what he wanted. He liked a bit of spit and fire in the bedroom. He liked a fight—it made the winning so much sweeter.

What he *didn't* like was the cuddling afterwards. Most women liked to cuddle—they wanted to snuggle and touch. But he liked to get up and away. Not because he didn't feel affection for the women but because touching seemed a little too personal, a little too close. He wasn't into close. And he suspected Brooke was the kind of woman who needed close.

'Jack.'

Brooke's angry tone brought him back to the hospital room. Brooke's long-sleeved shirt was open, revealing a tight white singlet. He'd had someone go to the house and get some clothes for the girls last night. They couldn't stay in their swimsuits. Jack's mind wandered back to Brooke's red bikini. It hadn't left much to the imagination. And her body was perfect. Small, tight and athletic. Strong. He imagined how athletic she'd be in bed.

'Jack.'

Again her voice brought him back and his eyes turned to hers. She was angry now. Clearly she didn't like being ignored. 'You need to send the cameras away until she wakes and fixes herself up.'

No. He didn't. The whole point was to see real reactions. The audience would love to see these two, just woken up after a night in hospital. But Brooke was right—no one would want a camera in their face right after they woke.

'This is what you both signed up for, Brooke—Alissa knows that.'

'Alissa had no idea she was going to end up in hospital. I'm sure she didn't sign up for *that*.'

'The cameras are staying.'

He was done arguing. The more she talked, the more sense she made—and he didn't want to change his mind. He knew what would rate best and he needed this show to work, so he didn't want her changing his mind. He couldn't modify this show—not for her or anyone else. It had to be raw and real and make people sit up and take notice.

'What do you care, anyway? You look great. And it'll make you look good to be here when she wakes up—people will love you.'

He knew he'd said the wrong thing even before he'd

finished his sentence. She stood up. White-hot rage seeped through her eyeballs at him. Her fists clenched and her shirt slipped off her shoulder but she was too mad to fix it. His eyes moved to the golden tan of her shoulder. Smooth, with a smattering of freckles from too much time in the sun.

'I don't care how people see me, Jack. This isn't about me—or you, for that matter. This is about Alissa and the fact that she almost died yesterday. Do you even *get* that? Or do you just think about ratings and audiences and everything else that doesn't matter?'

'That's *all* that matters right now, Brooke.'

Didn't she get that? Why couldn't she understand that this wasn't about her or Alissa? This was about making good TV.

'No, it's not what matters. You're so caught up in what people think that you forget what this is really about. Twelve women so disillusioned with love that they think coming on some badly conceived TV show will help them find it. I don't care what you think—that's what these girls are here for—to find love. Not be made fools of in front of the nation.'

'These girls are here to get their heads on the TV. If they weren't they'd find some other way to find love.'

'No. The problem is people like you, Jack. People who perpetrate the myth that men fall in love with looks. But they don't. There's plenty of beautiful women out there, but true love is not about what you look like on the telly or on Instagram or on Facebook. It's not about what people think about you, it's about who you actually are. It's about the type of person you are and the little things that someone notices. People aren't attracted to a perfect nose or the right shade of blonde in your hair. It's not that specific. You can't explain why you're attracted to some people but not others. These women think that if they look hot and do some cool things they'll be desirable, but that kind of attention attracts meat-heads and pathetic, insecure men who don't want a real women—they want the image of a woman. And those are the men these girls should be staying away from.'

She was right. This *wasn't* the place to find a decent bloke. This was a television show. Even though it was called reality it wasn't—you didn't live your life on a TV screen. But right now she seemed to be blaming him for the wrongs of the world. Putting everything that was wrong with society and modern dating on him. It wasn't his responsibility to make these women see themselves as more than just images. It was his job to deliver a TV show that would achieve high ratings. That was it. The end of his responsibility.

'They're all over eighteen—they can make their own minds up.'

'You have no idea, do you? Have you ever stopped to think of what goes on in the lives of these women outside this show? Do you even know anything about them? They could have no support. They could have a group of family and friends who make them feel less than they are. Have you ever thought about the reasons they're here?'

'No!'

That had come out louder than he'd wanted. But she was making him feel things he didn't want to feel. Like guilt. Why should he feel guilty? He hadn't begged these women to come on the show. He wasn't responsible. He couldn't be responsible. That just led to trouble and he couldn't afford trouble. Not this time.

CHAPTER SIX

Brooke had stopped talking. She was clearly surprised by his violent outburst. Good. He needed her to be quiet. He needed to think. Or not think in this case. He just needed this to happen.

'Mick, get the boys in here. We need to start taping.' Alissa was waking. He needed her reaction. He needed to get out of the way so the scene could get shot.

He stepped back, away from Brooke and out of the way, but Brooke stepped forward.

'Don't you leave. You want people to see the real reactions then you need to be here. You need to take responsibility. You were a big part of this—you sent Alissa into the ocean, you calmed her down, and I suspect you were the one to send all the clothes and supplies for us. Now you're here. You need to be in this, too.'

No, he didn't. 'I'm not on the show—you are. Now turn around and talk to your friend.'

He was sure that order would send her into a fit. He was sure that would make great TV and he was sure he only felt a slight twitch at the thought of that. But she didn't have a fit. She smiled. She looked at him, direct and hot in the eye. Then she turned and went to Alissa.

It took half an hour of Brooke talking to remind Alissa of where she was and what had happened. Alissa delivered a magnificent performance, forgetting where she was and then crying over the accident before declaring that she hoped her perfect match was worth the trouble. Perfect line. Perfect TV. But for some reason it didn't make Jack feel good. It made him feel old and jaded and uncomfortable. Uncomfortable because he knew he'd just done something his father would have been proud of.

The food in the hospital was terrible. Brooke pushed the plate away and it scraped noisily, echoing in the empty space. Brooke's neck ached and her shoulders hurt. A night spent sleeping upright in a chair had taken its toll. Especially after a day surfing and hours consoling Alissa, who was clearly OK but still sore and unsteady.

And the cameras wouldn't go away. They captured every word and every movement and Brooke was sure she looked about as cute as she did after a particularly hard workout. All she wanted to do was go home and have a shower and sleep. But she couldn't. Because Jack always wanted another shot, and the cameramen were always wanting her to sit and look this way or that.

The more Brooke saw of it, the more she realised there *was* no reality in reality TV. The reality was behind the camera. The reality was Jack. The man who said she was stunning. The man she couldn't stop thinking about.

What had he meant yesterday? Why had he told her everything about her was stunning? It made it so hard to stay angry with him. He made bad choices. He did things for the wrong reasons. But this show wasn't her responsibility and neither were the other eleven women. All she had to do was wear Wright Sports gear and get Wright Sports products on prime-time TV.

She needed to calm down. Maybe it was just the lack of sleep and the fact that it had been almost eight days since she'd had any contact with her sisters that was making her so angry. Brooke breathed deeply. Where the hell was her Zen?

'Here you are.'

Jack. Again. Brooke searched for the cameras. She was sick of them. Sick of watching what she said and thinking about how she looked. She just wanted a minute to herself—which was why she was down here in the hospital canteen.

'Jack. Seriously. I can't do this right now. I'm exhausted. I can't do cameras.' She was too tired to fight. She just needed him and his annoying cameras to go away.

'There are no cameras.'

Brooke looked up in surprise.

'I wanted to talk to you in private.'

In private? Jack never did anything in private. He was all about the show. Brooke was immediately nervous. He wasn't going to say she was stunning again, was he? Because she didn't know what he meant by that…and it was probably just a line…and he was probably lying to get his own way…and that would make her angry and she really didn't want to get angry again.

'What about?'

'About before.' Jack scraped back a plastic chair and the noise reverberated across the vacant canteen.

'Before?'

'Before. In Alissa's room.'

'Jack. I can't fight right now. I'm too tired.'

She *was* tired. Tired of Alissa's complaining and tired of being constantly watched and tired of this bad, bitter coffee. She put the cup down and made to stand, but Jack's arm on hers stopped her. That made her still. Jack rarely touched her. Not voluntarily. She'd noticed that about him. He didn't touch anyone and he stood well away from people. The couple of times she'd accidentally touched him he'd actually flinched.

'I'm not here to fight, Brooke. I'm here to apologise.'

That stopped her. Jack? Apologising? That just didn't seem right. Something about it didn't compute.

'You are?'

'I was an ass before. I made you do something you didn't want to do. I should have waited until you girls were awake and ready before I brought those cameras in there.'

Brooke sat heavily. Jack's apology stilled her tongue. She didn't know what to say. She'd never heard him say he was sorry—he didn't seem the type of person ever to apologise. This man had a real knack for confusing her.

'Brooke?'

'You're saying sorry?'

'Yes.'

'You're saying I was right?'

He paused. His mouth went tight, then his dark eyes set on hers. 'Yes.'

Yes. He was admitting she was right.

The shock was too much. She was tired and surprised and Brooke didn't know what else to do so she leaned forward and rested her head on her hands.

'Brooke?'

She felt Jack's hand on her arm. It was warm and he squeezed her firmly. She sat up quickly and grabbed his hand, squeezing back. Jack's face registered shock and he tried to pull away, but she didn't let him. He wasn't getting away that easily.

'You're sorry? You think I'm right? You're taking responsibility?'

'Yes.'

Brooke let her fingers lace between his and he tried to pull away again. Again she didn't let him. She just pulled her light plastic chair closer to him. So close their knees were touching.

'Where is Jack? What have you done with him?' she teased.

She knew he wanted to pull away, she knew she was making him uncomfortable, and she liked the power she had over him. But he didn't pull away. He actually smiled at her joke and leaned in closer. Brooke noticed his skin. It was dark and smooth and a sprinkling of hairs spread across his jaw, as if he hadn't shaved that morning. He looked a little dishevelled. He looked a little less than the put-together, in control Jack she knew. She liked it. It made him more real somehow.

She leaned closer, taking in his eyes, dark and dancing. His mouth had turned up at the edges. She watched it, then watched his eyes again. They were exploring her face. She suspected he was trying to figure out what she was doing and what she was thinking. She pulled on his hand, letting it rest on her chest. She liked it there. She liked this Jack. The Jack without the Instagram filter.

'I've got him locked up somewhere you'll never find him.'

'Good!' She laughed. 'Keep him there—I prefer this Jack.'

'Why?'

'Because he's real. He feels things. He touches me.'

Jack's smile disappeared. She felt his fingers tighten over hers. 'You like it when I touch you?'

'Yes. Very much. I like your hands. I like your fingers.'

She squeezed his fingers again, before letting go and allowing her own fingers to trail over his palm. When she looked up he was watching her fingers. Brooke's breathing became shallow. In this moment this wasn't Jack. In her sleep-deprived, hungry state this seemed to be someone else. Someone sincere and real whose warm hands she wanted to feel on her skin. Someone who thought she was stunning.

Jack's eyes met hers. Their stare was unbroken—both were having trouble breathing. Brooke wasn't sure if it was the lack of sleep or the gratefulness she felt for his physical touch, but that was what she blamed when she leaned forward and let her lips rest gently on his.

Jack didn't move. He didn't react. He let her press her lips to his and sat still, clinging to her fingers. Brooke opened her eyes, instantly regretting what she'd done. He still didn't move. Except his eyes. They darted from one of hers to the other, but he didn't pull away. Did he want her to do it again? His hand still clung to hers. Should she kiss him again?

She didn't know what to do so she kissed him again. And this time he did react. He pushed closer. He kissed her back, his tongue pushing on her lips till they opened, letting him in. He still didn't let go of her hand and it was hot in hers. His lips were hot too as he tilted his head so his kisses could deepen.

Brooke's heart pounded in her chest. The kiss felt wrong and forbidden. It was over in seconds, and it left her breathless and a little shocked and a lot embarrassed. She let go of his hand and sat back. She blinked, unsure as to why the hell she'd done that.

Brooke couldn't speak but she looked at his face, wondering what he was thinking. He looked back at her blankly before a slow smile spread over his face. A slow, knowing smile that made Brooke's heart drop.

'Nice kiss.'

Brooke shut her eyes tight. *Nice kiss*. That was all it was. He didn't feel anything. He'd just taken the opportunity. He hadn't been kissing her back. He'd just been kissing whoever kissed him. She was right about him—a total player. Incapable of real feelings. Despite his apology. Despite his 'stunning' comment. Of *course* he didn't really think she was someone special. She needed to stop doing that. Stop thinking that people meant what they said and that their actions meant anything. All that kiss meant was that she was tired and he would kiss anyone, anywhere.

Totally disappointed in herself, and extremely over it, Brooke stood.

'That was a bad idea.'

Jack stood as well, his smile now gone. 'Was it?'

'Yes. Very bad. I need to go.'

'Wait.'

Brooke turned back, stupid hope lifting her heart. 'What?'

'I came down here to talk to you. I wanted to ask you something.'

So that was it. He was only apologising because he wanted something. She was so naïve sometimes.

'What?'

'Meet me tonight at Lottie's, near the apartment. For a drink.'

Jack sat back, his eyes blank and his jaw tight again. Gone was friendly, affectionate Jack from moments back. Uncaring, unfeeling, business Jack had escaped from his ropes and was back. He wanted something. Not just a drink—something else. Brooke was sure of it. A hot rash spread up Brooke's neck and into her cheeks. Embarrassment—that was what she felt right now. She was embarrassed that she'd managed to let herself be played by a man she knew was a player. God, she must be tired!

'I'm not sure that's a good idea.'

Jack paused. He sat back even further.

'I mean, clearly we just broke some kind of contestant/producer ethical code or something. I shouldn't have done that.'

A slight vulnerability shadowed his dark eyes. Brooke's heart saw it before her eyes did. Did he actually *want* to take her for a drink? No. *No.* He wanted something. Information. Maybe he wanted to tape her getting sloshed. He definitely didn't want to take her for a drink because he felt something, otherwise he would have said something other than 'nice kiss'.

Brooke's stomach swirled and her head hurt. She wanted him to take her for a drink because he felt the attraction she did. She wanted him to take her for a drink so they could get to know each other, without the cameras and the lights and the direction. She wanted him to feel something—but she wasn't sure he was capable of that. Not with his aversion to closeness and his playboy reputation.

Brooke wanted to get out—away from him and his knowing eyes and his expert lips and the way he was making her move again. Move violently. She didn't want to feel for him. She just wanted to go home and sleep and forget about her recent lapse in judgement.

'But you did, and we should probably talk about it.'

'No, we shouldn't.' Brooke stood to leave.

'Brooke, I know why you're here. For your family's business. I've noticed that you wear Wright Sports clothing most of the time.'

Brooke watched his face. Was he angry? Did that mean he wanted her off the show? For some reason that didn't make her as happy as she'd thought it would. She didn't like the way this show was changing her, the fact that it was making her angry and aggressive, but she liked the other girls. And who would stand up for them against Jack and his outrageous demands if she wasn't there? He'd apologised to her just minutes ago—maybe she was getting through to him. What if she left and he just went back to his old ways?

'What...what are you going to do about it?'

'Nothing. If you come and have a drink with me.'

Brooke wanted to have a drink with him. She wanted to be alone with him. But she wasn't sure if that was such a great idea. Maddy had said this show would be good for her, that it would take her out of her comfort zone. Having a drink with bad-boy Jack Douglas was certainly that. Maybe she should do it.

'Will the cameras be there?'

'No!' he answered emphatically. 'No. It'll just be me and you.'

Her and him. And a drink. In a dark bar. This was dangerous, and so out of her comfort zone. But she wanted to do it. That kiss had made her feel something she hadn't felt in so long. Alive. Excited. No longer numb. Maybe this was just what she needed.

'I'll send someone to pick you up. You might get lost.'

'I don't need an escort and I never get lost.'

Brooke still wasn't sure if this was a good idea. She still didn't know what he wanted or how he felt, and she certainly didn't want any witnesses. No cameras, no one else. Just him and her.

'No, I bet a good girl like you always checks Google Maps.'

'That's right. I'm good, but when people screw with me I can get very bad.' She wasn't sure of that, but it annoyed her that he'd pegged her as a good girl. She'd been bad before. He had no idea.

Another lazy smile spread across his face. He slipped his hands into his pockets. 'Good girl gone bad? I'm looking forward to that.'

Brooke didn't say anything. He didn't deserve any more of her time and he looked too hot right now, all crumpled and lazily sexy, so she turned and left. Before any more bad thoughts could creep their way into her good head.

CHAPTER SEVEN

THE NIGHT WAS hot and still. Laughs rang out from the restaurants that lined the footpath. The smell of the sea lingered in the air and Brooke breathed it in.

Brooke had spent almost her whole life living in Sydney, but she'd never spent much time in Manly. Her family lived in the inner west and she worked in the city and there just weren't that many reasons to cross the bridge. But she liked it. She liked the laidback, casual charm of the coastal suburb. She liked the feeling that it was trapped in holiday mode. No one seemed to work in Manly—they just went to the beach and jogged with their dogs.

But she was missing her sisters and she was missing her work. The *Perfect Match* contract said they were to have no contact with anyone other than each other for the six weeks of taping. No internet, no smartphone. Which was harder than it sounded.

Although Brooke got along with the girls, she missed the comfortable ease of having her sisters on hand. It had been eight days now that they'd been holed up in the penthouse and, although the days had been filled with briefings and hair and make-up sessions and various staged tapings, Brooke was starting to feel very anxious and a little lost without her sisters.

Lottie's was one of those new Sydney bars. One of those discreet hole-in-the-wall places with almost no signage at the front—because signage was, like, *so* five years ago. It took Brooke a few laps around the Corso to find it. She almost wished she'd taken Jack up on his offer of an escort, but the more she thought about it the more she thought the escort would have been a spy.

She didn't know what to make of Jack. He was so confusing and he made her so angry. All she wanted to do was go back to the way things had been. Predictable. Easy. Dull. *Dull?* Where had *that* thought sprung from? Her life wasn't dull. She had her sisters and her friends and she had fun.

But as her heels clicked on the cobblestones she was remembering how she'd felt before she'd come on this hideous show. Numb. But she didn't feel numb any more. She felt anything but numb. She was on some mad, out-of-control rollercoaster and she was sure she wanted to get off. She had to concentrate on not letting her emotions get away from her and on not getting angry. And she had to concentrate very hard on not letting Jack get under her skin.

But as she slipped through the heavy wooden door and spotted Jack in the corner, sipping on a short glass of something dark, her focus went out of the window.

In the darkness of the bar, with the slow sexy beat of the music in the background, Jack was looking...delicious. There was no other word. This wasn't work Jack—this was night-time Jack. And all those rumours about all those women suddenly became so much more believable. He had on a dark shirt, open at the neck but not too far so as to seem sleazy. As she got closer she noticed his black pants were pulled tight at his knees to expose some very nicely developed vastus lateralis muscles. She'd been trying to develop those muscles for two years, but her knees were still knobbly and the muscles there pathetically small. His were anything but small. Hard, muscular thighs.

He saw her and smiled and she steeled herself against the anxious flutter in her chest.

Don't look at his smile, look at his teeth. White, straight—perfect. *No, not helping. Look away.*

His hair. Look up. It looked thick and wavy and he was holding it up over his forehead. Very nice hair. *Don't look at his hair.*

His eyes. Dark and velvety. Chocolaty. Sexy. Bedroom eyes. *Definitely don't look there.* Especially not now he'd said she was gorgeous. Stunning. She remembered the way he'd said it. The word had rolled off his tongue like a thick, sticky liquor and she'd become stuck in it. Even now the word stuck in her head and wouldn't get out.

A lazy layer of dark stubble sat on his jaw. Good—she preferred clean-shaven. Except on him… She liked the stubble. She didn't want to but she did. It made him look a little rougher, a little more manly—maybe even a little dirty.

Oh, crap.

Movement rattled her core. Annoying hot, sexual movement. She tried to force it away but it swelled and intensified—as did her confusion about Jack and what she was feeling about him. She wasn't into all that He-Man stuff. Sensitive. Caring. That was what she liked. Stubble was not her thing. *He* was not her thing.

Focus on something else. His hands. They were resting on his knees as he sat in that wildly confident way some men did. Knees apart. On show. Boasting. *No! Don't look there.*

Concentrate. His hands. His fingers were long and his

hands looked solid. As if they'd never let go. She imagined he'd have a great grip for rope climbs. She wondered if he worked out. He raised his hand to wave and his shirt pulled at his shoulder. Yep. Definitely worked out. So definitely not her type.

Brooke swallowed hard and pulled at the collar of her shirt. She'd undone a few buttons so her bra just peeked out. She'd wanted to look sophisticated, in charge and in control. But now all she felt was exposed. She tried to cover herself up a little before pushing her lips into a wide smile and attempting to saunter towards him.

He didn't get up. Bad, *bad* man. He just smiled and said, 'You look incredibly sexy tonight. Hot date?'

Thank God it was dark, because a hot blush spread up Brooke's neck and into her cheeks. Of *course* he'd think she'd dressed provocatively for him. For him to enjoy. But that wasn't why she'd done it. She'd wanted to look like a woman in charge—she'd wanted to look stunning.

'No. I'm meeting an arrogant player who thinks he can win me over with a few free drinks.'

He smiled. Slow and sexy. And lust licked up around Brooke's body.

'Well, if I see him I'll get rid of him, because I want you all to myself tonight.'

Brooke stopped. What was *that*? A line? She didn't want a line. Anger mingled with the lust and her lust for him made her angry. Brooke felt her emotions bubble to the surface again. Nope. Zen didn't exist when she was around Jack. She needed to fix this. She needed to find out why he made her so angry. Tonight. She had to stop this and go back to the way things had been. However dull that was. She couldn't keep getting angry. Anger never solved anything.

'Jack, why am I here? What do you want?'

He turned his head and smiled at her. One of his fake smiles she was so used to.

'Why do you assume I want something?'

'You think it's amateur hour? I know all about you. I know the kinds of things you get up to.'

'Sounds like you Googled me. You're someone who graduated with a high distinction in marketing and business management—I would have thought your research abilities were better than that.'

'I can do more than use Google, Jack. You'd be surprised at the things I manage to dig up about people.'

'Would I? You graduated in the top ten per cent of the state six years ago, then studied at uni by distance because you started working for the family business the day after you left school. One of five highly competitive and athletic sisters. Mother Mandy, a former Commonwealth hurdler, and father Mark, head coach at the Australian Institute of Sport. You run marketing for the company, which has a current annual turnover of almost a million dollars—a turnover that is mostly due to your sisters' bravery and your marketing skills. Your favourite restaurant is La Galleria on Norton Street and your favourite bar is Tio's Tequila Bar in Surry Hills. You drink green tea, never coffee, and your cup size is thirty-two B.'

Brooke knew her mouth was open but she couldn't shut it. He was good. *Very* good. But clearly he didn't know everything. Although he did know her cup size? *Really?* How had he found that out?

'The internet does *not* give out information on cup sizes.'

'No…' Jack's eyes moved to her chest. 'That one I figured out by myself.'

Heat. More heat. Spreading across her chest and up her neck. She suddenly wondered if he liked small breasts.

What was she thinking? Jack Douglas would like *all* breasts.

'Fine. You know all my secrets. Time to tell me yours—why am I here, Jack?'

The waitress arrived back with her drink and made a show of setting up a napkin and making sure the straw was facing the right way. She was taking an awfully long time.

'Thank you.' Brooke looked up into two very large breasts. Definitely not thirty-two B. The waitress was leaning forward, her eyes fixed on Jack. Brooke turned to see Jack smile back at her. Right. Sleazebag. *So* not her type. She needed to get this over with.

When the waitress finally moved away, swaying her hips ridiculously as she walked, Brooke spoke. 'When you're finished lining up your next conquest, I'd like to know what you want from me.'

'You're a pushy little thing, aren't you?'

She hated being called little even more than she hated being called pushy. Even though she knew she was. But it was condescending and rude, and coming from Jack after the way he'd just ogled their waitress it made her even angrier.

'Yes, I'm pushy. Because I'm suspicious. I'm suspicious about why I'm here and what your motives are. But don't worry, Jack, it's not you. I'm pushy and suspicious with everyone.'

She'd always been that way. Sometimes she wished she was more trusting and easygoing, like her little sister Melody. She wished she could put on rose-coloured glasses and expect people to treat her with respect and be gentle. But people weren't like that. They were selfish. And most of the time they were too concerned with what was happening in their own little bubble to worry about hurting the feelings of those around them.

Jack smiled slowly. He leaned back, putting the heel of his shoe up to his knee. His muscles bulged. Brooke looked away. Muscles meant nothing to her. She spent hours in the gym with muscle-heads, and most of them had less between their ears than she had numbers in her little black book. Although she wasn't sure Jack was one of those guys who spent the hours they worked out taking selfies of their muscles. Jack seemed a little more worldly—a little more aware. Which made him infinitely more dangerous.

'That's interesting. Tell me more.'

Brooke smiled. 'Why would you think I'd tell you anything?'

'Because you're alone and you miss your sisters. Because you're feeling abandoned and you're angry and you need someone to talk to.'

Brooke opened her mouth to deny it but she couldn't. He knew exactly how she felt. How did he do that?

'Maybe I should be more like you and talk to no one about anything? Totally independent. An island.'

Jack's eyes hardened. 'No man is an island—haven't you heard?'

'*You* are.'

'That's where you're wrong, Brooke.'

Something in his tone stilled her. Something was different. *He* was different. As if he wanted to say something he wasn't saying. As if he wanted her to know something but couldn't tell her.

'Why can't you stand being touched?'

'What?'

'It's fairly obvious. Your eyes get all shifty whenever someone gets too close to you. You cross your arms and step back, and if anyone touches you I can practically see the hairs on your arms stand on end.'

Jack shifted, moving his leg back down. He moved forward, then back, before reaching for his drink again. When he'd sculled the last of it he motioned to the waitress. 'We're going to need a bottle of tequila, some lemon and some salt. And beers. Lots of beers.'

'I'm not drinking.'

'Yes, you are. You and I are getting ridiculously drunk tonight.'

'Why?'

'Because, Brooke, you make me uncomfortable. And the only way I can tell you what I want to tell you is if my brain is swimming in tequila.'

That statement sounded almost honest and it took Brooke aback a little that he'd admitted a vulnerability. A weakness. It seemed so off for Mr Cool to admit he was uncomfortable. Which was probably why she threw back two shots with him as soon as the tequila arrived a few minutes later.

After a long sip of beer Jack shifted back and Brooke shifted with him, resting her head on the cool leather cushioning of the bench seat. She turned her head to watch the side of his face.

'So are you going to tell me why I'm here? What you want from me?'

'I know why you're here, Brooke. I know you're trying to promote your family business.'

'So you mentioned.'

'Every person on this show has an agenda. Most are fame junkies, some are attention–seekers, and I suspect there are one or two who really are looking for love. But your motivation took me a little longer. Until that day on the beach and the red bikini. Which you looked unbelievably hot in, by the way.'

'I'm too skinny.'

'Your body is perfect. Strong. Healthy. Athletic.'

'I have no boobs.'

Jack turned to look at her breasts. He stared at them. Brooke felt heat rise up her throat as he studied her chest. His head moved and his eyes narrowed. Then—to her surprise—he lifted a finger and used it to pull her shirt aside. She slapped his hand away and shot him a horrified, disgusted look which he held. Steady. Her eyes against his.

No words were spoken but a conversation went on regardless.

How dare you touch me without permission?

You wanted an honest opinion on your breasts. I have to see them to give you one.

But I don't even know you and I definitely don't trust you. It's weird.

It's not weird.

Don't touch my skin.

I won't.

Don't check me out...sexually.

I will. But I won't touch your skin.

Brooke sighed, which meant, *Do it.*

So he did it, and even though he didn't touch her skin every cell on her body throbbed. Small bumps formed on her skin as the fabric slid away from her body. She felt the heat of his finger as it slowly traced her shirt, opening it wider so he could look inside. She watched his eyes—they were so close now. Dark and mysteriously unreadable. Then his lips parted slightly and her core throbbed even harder.

She wished he'd touch her skin. Accidentally. His

closeness reminded her of how long it had been since she'd been with someone. Since Mitch. Almost twelve months. Twelve months since a man's hands had made their way over her skin. Twelve months since she'd felt a man's lips on the back of her neck. Too long.

Jack's bottom lip stuck out and he moved his head from side to side before letting his finger drop from her shirt. But he didn't say anything.

'What's that supposed to mean?' she asked, anxiety bubbling in her chest. What the hell did that movement mean? Did he not like her breasts? What was wrong with them?

'Eh…' He shrugged and poured another two shots before settling back onto the leather seat to throw one back.

'Eh? *Eh?* That's what you have to say about my breasts? Eh? What the hell does *eh* mean?' He thought her breasts were *eh*? They were small, yes. But they were better than *eh*. Pig. Sexist pig. Knuckle-dragging, Neanderthal pig.

Brooke grabbed a shot and flung it back, enjoying the burn as it flew down her throat and into her stomach. Her head shifted. She hadn't been drinking much lately as she'd been focussing on training and the booze was going to her head. *Good.* She'd be able to say what she was thinking.

'Want to know what I think about *you*?' She was leaning forward now—too close for him to be comfortable, she knew, but she didn't care. Indignation burned at her temples.

'Not really, Brooke. You see—I'm not like you. I don't need people. I don't need their approval and I don't need anyone to like me.'

'Clearly. Is there actually anyone that you treat well?

Do you have any friends? What about your family? Are you as mean to them as you are to me?'

'I'm not mean to you, Brooke, I'm honest. There's a difference.'

'Yeah, there's a difference. It's called tact. If you were being honest you'd have some. Without tact you're just mean.'

Brooke was angry. Somehow this man always made her angry. Which was why the fact that she found him physically attractive was so annoying. And right now the way he was leaning back, all relaxed and comfortable, his dark hair sitting perfectly and a layer of stubble swathed across his jaw, he looked even more attractive than he ever had.

Brooke reached for the tequila bottle and poured two more shots. 'How about I employ your brand of tactless honesty? See how you like it?'

'Go ahead.'

He turned to smile at her and Brooke wondered how the hell he could look so boyishly gorgeous at the same time as looking like sex on a stick. It truly was a gift.

'I think you're lonely. I think you have Daddy issues. I think you have no friends because you have no idea how to treat people. I think you're mean and you're bad and you use your looks and your money to make friends and bed women. You're a bad person, Jack Douglas. Bad and mean.'

Brooke sucked back her tequila, not taking her eyes off him.

There was a pause before Jack lifted his head, held her eyes and spoke—in that deep, calm voice of his. '"Bed women"? Do people actually *say* that?'

'What? Yes. They do. Bed women. That's what you do.'

'Pretty sure I have sex with them. Sometimes I kiss them too.'

He smiled and Brooke felt it all across her body. The way he said sex. The way his eyes held her steady when he talked. The way his smile said *good boy* and his eyes said *badass sex god.* Brooke knew her breath was becoming shallower. She could hear herself breathing heavily and she wanted to stop it but she couldn't.

Slowly he reached for the bottle and topped up her shot glass before topping up his own. Then he drank and so did Brooke.

He placed his glass on the table and leaned in closer, his voice now dark and dangerous and way too deep to be legal. 'Sometimes I go down on them—and if they're very bad I might even spank them. *Bed* them hardly seems to say enough, does it?'

'No.' Brooke heard her voice squeak a little. 'It doesn't.'

Brooke leaned back. Away from his voice and his eyes and his provocative scent and those hands and those arms and his muscles and tattoos and everything else that was making the tequila rush to her head much too fast. No, no, *no*. Not this man. No.

'Jack.' There was a slight wobble to her voice so Brooke sucked in a breath. 'Why am I here?'

Thankfully Jack leaned back, too. But not before pouring another tequila and handing it to her. Brooke paused. Getting drunk was not a good idea. Not when thoughts such as what those vastus lateralis muscles looked like in the flesh kept pushing into her mind. She put the glass down and picked up her mineral water. She was here for business, not pleasure. He wanted something from her. Maybe if she gave it to him she could get the publicity she needed. But how much was that going to cost her? she wondered.

The pause after she spoke seemed to last a very long time. Jack looked down at his drink, then back up, then at her.

'I like you.'

'You *like* me?' Brooke was confused. What was he saying? The tequila was making her a little dizzy. 'What do you mean?'

'What do you think I mean?'

He looked away and stared into his drink again. What *did* he mean?

'I don't understand?' She felt anxiety coiled, poised. Ready to strike when he delivered his blow.

'I mean I like you. I like how you tell me things I don't want to hear. I like that you argue with me and fight with me and stop me from turning into…well, stop me from making bad choices. I want you and I to be…friends.'

He liked her. He wanted to be friends. Her friend. Not her lover?

She didn't want to be his friend. She wanted to kiss him and sleep with him and have him go down on her and spank her and all those other bad things he said he did. She didn't want to be friends. She wanted more and he didn't.

His rejection hurt. Just as Mitch's had hurt twelve months ago. Just as it had hurt when her parents had rejected her. It hurt and he wasn't getting away with it. Not this time. This time she was going to take it.

'No.'

'What?' Jack turned to her, clearly surprised.

'I said no.'

'No? No, I don't like you?' Now *he* looked confused,

as if he'd never heard the word *no*, let alone had anyone say it to him.

'No. You *do* like me. And I like you. But I don't want to be friends.'

'You don't?' He still looked confused as he turned the glass around in his hand. 'You don't want to be friends?'

'Stop saying that word.'

'What word? Friend?'

'Yes. *Friend.* I'm not your friend. Nor will I ever be your friend. I have enough friends. Real friends. Friends I actually like. I don't need any more friends.'

The silence that followed dragged out for what seemed like hours. Jack spun the glass in his hand. His right leg shook as he tapped his foot on the ground.

'Right. OK…' was all he said.

The silence stretched out for too many minutes. Jack didn't speak and neither did Brooke. But she didn't want to leave either.

'We need more tequila.'

Jack's eyes hit hers hard. She took him in—his dark eyes, the stubble on his jaw, his full lips. Her eyes trailed down his chest to the dark hairs that whispered at his neckline. She wanted him. She wanted to put her hands on him and her lips on him. She wanted him to feel something for her. She wanted him to stay.

Jack breathed in, long and hard. She waited for him to refuse her, for him to get up and leave. But he didn't.

'Hit me.'

CHAPTER EIGHT

THE TEQUILA WENT down fast. As it did so Brooke found her shoulders relaxing. She also found herself moving closer to Jack. Drunk Jack was a lot more entertaining that sober Jack. When he smiled at her Brooke noticed the crinkles at his eyes. Sexy. He was *so* sexy when he smiled.

'Tell me about you, Brooke. What were you like as a teenager? Wait—let me guess? Straighty-one-eighty, Miss Goody Two-Shoes, I-didn't-lose-my-virginity-until-I-was-eighteen?'

Brooke tried to be indignant but it was true. 'Nineteen, actually, and, yes, I was a good girl. Still am.'

'Good girls make the best bad girls,' he teased, his arm resting close to her shoulder but still not touching. Never touching.

Brooke felt her body heat. Mitch had never made her stomach flip and the heat curl low in her belly the way Jack did. 'Good girls make terrible bad girls. We think too much.'

'That's what makes you so good at being bad. You know what you're doing. When you decide to let yourself go you do it completely and without any hesitation. Confidence and knowing what you want is incredibly sexy.'

Brooke knew where this conversation was headed.

She really should stop it but the tequila said no. 'Sounds like you've had plenty of experience.'

'I have. But that's not a bad thing. It means you don't have to worry when you're with me. I'd satisfy you. I wouldn't give up until I did.'

'Ha! You wish.'

'I do wish, Brooke. I *do* wish.'

It was the sincerity in his tone that did it. It was the way he seemed really to mean what he said. Her brain knew that he didn't, but her stupid, needy, desperate tequila-laced heart wanted to believe he did.

Which was why she leaned in. Which was why she stared at his lips. And which was why, when the hotness of his lips met hers, she let herself go. Completely.

Jack pulled her bottom lip in between his teeth. This was what he'd been wanting to feel all night. Her. Close to him. So close he could taste her. And right now she tasted like lemon and salt and warmth and comfort and it was just what he needed. Especially after his terrific failure at actually trying to be honest with her earlier.

He'd struggled in the past few days. He'd thought about her so much. About the way she exposed his faults. The way she made him want to be better. He realised now it wasn't just lust. He liked her. Who she was. He wanted to let her in.

And then she'd arrived in her sexy shirt, almost open to the waist, and she hadn't let him get away with anything. She'd made him accountable, and she'd made him want to actually *talk*. She'd told him what she thought of him. That was unusual. People usually told him what he wanted to hear. He was surrounded by people too scared to annoy him, but she seemed to have no problem with it. Which was why he wanted more with her. But she'd refused. She'd said she had enough friends. *Real* friends.

But now she was moving her soft lips against his and exploring his mouth with her tongue—and it felt very friendly. And he wanted her close. Her hands snaked up his chest. He grabbed her wrists and held them back. She leaned against him, trying to press her skin to his, but he held her away. Her mouth he wanted close, but not her skin.

'Jack, what's wrong?'

'Nothing,' he murmured as his kisses moved from her mouth and down her neck.

She made a little mewling noise in the back of her throat and he knew he'd found her spot. It was at the base of her neck, and as she arched her back he kissed it again, letting his tongue flick the spot and his teeth tease her skin before soothing it with a hard kiss. She said she didn't want to be friends. He wanted more. Not just sex. *More*. But she didn't want that. He had to hold back. He couldn't fall. He couldn't get too close. He needed to protect himself.

'Jack…let me touch you,' she whispered as she pushed against his hands.

He had them held still. No, she couldn't touch him.

'Relax. Let me touch you.'

When he felt her wrists stop fighting against his hold he lifted a hand to cup her jaw and moved his mouth back to hers. Taking her lips, kissing her deeply, allowing her bad girl every excuse to escape. She was proving to be a wonderful bad girl. Responsive. Passionate. The noises she was making were making him even harder. The way she tried to push herself into him made his body heat and his brain blur. But not enough to stop him keeping her wrists held so she knew not to touch.

Slowly, carefully, he let his hand explore her skin. Down her jaw and neck and further down still, till he hit the soft mounds of her breasts. They *were* small, but perfect, and when he'd pulled her shirt away earlier he'd glimpsed a flash of dark pink. He wanted to feel her nipple now. Twist it between his fingers before licking at its hardness.

He moved his head and she seemed to encourage him as he kissed down her chest, but a loud cough to his right brought him back to reality. They were still in the bar. There were people either side of him. Public displays of affection were not his thing. He hadn't kissed a girl in a bar in years—too many camera phones had stopped that habit. But the combination of Brooke and tequila was making him do some very stupid things.

Like trying to get her naked right here in front of everyone. Like sleeping with a contestant. Like wanting more from her. That was a monumental mistake. Even through the tequila he knew that was wrong.

Quickly and efficiently he pulled her shirt back to where it was supposed to be and sat up. Brooke's eyes opened wide, as if she were coming out of a daze, and she rubbed the back of her hand across her mouth.

What the hell was he thinking? He'd become too carried away. She was so easy to talk to and she laughed in all the right places. It was as if he'd reverted back to his sixteen-year-old self for a second. Thinking that this girl was different. Thinking he could actually trust her. Of course he couldn't. The only reason she was here was to get publicity for her business, and the only reason she'd agreed to meet him tonight was because he'd forced her. Bullied her into getting what he wanted.

No, that wasn't him. He wasn't going to be like his father and make people do what he wanted even when they didn't want to. If she was going to be with him it would be because she wanted to. He had to pull back.

'Wow. I think we got a bit carried away.' A shy smile spread across Brooke's face and she lifted her eyes to his.

Jack's body tensed when he looked at her. Her hair was loose and curling round her shoulders, her lips dark red and her green eyes glowing in the low light. He wanted her even more than ever but he couldn't do anything about it. He had to stop. He could easily throw himself at her in here, but he wasn't going to do that. He liked her too much and that meant it would cut him too much when she left.

'We did. My mistake.'

No more tequila, Jack decided. Time for a real drink. He picked up the discarded Scotch on the table and took a sip. He hated the taste. He hated the burn. And he hated the way it reminded him of his father. Wouldn't his father celebrate if he could see him now? *Another mistake, Jacko? I knew you'd slip up.*

Jack sipped again—before almost spitting it out when he felt Brooke's hand on his thigh.

'What if it wasn't a mistake? What if it's what we both need?'

Jack felt his chest rise and fall. Something about Brooke made him uncomfortable. Not in a bad way but a confrontational way. She made him feel things he didn't want to and think things he wished he didn't have to. But he'd been handling it fine because she always delivered her messages with spit and fire. Now she was touching him, and her smile had gone sexy, and her lashes blinked. His eyes slipped to her breasts again. He wanted to touch them. He wanted to feel her body beneath him. And she wanted him—that was clear. But maybe it was just the tequila talking.

'What I need to do is take you home.'

Brooke's mouth drooped a little at the edges and he didn't like it that he'd done that. He liked it when he made her laugh. She had a wide smile and deep dimples, and when she flashed her white teeth she looked carefree and fun and everything he wished he could be.

'What's the matter? Are you scared?'

'Not scared. Sensible. You're a contestant. It's unethical.'

'What do you care about ethics?'

She had a point. 'I don't like messy.'

'Messy?'

Her eyebrows shot down and her hand moved away. Strangely, he missed it.

'It wasn't "messy" when you wanted to be friends—why would this be messy?'

'Because one of us would want more.'

Her smile was back. Wide and gorgeous.

'More? From you? I know better than to expect anything more from *you*.'

There it was. The reason she didn't want more. He wasn't good enough for her. Well, maybe he wasn't. But she didn't know that. She assumed she knew him. Had read about him in the papers, heard the rumours. But she didn't know him. She thought he just wanted sex. Well, he might as well live up to his reputation—she was determined not to like him anyway.

'Well, seeing as you expect the worst—let's go.'

She stared at him but didn't move. Just as he'd suspected. She hadn't meant what she'd said. She didn't want anything from him. He'd had enough. He wanted to go to bed. The tequila had given him a headache and with a staff meeting scheduled for tomorrow he was in for a big day. This woman was doing his head in. She was complicated and confusing and he wasn't in the mood any more.

'OK.'

It was so quiet he thought he'd misheard, but then she repeated herself.

'OK. Let's go.'

At those three words, Jack's whole body fired up. She'd said OK. She wanted to go home with him. The woman he wanted actually wanted him. But he shouldn't. She was a contestant and she was fiery and she could make trouble. *Sensible*. That was what he had to be.

But her hand was back on his thigh and she massaged the muscle just above his knee. Then he watched as her hand slid up his leg, closer and closer to his groin. Her pink-painted nails glowed against the lighting in the bar. He couldn't believe he wasn't throwing her hand off. He didn't want her to touch him. He never wanted anyone to touch him. But her hand was firm and confident—as if she knew what she wanted. Good girl gone bad. They were hard to find, but when you found one…

Brooke's hand expertly cupped him and he felt as if he was going to explode. He wanted to stop what she was doing but her hand moved again, up past his buckle and over his chest. As if she was feeling every inch of him. He didn't want her hands all over him but he couldn't stop her. He was mesmerised by her fingernails.

When her hands hit the skin of his neck he finally looked into her eyes. He saw lust and something else. Something deeper. She lowered her chin and her mouth was close again. He wanted to throw her back and kiss her. He wanted to have his hands all over her. But he held steady. He still couldn't figure out why he felt so much for her. It was almost chemical—like a magnet attracted to iron. He couldn't stop thinking about her and his mind refused to let him forget about her. Even though the logical part of his mind knew he shouldn't like her—the rest of him didn't care. He liked her. He wanted her. He had to have her.

Slowly, seductively, she leaned forward, and he felt her words on his ear before he heard them.

'Take me home, Jack, and make love to me.'

Jack didn't care if she was playing games. He wanted her and tonight she wanted him. He leaned in, catching a glimpse of her breasts, and touched his cheek to hers, wanting to feel her skin on his but needing to tell her what she needed to know. Needing to warn her.

'I want you *bad*.'

CHAPTER NINE

BROOKE LOST IT. She dropped her glass and it clattered onto the hardwood floor. She felt the breaths in her chest come way too fast. She needed air. She needed to breathe. But most of all she needed Jack Douglas. Tonight.

She didn't care what he meant about being friends. She didn't care that he was the producer. And she didn't care that soon she was supposed to meet her 'perfect match'. All she cared about was her skin being right next to his skin and his tongue sucking on her '*eh*' breasts.

'We need to leave.'

She didn't want to wait for the tequila to wear off or for herself to change her mind. Jack was bad and mean and no good. Perfect for one night of hot sex—which was exactly what she needed. No wonder she'd been so angry lately. Sex. That would fix it. After she had hot, hot sex with this very bad man she'd go back to being her normal, calm, sweet self. She could finish this stupid show and get the hell out of here.

'Leave?'

'Right now. We need to go.'

Brooke stood. If she didn't take him home right now the waitress would, and tonight *she* wanted him. She wanted to have sex with someone who knew what the hell they were doing. It had been too long. She'd been good for too long. Her sisters were right, she needed to do something mental to bust her out of the rut she was in. And Jack Douglas was certainly mental.

'Now.'

She didn't touch him but she gave him a look that she hoped left him in no doubt of her intentions. And if he was as bad as she suspected, and—let's face it—she knew he was, he'd follow her. He'd take her home and give her a seeing-to until she couldn't stand straight. Which was just what she needed, she'd decided. Or maybe the tequila had decided for her. Either way—it was happening.

Brooke walked out through the door with only a sliver of doubt that he'd follow. The doubt disappeared as soon as she felt the warm breeze hit her outside. She felt him behind her, heard his footsteps on the cobbles.

'Where are we going?'

Brooke turned, stopping but not touching him. 'Your place, obviously. There are eleven other women at my place.'

He smiled but didn't say anything. He didn't have to. She knew what he was thinking.

'I'm sure twelve women at once is a mild night for you, but tonight I want you all to myself. Just you and me—and you know what?'

'What's that, Brooke?'

She didn't miss the satisfaction in his voice.

'You're going to enjoy it. And you're going to make me enjoy it. You're going to pull out every trick you have in that bag of yours because I haven't had sex in twelve months and I need unbelievable sex tonight. Not good. Not even great. Un-freaking-believable. And, Jack? We're not friends. Can you do that?'

'I can try.'

'There's no *try*.'

Brooke turned to walk again. She wasn't sure where he lived, or where he was staying, but she wasn't about to stop and ask because if she did she might change her mind. She might think about tomorrow and how awkward it would be. She might also think about how she would probably enjoy it and might want to do it again, but he wouldn't, and then she'd get mad and offended and probably say something to him, and then he'd think she liked him and she'd try and explain that she didn't, and then he'd think she *really* liked him, and then she'd get really angry and start thinking about it and obsessing, and then she'd probably convince herself she actually wanted to see him again, and then he'd break her heart. *Sigh.*

Brooke stopped. This was going to end in tears, wasn't it?

'Something wrong?'

He was so close behind her but still not touching her. She wished he would touch her. Something to encourage her. Something to stop her from thinking and to remind her that this was about a bad boy and a night of fun.

Brooke breathed in a big gulp of muggy sea air. The tequila swam in her head. It was telling her things. Telling her to say things she didn't want to. But the tequila was strong.

'I haven't had a boyfriend in almost a year.'

Don't say that!

'Then you're well overdue for some attention.'

'My boyfriend left me.'

No! Not sexy.

'Your ex sounds like a jerk.'

'He's not. He wasn't. He was perfectly lovely and we were perfectly happy. One day he just didn't call. And he didn't answer my calls. And he was never home, and I couldn't get hold of him, and his friends kept feeding me excuses. I didn't know what the hell was going on until I saw a Facebook post a few weeks later. It was a picture of him and "his love". That's what he called her.'

Brooke didn't cry. She'd shed so many tears over Mitch that there were none left, but somewhere deep in her heart something twisted.

'He left me. Then he got someone else and posted it all over social media. Didn't even have the balls to tell me. Couldn't even give me a heads-up. Just humiliated me.'

Jack was silent behind her and she knew what he was thinking. She'd said too much. He didn't want to know. He didn't want heavy. He was a bad boy—he wanted light, fluffy bimbo. Not feelings. Bad boys didn't *do* feelings.

Bloody tequila!

Brooke started to walk before she thought about what she'd said and before he could say anything to her. She'd blown it. There'd be no hot sex with Jack tonight. She'd been humiliated by a man in the past—why the hell would she want to do something that was sure to lead to more humiliation?

Brooke's feet started to move faster and so did her anger. It escalated as she remembered every sexist, horrible thing Jack Douglas had done to her. It escalated when she thought of the girls back at the penthouse. All believing they were going to find their perfect match on the show. All believing that there was a man out there who was going to make them happy.

It seemed only she knew the truth. Men didn't make you happy—they made you miserable. The only person you could count on was yourself.

Brooke's feet stopped and a massive lump caught fiercely in her throat. Then why had she been so miserable since Mitch left? Why had she let her happiness depend on him being around? Mitch. Who had left her for no reason. Who hadn't even said goodbye. Who hadn't even had the decency to tell her it was over to her face.

He'd left her a message. A very public, very humiliating Facebook message on her wall. Everyone had known he'd left her. *Breathe in, breathe out.* She'd been humiliated. Exposed. Which was exactly what she was going to feel in a few weeks, when this show aired. When the men arrived tomorrow and she failed all the challenges and didn't get to meet anyone. When it was her time to fail, like Alissa had at the beach. *Keep moving. Keep walking.* She started to walk again.

'Brooke. Stop.'

Jack's deep voice was close behind her. Only a few steps away. The sound of it made her move. Quickly. But his long legs against her short ones meant he was keeping up. So she walked faster and faster, until both her feet were off the ground and she was jogging. But he was still keeping up.

'You can't outrun me, you know.'

Challenge accepted.

Brooke paused to slip off her heels and broke into a run. An all-out pelt up the Corso and across the road to the beach. The sand would slow him down. But it didn't. Once she reached the bottom of the stairs and her heels started to dig into the sand he was right beside her, arms pumping.

'Faster Brooke, faster!' She heard her father's voice ringing in her head.

She ran faster. Faster and faster towards the water. Wanting to get away. Wanting to forget. Wanting not to think, just to breathe and pump her legs.

When her feet hit the water it was cold and she braced herself as she dived in. She dipped her head, allowing the noises of the ocean to take all her thoughts and worries and anxieties and humiliations away. She swam and stood and dived and swam until her lungs burned. Then she stopped. She was a long way out. Past the breaking waves. The water was black and everything around her was black. She was alone, and the exhilaration she'd been feeling as she swam was quickly replaced with fear.

When Jack's arms grabbed her from behind her first feeling was an irrational terror that it was a shark. When she turned and looked at his face she realised he was a shark. He was beautiful. Wet and dripping, his face shadowed, his eyes hooded. He had his shirt off and he was panting and his eyes were fixed on her lips.

'I know you're angry, Brooke.'

His voice was low and deep and Brooke felt it rumble through her chest.

'I can make you feel better.'

Jack Douglas was a bad man. A man who partied hard, broke hearts and didn't care about anyone or anything. He *was* a shark.

'I want to make you feel better.'

Right now he was telling her exactly what she wanted to hear. He knew what he was doing. *She* knew what he was doing. But for some reason she couldn't stop pressing her lips to his and kissing him as if it was her last day on earth.

Brooke's body felt as good as it looked. Her skin was smooth where his hands explored her wet flesh. Jack pushed the fabric of her shirt out of the way so he could come into contact with her skin. His aversion to touching was forgotten as his other hand came up to cup her chin. She was beautiful—but here in the ocean, all wet and frantic, she was out of this world.

Her eyes closed as he let his mouth press to her lips. He pushed in hard and she met him. Her kisses weren't soft or tender, and her passion was turning him on. She wanted him badly and he felt exactly the same. Their tongues explored and her hands were moving as wildly as her lips, touching everywhere. He didn't mind. He wanted her close.

He pushed and she pushed, and while his legs paddled wildly to keep them afloat he pressed closer, making sure they were as close as two people could be. He wanted her close. He wanted to hold her up and keep her afloat. He wanted to take her anger away, make her forget.

Brooke wrapped her legs around his waist. She clearly wanted to get closer to him, and her desire was unexpected and all the more sweet because of it. He suspected that right now she was hurting and wanted to hurt him as well. She wanted to make him feel how angry she was.

Her teeth bit at his lip and he growled a little. He tasted the salt on her skin as he kissed past her lips to her ear, then down the milky column of her neck. She threw her head back and moaned wildly as his kisses made their way down her chest.

He needed more traction. He wanted to do more with this beautiful mermaid. He wanted to lay her in the sand and kiss her all over. He wanted to take her anger until she wasn't angry any more—just wild with passion. For him. And only him.

Jack pulled back quickly. What was he doing? She wouldn't want to be with him. Not when she met her perfect match. Not when she realised he wasn't good at communication and feelings and all the other things that went on in relationships.

'Don't stop.' Her voice was soft and demanding.

'We should go back to shore.'

'No!'

Her legs tightened around his waist, making his erection painfully hard.

'I want to stay here. With you.'

She kissed him again and he felt as if he were drowning in it. Every thought and reason flew from his head. All he could concentrate on was the way his heart was beating faster and how he wanted to get close, closer to her and her skin, and her mouth and her hands. Her small body clung to him and he wrapped his arms around her, holding her close, wanting this to be something that it wasn't. He knew what this was. A fleeting moment of lust. He had to stop it before he got in too deep.

Pulling her arms from around his neck, he met her eyes. 'Brooke, we have to go back.'

She understood. He saw her eyes searching his. She was thinking, but he didn't know what.

When she let him go he felt cold and bare and he hated that he felt it. This was why you couldn't get close. The confusion and the wondering what the other person was thinking. He'd not had a relationship yet that was honest and he was sure it would be the same with Brooke. She confused the hell out of him already, with her arguing and fighting and then her unexpected kisses.

He watched as she took skilful strokes through the water to the shore. He wasn't a strong swimmer. He hoped she didn't turn around when she reached the sand to watch him. She was athletic—good at everything. He wondered how she did that. And she was smart and hot. She was stunning and special.

But not *his* special, he reminded himself as his feet finally hit the sand and he was able to stand and step over the gently rolling waves to the shore. His breathing was heavy. He hadn't been to the gym in three months. Ever since work on this show had started.

He missed it. He missed seeing his workout on the board and thinking there was no way he'd complete it in time, then the satisfaction when he did. He felt unfit right now, and he was sure Brooke would want someone fit. She was so fit herself. Women like her put value on health and fitness and he caught himself wishing he were fitter. Wishing he could impress her—because so far he hadn't been able to, and that was starting to bother him.

When he made it past the water she was waiting for him. Soaking wet. Her hair was pulled back and her face was shining in the moonlight. He'd never wanted to kiss anyone more, but he didn't. He couldn't. This would never work. She'd get hurt, and something deep inside him knew he didn't want to hurt her.

But she didn't give up that easily. She stepped forward, wrapped her arms around his waist and leaned her head on his chest. That was all. Just quietly stood there, hugging him tight. It was an intimate feeling and he wanted to push her away. Explain that he didn't *do* intimate. But right then it seemed as if she needed him and he liked it. She needed comfort and warmth and understanding and he wanted to give it to her.

He let his arms envelop her. Maybe he couldn't give her a lifetime of happiness, but he could give her a moment. He could make her feel better for now. As his arms tightened she looked up. The smile she gave him was relaxed and grateful and he was so glad he'd done that. He liked to make her smile even more than he liked to fire her up. Which was why he leaned down to kiss her.

But the comforting kiss soon turned into something more. Her hands explored his chest, her tongue eager and exploring. He let his hands rest on either side of her face, keeping her still, keeping her there—not letting her go. Something wild and frantic built inside him. He wanted her. He needed her. He had to have her. Here. *Now.* Carefully and quickly he wrapped one arm behind her back and let her fall to the sand.

Brooke wasn't angry any more. The emotion she was feeling now was something else. Something much more desperate. She wasn't sure if it was still the tequila doing the thinking, but right now she felt something from Jack she hadn't felt in a long time. He wanted to please her. He wanted to comfort her. And she was grateful—because she was lonely and sad and angry and his comfort was exactly what she needed.

When he pushed her back into the sand Brooke felt strangely safe. He was strong and he was leading her to where she needed to be. She didn't have to think—all she had to do was feel.

'Are you sure you want to do this? With me?'

When she looked at him she was surprised at the uncertainty in his eyes. She'd never seen that look before. She hadn't ever considered he'd be insecure. Didn't he realise how much she wanted him?

'Yes. I want this. I want *you*.'

He didn't smile, but he held her eyes before kissing her. His soft lips soothed her and Brooke's head swam. She thought of nothing but him, and the weight of him on top of her, and the feeling of his hands running over her body.

Keeping one hand on her waist, with the other he pulled at her shirt. Moved the wet fabric aside, as well as the bra underneath, to expose her thirty-two B breasts. His tongue laved at her nipple and any residual anger in Brooke's head gave way to something else. A pleasure that made thinking impossible. That made reason vanish. She just wanted more. More of his mouth and more of his tongue and more of *him*.

The cool night air hit her nipples and they hardened. He took them in his mouth again before allowing his lips to trail further down her stomach. With a tug he managed to get her wet jeans off. He threw them in a heap on the sand and Brooke clawed at him, trying to get him back up to kiss her again. But he didn't. He stayed where he was.

'You're beautiful,' he murmured as his tongue licked around her lower stomach.

Brooke lay still in anticipation of his touch. Of his tongue. His kisses moved lower and she opened her legs, allowing his head to get closer. She watched him. Watched the way his eyes eagerly drank her in. She watched his hands as they stroked her thighs, and then she watched as he trailed one finger through her wetness.

'So wet… So hot…' he murmured, before allowing his face to fall and his tongue to push in, searching for her clit.

Brooke arched her back in delight. She moaned, grabbed at the sand, trying to get some traction—but there was none so she reached for his shoulders instead. Looking down, she watched him as ripples of pleasure shuddered through her. She pushed her pelvis up, wanting to get closer, needing him to go deeper, and he obliged. His tongue worked like magic and he sucked gently, making her groan even louder.

This was what she needed. Pure release. With a man who knew what he was doing. Mitch had never done this properly and he'd certainly never been this enthusiastic.

Jack's head moved a little from side to side and Brooke almost screamed. That slight movement had his tongue hitting every G-spot she had. She wanted more…she needed more. She was building fast.

'Don't stop,' she moaned, pushing herself closer and closer to him.

He didn't stop. His movements became more frantic. His tongue started to move in and out and up and down and then he made a low, growling noise that she felt reverberate through her whole body.

That did it.

The orgasm started down low but once it took hold Brooke couldn't stop it. It grew inside her like a werewolf howling at the moon till she felt it burn through her veins, up her stomach and into her arms. Her whole body shook and still he didn't stop. She felt him suck and the orgasm shot through her again, even more powerful than before.

'Stop, stop! You have to stop.'

She pushed on his shoulders, trying to get him to release her. She was swollen and sensitive and her brain felt as if it were about to burst.

With one last tender kiss, Jack moved. He looked up, his face flushed and his eyes glowing.

Brooke didn't move. She couldn't. Her body lay in satisfied pleasure.

'That was…that was…' She couldn't speak. She couldn't explain how good she felt.

Then she felt him next to her. His arms weren't on her, but he lay next to her. His skin was still wet but she was hot so it felt good.

Brooke lay panting for a few more minutes before she turned in the sand to look at him. He had one hand behind his head and was staring up to the moon, but he turned when she looked at him. A slow smile spread across his face.

'Feeling better?'

'Much better.'

Brooke shifted and spread an arm across his chest. She felt him immediately stiffen beneath her so she withdrew her arm. Even after what had happened he still didn't want her to touch him. She should have been offended, but she was too relaxed and relieved to feel anything but curiosity.

'Why don't you like being touched?'

'I do. I was enjoying you touching me earlier.'

He was smiling, but she wasn't fooled.

'That's different. You don't like anyone hugging you or putting their hands on you. You get nervous when I touch you. Like right now—you went stiff when I tried to cuddle you. And today, in the hospital, you hated that I was holding your hand.'

He was quiet and Brooke turned to face the moon, wondering if he'd answer.

'I don't like insincerity.'

'Touching is insincere?'

'It is when you hardly know someone. I just don't understand why you would want someone that close to you.'

'Because it feels good. Because everyone needs physical touch. Because people like to feel loved and cherished and they want pcople to show them.'

'I just don't like lies.'

That made Brooke turn. 'That's hilarious, coming from you.'

His eyes met hers. They were hard and challenging. 'I may be an emotionless, indifferent, unfeeling, apathetic bastard—but I'm not a liar.'

Brooke laughed. She couldn't help it. There clearly was no one who could abuse Jack better than he could himself. 'You're a bit hard on yourself, lover.'

Jack propped himself up on his hand and looked at her, his smile back. 'Lover? Is *that* what I am?'

'Yes. You are. If you think we're not going to do that again you're wrong. That was…you were…magnificent. And I *don't* think you're emotionless and indifferent and unfeeling and—what was the other thing?'

'Apathetic.'

'Right. Apathetic. I think you're passionate and thoughtful and you care more than you think you do.'

Jack didn't take his eyes off her. He watched her watching him and Brooke started to feel an uncomfortable feeling settle over her. As if she was thinking too much about him and wanting too much of him. But then she felt the warmth of his hand on her shoulder. Brooke held her breath as his hand slid down her arm to her waist, where it rested. She knew what this was. Jack's form of post-sex snuggling.

Brooke sucked her core in tight. She didn't know what it meant, but it made her nervous. Something was happening and she was very afraid it was another thing she wouldn't be able to control.

CHAPTER TEN

TODAY THE MEN were arriving. The tone of the show was about to change. Testosterone was about to be introduced, meaning more aggression, more competition and even more drama. Perfect. Just what the show needed.

Jack sat watching the reel Mick had edited so far. It had the lot. Dramatic scenes, backstabbing, lots of flesh and a few tears. His blood was running hot. He was sure this time he'd have a hit. He'd managed to find that perfect combination of personalities and format. This show would be a success and then he could get out. For good. Away from this lifestyle, away from these people and away from the rumours.

But Jack's shoulders were still tense and tight. This wasn't over yet. But—surprisingly—he wasn't worried. Far from it—he was excited. He was fired up. He kept shooting questions and suggestions at Mick. He wanted to watch the reels again and again. He felt buzzed, as if he'd spent the night drinking coffee. But he hadn't. He'd spent the night alone in his bed. Not sleeping, but being kept wide awake by the memory of two green eyes, a petite body and a pair of thirty-two B breasts.

Brooke Wright shouldn't be stuck in his head. But she was. The way she tasted when he kissed her salty skin. The way her frantic kisses made him feel bigger, stronger and needed. She was desperate for him, angry and crazy, and he shouldn't even be thinking twice about her, or that kiss, but it was stuck in his head. *She* was stuck in his head and he couldn't shake her. And somewhere in the night he'd had an epiphany.

'It's good, Jack, but…'

'But what?'

'The female audience are not going to like the men calling the shots.'

'No, they're not. Which is why we're switching it up. The women are going to determine the challenges.'

Mick didn't move. He was waiting.

'We've been concentrating too much on drama for getting our ratings, Mick, but we were wrong.'

'We were?' Mick asked quietly.

'We were. We need to focus on emotions. On relationships. We need the drama to come from the way the women *feel*. If we leave it up to the men this will all be about ridiculous and demeaning challenges. That's surface stuff. We're going to dig deeper—and who better to dig deeper and get to the core of something than a woman?'

Mick stayed silent.

'The women will determine the challenges—they'll make the men work for them. They'll force the men to talk and to feel and to try harder. That's good TV.'

Mick breathed in through his nose quickly, then released it slowly. 'It's risky, Jack. It's harder to capture emotion on tape. It's harder to edit. It'll take longer, and it'll cost more.'

'But it will make better TV and that's the point.'

Jack waited. If Mick didn't agree he wasn't sure what he'd do. He respected Mick. His opinion was like gold in this industry. He'd been around for ever, had seen everything. He knew what worked and what didn't. And Jack wanted this to work. Not just because he believed in it but because it was the right thing to do. He'd forgotten what TV shows were about as he searched for ratings and audiences and advertising dollars. Storytelling. Emotions. Human reactions. And that was what he needed to get back.

'Let's give it a go.'

Jack breathed out and slapped Mick on the back. Today was a good day.

Jack paced his office floor one more time. The sound of Brooke's heavy breathing in his ear rang through his brain. He thought of the feel of her skin under his hands, smooth and wet. His chest actually hurt, thinking about her. He was seventeen again and finding it very hard to control himself. He'd tried not to think about her, tried to distract himself as he sorted out the last of the male contestants and rewrote the format. But it wasn't working.

He found himself reaching for his car key, determined to drive over there and find out what she was thinking and if she'd changed her mind about being friends. But he stopped himself. She didn't want more. If she did she'd have contacted him. She'd have let him know. But she didn't. He had to get that through his thick head.

With the editing done it was time to get to the penthouse and start getting the girls ready for the big scene later on today. Meeting the men. And letting them know that *they*—the women—were now determining the challenges. He was looking forward to it, but more than that he was looking forward to seeing Brooke again. Which he knew he shouldn't be.

Ever since they'd met he'd known there was something between them. A little spark of sexual energy that he'd thought would go nowhere. She had seemed too uptight to do anything like she had the other night. And the other night she had been anything but uptight. No—stop. He had to shake this off. He needed to go for a workout, a run—or maybe go and have sex with a beautiful stranger. Anything to get Brooke and her green eyes out of his head.

But he didn't want to have sex with anyone else. He wanted to finish what he'd started with her.

He drove silently through the city and back over the bridge to Manly. The sun was out and burning even brighter today. A perfect Sydney Sunday. Jack hadn't felt this fired up in years. Today's shoot was a big one. The girls were spending most of the day in hair and make-up—getting styled for the big meet-and-greet this afternoon. The men were being bussed in at three. This scene was important. He needed to make sure there was enough sex in the air to make it spicy and enough tension to have everyone almost wetting themselves in anticipation.

He didn't usually get this involved in the day-to-day of any show. But this time he was determined to be there every step of the way. This time there would be no mistakes like last time.

A flashback of the fight scene ran through his mind. If he had been there he would have stopped it from getting out of control. The scene had rated well, but the complaints afterwards had seen the show pulled off the air and millions go down the drain. His father hadn't been impressed. Jack had dreaded the call from his house in Italy.

'How the hell did you let that happen, Jack?'

Useless, stupid idiot...should have known better than to leave you in charge...

It had been his father at his worst.

The names and jibes hadn't bothered him. He'd already heard everything his father could possibly call him throughout his life. But the way he'd felt afterwards had. He'd been used. Manipulated. He'd assumed someone needed him and they hadn't. He should have known not to get so close. But he'd been younger then. Filled with ridiculous heroic tendencies. Now he was older and knew that getting too close always ended in disaster. You couldn't trust anyone.

He could see some of the girls up on the balcony as soon as he pulled up. He'd collected twelve of the most beautiful women in Australia for this show. Blonde, brunette, redhead—they were all gorgeous. But none was more stunning that the woman he was now trying to forget.

Brooke's chest hurt from the rapid beating of her heart and her dry throat itched. She checked the clock. Ten minutes till Jack Douglas arrived. Ten minutes till he walked through that door, all smiles and cockiness, and ten minutes till all her pride disappeared. Her entire insides felt as if they were going to come up out her throat.

Why the hell had she done that the other night? Why the hell had she let her emotions turn into something she really didn't want? Before, Jack Douglas had been a player, but she had had his number. She'd been driving the bus. But now she'd kissed him. She'd opened her legs for him and pushed her nipples wantonly into his mouth. Now *he* was driving the goddamn bus and she wanted to get off.

It had been three days since they'd had fun in the sand. He'd taken her home. Kissed her goodnight, then left. She'd waited to hear from him—sure he'd felt something. But clearly he hadn't. She hadn't seen him or heard from him and now she felt stupid. He'd been drunk on tequila that night. He hadn't really wanted to do that and he didn't want any more. He'd made no promises, but she'd assumed. She'd assumed he wanted as much as she did. And now here she was—disappointed and angry and feeling like a fool.

Breathe. Deep breaths. That was what she needed.

Around her nervous excitement was almost making a fog in the air. The other girls were sipping champagne and their voices were getting higher and higher. The men were arriving today. Their competition on the beach had been a warm-up. A prelude to the *real* competition. She suspected the producers—or Jack Douglas—had wanted the girls to bond and make friends before the men arrived. That way, when they started getting their hearts broken and getting rejected, their responses would be even more dramatic.

She knew what he wanted. A few 'That-Bitch-Stole-My-Man' moments. Great TV. But an awful, awful thing to create. Did the man have no shame? No. Of course not. He didn't even *know* her. He'd known she'd had too much to drink. He'd known she was angry and upset and he'd taken advantage of her. He had no morals. No idea of consequences. Just as she'd assumed, Jack Douglas was a take-whatever-he-wanted kind of guy.

And in ten...no, *eight* minutes he was going to walk through that door, throw her a knowing wink and shatter her confidence. Which was something she didn't really need. Not now the men were arriving. Twelve tall, handsome men. Twelve men and one perfect match. Twelve men she wouldn't even get a look-in with. Because she would only be able to go on dates with them if she won the challenges—and she never won anything.

If there was ever a time she'd needed to talk to her

sisters it was now. She needed Maddy to calm her down, Melissa to tell her she was awesome, and Melody to… Well, Melody would just ignore Brooke's problems and talk about her own. But that would be fine! At least Brooke wouldn't have to talk about her own problems then. She'd be distracted and she wouldn't keep checking the clock…

Seven minutes. She started to pace. She joined a small circle of three women in the lounge. She needed to find her Zen. Jack could throw whatever he wanted at her, but she was going to remain Zen. *Breathe.*

'I wonder if they'll be hot?' Katy looked at the other girls anxiously.

'Of course they'll be hot. They don't put *fuglies* on a show like this. Who wants to watch fuglies?' Alissa was back to her normal self and completely over her near-drowning experience.

'I don't care what they look like. I'm after a man with a good heart,' another girl said.

'What about you, Brooke? What are you hoping for?'

Brooke almost spat out her sip of water—she didn't trust herself around alcohol any more.

'What?'

'What are you hoping these men are like? What's your perfect match?'

Her perfect match? Jack's face swam in front of her eyes. His muscled body and those tattoos that skipped all the way down his arm to his wrist. She remembered how good it had felt when he'd finally let his palm run over her arm to her waist. Then, when it had travelled back up and his thumb had rested on her bottom lip, he had kissed her. Long and hard and deep.

Everything in Brooke's core suddenly went hot and heavy. He wasn't her perfect match. He was careless and thoughtless and he hadn't called in three days. She *hated* him.

Brooke shifted her eyes, aware of the cameras all around them. There were even more than normal here tonight. Set up right in their faces. Waiting for every word. Brooke smoothed down her skirt and shifted. She was wearing a Wright Sports watch tonight. She moved her hand, trying to get it into the shot. That was what she was here for, she reminded herself—not to meet her perfect match!

Everyone was waiting for her response. She checked her watch. Three minutes. What was she going to say? What would her sisters want her to say? What would be the best thing to say for the sake of the business? What could she say that wouldn't make her look like a fool in front of the man who was now making her armpits feel like the inside of a Swedish sauna?

'My perfect match is a nice cup of tea and a piece of chocolate cake.' She smiled.

The women laughed. Except for Katy.

'No, really, Brooke—what are you looking for?'

Brooke glanced at her. Katy *knew*. She knew Brooke was avoiding the subject. She wanted the truth.

Katy had been up when she'd got home the other night, and even though Brooke hadn't told her what had happened Katy had known something was wrong. She'd been asking her for days if she was OK.

'It was a joke, Katy.'

'You're so funny, Brooky,' said Alissa, giving her an embrace.

Katy didn't say any more. Brooke's shoulders relaxed. She still missed her sisters, but somehow these women had become her temporary family. She wasn't even as angry any more. The girls had begun to recognise when she was firing up and now they helped her calm down. Backed off. Gave her food. Told her a joke. She'd even started to enjoy herself.

Until she saw a camera and realised that none of it was real. Just as the other night hadn't been real. Nothing Jack had said or done had been real.

Except that orgasm.

Brooke folded her legs tighter as heat surged there. That had been real—and unbelievable—and the most stunning orgasm she'd ever had. And, although it annoyed her, she wished she could feel it again. But she knew she couldn't. That was over.

Brooke's thoughts were interrupted by a flurry of activity at the door. More cameras had arrived. Producers had started to make their way through the door and Brooke held her breath, waiting for her first glimpse of the man she'd decided she'd never wanted to see ever, ever again.

Jack's eyes scanned the room from outside the door. He looked at each of the faces of the twelve women assembled but saw none of them except the one face he couldn't get out of his mind. Brooke—like the rest of the women—looked angry and shocked.

Something about her look made his stomach drop. What had happened *now*? He wanted to go to her. He wanted to put his arms around her, make her laugh—take her anger away. But he couldn't Not here.

'Jack, we've got problems.'

Mick was at his side and his quiet voice sounded anxious. Mick was never anxious—which put Jack immediately on alert.

'What's happened?' Jack looked around. Some of the

women looked noticeably shaken. A couple were on the couch, comforting each other.

'Rob Gunn was here before you.'

'What?' Rob Gunn? His father's hotshot producer? What the hell had *he* been here for?

'The format is staying as it is, Jack. The men are determining the challenges. Rob announced it all to the girls—said they had to fight for their places. Told them to consider their friends their enemies and reminded them this is a competition. It wasn't good, Jack.'

Jack's blood burned red. His father had done this. His father had sent Rob here. He'd known it was a mistake to have told him about the revised format. He'd known he should have done this on his own.

'Where is he now?'

'Gone. But he showed me his contract, Jack. Signed by your father. It's legit. He's in charge now.'

Anger burned white-hot in Jack's ears. Not this time. Jack was in charge and his father wasn't calling the shots here. *He* was. He'd had enough—enough of playing his father's game, enough of putting up with his father's demands and enough of not getting angry. Tonight he was taking control of his life.

'Get him on the phone, Mick. This ends now.'

'This is ridiculous.'

When the door had opened and the stranger had appeared Brooke had known immediately that something was up. Where was Jack? Who was this new man? And when the perpetually happy man who'd said his name was Rob Gunn had announced that the men would be setting the challenges, and that there would only be four men, Brooke's anger had fired up again. It was bad enough she had to compete in challenges, but challenges chosen by four men who all seemed as if they shared half a brain between them was quite another thing.

'Since when do the men get to choose the challenges? The original format said we'd complete challenges set by the producers and we'd get to choose the men. What's going on?'

Rob Gunn had left now, but Mick had just come back into the room. He didn't appear to have much to say.

'Where's Jack? Does he know about this?'

'Look, ladies, I don't know what's going on right now. This was Jack's original idea but…'

This was *Jack's* idea? Of course it was. He was a sexist pig, she reminded herself. No matter how good he was at convincing her that he wasn't. No matter how talented he was with his tongue.

'This is embarrassing and demeaning. You can't make a major change like that without telling us.'

Mick stood. He rushed over to her and the cameras fell back.

'No, Mick!' Brooke's voice was getting louder. 'It's not right. Do you mean to tell me that now only four women will have the chance to meet their perfect match? That now we'll have to fight each other for the chance? This is silly.'

Mick was trying to calm her down, but she didn't want to be calmed down. This was outrageous.

'Calm down, there, love. All you girls have an equal chance of getting to meet us. There's no need to get your knickers in a knot—*you* might be one of the lucky ones.'

One of the four men Rob Gunn had introduced earlier spoke up.

Brooke turned slowly. She stared at him. 'My knickers are none of your business—*love.* And I can tell you right now I would be anything *but* lucky if I ended up with *you*.'

'Brooke, calm down. Jack will be here soon. I'll talk to him. We'll get this sorted. Just wait. Sit. Wait. I'll talk to Jack.'

'You'd better.'

She knew this wasn't Mick's fault, but her blood was boiling and her bones were shaking. She *wouldn't* fight the other women for these men. She *wouldn't* pit herself against women she'd become friends with. And if Jack thought he was going to make her he clearly didn't realise how angry she could get.

CHAPTER ELEVEN

JACK'S ANGER HAD subsided. A little. He'd managed to gain back a little control. He'd finally tracked down Rob Gunn, who was hiding in a luxury apartment owned by Jack's father. Jack had laid down the law. Told him to stay the hell away from the set *and* the girls.

Rob Gunn had reached for his phone, but Jack had reached for his as well. He'd done his research. He knew about the formal complaints of sexual harassment brought against Gunn in his last job. He knew Gunn wouldn't want that made public.

It had been enough to get rid of Gunn, but not his father. His father was adamant the format stayed the same, determined that the men would be calling the shots. Jack knew that was suicide. Women would hate it and they were the ones watching. It would turn them off. There'd be no chance of a spin-off. And, more important than that, it wasn't the right thing to do. Brooke had made him realise that.

The next person he wanted to see was his mother. He wanted to make sure his father didn't get to her first.

But he was too late. When he got to his mother's house her eyes were bloodshot and her normally perfect hair was in a mess.

'I yelled at him, Jacky…'

Jack remembered the way his mother's eyes had used to look. Soft and blue and wrinkled at the sides. Now she used Botox. It kept the wrinkles at bay. She didn't need it. He preferred the way she looked without it.

'It's all right, Mum, you don't have to worry about it. I have it under control.'

His mother had been pouring herself a drink and Jack jumped as he heard the glass smash against the wall. Quickly he went to his mother. It wasn't like her to lose her temper. His father must have really rattled her, Jack fumed. Right then he made his mind up to get on a plane to Italy and sort that man out once and for all.

'No, Jack, I *do* have to worry. I don't want you to fight for me. You're my son—not my protector. It's time I fought for myself.'

Jack stilled. His mother's voice was raised. She never raised her voice. She was always cool. Always calm.

'Mum, what's wrong? What did he say to you?'

'Nothing! Nothing more than what he usually says. It's not him that's making me angry now, Jack, it's *you*.'

'Me?' He'd done everything to try and fix this.

'Yes—you. When are you going to learn? When are you going to grow up? When are you going to realise that you can't control your father? He's the type of man who does whatever he wants.'

'I know who he is, Mum, but that doesn't mean he can treat you like he does.'

'Oh, Jack…' His mother poured the drink and fell into a nearby armchair. She lifted her arms, took her earrings out and placed them on the table next to her. 'Honey, sit down. It's time we talked.'

So Jack sat. And he listened.

'Your father is a passionate man. He throws himself headfirst into things. That's his charm. That's what I fell for. When we met he chased me. He pursued me and made me feel I was the only girl in the world. I felt like the most important person in the world. I thought that meant he loved me. But I was just something he wanted. After he had me the novelty wore off. He moved on. I could have left. I considered it. But you were so young and you loved him—he was so good to you then. He'd take you everywhere with him and lavish you with presents and attention.'

'And then he'd leave.'

'Yes, then he'd leave. But you have to realise that people don't always stay. People like your father have a full tank of love but they use it up quickly and madly. Then they need to leave and go and fill that tank again.'

'That just sounds like an excuse for him to do whatever the hell he wants.'

'I could have left, Jack, but what would have been the point? I loved your father. I wanted him so badly I was willing to put up with him going elsewhere because I knew he'd come back. He always came back.'

'You *knew*?' Jack felt the blood drain from his face.

He reached for his mother's hand but she pulled it away. His mother didn't like touching either.

'Of course I knew, Jacky.'

She knew. He'd been trying to protect her, but she knew. And she didn't look sad—just exhausted.

'I should have ended it years ago. I should have been more angry. I should have yelled and screamed and demanded he stay with me. But I didn't. I shut up and I put up.'

Jack finally really saw his mother. For the first time. Not as someone who needed his protection, but someone who needed his love. His mother had lived for thirty years with little affection. Always feeling second-best. He saw how lonely she was. She was right: she should have got angry years ago. Just as he was angry now.

'Never again.' When she looked at him determination lit his mother's eyes. 'Your father will be back—when this affair is over—but this time I won't be there. I'm tired, Jack, and I'm lonely. I need to find someone who cares about me. I need to be happy and it's taken getting angry for me to be able to do that.'

'Do you love him?'

'Do I *love* him? I have no idea—I'm not sure I even know what love is any more. Or if I'll ever meet anyone I love as much as your father. But the truth is all you can really hope is that you'll meet people to spend a few moments of your life with. Share some good times. Make some wonderful memories. I don't know if I'll love again, Jack, but it doesn't matter because I have you. I love you, and you love me, and our love is stronger and more real than any love I'll ever have with a lover.'

Jack stared out of the window as he approached the bridge. He'd spent so many years worrying about his mother, thinking she needed his protection. But that wasn't what she needed. She just needed *him*. Being there and making her laugh when she needed it. Letting her know that she was loved when she'd spent so much time feeling unloved.

He wished his mother had got angry years ago. He wished she'd realised years ago that his father was never coming back. But she was angry now and Jack was pleased for it.

The girls looked nervous when he arrived for the challenge. They were being kitted out in climbing suits and ropes. He wasn't sure if Brooke looked nervous or not because he didn't want to look at her. He remembered the sadness in his mother's eyes. Loving someone who didn't love you back was pointless. He wasn't going to make the same mistake his mother had made.

'OK, ladies. You're all ready—it's time to climb the magnificent Harbour Bridge!'

The girls tittered and giggled and they set off, led up the stairs by the climb leader. Only one woman remained behind.

'Come on, Brooke, we have to stick together—we're all joined.'

Finally Jack looked at Brooke's face. This wasn't just nerves. Real fear spread across her features. Brooke was scared and he couldn't just stand back and watch. Not when he knew how brave and strong she normally was.

'Brooke, what's wrong?'

Brooke didn't look at him. Her face had gone white and she was gripping the rails on either side of her.

'Nothing.'

'Brooke, it's OK. It's safe. You're connected by ropes. You can't fall.'

Brooke finally met his eyes. 'Yes, I *can* fall. It's too high. I can't do this,' she whispered.

Jack had never seen Brooke like this. She was genuinely frightened. He wanted to tell her not to do the challenge. He wanted to take her away and make her feel better, But he couldn't. The cameras were rolling. He shouldn't even be talking to her. But he couldn't leave her. He knew no one else would be able to help.

'You won't fall. I'll come with you. I'll stand right behind you.'

He could see in her eyes that she wanted to say no. She wanted to tell him she could do this on her own but the fear was clearly too much. She took one hand off the rail and grabbed his forearm, holding him tight. He reached out and held her arm, not once wanting to throw her hand off.

It had been over a week since he'd touched her. Over a week since he'd felt her skin. He missed it. He missed her. But he had to push all that away.

'Don't let me fall.'

Jack held on tight and let his gaze fix hard on hers.

'I won't.'

The view from the top was not what Brooke was expecting. She'd expected to open her eyes, look down and see death swirling beneath her. But when she opened her eyes she didn't see death—or near-death. She saw sky. Wide, blue sky. She felt the wind as it picked up her hair and the breeze as it tickled behind her ears, cooling her body.

'Just breathe it in.'

Jack's voice was calming her. Like it always did. But it shouldn't. His voice should mean danger and warnings and everything that was bad. But it didn't.

'Don't look down. There's nothing interesting there. Look up. Out there—past the city.'

Brooke looked up and saw the clouds as they moved slowly. She couldn't hear anything but Jack's voice, and the hum of the traffic below muffled the squeals and giggles and conversations around her. Jack moved a little closer. Not close enough to touch—he'd never do that. But close enough that she could feel him. Big and strong and solid. If she fell he'd reach out and stop her.

Brooke breathed in deeply. The air was different up here. Cleaner, crisper—but thinner. She needed to breathe again and again just to stop her heart beating so fast. She was angry with him for not calling. For forgetting about her. But the emotion running through her right now wasn't anger—it was fear.

'It's different to what I thought it would be.'

The city didn't look real from up here. It looked like an animation. A pretend city you'd see in a boy's train set.

'Everything looks different when you conquer something you thought you couldn't.'

'Wow.' Brooke whipped her head round to face Jack. 'Those are wise words from a self-confessed emotionless, indifferent, unfeeling, apathetic bastard.'

Jack blinked at her and twisted his mouth into a half-smile before looking out to sea, then back at her. 'Is that what I said?'

'Word for word.'

'You have a good memory.'

'Sometimes. When I know someone is saying something untrue and I want to use it against them later.'

'I should have known you had an ulterior motive.'

'Well, at least I put my motives on the table.'

'I think I've made *my* motives pretty clear.'

'You're right—your motives *are* clear.'

Jack blinked in the wind, his hair blowing across his forehead. His eyes were dark and set on her, making her feel unable to move. She wanted to reach for him, wanted to feel him hold her, but he just wanted to be friends. She didn't need a friend.

'I don't have motives, Brooke. I just want to get through the next few weeks of taping. That's all.'

That's all. That was all this had ever been about. The show. Ratings.

'That's right—you don't think, do you? It's all about you and what you want.'

His eyes didn't leave hers. 'Is that what you think of me?'

She was angry. She could feel it burning at her. But this time she wasn't going to let it out. She wasn't going to show it. She would find her Zen if it killed her.

Brooke gripped the rails and looked up. 'I don't think about you, Jack.'

It was a lie. A terrible, awful lie. But she had to lie because if she let the words she wanted to say out of her mouth she wasn't sure she'd be able to stop.

'Yes, you do. I know you do.'

'I don't.'

She looked at him then, straight into his eyes, refusing to believe that when her stomach flipped it was from anything but hunger. Refusing to believe that she could possibly smell him as she thought she could. They were hundreds of feet up and the wind was blowing. She couldn't smell *anything*. It must just be the memory of his scent. Because his scent had been all around her the other night and hadn't left her mind for the past three days.

Brooke thought of the other night. Again. She was hot now, and heavy, and she knew what she wanted. But she didn't want to remember his scent.

'You're nothing to me.'

Good. Cool. Nice response. He would have no idea what she was thinking. And that was a relief, because right now she was realising what it was about bad boys that women found so attractive.

It wasn't just their muscles and their tattoos and the dirty way they spoke, or the passionate, almost disrespectful way they pushed you down to kiss you. It was a pathetic female need to believe that inside every bad man was a *good* little boy, waiting for the right girl to find him. Which was complete rubbish. Jack wasn't good. He was bad. *Very* bad. She just needed to remember that—not his incredible sexy smell.

He didn't answer her and he didn't move.

'What's supposed to happen now?' Brooke moved away, still gripping the rail in front of her. 'Are we supposed to say how beautiful Sydney is? How much is Sydney Tourism paying you for this segment, Jack?'

She knew she was being cynical and flippant and rude but she had to be—because if she didn't she'd tell him what she really thought. And she wasn't going to do that. She wanted to get away from the memory of his smell and the flashing reminders of the way he'd kissed her and the words he'd growled into her ear that night. Of the way he'd made her feel as if she was the only woman he thought about and the only one he wanted.

No. She pulled her core in tight to stop the heat there from spreading. She needed to get the hell away from here. *Right now.*

'They're paying plenty. So you should take some photos, enjoy the view. Make it look as if you're having fun. You may as well settle in—we'll be here for another twenty minutes.'

'Then don't let me hold you up—I'm sure you have work to do.'

Jack leaned back to peer behind her. 'Nope, I'm good. Looks like Mick's got everything under control there.' There was a new anger in his voice now. As if he was holding back too.

Maybe if she didn't say anything he'd walk away.

'It's better up here, don't you think?' he said.

No, she didn't think that at all. Up here was beginning to feel a lot like torture. 'Mmm…'

'Nothing matters for a few minutes. You can just stop and breathe, you know…and think.'

She heard something in his voice. He was trying to tell her something but she had no idea what and she feared it was something she didn't want to hear. Some pathetic excuse. Some patronising brush-off.

Brooke breathed in. He was right. They were so far up and so far removed from anything it really *did* feel as if they were somewhere else and nothing else mattered. She had to calm down. She didn't want to hear what he had to say. She could tell he was angry too. Anger only got you into trouble.

Talk about something else. That would stop him from saying whatever it was he was going to say.

'When I was little I used to hide in a cupboard. It was dark and quiet and no one could find me. It was the only place I felt safe. That's what this feels like. Like I'm in the middle of everything but hidden away.'

'You hid in a cupboard?'

Crap. She shouldn't have said that. She needed to think of something else.

'Only a couple of times.'

'Why? I thought you and your sisters were best friends—why would you want to get away from them?'

Brooke licked her lips and lifted her hands to her hair, pulling it to one side. The anger was still there and it was starting to build again. 'We were…the cupboard-hiding business was…'

What was she *saying*? She needed to zip it.

'Was what?'

He was looking at her now. Intently. She could feel his dark eyes boring into her. Brooke tossed her hair, then gripped it again, pulling it into a ponytail at the back of her head.

'Well, it was…before.'

'Before?'

'Before I met my sisters.'

'You hid in a cupboard before you met your sisters?

Maybe it *is* time to go down, Brooke—clearly the air is too thin for you up here.'

He thought she was crazy. She knew she wasn't making any sense. But she didn't want him to think she was crazy—or angry.

Still pulling at her hair, she turned away from him. 'I didn't meet my sisters till I was six. I was adopted.'

The words came out soft, her lips barely moving. Her anger evaporated in an instant and was replaced with another emotion she hated even more. Sadness. Being adopted wasn't something she was ashamed of—it was just something she didn't like to talk about. People always asked questions. and she didn't like the answers she had to give.

But Jack was silent. He didn't ask any questions.

Brooke turned back. 'Did you hear me?'

'Yes.' He was still looking at her. His eyes dark, his long lashes still.

'Aren't you going to ask me about it?'

'No. Not unless you want me to.'

Not unless she wanted him to.

He *wasn't* considerate and lovely and thoughtful. Even though he'd taken away her anger in the sand the other night. Even though he'd helped her get up this damn bridge. Even though he was still here, talking to her, when she was saying things he didn't like. No, he was selfish and self-centred and he only wanted to be friends and didn't call. She was angry with him.

Brooke's mouth clamped shut and she turned back to the sky, resting her hands on the rail. Jack moved next to her, his elbows on the rail, fingers clasped—looking out at she wasn't sure what. They stood like that for a while. Not talking, not touching. Just looking.

Brooke wanted to tell him. She wanted to confide in

him. She missed her sisters, and she was lonely, and he was paying her attention so she wanted to tell him. She wanted to have this moment with him even if it was the only moment they'd ever have. Possibly *because* it was the only moment they'd ever have. After this was all over he'd be gone. It was safe to tell him.

'My birth parents put me up for adoption when I was five. I had to go to a foster home. I don't remember much—except that I would sit in a cupboard for hours. The old lady who was looking after me—Mrs Edwards, her name was—tried to get me to come out, but I didn't like her. I don't know why—looking back I'm pretty sure she was perfectly nice, but I hated her. So I hid in the cupboard.'

Jack still didn't say anything, but he turned to face her, one elbow still on the rail.

Brooke didn't look at him. She kept staring out to the ocean. 'One day she asked me if I wanted carrots with my dinner and I screamed and screamed at her, saying, *No! I don't want carrots!* That's all I remember saying—*I don't want carrots!* I was so angry.'

Brooke tried to smile. It sounded ridiculous now. But the smile kept disappearing, no matter how she forced her lips to move upwards. It wasn't funny. Not even now.

Brooke stopped and took a breath, pushing down the hard lump that was in danger of moving up from her chest into her throat. That had happened a long time ago. All that anger…all that hate. Brooke stared into the black water of the harbour below. When she spoke again her voice was quieter.

'She had all these porcelain cats everywhere and I started picking them up and throwing them. Smashing them. She grabbed me and tried to cuddle me but I fought her off. I threw the cats at her and they hit her in the head.

She was bleeding. There was so much blood. I remember all the blood.'

Still Jack remained silent. His silence was somehow comforting. She needed it. Slowly Brooke turned her body towards him. She still couldn't look at him, though, so she looked over his shoulder instead.

'I got moved then—to a house with two boys. I can't even remember their names. They didn't want me there. They would go off on their bikes super-fast so I couldn't catch up. They called me names. Sooky Brooky...The Girl That No One Wanted.'

Brooke felt Jack stand a little taller, his eyes still on her. She still couldn't look at him.

'One day I got angry because they were throwing rocks at me. I picked up the biggest one I could find and threw it back at them.'

Brooke pushed at her lips again and one of them managed to tip up half-heartedly. She looked down at her hands and picked at her nails. Something she hadn't done since she was a child.

'It hit one of them and he fell. He ended up in hospital.'

Brooke's heart stilled. Those boys had hated her. They'd told her that her father had got rid of her because she was too ugly and her mother hadn't wanted her because she couldn't do anything. But they didn't deserve what she had done. All because she'd got angry.

'Brooke...'

When Jack finally spoke his voice was deep and soft. As soon as she heard him say her name she wished he hadn't. It wasn't emotionless and indifferent and unfeeling at all.

She didn't look at him. She remembered those boys. She remembered the way they'd left her out and the way they'd only played boys' games and wouldn't let her join in. She remembered the boy splayed out in the dust. She'd thought she'd killed him. She remembered running away as fast as she could. They'd come and taken her away that night. She'd been so scared and so angry.

'Brooke. You were just a little kid.'

Brooke shook her head. She'd been a kid but she'd known what she was doing. She'd wanted to hurt them. The way she had hurt. Still hurt. The lump rose and Brooke choked it back down. She swallowed hard, trying desperately to stop the sob from falling out. She wasn't going to cry. Not about that. Not now—and not in front of Jack.

'Brooke.'

When his hands touched hers the sob stuck in her chest. He wasn't touching her the way he had the other night. It wasn't fast and hard and fleeting. It was firm, but tender. His fingers wrapped around hers, stopping her from picking at her nails. The air stilled for a moment and breathing became difficult. When Brooke looked up she met Jack's eyes. Dark and soft and full of concern. But almost as quickly as he came he went away. He pulled his hands back and shoved them in his pockets, breaking his gaze and searching the ocean for something.

'It's natural for someone to get angry when they're hurt.'

Brooke's heart jumped and started beating again. That small intimate moment had made the sob disappear. Somehow that second of recognition behind his eyes, the very small show of concern she hadn't been expecting, had given her whatever it was she'd needed to become unstuck from that memory and move on to another one.

'Getting angry doesn't solve anything.'

The burning behind Brooke's eyes stopped. She kept her eyes on him. On his nose and the way it jutted from his face. On the way he tilted his chin up almost defiantly. But mostly she watched the way his jaw was working… up and down and up and down… As if he was thinking and trying to hold back his own emotion. The idea that Jack could get emotional made her focus. Jack…? Emotional…?

'I hurt them because I was angry.'

'You were angry because they hurt you. I'm not saying you should have thrown things or made people bleed…'

He turned his dark eyes to her and held them steady. They were almost black. She didn't know him well enough to know what he was thinking, but he was definitely thinking *something.* What she'd said had affected him in some way and it surprised her.

'But sometimes you need to get angry. You need to let people know that you've had enough and you won't be treated like that. Sometimes you need to get angry so people know you're hurting and that you need help. And just think—if you hadn't got angry and done those things you never would have ended up with your sisters.'

The words of those boys still rang through her ears every now and again. So did visions of the old lady bleeding or the little boy lying in the dust. When something bad happened or when she was sad or lonely. But mostly they were drowned out by the things her sisters had said to her since. The good things and the happy things, the sweet things and the encouraging things. She knew how lucky she was to have her sisters. She'd seen what it was like to live without love, and the chaos and bickering she'd grown up with from her sisters was infinitely better. Without a doubt.

'Anger isn't always bad. It's just something we need to feel sometimes so we know what we don't want. Just like we need to feel sad so we can appreciate when we feel happy. You shouldn't be scared of how you feel.'

Jack was looking at her. For too long. His hands were still in his pockets and his eyes were on her. He was not touching, not coming close, just watching—almost warily.

'But *you* get scared, Jack. Maybe not of anger or sadness, but you're scared of getting close. Of being happy.'

There was something Jack wasn't saying. She needed to tread carefully here. If she was going to get him to reveal anything she'd need to be gentle.

Jack watched her, his eyes not leaving hers. She was right. He *was* scared of getting close. Scared of being happy. Because happiness never lasted. He'd known moments of it. Short, hard, fast moments of happiness that would disappear into puffs of smoke. It never lasted.

'Getting close means getting hurt.'

'Is that why you didn't call?'

Her face had changed. Her eyes dipped, then met his again. They widened, then she turned to look out at the water again. She was upset—he could see that. He hadn't meant to upset her. He'd meant to give her space. That time in the sand had just been comfort. She hadn't wanted more. He hadn't called because she didn't want more.

'What would I have said if I *had* called?'

Her head whipped back and she faced him, her green eyes bright and narrowed. She crossed her arms over her small body and stared at him, anger obviously simmering on the surface. 'How about, *How are you?* How about, *I'm thinking of you*? How about, *That meant something to me*?'

Her cheeks pinkened and her eyes challenged him. She looked beautiful. Petite and defenceless but Amazonian and capable all at once. He liked that about her. He liked her contrasts so much it made his chest ache. He wanted to know more—he wanted to reach out and touch her hot cheeks, he wanted to kiss her. But he didn't because he had no idea what she wanted. She was confusing and beautiful and it made his head spin.

Jack clung to the rail, planting his feet so he wouldn't sway. He had to just tell her. He had to just let her know what he was thinking. If his parents had taught him anything with their messed up fallacy of a marriage it was that he needed to say what he was thinking.

'*You* mean something to me.'

Brooke opened her mouth, then closed it. A line creased her forehead between her eyes. She opened her mouth again and closed it again. Her eyes remained on his, searching.

'What?'

'I think about you all the time. I think about your eyes and your smile, and I think about your gorgeous body and how it moved in the sand when I was kissing you.'

Brooke sucked in a deep breath.

He needed to stop. He had no idea what she was thinking, but he couldn't stop. Not now he'd started.

'I think about how you fight with me about everything and how you don't let me get away with anything. I think about that dimple in your left cheek.'

She let out a little puff of air and that dimple appeared. It swelled his brain. He had to keep going.

'I think about how you always say what you think, even when you know it'll probably get you into trouble. But the thing is—mostly I just think about *you*. Just you.'

Brooke stared. Then her hands flew to her eyes and she rubbed them, before taking them away and staring at him again.

'But you didn't call.'

'No. I didn't call. Because I didn't think you wanted me to.'

There—she had it all. It was on the table and now it was her turn. The idea filled him with a fear that made him go cold. He *never* gave his power away. He never gave anyone the ammunition to hurt him. But he'd given it to her. She'd give him the speech now. The 'let's be friends' speech. He hadn't heard that in years, because he'd always been the one giving it.

His stomach ached and his head hurt. He gripped the rail hard and held his breath.

Slowly, carefully, she moved her hand. It rested on his forearm and he shivered. Then she let her fingers trail down to his and he watched their journey. Her touch wasn't uncomfortable. It made his skin tingle. It made the hairs on the back of his hand stand up. But it wasn't uncomfortable. Exciting, erotic, electric—but not uncomfortable.

'I wanted you to call.'

'You didn't want to just be friends the other night?'

'No.'

Finally her fingers met his hand and she looped them underneath his palm. Relief coursed through his body.

'I didn't want to be friends. I wanted to be more than friends.'

More than friends? 'How much more?'

Her fingers moved until they were holding his hand tight. She stepped in closer and he felt her, warm and soft against his chest. He carefully moved his other hand till it was behind her neck. He pushed and she came closer. His body was hard and he wanted her there. Close and soft and pressing up against him. He moved forward until the whole length of him was pushed up against the whole length of her. Her free hand moved to his waist and curled around his back. She moved even closer, her breasts pushing against him and her hand pushing on his back.

Everything in his body screamed at the contact but he ignored it. He wanted her close, he needed to feel her, and he needed to feel the way she wanted him back. *More.* He could give her more. He could give her anything she wanted.

Her chin tilted up to him and her hair fell off her shoulders, tumbling down her back. He let his fingers thread though it—soft and fragrant. He leaned down to bury his face in her hair before finding her hot neck with his lips and kissing her. Tenderly, softly, and with a passionate reverence he hoped she'd be able to feel.

The low moan that escaped her lips was enough. His whole body fired to attention and the kisses on her neck became harder and faster and more desperate, until he'd kissed his way up to her mouth and was taking her in. Desperately kissing and moving to get as close as he could.

And then he realised she was doing the same.

CHAPTER TWELVE

'WHAT I REMEMBER…'

Max Douglas's voice boomed off the screen. This was Max at his bullying best. The veins in his forehead bulged through his reddened skin. Jack knew his own veins looked exactly the same.

'…is that you let your heart rule your head—even after everything I taught you. You let some woman manipulate you and change all the rules to suit *her.* And what happened in the end, Jack? She lied to you. She didn't want you. She wanted that other tosser. All that happened was that you caused an on-air fight that got us chucked off the air.'

Jack tried to breathe. Once again his father had got it wrong. No matter how many times Jack told him what had happened his father always preferred his own version of events. Jack hadn't been in love with Kayla. But she'd been young, and had seemed innocent and frightened and unsure what to do. So he'd helped her.

She'd said she was frightened of one of the other contestants—said he intimidated her when the cameras weren't there. Jack hadn't been able to have him thrown off the show so he'd adjusted the editing to 'out' the man, ensuring he would be voted off because of his bullying. What he hadn't known was that Kayla was in love with the bully and he'd rejected her advances. He'd made her feel small and unworthy. And then he'd started something with her on-screen best friend.

Jack should have known what a woman scorned in love was like. But he'd believed her. He'd wanted to protect her.

When the new edits had been shown the truth had come out: Kayla wanted her best friend's man. She'd lied and manipulated until she'd managed to get the man in bed and had waited till the cameras had caught them. She'd wanted her best friend's man and she'd got him—with Jack's help.

The other contestants had got involved—people had started taking sides—and when the punches and the hair-pulling had started things had got ugly. And it had all been caught on camera. Jack had thrown Kayla off the show but it had been too late—the TV authorities had shut the programme down, the company had lost millions, and Jack's father had nearly come through the phone line.

That had been five years ago. Jack had learnt his lesson. He'd learnt to keep everyone at a distance—that way he couldn't get sucked into any of their lies. Except now he'd let Brooke in. Was his thinking screwed up because of her? Were his father and Rob Gunn right? *Should* he let the men choose? He didn't know—and that made him angry.

But what made him angrier was his father on the line—telling him what to do. Overriding his decisions and making everything so much harder.

'This is *my* show, Max. I came up with the concept, I wrote the format, I got all the funding together and I handpicked the team. You're not going to take over.'

'I couldn't care less what you've done, Jack. You're wrong. I'm right. Gunn stays.'

'No. *You're* wrong. Gunn is banned from the set. If I see him again I'll have him escorted from the building and there's nothing you can do about it—unless you come here yourself, and we both know you won't do that.'

His father had been living in Italy for over four years now. He'd been home maybe five times. He'd told Jack's mother he was setting up a new company. Jack knew he was living with his mistress.

'I still own this company, Jack, and the last time I checked you were on my payroll. The format stays as is. The men choose the competitions. The men choose the women. The men control the show. The women are there for decoration and drama and if you don't like it you know where the door is. Be prepared to pay me back every cent. And don't think I won't come after your mother for it if *you* can't deliver.'

Jack's blood steamed. Not only was his father at his intimidating, bullying best, he was pointing out the very reason Jack couldn't leave. His father would target his mother if he did. But, he reminded himself, his mother could take care of herself. Or could she? And what would happen to Brooke and the others if he walked off the show?

No, he had to stay. He had to stay and try and protect Brooke and the others as well as he could. At least from within he could do something—if he left he would be powerless, and right now he was angry and he wanted to fight. For his mother, for Brooke, and against the man whose voice made him feel as if his hands were squeezing tight around his throat.

'You win, Max. You have me where you want me. I'll stay.'

* * *

When the girls received the envelope explaining the next challenge Brooke's heart sank. A cheer-off. Of all the demeaning, humiliating things…

The men had demanded they dress in skimpy cheerleader outfits and dance and sing and run around like chooks with their heads cut off. All for their amusement. How this determined who was their perfect match she had no idea. But she wasn't calling the shots—Jack was. The man who confused her more than anyone ever had.

After their mind-blowing kiss on the bridge they'd said goodbye with smiles full of meaning. He'd called the apartment the next day. Said he was thinking of her. She'd clung to the receiver so it wouldn't fall. Her heart had beat so fast she was sure the other girls would be able to see it.

Their conversation had been short—she hadn't been able to talk anyway, with the other girls listening in—and then she'd got mad, because she'd realised he was able to shift her emotions so severely. As if she had no control over them. She didn't want him to be able to control her like that but he did—and that made her angry. Except it was hard to be angry when she thought of his mouth and his kisses and the way he'd told her she meant something to him.

And now she gripped the envelope in her hand and her stomach rose to her throat as she thought about Jack making them do this. He surely knew how much she'd hate it? Did he not consider her feelings? Or were her feelings second to the ratings?

But one thing she'd learnt over the past few weeks was not to assume anything, and the moment she saw Jack she was going to sort this out. There was no way she and the other girls were going to endure a series of embarrassing challenges only to be chosen or rejected by four meat-heads who hadn't even taken the time to get to know them.

The night they'd been introduced the men had zeroed in on the women they'd clearly thought were the hottest, then got bored and spent the night talking to each other and drinking before disappearing. Probably to visit some seedy strip club and talk about what a sweet deal they had.

Heat rose from Brooke's legs up to her head. How *dared* they do this? How *dared* they assume that the twelve of them would just sit back and accept this new twist? If her sisters had taught her anything it was to respect herself and make her own choices. She wasn't about to let four strangers make her feel rejected or less than she was. And as she looked at the other women, still talking about the cheerleading challenge, she knew she wasn't going to let those strangers do it to these girls either.

Some of these women were vulnerable and shy and didn't have a lot of confidence to begin with. She wasn't going to let their confidence be shattered by a few bad men with perverted control fantasies. Jack had once said that anger could be a good thing, that you should speak up for what you believed in. She'd never thought about that before. She'd thought that anger always got you into trouble. That was why she'd spent years trying to keep her anger tucked away. Now she realised that anger could be good.

But instead of lashing out, and providing Jack with 'great TV', she needed to channel that anger into something much more productive. Like forming a plan to let these men—*and* Jack—know exactly what she and the other girls thought of their challenge. A plan to let them know who was really calling the shots on this show.

Brooke's body buzzed with the anger that flowed through her veins. She needed to release it—that was the only way she was going to survive this.

'Jack, it's humiliating!'

'Brooke. Listen to me—'

'No! You listen to *me*. We're not here to be humiliated and made to feel like pieces of meat. We won't do this.'

This time the girls were behind her. She'd spoken to them. They hated the idea of there being only four men. How were they supposed to meet their perfect match when there were only four men to choose from? They were united. They weren't going to take it. The girls were ready to rebel—they were just waiting for their fearless leader to give the word.

'You *have* to do this. Trust me—it could be a lot worse.'

'Worse? How? How could it be *worse*? We'll be on national television with our butts hanging out, dancing and chanting with no idea what we're doing! What are you hoping for—that we'll all fall and break our necks? That would be great TV, wouldn't it!'

Brooke stood up. She needed to be above him. She couldn't look into his calm eyes any longer. He wasn't getting roused at all. He wasn't even getting defensive. He was just sitting and watching her. She knew what he was doing—trying to calm her down. Well, she didn't want to be calm. He'd told her getting angry was good, so she was getting angry. She was going to test his theory. She had a plan.

She wasn't going to tell him about it, though. She had a plan to turn the tables on the men and let them know what the women all thought of their 'challenge' and the new rules. But that wasn't what was making her angry right now. It was Jack.

Was this who he really was? Where was the sensitive man on the bridge? Or the comforting man in the sand? This emotionless, unfeeling Jack infuriated her. She didn't want him.

'Brooke, I know you're angry, but you have to trust me.'

'Trust you? How can I trust you? What are you *doing*, Jack? This is ridiculous—and awful. How can you think this is OK?'

How can you think this is OK to do to me? She didn't say it, but she was thinking it—oh, was she thinking it!

'I *don't* think this is OK.'

'Then why are you letting it happen?'

'I have to. I have no choice. You have to trust me, Brooke—the first suggestion was a lot worse than this…'

'What do you mean, you have no choice? You're the producer!'

He didn't move. She watched him still, and then he retreated. His eyes blanked. He turned away.

'Jack. Tell me what's going on.'

'Just trust me, Brooke.'

He didn't reach for her. His hands stayed where they were. She knew what that meant. He wasn't touching her because he was feeling out of control. Keeping her at a distance was his way of regaining it. But this couldn't be about control. If they had a chance of working Jack had to realise that they were a team. He didn't have to do this on his own.

So she sat back down—this time next to him—and reached for his stiff hand. She curled her small fingers through his and didn't let go, even when he didn't squeeze back. She just moved closer.

'What's going on, Jack? Tell me.'

* * *

When Jack looked into Brooke's eyes he saw something he'd never seen before. Someone who wanted to know what was wrong with him. Someone who was concerned with what he was going through. Someone who was shattering his walls and wanting to see the man behind.

It made his chest ache. He felt exposed and uncomfortable, but he wanted her to keep looking at him like that. He wanted to feel her warm hand in his and he wanted her to smile again and then kiss him. So he told her. *Everything.* About his father and his mother and the deal he'd made when he was nineteen.

Brooke didn't speak. She just held his hand and listened as no one had ever listened before. When he'd finished he felt sick and completely exhausted. As if everything that he'd been keeping to himself was physically weighing down on him. He looked into her eyes, worried he'd said too much. Worried that she wouldn't understand.

But he shouldn't have worried. The fierce little nymph sitting next to him moved closer, her perfect breasts brushing his arm, her dimple getting deeper as she smiled, moving in closer to his ear. And when he felt the warmth of her breath on his ear as she whispered his whole body stood to attention.

'Sounds like it's time you got angry, Jack.'

The girls were buzzing. They'd been up half the night working out their routine, chanting the words and practising the lifts. For most it was hard work. Many of these women hadn't ever done anything more strenuous than running on a treadmill.

Despite being the least athletic in her family, Brooke excelled at the cheerleading routine. She was strong, so she could throw the other girls in the air and catch them with ease. She was also agile enough to flip when she was thrown up herself. She supposed that all those years of training had achieved something. Perhaps comparing herself to her sisters was not the best idea—they were freakishly good, after all—but compared with the rest of the population Brooke realised that her persistence and dedication had actually paid off. She was *good.*

They were all dressed in ridiculously brief outfits—although Brooke *had* managed to convince the wardrobe consultant to purchase everything from Wright Sports. Maddy was going to flip when she saw it all on screen.

For a moment Brooke wondered if her plan would perhaps show the brand in a bad light. But how could it? Standing up for themselves and turning the tables on men could never be bad. And if some people didn't like it then Brooke didn't care. She didn't want them as customers anyway.

One of the goals of Wright Sports was to promote women in sport. As professionals who demanded as much respect and money as their male counterparts. Her little cheer today would only help their cause. No—this was the right thing to do. Channelling her anger into a well-thought-out plan was a *good* idea. And Brooke couldn't wait for this thing to start.

The crowd at the football game was pumped. It was a big game—a fierce battle. Screams and whoops echoed around them as the girls stood waiting in the tunnel and the ground's announcer started to talk.

'Make some noise, everyone—we have over eighty-five thousand fans in the stadium tonight and we want to hear each and every one of you!'

The crowd howled in delight. Excitement turned to

flutterings in Brooke's stomach. She turned to the other girls and knew they were feeling the same.

Katy was looking a little green. She reached for her hand. 'We're going to nail this, Katy,'

'Do you think we're doing the right thing?'

'Yes, absolutely. One hundred per cent.'

Katy's eyes flickered with doubt. 'But what if one of those men actually is my perfect match?'

'Katy—look at me.'

Katy's big brown eyes stared into hers. Brooke saw her fear. She saw her doubt. She saw twenty-seven years of wondering if she was good enough. Wondering if she'd ever meet 'the one'. Wondering what she'd done every time it went wrong. Wondering if one of the men she'd let go because he'd treated her badly should have received a second chance.

'Your perfect match doesn't exist. That's not what it's about. It's about meeting someone who helps you on your journey. Who heals your heart and sees through your pain—who sees who you are and loves you anyway. Who holds you when you're sad and celebrates with you when you're happy. You'll meet that person when the time is right. And it may not last with that person, but then you'll meet someone else. And if you don't—it's OK. You'll have family and friends and people who love you and you'll be happy. Love isn't perfect, Katy—it gets messy and complicated because *people* are messy and complicated and we're all just muddling through together. There's no destination to get to. And there's no guarantee that finding the perfect man will make you happy. But I'll tell you something...'

Brooke reached up high to put her hands on Katy's shoulders before pulling her into a hug and whispering in her ear.

'The next five minutes *will* make you happy.' Brooke smiled. 'I promise.'

The loud voice of the announcer boomed across the field and into the tunnel. It was time. They were supposed to go out there, dance and cheer, and let four men they didn't even know assess their abilities and choose which one of them he wanted to go on a date with.

Brooke couldn't wait to see their faces. And she couldn't wait to see Jack's.

The girls rushed onto the podium in a hurry. Brooke called out to them to get ready. She looked each of them in the eye. They looked back. It was time. They were ready.

With a whoop and a cheer they began their chant while simultaneously flipping each other up and around.

You might be good at cricket
You might be good at that
But when it comes to football
You might as well step back
Might as well step back
Say what?

The crowd roared in appreciation and started to clap along. Brooke smiled as she flew into the air. They shouted louder this time.

You might as well step back
Cause we ain't gonna play no more
No, we ain't gonna play your way
Cause we're the girls of Perfect Match
And we're about to say
Say what?
We're about to say...

The girls stopped flipping. They formed a line. Their voices boomed through the microphones attached to their tiny crop tops.

You can take your silly cheering comp
Cause we think it's corrupt
Say what?
We hate to disappoint you
We hate to interrupt
But this is what we think of you
It's time you all got...

They turned, flipped up their skirts and bent over. An audible gasp filled the stadium and the clapping stopped. No one moved. Then suddenly there was a flurry of activity as photographers rushed from the sidelines to take photos of the girls butts. They stayed where they were.

Brooke turned her head. 'Done!' she called, and they stood up, turned around and faced the crowd, who had started to twitter.

They called out, then clapped, and finally they roared and cheered. Relief rushed through Brooke's body. They *got* it. They understood.

Brooke clasped the hands of the girls either side of her and squeezed and then, holding their hands aloft, the girls took their bows before bouncing offstage as if they'd just been fed a truckload of red frogs.

The conversation Jack was having with his father that afternoon wasn't pretty. His father was roaring. He wanted to know who had organised it. He wanted heads to roll and blood to be spilled. He blamed Jack, of course, and Jack was taking great pleasure in the rant his father was giving him.

'Which one was it?' his father demanded, the angry purple veins in his neck popping. 'It was the little one, wasn't it? Tell me! It was her, wasn't it? She's been causing trouble from the beginning. You need to get rid of her!'

Jack's throat closed. His father couldn't get wind of Brooke's having anything to do with this. The thought of his father saying anything to her made his body fill with a rage he hadn't felt in years. Not since he'd found out about his father's first girlfriend.

'The girls were never going to put up with this, Max, you had to expect rebellion.'

'If I find out it was her she'll be sorry she ever opened her stupid little mouth…'

'That's enough, Max.'

Jack's blood pumped. *Calm*. He had to stay calm. He couldn't let his father know how he felt about Brooke. If he knew Brooke would pay…big-time.

'It's not enough. That small-titted little troublemaker had better watch herself. I can make her life miserable—you tell her that.'

Jack stood up. White spots danced before his eyes. 'First of all, you don't speak about her like that. And second—if you hurt her in any way I will hunt you down, Max, and you'll be the one who's sorry.'

As soon as the words left his mouth he regretted them.

'Geez, Jack, don't tell me you're having a fling with her? Is *that* what this is about? You've let *another* woman manipulate you?'

'I'm not having a fling with anyone.' That was true. Brooke was not a fling. 'But you're not going to threaten *any* of the contestants like that. I'm still in charge here.'

'If I find out you've become involved with this girl…'

Jack had to dig himself out. He couldn't let his father

know—couldn't let his father turn his anger and hatred on Brooke. That wasn't going to happen.

'I'm not. Do you think I'd send her on a date with the biggest jerk on the show if I was involved with her?'

Jack was thinking on his feet. He wasn't sure if he was doing the right thing, but right now he just had to steer his father off-course.

'Brent?'

'Yes. I've teed it up for Brent to choose her. She'll hate it. It'll make great TV.'

It would. But what would make greater TV was what she was going to say to him after that date. Brent was the most stupid, sexist loser Jack had ever met. All muscles, no substance. Brooke would hate him. And hate Jack for setting them up. But he had to get his father off the trail. He wouldn't be able to stand what would happen to her if he didn't.

'Nothing had better go wrong this time, Jack. Get it together. I'll pull it off the air myself if *anyone*—including that troublemaker—does anything to jeopardise our ratings or the show's future. Do you understand?'

Jack understood. He understood that he'd had enough. He was getting out. He'd pay his father back any way he could, but after this show was done and Brooke was safe—he was out.

'I choose Samantha Draper.'

'I choose Dimity Lee.'

'I choose Brooke Wright.'

The whole room fell silent. In their wisdom, the powers-that-be had decided that the dates would be doled out on a boat in Sydney Harbour. Brooke suspected it was so no one could run.

They were dressed in full formal regalia. They'd been

in make-up for hours, getting their hair to sit just right and creating the perfect winged eyeliner. Brooke had never felt less like herself. When she looked in the mirror a stranger stared back. A beautiful stranger—but someone Brooke didn't recognise. False eyelashes hovered over her eyes—she longed to rip them off.

Someone shifted. The women were standing in a row on the top deck of the boat, their backs to the magnificent Harbour Bridge. The four men stood before them, smiling in their suits. One leered at her. He'd just called out her name.

A gust of wind blew a strand of hair into Brooke's open mouth. Someone had chosen *her*? Why? He was smiling at her. Big and muscly, clearly a bodybuilder. *So* not her type. He was dressed in baggy jeans and he had a flat cap on his head. Clearly he was trying to look younger than he was—she was sure he was bald underneath that cap he never took off.

He held out a brawny hand to her and she took it, wondering what this meat-head saw in her. His eyes trailed over her body and she knew.

'You looked hot out there today, Brooke.'

Brooke didn't answer him. She turned back to the other girls, who offered a few sympathetic smiles.

What the hell had she got herself into?

The date started badly. His name was Brent and he was thirty. Although he dressed as if he was twenty-one. He laughed a lot, but conversation clearly wasn't one of his strengths. His biceps bulged out of his too-small shirt. A faint smell of fake tan lingered around him.

'Your arse looks hot in that dress.'

Brooke gulped down the water she'd just taken a swig of. He'd chosen an oceanside bar for their date. It was packed, but the producers had managed to set up a secluded set of stools for them so they could tape without too much noise. Brooke had a headache from the thumping music and her patience was incredibly thin as she watched this thick-head eye up every woman who walked past in a short skirt.

'Thank you. Your biceps look ridiculous in that shirt.'

He laughed uncertainly, clearly not sure if she was joking. She wasn't.

'What do you want to eat? This mob are payin', so order as much as you want.' He smiled.

The man was attractive—she'd give him that. Nice teeth. A wide jaw. He was manly-looking. Big and handsome. But it was his personality she was struggling with. Or rather she was struggling to find one.

'What do you do, Brent?'

Brent's head turned as another pretty young thing walked past.

'I'm a project manager.'

Brooke rolled her eyes. If she had a dollar…

'So you're a tradie?'

'Ah…yeah, I s'pose you could say that. I'm a sparkie.'

An electrician. Good job. Steady. Reliable work. OK—one good thing.

'And where do you live?'

'Bondi.'

Brooke smiled, waiting. But the silence was long-lasting. He sipped on his drink and pulled out his phone. Brooke waited while he checked it, quietly annoyed that *he* was able to have contact with the outside world while she couldn't.

'What made you come on this show?'

'What is this? A police interview? Just relax, darl, and enjoy your drink.'

Brooke felt frustration swell in her chest. So he didn't want to talk… What the hell were they going to do till the food arrived?

'I'm in marketing.'

He didn't look up but he grunted a little. The waitress came to take their order and he finally put his phone away, slipping it into his back pocket. Brooke was actually in pain now. This was without doubt her number one worst date *ever.*

'Are you looking for love, Brent?'

'Geez, slow down. You're pushy!' Brent took another sip of his drink and pulled out his phone again.

Brooke felt heat rise in her head. She could hear it fizzing in her ears. 'Look, mate. I don't know why you asked me on this date. You don't want to talk—you just want to check your phone and every girl who walks past. Clearly I'm not your "perfect match", so what are we doing here?'

Brent looked up and for the first time looked into her eyes. 'Jack said so.'

A breath expelled from Brooke's chest. *Jack?*

'What do you mean? I thought you chose me?'

'You're hot and all that, babe, but Jack told me to pick you. He said we'd be a perfect match. Look…' He leaned in to whisper in her ear. 'I have a girlfriend, but I'd be willing to forget her for one night if you want to have some fun.'

Brooke closed her eyes. She breathed deeply. *Don't go off,* she coached herself. *Don't go off.* This is what Jack wants. *Great TV.* Brooke going off about something else. Brooke being humiliated on national TV. *Don't go off—that's exactly what he wants.*

Every time she thought she had him figured out—every time she thought she'd got through to him—he did something else to make her anger flare her.

'Thank you for the lovely date, Brent, but I have to go.'

'Not yet! We haven't even eaten! I'm starving!'

'You stay, tiger. Eat all you want. I have somewhere I need to be.'

Brooke moved fast. Her feet barely hit the ground.

She grabbed the cameraman by the arm. 'Turn it off. *Now.* And take me to Jack.'

She was mad. A white rage had made spots appear before her eyes.

The cameraman didn't argue. He put down the camera and took her to his car.

CHAPTER THIRTEEN

SHE WAS HERE and she was angry—that much he could tell. And he knew *why* she was here. The unwatched footage sat leering at him on the computer screen. Mick had just emailed it over. Mick's promise of it being a great scene rang in his ears.

He wanted to watch. Not for the scene. Not for the drama. But he wanted to know. How had her date gone? Somewhere in his jealous heart he was worried that she might have enjoyed her date with that meat-head.

'Open the door, Jack. I'm not going anywhere until you do.'

Definitely angry.

Jack's heart leapt ridiculously. Maybe the date hadn't gone well. Maybe she'd realised the man was a jerk and she'd given him a serve and now she was here to declare her feelings for him.

Jack stepped back. No, she was angry. He knew what she was here for. To tell him off for forcing her to go on a date with Brent. She'd hate him. She wouldn't want 'more' from him now. But he'd had to do it—it was the only way Jack's father would leave her alone.

Reaching the video entry system, he swiped the screen to allow her face to show. 'What's wrong, Brooke—what are you doing here?'

Her face turned to the camera. 'Let. Me. In.'

She was mad. Madder than ever. And he knew he had to let her in. He *wanted* to let her in. She was angry and she needed to yell at him and, strangely, he wanted her to. He wanted her to take her anger out on him—as if he could absorb it for her and ease her pain.

Two short minutes later Jack opened the door to reveal Brooke. Dressed in a body-hugging black dress and pushing her way past him.

'This is *it*, Jack. The very end. I'm not putting up with this any longer. You've had your fun—I want out.'

'Brooke—'

Her arms were folded tight across her chest, making her breasts rise up and peep out from the top of the dress. Her cheeks were flushed and her hair was pulling free from the tight style she had it in. She looked angry and beautiful all at once.

'Don't "Brooke" me. I *know* what you did. I know why you chose Brent. You wanted the exact type of man that would annoy me the most. A misogynistic, stupid man-slut who has no self-worth and absolutely no idea how stupid he is.'

'Are you talking about your date, Brooke?'

'Yes, I'm talking about my date! The big knuckle-dragging caveman *you* set me up with. He spent all night checking out every other woman in the place. Then he suggested we go back to his place after they finished the taping because his girlfriend was away. You couldn't have found a more repulsive man and you know it.'

'I didn't know he had a girlfriend.'

'But you *did* know he was a pig? You told me that you wanted the best for us. That you really cared about us finding our perfect match. But you don't, do you? You just want to make entertaining TV.'

'I thought you liked the bodybuilder type.'

'Since when do I go for the stupid bodybuilder type? Since when do I seem like the type of woman who puts up with a man who thinks monogamy is a pizza topping? You don't know me at all and neither does anyone on your team. Do you even know what you're doing? Maybe your father was right and they *should* have brought in that hot-shot producer. Maybe *he* would have found a man who was even close to being my type.'

'I thought you didn't want to find a man? I thought this was all about your family's business?'

'It is…' She hesitated, looking away.

She wanted a man. She was *disappointed*. Something burned hot in his gut and he knew what it was: jealousy. Stupid, worthless jealousy—for a man who wasn't even worth her notice.

'Is that the problem, Brooke. Did you get all excited when you saw Mr Muscles and hope he was the one for you? What happened?'

Brooke's eyes were wide and to his horror they were filling quickly with tears. He'd hit a nerve and he knew it, and he wished he could take back the stupid thing he'd just said.

'He has a girlfriend. He just wants to have some fun. He told me you told him to choose me, so I left.'

'Good.' *Good*. He felt better, but his chest was still pumping with blood. 'That's what you should have done.'

'He was a pig, Jack. He was mean and thoughtless and stupid and completely out of touch with the real world—and you sent him to me. You chose him for me.'

He had. She was right. He'd known they wouldn't go well together. He'd known she would hate him and he'd sent him to her. He shouldn't have done that. He should have found another way. Because now she was upset and it was his fault and he felt as big as an ant.

'Brooke, that's not what I—'

'Not what you *what*? Meant to do? You didn't mean to hurt me? Well, you did. You humiliated me and you treated me like any contestant on the show and you've never done that before. You treated me like I was a puppet to be manipulated and you made me feel used and dirty and stupid—and now I can't trust you.'

But that was what she'd signed up for. She knew that. She had to expect that. She *was* a contestant. This *was* a TV show. So why did he feel so small?

His chest with heaving with the heavy breaths he was taking. She wasn't just mad at him—she hated him. He could see it in her eyes, in the way she didn't come anywhere near him. Brooke always wanted to touch, she always came too close, but right now she was as far away from him as she could be and it made him feel cold and desperate. Desperate because he'd pushed her too far.

And the desperation that was prickling like a cold heat all over his body was a feeling a lot like something he hadn't felt in a long time. *Love.* He saw it in a flashing instant. He loved her. He wanted to protect her because he loved her. And that thought scared the hell out of him.

'You *are* a contestant, Brooke. That's what you're here for.'

The look she flashed him made his whole body go cold. *Hate*. Hate and disappointment and utter repulsion. The breath stopped in his throat. He sucked in air through his nose.

Time ticked by slowly. She stared at him, her eyes darting around his face as if trying to read him. Then they were still, and the mouth that had been held in a tight white line moments earlier opened.

'That's good, Jack. I needed to hear that. I needed to know what I am to you and how you really feel about me. I needed to be reminded what a selfish, narcissistic man you are before I started believing that you were actually one of the good guys. But you're not, are you? You're just as bad as the knuckle-dragger. No—you're worse. At least *he* was obvious about it. He let me know what a pig he was up-front. But you're stealthy, aren't you? You come across all sympathetic and kind and thoughtful, make me think you actually feel something for me—but it's just lies. You are a *liar*, Jack.'

Brooke had felt her body shake as she delivered her speech. She watched his face—unmoving and unemotional—as she spewed out her feelings. As she put everything out on the floor, waiting to see what he would pick up. But he didn't move. He just stood there. As if she were a stranger in the street. As if they hadn't shared the moments they had and as if they hadn't…

She'd wanted more from him—but not now. Now she was glad she hadn't let herself get carried away, because she knew if they'd gone further she would have let herself fall and she'd be feeling even worse than she was already.

'I told you before. I'm bad news.'

He delivered his statement so quietly she almost didn't hear him.

She wanted to walk out. His coldness and the way he wasn't even trying to apologise or salvage anything was hurting her physically. She wound her arms tighter to her body, pinching herself under her arms.

'So that's it? You just absolve yourself from any responsibility by saying you're bad news? You warned me so it's *my* fault when I get hurt? There's low, Jack—and then there's you. For you to deliberately hurt me—deliberately want to humiliate me—makes me think you're so much more than bad news.'

She wasn't sure how she could hurt him as much as he had hurt her but she wanted to. She wanted that frozen look on his face to change. To something. *Anything.* Anger, even—she didn't care. She just wanted him to react—to acknowledge that he'd hurt her.

She let out a little huff of ironic laughter, searching for the most hurtful words she could find. Her mind was blank. She could only tell him how she felt—it was all she had left right now.

'You're worse than your father. You are possibly the most horrible person I've ever met. No. Not possibly. You *are*.'

His face didn't move. She waited for his reaction—his anger—but there was none.

She opened her mouth again. 'You're disgusting. I know why you're single now, Jack—you're a horrible, horrible person and I hate you.'

The words came without her thinking. She didn't even mean them any more, but a blinding need to hurt him had taken over her brain and her mouth.

'I feel sorry for the people who work for you and I feel sorry for your family and anyone who has to put up with you. You're cold and mean and a terrible person. I hate you and I wish I'd never met you and I *definitely* wish I'd never kissed you and I'm glad we didn't become friends or anything else. You make me sick.'

Finally Brooke took a breath. The fog cleared and she tried to remember what she'd said. Still Jack stood before her, starting at her. Unmoving. Her heart hurt. Her arms hurt where she was pinching them. Everything hurt and nothing she was saying was working. She needed to leave. *Now.* She wanted to see her sisters and not to feel like this any more.

But just as she unfolded her arms to move she felt him. He moved quickly and he was in front of her, not touching, but standing so close she couldn't move. When she looked up his face was still hard, his mouth turned down at the edges, but his eyes were different. They were hot and angry and set on hers.

'Are you finished?' he asked, his voice a low, threatening growl.

He was too close and he stood over her. She didn't feel scared of *him* but she did feel scared. She'd wanted this reaction. She'd finally made him feel something—that was what she'd wanted. He felt…what? Anger? Something… This was just what she'd wanted but right now she wasn't sure if she'd done the right thing. Her mind flicked back to what she'd said. She couldn't be sure of every word but she knew she hadn't meant most of it. She'd just wanted him to react and now he had.

'You're angry, Brooke. *Good.* Get angry. Get angry at that jerk who didn't deserve you—get angry at me.'

Her breathing was now so heavy her breasts were moving up and down against his chest. She didn't answer him right away—she'd used up all her words and she just wanted to look at him. She wanted to watch his reaction. She wanted to know if he was as angry as she was.

The answer came seconds later when she felt his mouth, hot and hard against hers. His tongue pushed against her lips violently. His teeth nipped and he pushed at her, his arms coming around her back to pull her closer. Brooke pulled back, shocked, but he didn't let her go. For a second their eyes met, and she saw the anger in them before he closed them and set about kissing her again. Even harder. Even more passionately.

They weren't nice, loving kisses. They were genuine I-hate-you kisses. She felt his hate and his anger and his need to hurt her. She felt it in his lips and in the way he flicked his tongue as if the pleasure was all his. She wanted to push him away. She hated him even more. He had hurt her and she didn't want him to think she wanted this. But for some perverted reason she did. She wanted him pushing against her and kissing her and her stupid brain wouldn't let her pull away.

She pushed her lips closer, pushed her hips and her breasts and everything she had closer to him, snaking her hands up to his big shoulders and gripping them tightly, digging her fingernails in hard. His free hand moved up to her cheek and he cupped it as he kissed her, deeper and deeper, pushing her back further and further, till she was against the wall.

Before her brain could even register what was going on her body had reacted and she'd hoisted herself up, straddling his waist, which made him push her even harder into the wall. She felt him, long and hard against her, and moved her hand down till she felt him through his jeans. A deep growl escaped from his mouth and he left her lips for a second so he could kiss her neck, underneath her ear and further down. But these weren't gentle kisses either. They were hard, and he sucked as he went, his hands expertly moving behind her back to unclip the clasp on her bra.

There was no stopping now. She knew that. She accepted that. She didn't want to stop. She needed him close. She wanted to hurt him—to make him feel the violence of her kisses. When his face moved back up to hers she didn't give him time to look into her eyes. She kissed him again, biting his bottom lip and sucking it in, letting him know that she hated him as much as he hated her.

'I know you don't hate me, Brooke.'

His voice murmured in her ear as he kissed her neck. Brooke's blood was running hot and heavy. She *did* hate him. So much.

'I do hate you.'

'You don't hate me.'

He didn't stop kissing as he spoke. His hands explored her body and she responded with a loud moan as she arched into his touch.

'I do. You won't give me what I want.'

'What *do* you want?'

Jack pushed her skirt up and out of the way. His fingers explored beneath her underwear. She felt him gently sliding against her wetness.

'That—I want that.'

She wanted that. She wanted him. She wanted comfort. She wanted everything he had to offer.

Brooke kissed him hard. She bit his lower lip and he responded by pushing her against the wall. Her legs clung to him. She pushed into him. Angry and sad that she couldn't get what she wanted. Annoyed that she even wanted it. She should have known better than to fall for the wrong man.

Jack kissed her back, just as hard, and with the strength she knew he had lifted her up against the wall. She clawed frantically at his buttons. She needed to feel his skin. And when her hands found what they were looking for relief rushed to her head. She let her hands wander across his muscles and up to his shoulders as his large palms wrapped around her thighs and pulled her closer to him.

Their mouths didn't stop. Not for a second. When he wasn't kissing her mouth he was kissing her eyelids, or her neck, or her jaw, and she threw her head back to allow him access to every part of her. The only sound was the heavy breaths they took and her groan of pleasure as he finally removed her underwear.

Finally they paused. Made eye contact. This wasn't just sex. Couldn't be just sex. She wanted more, and when she looked at him she knew it *was* more.

He lifted a hand, dragged his thumb across her bottom lip, then kissed her. Long and hard and deep. Brooke forgot to breathe. She kissed him back, forgetting the sex, forgetting everything else except that kiss and the way they seemed to be drinking each other in, taking away each other's anger and leaving themselves with something more pure. Something much deeper.

By the time he pulled back she was ready. She had to have him. With a quick movement he was naked from the waist down and pushing on her, asking for permission. Which she gave, with a push and a long, hard slide.

Brooke couldn't help it. Her head flew back and the moan was out of her mouth before she could even think to stop it. His noises were much deeper, much more guttural, and they came from the back of his throat.

She focussed on the noise, on the way he was sliding up and down, and then on how he was using one finger to circle her clit before plunging into her again. She kissed his neck, now clammy with sweat, kissed his jaw, until finally she put her mouth over his and let her kisses match his strokes, faster and faster and deeper and deeper, until she felt it burst and shatter and she had to tell him to stop.

He stilled. He wasn't done. He hadn't finished and he wasn't going anywhere. He shifted as she shook and she held tight, not *wanting* him to go anywhere.

'Is that what you needed?' he growled into her ear.

'Yes. That. *Again*.'

She moved to allow the sparks to subside and then

start all over again. She was sensitive, and her orgasm sat right at the surface, so when he started to slide again she felt herself shudder and shake. But he didn't stop. He kept going. Pushing and going deeper, pausing to look down—clearly turned on by what he was seeing. She looked too, and watched as he slid in and out. Her fire sparked again. So close to the surface. But she didn't have time for release because it was his turn and he pushed into her with a force she wasn't expecting, banging her head on the wall behind her.

'Ouch!'

'Sorry…sorry!' His eyes were glazed but his hand came up to cradle the back of her head.

She felt his legs buckle a little, but he held her up. She lifted a hand to cover his on the back of her head. Warm, big… She put her small hand over his and he met her eyes.

'I'm sorry,' he whispered, his voice deep and hoarse.

'I know,' she whispered back, waiting for him to let her drop. But he didn't let her go. He wrapped his big arms around her and she buried her face in his warm skin, breathing in his scent and placing soft, tender kisses on his biceps.

They stood naked and silent for minutes before Brooke pulled away, brushing the hair from his forehead where it had fallen. She lifted herself up onto her toes and kissed his lips. This kiss was different. Soft and tender. He'd taken away her anger. He'd let her rage and allowed her to release herself without judgement. Without argument. And she was grateful for that. She'd needed that. She'd needed *him*.

'That was a bad thing you did, Jack.'

'I know.'

His voice was soft and she felt it travel through his chest and into hers.

'Are you going to tell me why you did it?'

She watched him, watched his eyes, sure he was going to tell her. That he had a plan. That sending her on that disastrous date had a hidden meaning she didn't know about. Maybe hoping that he'd sent her on a date with that dope so she wouldn't fall for anyone else. Because he wanted her to himself.

It couldn't be for ratings and great TV. She understood him now. She knew about his father and what he was making him do. All she wanted was to know that they were in this together. But he didn't say anything. He just shook his head.

'No?'

He still didn't say anything. Just lifted a hand to her hair and pushed it back, away from her face. It was a tender movement that didn't make any sense when he still wasn't letting her in. Brooke felt she was on a roller-coaster. Up and down, frightened and happy, exhilarated and angry—and right then, after what had happened, she just couldn't take it.

Brooke pushed against him till he released her. As she righted her clothes and retrieved her handbag from the floor a weakening sadness spread over her. Would Jack ever give her what she needed? Would he ever really get rid of that wall he'd built up in front of himself and let her in? Trust her?

'Brooke. Don't go yet.'

He didn't reach for her, just stood with his hands by his sides. Brooke looked into his eyes. More sadness. He was sad too. But, as much as he was sad, he wasn't offering her any more.

'I have to, Jack. I'm afraid my broken old heart can't

handle this. I don't know why you're holding back, and I don't know why you don't trust me, but you don't. I don't think you ever will. And I can't just have meaningless sex with you—I like you too much.'

'I can't tell you what's going on, Brooke.'

'Yes, you can. But you won't. And if I'm not on your team, Jack, I'm on the other side.'

She didn't wait for his reaction. She just turned, took a deep breath and walked out through the door.

CHAPTER FOURTEEN

WHEN THEY FINALLY reached the peak Brooke was panting. Sweat dripped down her neck and between her shoulder blades. It had to be almost forty degrees. Everything on her was hot and she needed a drink. The girls around her were sighing and breathing heavily too. They were exhausted.

The last day had come. The last challenge was over. And Brooke was so relieved she almost felt like crying. But she didn't have time to cry, because in the distance was a table laden with food and drinks, and standing around the table were some men.

Brooke counted them. Twelve. One for each woman. Who *were* these men? The girls started to twitter in excitement. Brooke felt an arm loop through hers and her stomach started to swirl as well. What was going on? Weren't they done?

After last night's party Mick had come to see them. He'd said they only had one more challenge left. He'd said the men would then make their choice. The challenge was supposed to be a hike to the top of the Curl Curl peninsula. Mick had said nothing about anyone else being there.

Brooke couldn't ask Jack. She wasn't even sure where Jack was. Typically, Jack hadn't been in contact. She missed him. She wanted to know how he was and what the hell was going on. But, as usual when it came to Jack, she was left in the dark. And now there was a crowd of people waiting for them.

What was going on *now*?

Brooke was exhausted. Physically and mentally. She was confused and starting to feel angry again. Angry that Jack was leaving her in the dark and frustrated that she was so close to seeing her sisters again but still so far away.

As they walked closer the girls' steps started getting faster. Excitement was starting to build. There were about ten cameras facing them as they climbed the last of the slope and came to the table and the strange men.

'Oh, no.'

Someone stopped.

'You can't be serious.'

Brooke looked around. Some of the girls had gone white. They didn't look happy. Brooke turned back to the table and squinted in the sun. She scanned the faces of the men until finally one of the faces registered. Brooke's blood rushed cold in her veins. Pinpricks touched her skin in a rush. *That face.* That wasn't a strange man. That was the man she'd hoped never to see ever again. *Mitch.* Standing behind the table. Smiling. At her.

Brooke wanted to run. She wanted to get the hell out of here and away from that face. But she couldn't. The cameras were close now, and all but two of the women had stopped. Those two had rushed to the table and embraced two of the men waiting. But the other women didn't.

Brooke realised what this was. Everyone's exes were here. *Great TV.* What better finale than forcing the women to come face to face with the men who had led them even to come on this ridiculous show? The drama was sure to be top level.

As she finally reached the table Mitch smiled at her. A smile that had once been so familiar and dear to her. Now it just seemed as if he was mocking her.

'Brooke. You look great!'

He was talking to her. How *dared* he talk to her? Around her, things were not going well. Someone was crying. There was shouting at one end of the table. Most of them were stiff and unsure.

'What the hell is going on? Why are you here, Mitch?'

'It's all about moving on, Brooky. I'm here to release you, so you can move on.'

Brooke's ears burned and she gripped the chair in front of her. 'Excuse me?'

'They thought it would be a good idea if you faced your demons. If you met up with the men you'd loved the most and had the chance to talk.'

'*They?* Who is they?'

Mitch's eyebrows furrowed. 'The people in charge—I don't know.'

Jack. Jack was in charge. Jack had arranged this.

Brooke didn't want to believe it. As she listened to the words coming out of Mitch's mouth she thought maybe it had been Mick's idea. Or even Jack's father's. But it hadn't. Jack had done this. Jack had sent Mitch back to her. *Jack*. Who knew what Mitch had done. Who knew how Mitch had made her feel. Why would he do this?

A woman's voice boomed out across the table.

'Ladies and gentlemen, it's time to sit. Today is all about breaking bread with someone from your past who has caused you pain. The aim is to get everything out in the open so you're able to move on to your own *Perfect Match*.'

People started to sit, but Brooke didn't want to sit. She wanted to leave. But then she saw the cameras. She wasn't going to make a scene. That was exactly what Jack wanted. That was exactly what Mitch wanted.

Why would Jack do this? How had she got him so wrong? How had she thought he was different? He *wasn't* different. This was all about ratings to him. And it didn't even matter if the show did end—Jack would always put success above her. She realised that now. This dirty trick had shown her the truth. Jack wasn't true and sincere. Jack would do anything to get what he wanted. Right now—he wanted a reaction. Well, Jack could go jump.

Brooke sat down and piled food on to her plate. Her appetite was gone but she was determined to eat and smile and pretend that none of this mattered.

'How have you been, Brooky?'

Mitch's voice had a high-pitched twang to it that she never noticed before. It irritated her. She shoved a piece of bread in her mouth and chewed.

'Don't talk to me, Mitch. Don't make polite conversation,' she hissed through the food and through her teeth. 'Just sit there and shut up.'

Mitch stopped eating. 'You know, Brooke, that was always the problem with you. You were always telling me what to do.'

What? The man had a hide. She'd never told him what to do. Perhaps she should have. He might have treated her better. Brooke remained silent. She didn't want to fight. She didn't want any reason for the camera to come her way.

'Still cold, Brooke? Still not letting anyone in?'

Brooke told herself to breathe. Cold? Her? She'd given Mitch *everything*. All of her. She'd been there for him when he was down. She'd pumped him up when his ego was low. She spent all her time and all her energy on him and then he'd left. As if she hadn't mattered. He'd replaced her and moved on.

'You know, Brooke, if you talked to me instead of projecting all this anger we might be able to work things out. I still care about you, you know.'

The spots of anger were back in front of Brooke's eyes. Her breathing was shallow. She sucked in a breath and chewed the remains of her bread.

'If your sisters butt out, that is.'

Brooke put her hands to her eyes and rubbed. She knew what she was about to do and she couldn't stop herself. She'd had enough.

Brooke stood up and banged her hands on the table. 'Ladies, this is *enough*. We've gone through enough. We don't have to sit here with these…men. These people who didn't understand us, didn't care about us. We are the authors of our own stories—not these sad excuses for men here at the table.'

'You're right, Brooke. I don't want to eat with you, Grant. I don't even want to look at you. I don't like you. I don't think I ever did.'

'And I won't sit across from *you*, knowing how many times you cheated on me. How many times you lied to me, Patrick.'

Alisssa's voice rang out across the table. 'And you know what, Matthew? I *did* cheat on you. You want to know why? Because you're bad in bed!'

Another woman stood and said her piece, then another, and another. Then it was Brooke's turn.

'You listen to me, Mitch, you little weasel. My sisters *knew* what a lying, cheating arse you are. They tried to warn me but I didn't listen to them. I believed *you*. And you betrayed me. You took everything I gave you, sucked up all my goodness, and then you walked away. You humiliated me and you treated me like I meant nothing. You are low, Mitch. Lower than low. But you're not my demon. You're nothing to me now. I don't even think about you, except to think how lucky I was to get away from you. I don't like you, I don't love you, and I've realised I never did. You were what I needed at that time in my life. But I don't need you any more. I don't need *any* man. I deserve to be treated with respect. I deserve a man who isn't afraid to love me madly and deeply. And I am way too good for you. I won't sit with you, Mitch. You don't deserve my time.'

By now she knew all the cameras were on her and she didn't care. Mitch needed to know that she wouldn't be treated like this. He needed to know that she was angry and that she was done. Done with bad men and bad relationships. And right now she needed to tell another man that too, because she was angry and she was worth it and *she* was calling the shots around here.

CHAPTER FIFTEEN

JACK GRABBED HIS bag and headed for the door. The taxi was here. He had waited as long as he could. He knew they were still taping the last scene. He'd tried to tell himself to stay away but he couldn't. He couldn't stand the thought of Brooke being there—without him. The need to protect her was too strong. He couldn't just leave it.

He'd just called his father and informed him that he would not be screening the last two scenes and the show was finished. All he wanted to do now was go and see Brooke and tell her how he felt—even though he knew she probably hated him. Even though he knew she wouldn't want anything to do with him. He wanted to be there after she'd faced that dirt-bag of an ex of hers.

The buzzer went again. The taxi driver was impatient and so was he. With a click of the door, Jack left. He took the stairs two at a time. His stomach was still lodged in his throat, but it dropped quickly when he saw who was at the door.

Brooke.

Standing next to four tall blondes. Somehow, even among that bevy of beautiful Amazonian women, Brooke stood out. To him she always did. Her eyes. Her dimples. Her body. It all made sense to him. It was as if someone had reached into the depths of his mind and pulled out everything he'd ever wanted in a woman and now she was here.

She looked calm. His heart leapt into his throat. Brooke didn't do calm. Something was really up.

The tall blonde standing next to Brooke spoke up. 'Are you Jack Douglas?'

He turned to her and nodded. He didn't want to talk to her—he wanted to talk to Brooke. He wanted to calm her down. Had she seen her ex yet?

'Then I have something to say to you.'

'Maddy, wait…'

Jack turned eagerly towards Brooke's voice. It was quiet and soft and so unlike her that he wanted to step forward and take her in his arms. He wanted her to be his. But he had no idea what she was feeling. Calm Brooke was not someone he'd experienced.

He gripped the strap of his bag hard. 'Brooke. Are you all right?'

'No, she's *not* all right. How could she be all right after what you did?'

'Melissa, stop.'

There it was. Tough Brooke. *His* Brooke.

'I can handle this. Go and wait in the car.'

'We're not leaving you.'

'Go.'

Her voice had become louder. He saw her spark again. His body went tense in anticipation. She was going to tell him off. He hadn't realised till now how much he missed that.

The tall blondes each threw him a look of disdain but they stalked off one by one—the last one putting her fingers to her eyes and then pointing to his before finally leaving him alone with Brooke.

'Jack. We need to talk. Not because I want you back. Don't think that's what I'm here for.'

Jack's heart sank and he had to suck in a few deep breaths. She didn't want him. Now he knew.

'I'm here to ask why? Why you did it?'

'Why I did what?'

She made a sniffing noise and looked away, folding her arms across her chest. When she looked back there were tears in her eyes. She was sad. Angry he could do—but not sad.

Jack stepped forward.

Brooke stepped back. She tried to harden her heart, to keep her emotions in check. It had been easier with her sisters standing beside her, but here alone with him she felt herself waver.

'No. Don't touch me. Don't think you can touch me and make this OK. I want to know why you used what I said against me. Why you lied to me. Why you made me feel like we had something and then threw it all away. For ratings? Or was it for fun? Why would you *do* that? Why would you make me feel like that?'

'Brooke, I did the wrong thing. I thought I was protecting you. I thought that by staying in the background and preventing my father from doing even worse things I was helping you.'

'How did they find out about Mitch? Did *you* tell them?'

This was the question she wanted to know the answer to the most. Had he used the information she'd given to him when she was upset against her? She wanted to hear him say no. She wanted to believe he was good deep down inside.

'Yes, I did.'

Brooke's heart shattered and she stumbled, her act of bravery forgotten for a few seconds.

'But if I hadn't they would have found out some other way. It was going to be worse, Brooke—a lot worse. My father came up with a scheme to trick you all into revealing your feelings about your exes before having them appear. You have no idea how much I fought him on that.'

'You should have fought harder.'

She understood now that he had been trying to help her, but it wasn't enough. He'd let her fall.

'I know I should have. But I realised that too late.'

The tears that threatened Brooke's eyes leapt to the surface. She'd wanted him to fix this. She'd wanted him to be the one. But he wasn't.

'I realise now I'm on my own, Jack. There's no prince coming to rescue me. There's no perfect match for me. I'm going to have to save myself.'

'We all have to save ourselves, Brooke.'

The first teardrop fell. That wasn't what she'd wanted to hear. As much as she knew that she was in this on her own, and that there wasn't a perfect match out there for her, she hadn't wanted it to be true. But it was.

'But that doesn't mean you have to do it on your own.'

Sobs threatened Brooke's chest. She didn't want to listen to him any more. She just wanted to be back with her sisters and hear their comforting words.

'Sometimes you have to be taken out of your comfort zone and be thrown into a completely new situation to see if you sink or swim. And you, Brooke—you're a swimmer. You fought the whole way. For yourself, for the other girls—for women everywhere. There's no doubt in anyone's mind that you are the bravest, toughest woman in Australia right now.'

She *was* brave—he was right. She was tough. But she was still sad that she was alone.

'But no one will ever know how tough you are because I'm not letting the last two episodes go to air. I've cancelled the show. It's over. Everything beyond the football match will never be seen.'

'What?'

Brooke stared at him. What was he saying?

'I told my father to stick it. He can sue me, but those episodes will never see the light of day.'

Brooke's heart leaped. That rollercoaster rocked into view. 'You did that? For me?'

'Of course. I'd do anything for you, Brooke. Because—well, quite frankly, I'd be too frightened of what you'd do to me if I didn't.'

His smile was shy and quiet and genuine. She felt his arms around her, his lips landing on her forehead, her eyelids and her mouth.

'And because…'

Jack stepped forward, but Brooke stepped back again, into the gutter on the street. She was now even tinier. He moved swiftly and grabbed her arms. He wasn't letting her go—not until he'd told her how he felt. She had to know. Everything he'd done was because of her. Because he wanted to protect her. And maybe he was an idiot, and maybe he'd gone about it the wrong way, like he had with his mother, but he wasn't making the mistake of not letting her know how he felt. Not this time.

'I love you.'

Brooke didn't want to cry but she couldn't stop. She was confused and frightened and angry. And Jack was here, telling her what she wanted to hear, and it seemed too good to be true.

'Brooke—listen to me.'

His hands were hot on her arms. He was so close she could smell his scent and it was making her weak. She wanted to fall against him, have him tell her everything was OK, but she wasn't sure. Was this real? Was he telling her that he actually loved her?

'You don't love me, Jack. If you did you wouldn't have let me go so easily.'

Brooke gasped when she felt Jack's arms around her. He lifted her up until her face was level with his.

'Let me tell you something, Brooke. You have no idea how hard it's been for me to let you go. I thought that was what you wanted. I thought you hated me—that you were too angry with me to ever want to be with me again. I thought you didn't want me.'

'I *did* want you.'

She was looking into his eyes now and she saw something. Hurt. Pain. Loneliness. And she knew that was what he could see in hers.

'Do you still want me?'

He was unsure. Big, bold confident Jack was unsure. Brooke's broken little heart started to beat again. Maybe he was telling the truth. Maybe he did love her.

'Yes.' The word came out as a whisper. 'Yes. I still want you.'

The kiss landed on her lips with a force she hadn't been expecting, but he held her steady. Strong and steady. He wanted her. It wasn't over. He hadn't betrayed her. Brooke kissed him back. Hard and furious. She was angry he'd let it come to this and she needed him to know. His kisses trailed down her neck.

'I know you're angry, Brooke. I can feel it.' His lips moved back up to hers. 'And I hope to spend my life making you angry so we can constantly enjoy making up.'

Brooke punched his arm with her fist. Then she kissed him again. Hard.

'Then you need to know one thing, Jack Douglas.' Brooke drank in his smile, his eyes, and the feel of his arms wrapped around her. '*I'm* calling the shots around here.'

* * * * *